EDDIE'S GIRLS

ROGER WOODTHORPE

UK Book Publishing.com

Editing, design, typesetting and publishing by UK Book Publishing

www.ukbookpublishing.com

ISBN: 978-1-917329-38-5

EDDIE'S GIRLS

This book is dedicated to my wife *Sandra*
– without her help and encouragement
it would never have been written.

CHAPTER I

An unsmiling man with a bad reputation

EDDIE

It took a second suicide to stop the bullies that plagued Broad Street School. Juliet Morris was a lovely girl, sensitive and caring, but heavily built and ungainly with a head seemingly too small for her large frame. A lisp left her unable to pronounce her own name properly and Vinnie Proctor, Ray Powers and their team of sadists terrorised her, named her 'Pinhead Morrith' and turned her into a thief.

Shortly before ten o'clock on a warm September evening, Juliet kissed her parents goodnight and went to her room. It was a little early and she didn't always kiss them goodnight, but they weren't worried – she'd been busy in her room all evening and was probably tired. They knew she'd been unhappy since the beginning of the new school term and had decided to speak to her after the weekend; they didn't want to spoil Sunday with their new grandson.

In her room Juliet put on her best blue dress, spread a plastic sheet on her bed and swallowed most of the contents of her mother's medicine cabinet. She then lay on the bed, surrounded herself with her most precious things and waited patiently to die. The plastic sheet was uncomfortable, but Juliet had heard that bodies often leaked after death and she wanted to make the disposal of her heavy body as easy as possible.

Earlier that day Ray Powers had given her a note naming a video game she should steal for him or suffer the consequences. Times had changed since she'd last shoplifted, and as she ran from the store a CCTV camera flashed at her. It would only be a matter of time before her shame was paraded before the world and Juliet couldn't take any more humiliation. She remembered Neville Webster – he'd hung himself in his father's garage rather than return to Broad Street School, but his death had changed nothing; he'd not left a suicide note. To ensure her death served a purpose, Juliet left three notes. The first was an open letter giving graphic details of the indignities that she and so many others had suffered. She named the ringleaders, Vinnie and Ray, but not their targets; she didn't want to brand them as victims and thieves like her. She named Eddie Stagg as the only person who'd helped her and paid tribute to his kindness. The second letter was to her parents, apologising for the shame she would bring them and for being such a disappointment as a daughter. The third was to Eddie.

On that same September evening four years ago, Eddie had moved from the grubby room in an HMO in Cromwell Court provided by Social Services to a privately rented room in Gladstone Street. His new home, a converted loft over a lock-up garage, was in a better part of Canley's West Town – fewer

2

addicts and winos, just prostitutes plying their trade on street corners. Eddie's pride in his new room was short lived: an early visitor was Mrs Morris bringing news of Juliet's suicide and her letter. She watched him open it and saw the shock on his face as he read the first sentence, Juliet loved him!

Mrs Morris' voice was calm. "You didn't know, did you?"

Eddie shook his head, he didn't know, and had no idea what to say to a grieving mother. He spoke a few words to Juliet every day and sometimes they sat together in his bus shelter and talked about music, but that was all. When he finally grasped what she'd done he realised it was his fault – he'd protected her and given her hope then abandoned her; his head full of his own troubles.

He wanted Mrs Morris to shout and scream at him, but she didn't; as he tried to read beyond the first few lines, she looked around his room and started to cry. Moments later she was gone, clearly unable to bear the sight of him. The shame he felt that night would never leave him, Mrs Morris had suffered the cruellest loss of all, yet was still functioning and thinking of others. So, his parents were dead, but he didn't love them and they hated him. So, his brother had put him out on the street without a penny, but Social Services had found him a place to live. So, Janice, the girl he loved didn't love him, but she had no reason to. Compared to Mrs Morris, he'd lost nothing and he hated himself for his self-pity.

A week later he added guilt to his shame. If he had no idea of Juliet's love for him, then Janice probably had no idea of his love for her. When she came to tell him of her boyfriend's treachery, he was able to look her in the eye as a friend, not a pathetic lovesick suitor and be kind. He salvaged the remnants of his pride, but the price was Juliet's memory.

He and Janice remained friends and continued rehearsing their fledgling band in Mike's garage, eventually playing gigs using a succession of mediocre singers. A year ago he'd made the stupid mistake of allowing himself to hope; in three years of relentless hard work he'd achieved and acquired, he had a house, a car and earned more dealing than he did as a porter/handyman at Fultons Auction House. It made no difference, he was still Eddie, monster and unrepentant street fighter and he wasn't considered. Nice girls like Janice didn't want an unsmiling man with a bad reputation.

Then, just when he thought she couldn't possibly hurt him anymore, she did: her new boyfriend Andy was a bass player and she wanted him to take her place in the band. It was a hurt too far, Eddie became a free man!

The next change in the band was for the better: mediocre singer number three left and was replaced by tall, dark, handsome and wealthy Dave King. Dave wouldn't stay long; he would sing for the psycho for a few months then leave and dine out on the experience for a few years. No matter, in the meantime Dave was a good singer, a passable guitar player and a surprisingly decent guy. Eddie wished he could say the same about Andy, but couldn't. Andy was a salesman, and not a particularly good one despite his bragging; at thirty he'd achieved and acquired nothing, even his precious bass was on credit. In contrast, Janice was a clever girl with a good job and prospects; Andy had found a meal ticket.

For a few weeks after Juliet's death, Eddie was almost a hero, a boy fighting a lone battle against a hideous school bullying regime. However, Juliet's compassion in not naming the victims rebounded: no-one spoke up for him at the enquiry into her death. Victims wanted to forget they'd been terrorised and turned into thieves. Other pupils wanted to forget they'd looked the other way, thankful it wasn't them. Teachers wanted to forget they knew what was happening, but wanted someone else to point the finger at the sons of wealthy businessman Jerome Proctor and Chief Superintendent John Powers, Chairman and Deputy Chairman of the School Governors. Parents wanted to forget they'd allowed their sons and daughters to be terrorised by refusing to believe that children from rich and powerful families could be depraved sadists. Juliet and her cause were soon forgotten, but not Eddie, a violent maniac who'd 'massively overreacted' and hurt so many boys. And anyway, a psycho fighting a good cause was still a psycho!

Juliet hadn't died because Eddie was too violent, she died because he wasn't violent enough. If the bullies had been more frightened of him, they wouldn't have started up again as soon as his back was turned. Well, he'd learned that lesson, and in a world that made Broad Street School seem like a Teddy Bears' picnic. Roxy and the girls were safe because he'd smashed faces into brick walls, broken arms and legs, hurt grown men so badly they'd cried like the girls they'd abused with so little conscience. And he'd got away with it for the same reason he'd turned vigilante in the first place – there were no police patrols in West Town and no CCTV cameras, Chief Superintendent Powers and City Council leader Jerome Proctor had diverted resources to protect 'decent' people in 'decent' areas.

JILLY

Eddie's band 'The Roadrunners' had played their first set at a Sixties dance in Broad Street School hall; it was now the interval. A glance at his watch showed Eddie he'd been sitting, brooding, on a low wall outside a fire exit corridor for half an hour, and the second set was due to start in ten minutes. He removed the watch, turned it over and examined the back. The engraving on his 21st birthday present 'To Eddie with love Janice' would confuse a girlfriend when he got one. Eddie smiled grimly; positive thinking: he'd thought when not if.

Eddie usually sat with Janice during intervals at gigs but not today; Broad Street held too many unhappy memories. The only untainted one was of Mike's unwavering loyalty, those of Juliet and Janice were bitter and the distant ones of Jilly, his crush at fourteen, were bittersweet. He'd told Janice about the girl once and she'd given him the strangest look, but then Eddie didn't understand girls, and certainly not ones as complicated as Janice.

He stretched, sipped from his can of Coke, and looked round. It was dark, with light from a nearby street lamp filtering through a bush just inside the school railings. As he put his can down he heard shouting in the fire exit corridor – it sounded like Pete Lomax; that arsehole was always shouting at somebody. The shouting reduced to a loud hiss. Was it something in the air at Broad Street that turned people into bullies? Eddie contemplated intervening but didn't; he might 'massively overreact'!

Then his ears pricked up, he thought he heard a sob! The hissing continued and there it was again, a sob. The bastard!

Eddie jumped to his feet, ran towards the fire exit door and tripped on the edge of the path obscured by the shadow thrown by the bush. He picked himself up, wrenched the door open and tripped again, this time on the brick he'd used to prop the door open. As he recovered, he saw Pete disappear, turning right at the end of the corridor.

To Eddie's left a small, dark-haired girl was pressed against the wall where Pete had left her, head down, sobbing into a tissue. Eddie walked forward slowly, she must have heard him crash through the door but he didn't want to startle her.

Out of breath he gasped. "Are you OK?"

The girl didn't look up, she was sliding along the wall trying to hide in a shadow. Between sobs she murmured, "Yes, thank you."

How could she be polite after such an ordeal? Eddie wanted to hold her, tell her she was safe, but knew it would frighten her. Instead, he took a deep breath and used his best slow, controlled voice.

"Don't worry, he's gone, and he won't come back while I'm here."

As he spoke the girl jumped – was it what he'd said or how he'd said it? She looked up briefly, and even with her eyes red from crying she was pretty, and familiar. Eddie was transported back seven years to a pretty girl with trust in her eyes.

"You're Jilly, Jimmy Orton's sister."

She gave a tiny smile. "And you're Eddie, you used to do my homework."

Eddie stammered, "That Christmas, I went to your house, it was empty, you'd gone…"

Jilly lowered her head. "My Dad…"

She stopped abruptly as Pete Lomax's voice boomed out from the main corridor, shouting threats at someone else. She was terrified and started sobbing again.

This time Eddie did hold her. "Don't cry, sweetheart, I promise he won't hurt you."

The word appeared from nowhere, he'd not called anyone sweetheart before in his life. Incredibly she didn't pull away, the sobbing slowly subsided and she tried vainly to dry her face with her tissue.

Eddie handed her his large white handkerchief. "It's a bit crumpled, but it's clean, honest!"

"Why was Pete Lomax shouting at you?"

Jilly hesitated. "My Dad owes him money, but can't pay because he lost it betting on a horse. Pete knows I've got a job, he says I've got to pay him or he'll hurt Jimmy."

Eddie felt dangerously calm. "Did he threaten to hurt you?"

She hesitated again. "I don't think he meant it." The tears came again. "I can't pay him, I gave my money to Mum."

She began moving towards the exit. "I've got to warn Jimmy, there's a bus soon."

"No." Eddie shook his head. "I'll take you home later." He hurried on. "I know Pete, I'll talk to him, persuade him to leave you and Jimmy alone."

Then she was staring at him, eyes full of trust. She was incredibly pretty, so pretty it was hard to think.

He gulped. "Here's what we'll do. In a moment we'll walk to the main corridor and, if it's clear, I want you to go back to the main hall." Jilly gave a questioning look. "I'm with the band, we've got a table at the front near the stage. There'll be a girl sitting there, her name's Janice and she's really nice." Eddie paused, picturing Janice at the table. "Tell her you're with me and that I want her to look after you until I get back, OK?"

Jilly gave a coy smile, head down, huge dark blue eyes looking up. "Is Janice your girlfriend?"

Eddie shook his head. "No." It was the first time he'd answered that question without bitter pangs of regret. "I don't have a girlfriend."

A smile, instantly replaced with concern. "Please be careful when you talk to Pete, he's rough and horrible."

Eddie was genuinely unconcerned. "Don't worry, I'll be fine."

Time to move, Jilly held out her hand, a startled Eddie took it and they walked together to the main corridor. Apart from a group of giggling girls it was clear.

Eddie turned to her. "Promise me you'll stay with Janice until I get back."

"I promise."

He reluctantly released her hand and watched her hurry towards the main hall, still clutching his handkerchief. He waited until she reached the door, hoping she'd turn and smile. Better still, she turned, smiled and waved, then she was gone.

Now, Pete fucking Lomax, your time had come!

JANICE

Janice felt conspicuous sitting alone at the band table, but knew she'd feel even more conspicuous standing at the bar. Six foot was too tall for a girl, and even though Andy was taller than her, people still stared. Anyway, Andy liked to drink beer and talk football with Dave in the intervals, he didn't want her hanging around.

When she was thirteen, Janice used to daydream, build a picture of her ideal man, and Andy was close to that ideal: tall, mature, confident and good looking. More importantly, he said he loved her and she thought she loved him, or at least loved him as much as she could love anyone who wasn't Eddie.

Eddie usually sat with her during the intervals at gigs, but today he'd taken his can of Coke and gone for a walk outside. He was depressed – not that Eddie would admit to being depressed, or tired, or unhappy. Janice was worried about him, he was becoming more and more withdrawn and looked ill with tiredness. He needed someone to look after him, but someone special, not her.

She should have known Eddie was special when he rescued her from the bullies and told her she was Lizzie Bennet come to life. She didn't, she thought he was weird. She should have known he was special when he pretended to be a monster to protect her from the bullies. She didn't, instead she enjoyed her freedom and new-found friends. She should have known he was special when, consumed with guilt after Neville Webster's suicide, he offered to protect anyone and everyone. She didn't, she thought he'd become the monster.

Janice resented the fact that he never took her home, and assumed he was ashamed of her. Worse, she thought he was callous because he sat in a bus shelter on Mayors Road after school instead of going home to care for his invalid mother. Mostly she distrusted him because he never opened his eyes properly, Janice believed that eyes were windows to the soul and thought he was hiding something. The final straw was getting involved in his final showdown with Vinnie and his henchmen and being splattered with blood when Eddie broke the nose of the boy nearest to her. And it hadn't helped having that stupid girl Deborah Aston standing nearby screaming and throwing up.

Ian was a young locum solicitor at the practice where she had a holiday job. He was mature and charming and she fell for him, fancied herself in love. She'd avoided Eddie, shocked by his violence, and couldn't understand why he'd moved to that awful room in Cromwell Court. But her head was full of Ian, convinced he would take her back to Oxford with him. How wrong she was – when she found him at his flat packing a suitcase, her questions brought a mocking response.

"Oh for Christ's sake, Janice, you were just a bit of fun, I've a fiancée in Oxford." He'd laughed. "You didn't actually believe I was serious, did you?" When her face fell his contempt became obvious. "Look at yourself, you're just a tall, thin girl with a big nose." He'd snorted with derision. "But you were easy, a bit of flattery and you were gagging for it. You were cheap too, no fancy restaurants, just a pizza and a couple of takeaways, how stupid are you?"

Her Nan was unsympathetic, so she'd turned to the normally gentle and caring Mike. He was furious, telling her that Eddie's mother had died and on the day of her funeral Eddie had told him the truth. His mother wasn't an invalid, she was an alcoholic who hated the sight of him, and Eddie sat in a bus shelter after school because he wasn't allowed home. The day after the funeral, Eddie's brother had thrown him out – he was in the awful room in Cromwell Court because he had nowhere else to go.

"Eddie screwed his fucking head up creating a monster to protect you and you didn't give a shit!"

Mike, the perfect gentleman who never shouted or swore, had just done both. The next day he calmed down and gave her Eddie's new address in Gladstone Street.

The converted loft over the garage in Gladstone Street wasn't much better than the room in Cromwell Court but Eddie seemed pleased with it. She expected him to be angry but he wasn't — he was incredibly kind. She told him about Ian and cried on his shoulder, not the bit about being easy, cheap and stupid, just about being tall and thin and having a big nose. He tried to smile, told her she was slender and elegant, and opened his eyes right up. They were half closed again in an instant, but it was enough: Eddie wasn't hiding anything, his eyes were brilliant blue and full of nothing but kindness.

He persuaded her to return to school, promising to help with her coursework as he'd always done. Before she left, he told her about Juliet, how they used to sit in his bus shelter and talk about music. It was then that Janice knew she'd lost him — an ordinary girl like Juliet knew Eddie was special, but she didn't. Eddie would go out with her if she asked, not because he loved her but because he was kind and wouldn't want to hurt her. That must never happen because one day he would find a special girl, realise Janice wasn't special, and look at her the way Ian had done. She could bear anything but that.

Eddie had the cool of Mr Darcy, the mystery of Heathcliffe and the brooding intensity of James Dean. He was clever too: in the last four years he'd passed four A levels with distinction, gained a Diploma in Building Management and started successful antiques and band equipment businesses as well as working full time at Fulton's. Eddie should be beating the girls off with a stick, but he wasn't — everyone remembered the monster he'd created to protect her. Nice girls avoided him and she didn't want him taking up with that awful Roxy or one of the other trollops he insisted were his friends. A special girl would know Eddie was special – it was just a pity she didn't know all those years ago.

Janice fingered her locket, something she did when she was upset or thinking of Eddie. It was slim, and the wide hoop at the top for the chain was set with five stones, a sapphire surrounded by diamonds. Eddie had given it to her for her 21st birthday last September and showed her how to open it by depressing the hoop and twisting it. He was embarrassed when she read the inscription inside 'To Janice with love Eddie' and his kindness inadvertently caused her first and only argument with her Nan.

A few days ago she'd had a furious row with Andy about money – he was hopeless with money – and she was fingering her locket when he snapped.

"You're always fiddling with that bloody locket." He'd paused then erupted with rage. "He gave it to you, didn't he? That fucking Eddie."

As he tried to wrench it from her neck, she said the first thing that came into her head. "It's not a locket, it's a pendant. It was my Nan's, it's antique."

The last part was true – Eddie had told her it was hallmarked in Chester in 1898. Andy wasn't convinced so last night she went to see Nan to warn her in case he asked.

She'd never seen Nan so angry. "You're a cruel, heartless girl. I didn't think you were like your mother, but I was wrong. You broke that poor boy's heart four years ago, you've played him along ever since and now this."

Then Nan slapped her, really hard, and ran into the kitchen. It was laughable: Eddie didn't love her, she would know if he did.

A few minutes later Nan came back. "My pendant it is then, but I'm doing it for Eddie, not you."

Janice peered at her watch, almost time to start the second set, Eddie wouldn't be back in time for them to talk about what her Nan had said. She stared down the hall, no sign of Eddie or the others, just a small, dark-haired girl who seemed to be walking directly towards her. The girl was pretty, picture book pretty, and had obviously been crying. She stopped, caught Janice's eye and gave an uncertain smile.

"Excuse me, are you Janice?"

A DEHUMANISED PSYCHO

Eddie watched the door into the main hall close. A few seconds ago the prettiest girl in the world had smiled and waved at him. A few minutes ago he'd called her sweetheart and held her while she sobbed. Pete Lomax had terrified her, so Eddie would find Pete and terrify him. He gave a grim smile; he knew people called him a psycho and perhaps he was. Dave called him dehumanised but sounded vaguely concerned when he said it. Well, dehumanised psychos had their uses.

Pete hadn't come back past the fire exit corridor, so he had to be in the gents' toilet. Eddie pulled a wooden stacking chair from a pile in an alcove before pushing quietly through the toilet door. Pete was at the far end, combing his lank hair in a mirror above a wash basin. Two youths drying their hands

14

under hot air blowers understood his pointing finger and left hurriedly. Eddie wedged the chair under the door handle and turned to face Pete.

"What!" As the hot air blowers stopped, Pete swung round, sensing someone behind him.

Eddie's face was expressionless. "Hello Pete, remember me?"

Pete gasped. "Jesus Christ!"

Eddie shook his head. "No, he'd be older than me, beard, long hair, sort of kindly looking."

It took a moment for Pete to grasp the sarcasm. "Don't you get fucking smart with me."

He lunged forward menacingly then stopped abruptly. Eddie was smaller than him but was a man with a serious reputation, and Pete still had painful memories of their fight years ago. His voice took on a whining tone.

"What do you want with me?"

Eddie repeated his question. "I said, do you remember me?"

A flash of anger. "Of course I do, you fucking maniac, you nearly crippled me." Anger over, back to whining. "What do you want? I've done nothing to you."

Eddie's voice was slow and controlled. "A few minutes ago, you shouted at a girl and frightened her."

"What's that to you?" Pete hesitated. "It's none of your business."

The controlled voice continued. "I'm making it my business, so tell me about it."

Pete's whining was becoming annoying. "I did some work for her father, and he hasn't paid me."

Eddie remembered Stan Orton, he hadn't liked him seven years ago and, by the sound of it, he hadn't improved.

He moved within touching distance of Pete. "If Stan Orton owes you money, then go and shout at him." He paused. "But leave the girl and her brother alone."

Pete smirked; he thought he'd got away with it.

He hadn't, but Eddie had to be careful not to hurt his hands – he had to play guitar in a few minutes' time.

"Don't drop your comb!"

Pete glanced down and the first he knew of the flashing right hand was it hitting the soft part of his face under the cheekbone. The blow knocked him off balance, nicely set up for a crunching left to his midriff. There was a gust of foul breath as he folded over, face falling towards Eddie's upcoming knee. Normally Eddie would aim for the nose, but not this time – he didn't want blood on his good jeans. Instead, his knee struck Pete's mouth and chin, driving his head back upwards until a second blow to the midriff brought it down again.

Eddie caught the back of Pete's shirt as he dropped – he was a bully but not a monster; Eddie didn't want him breaking his head open on the tiled concrete floor. The blows to the midriff disturbed the beer Pete had consumed during the evening, and he started to retch. Eddie dragged him into a toilet cubicle and thrust his face into the pan in time for it to collect a stream of beery vomit. When the stream stopped Pete started to writhe under Eddie's grasp; he must be feeling better. Time for a final lesson: Eddie lifted Pete's head and banged it on the toilet seat. Not hard enough – the nose didn't break, so he lifted his head and banged again. This time there was a crack and a spurt of blood.

"Can you hear me, Pete?" Silence from Pete. "I said can you fucking hear me?" A groan signified hearing. "If you go near the girl, or her brother, or her mum again, I'll come looking for you, understand?" Pete groaned again and Eddie released him, walked to a basin and washed his hands. Now to find Jilly.

TAKE A NICE GIRL HOME.

Dave King was standing by the band table, feeling confused. During the interval he'd pulled, and asked the object of his lust to join Janice at the band table towards the end of the second set. Unfortunately, Cherie was a bit of a trollop and as Janice was notoriously ill disposed towards trollops, Dave thought he'd better warn her of Cherie's likely arrival. He expected to find her talking to Eddie as usual, but there was no Eddie, just Janice fussing round an impossibly pretty girl whom she introduced as Eddie's girlfriend!

Despite her studied indifference, Dave suspected that Janice was Eddie's number one fan – she should be scratching the girl's eyes out, not fussing. A remarkably composed Janice gave him precise instructions; she and Jilly were going to the ladies to adjust their make-up and he was to wait for Andy and Mike, then stall for time because Eddie had been delayed. She didn't say why he'd been delayed, but as the girl had obviously been crying, somebody, somewhere, would be hurting.

An impassive Eddie had arrived and the second set was underway. He was the rhythm guitar player with the band's sound built round the wall of sound produced from his elderly Marshall Super Lead 100 amplifier and matching 4 x 12 speaker cabinet. The band, including Mike their tiny drummer, followed his crashing chords, his timing was impeccable and he didn't make mistakes, until now. Two numbers in and he'd muddled an intro and missed a chord change – was the iceman worried about the girl?

The third number brought the rare sight of Eddie walking out of the shadows at the back of the stage, trailing his guitar lead behind him like an umbilical cord. The girls were back but he hadn't seen them, Jilly had waved and when Eddie hadn't waved back she'd grabbed Janice's arm and said something. Now Janice was waving at Dave, pointing to Jilly then Eddie.

Dave understood and turned to Eddie. "They're back, she's waving at you."

Eddie nodded, moved to the front of the stage, smiled and waved, then retreated back into the shadows.

Dave desperately wanted the set to finish, eager to see Eddie and the girl together. They were about to play Mr Tambourine Man, the Byrds version with Eddie playing twelve-string guitar. Another enigma: Eddie used a Rickenbacker 360/12, a seriously expensive guitar for a porter at an auction house. His other guitar was an equally expensive Gibson, and the big Marshall wasn't simply old, it was all valve and vintage.

Dave glanced at Jilly and approached the microphone. "Eddie's changing to his twelve-string, he says this song's for Jilly."

Jilly almost jumped out of her skin, then did it again when the huge jangle of the twelve-string filled the hall. Dave sniffed; he'd made a pretty girl happy without intending to.

Music over and Cherie had arrived, all bleached blonde hair and cleavage. On second sight Dave wondered if she'd seen one too many ceilings, or was it just the contrast between her and the girl. Jilly was hanging onto Eddie's arm, chattering excitedly to him and Janice. They were together, Eddie was taking her home, and Dave still couldn't believe it. He shrugged; perhaps one day he would take a nice girl home full of hope for the future, but in the meantime he had Cherie. If Eddie was lucky, he'd get a kiss on the cheek as Jilly disappeared through her front door. Nice girls used the front door, more light than at the back, less chance of any funny business. In contrast, Dave was onto a sure thing, Cherie would bang like a shithouse door in a gale. He shrugged again – given the choice, he would opt for a kiss on the cheek.

Eddie was loading the big Marshall into his battered white estate car when he heard Janice behind him; her smile was false.

He smiled uncertainly back. "Well, what do you think?"

"I think she's lovely."

"Yes." Eddie nodded slowly. "But what's the chance of her having anything to do with the likes of me?"

Janice looked puzzled. "She told me she was your girlfriend." She saw the surprise on Eddie's face and asked: "When did you meet?"

"In the interval, but we first met a long time ago."

Then Janice knew. "It's her, isn't it? That boy's sister, the one you told me about years ago?"

She turned away, then hesitated before fleeing back into the hall.

Dave was preparing to leave when he heard raucous laughter behind him, Cherie was guffawing at one of Andy's lewd jokes and he was taking the opportunity to peer down her cleavage. She leaned forward to give him a better look and Dave grimaced; she was probably more generous with her favours than he'd thought, he'd better visit the Johnny machine in the gents before leaving. To his right Janice was saying goodbye to Eddie and Jilly, and the good guy in Dave sensed she might need support. Andy wouldn't know or care – he was too busy with Cherie's cleavage.

Janice turned to him. "I'm pleased for him, she's lovely." She was close to tears, her face and voice telling different stories. Dave put his arms round her and gave her a hug, then she was crying on his shoulder. "He hasn't rejected me, Dave, he knew her long before he met me, he's been waiting for her to come back."

Dave didn't understand.

CHAPTER 2

Eddie

CIGARETTES AND ALCOHOL.

"**W**here's my vodka?"

"They wouldn't sell it to me at the supermarket." Eddie evaded a vicious blow and added, "Anyway, the doctor said you shouldn't mix drink with your asthma tablets."

"You judgmental little bastard, a drink helps me sleep." Margaret Stagg aimed another blow at her son before continuing. "If you hadn't come along your father would still be alive and about to retire, isn't it enough you killed him without making my life a misery as well?"

Eddie cringed – surely it was heavy drinking and a sixty-a-day cigarette habit that killed his father, not working to support him?

For once he defended himself. "At least I do the shopping, the cooking, the cleaning and the gardening, you only see Charles and Angela on Sundays when you go to theirs for lunch." Brother Charles was nineteen years older than Eddie and the apple of his mother's eye. "And Angela drives past every day taking Charlotte to and from school, but she doesn't call in, does she?"

Margaret's tone was spiteful. "She doesn't call because you're here…" A malicious smile appeared. "As of now you don't come home from school until after five o'clock then Angela will bring Charlotte to see me."

Broad Street School was as dysfunctional as Eddie's home life with two gangs vying for control. Pete Lomax was a simple thug who regarded the money he extorted as legitimate income. Vinnie Proctor and Ray Powers didn't want or need money – they were sadists on a power trip. Their team selected targets from the weak or physically different and terrorised them. After a while, they offered their victims protection if they stole for the team, the object being to turn them into thieves who wouldn't dare complain. Ordinary Eddie with his non-confrontational habit of viewing the world through half closed eyes wasn't selected, but Pete Lomax chose his victims at random.

July, the penultimate day of the Summer term, and Eddie was simply in the wrong place at the wrong time. He was startled by Pete's approach and indignantly refused his demand for money. The next day Pete, his brother Bob and two others stopped Eddie on a piece of waste ground by the school's East entrance – he was to be taught a lesson. Eddie was used to being beaten, but not out in the open where anyone might see his shame. Odds of four to one soon overcame his spirited resistance then a sneering Pete was standing over him, repeating his demand for money.

Later, in the bus shelter that had become his after-school home, Eddie licked his wounds and relived his humiliation.

Rather more he relived the thrill of fighting back – not all the blood on his shirt was his, he didn't have to be a victim.

Eddie was excited, his third boxing lesson at Jim's Gym and Jim himself was taking an interest. The first two lessons had comprised basic fitness training, group instruction and individual sparring with Jim and some of the experienced regulars. Today a small, older man in a smart suit had arrived – everyone called him Mr Wells except Jim who called him Billy – and the two were watching him spar. Eddie knew he was doing well, he could hit experienced opponents at will and had found a big left hand that was knocking them over. The bell sounded and Billy approached with a friendly smile.

"Hello Eddie, I'm Billy Wells." Eddie smiled uncertainly back. "Jim's suggested I spar a couple of rounds with you?"

Billy changed into a tracksuit and climbed into the ring. They circled for a while, neither landing any significant blows, until Eddie threw a fast, straight right. It landed cleanly on Billy's face and Eddie saw him grimace. A few seconds later Billy feinted with his left and followed with a sequence of body punches. Eddie blocked the first two but the third hit home, and it hurt. He felt Billy's eyes linger on him, assessing the effect of his punches. It was a chance; Eddie jabbed with his right and followed through with the big left hand. Billy staggered, covered up and backed away, shaking his head.

Round two and an emboldened Eddie was moving forward, throwing punches, when his head exploded. It had happened once before when he was sparring with Jim – Eddie remembered the darkness closing in as he dropped to the canvas. He saw concern on Billy's face as he struggled to his feet, then Jim was ringing the bell.

Eddie was sitting in Jim's grimy office watching Billy's face swell where he'd hit him with the big left hand.

Jim's first words were a blow. "You've got talent, Eddie, but you'll not make it as a boxer."

Eddie couldn't hide his disappointment; he desperately wanted to fight.

Billy took over. "I don't suppose you've heard of me, but I used to be good, a title contender." He paused. "Jim's right, you've got fast hands, and I mean incredibly fast. You think quick, you move quick and you've got that huge left hand." Eddie waited for the but. "But, you can't take a punch, not even a little one, and that's dangerous. If you fight for a living or even as an amateur, you'll end up a cabbage."

As Eddie shook his head Jim interjected sharply: "Why do you want to box?"

Eddie told the truth. "I don't want to box, I just want to fight."

Jim snapped. "I teach boxing to stop boys fighting, it's stupid, you must know that?"

Eddie was choked. "I don't want to fight for the fun of it, I'm just sick of being pushed around."

It all spilled out, his parents and brother, the bullies, even the newsagent. Other boys got normal paper rounds, he got the tower block where the lifts didn't work.

Billy grunted. "I thought you seemed fit for a beginner."

Eddie tried not to sound bitter. "Running up and down stairs carrying bags of papers keeps you fit."

The gym was closed, Billy was holding an ice pack to his face and talking to Jim about the boy who'd done the damage.

"Will he listen?"

Jim gave a sad smile. "No chance, he's been a punchbag for too long. He's so screwed up with guilt about it, he'll fight to prove he's not a coward."

"Well, give him some rules before he kills someone."

September, the first day of the Autumn term and Eddie could see Pete and Bob Lomax waiting for him on the waste ground by the school's East entrance. Eddie was frightened – nothing new there: he'd been frightened of anything and everything most of his life. Today he had to confront the snivelling coward that was in him and walk towards the waste ground. Five paces, ten paces, twenty paces, then Pete was with him, demanding money, threatening another beating.

The fight was short and brutal – Pete wasn't expecting resistance and reeled back under a flurry of blows. Eddie was wearing a pair of fine quality leather-soled, black lace-up shoes he'd bought in a charity shop. Thugs wore boots to use as weapons, Eddie wore beautiful shoes because he liked beautiful shoes – the fact they made effective weapons was a bonus. He couldn't believe how slowly Pete moved compared to Jim and Billy, he had ample time to position himself and kick before he showed any sign of recovery. The result was almost comical – as the rigid sole of Eddie's shoe struck Pete's kneecap, he peered down with surprise, feeling the impact but no pain. Moments later the pain came and it was excruciating.

Bob was hanging back as he'd done during the first fight. Eddie suspected it wasn't cowardice, more that he disapproved of Pete's bullying. As Eddie moved towards him, Bob stood motionless, mouth open with surprise, and let Eddie kick him. Within seconds both Lomax boys were down, screaming with pain, and all Eddie felt was guilt at hurting Bob.

JILLY

The bus shelter on Mayors Road faced south. It was an old wooden structure with filled in back and sides and a wooden bench seat at the back. The green felt-covered roof overhung the front so unless the wind blew directly from the south, it was dry and almost cosy. Eddie was warm in his new coat and if it had been light enough to read would have been almost happy.

There had been no repercussions from the fight with Pete and Bob – to protect his reputation, Pete invented a tale of being beaten by a group of men after stealing their car. It saddened Eddie to think that Pete would rather brand himself a thief than admit to losing a fight. Shortly afterwards, fiction became fact when, after a spate of real car thefts, Pete was sent to a Young Offenders' Institution. His departure exacerbated Broad Street's bullying problem, his leaderless thugs joined Vinnie and Ray as enforcers, making them all powerful. Bob didn't join them; away from Pete's malign influence he kept his head down and his mouth closed. Eddie did the same and unwittingly became the psycho who'd beaten the Lomax brothers and couldn't be bothered to boast about it.

The fight didn't improve Eddie's self-confidence, but did teach him how to focus his willpower. He started with the newsagent who caved in immediately to his demand for a pay rise. It was too easy, they both knew no-one else wanted the tower block paper round, and Eddie hated himself for his weakness in not speaking up before. Asserting himself with his mother was more difficult – whatever her faults it was his duty to care for her. She was intransigent about the five o'clock curfew, but he gained the use of the garage. Not a great success as after a second drink driving conviction she'd sold her car, but Eddie now had somewhere to store and repair the finds from his bargain hunting. Initially he'd spent time in junk and charity shops because they were warm, but soon acquired a taste and a talent for dealing.

A lesson in life: his mother and the newsagent only tolerated him because they needed him, and he tolerated them because he needed a place to live and money to buy a new coat.

Eddie bought another pair of beautiful shoes from a charity shop. The ladies running the shops were mostly retired and seemed to like him, but he'd learned that lesson – they liked him because he carried their heavy boxes of books and bric-a-brac. Mrs Popplewell, the nicest of the ladies, told him the history of his new shoes and he wished she hadn't. They came from a house clearance where an elderly couple had died within days of each other. She explained that a good pair of shoes in the wardrobe were as much a part of the old couple's pride as a china tea set and food in the pantry. He was wearing a dead man's shoes, an old man's pride.

There had always been nightmares – Eddie couldn't remember a time when he hadn't woken sweating with fear after being chased, running and falling in the dark, from someone or something. Specific events triggered new nightmares, unusually severe beatings, his father's death, his mother's violent rages and descent into alcoholism, the fight with Pete and now his new shoes. Last night an old man, grey with death, had forced his way into Eddie's bedroom to reclaim his shoes. Eddie now slept with the light on – he wasn't afraid of the dark as such, just afraid of what filled his mind when he slept.

Five o'clock, Eddie could go home if he wanted to, and at home he could read and he loved reading. He no longer watched John Wayne western films – their only television was now in the room where his mother sat with her vodka, and he only went in there to clean or take her meals on a tray. It was no great loss; Eddie had never identified with John Wayne's confident hero figures and had noticed he rarely got the girl – he rode into town, shot the bad guys, then rode off into the sunset alone. Eddie had found C S Forester's Hornblower novels and could identify with Horatio Hornblower, a troubled hero struggling with his confidence and courage. Hornblower also got the girl, or three girls to be precise, but Eddie wasn't inspired by Maria, the Countess or Lady Barbara. It also troubled him that there were three girls – he needed a new author, a new hero.

The rain had stopped, it was bright and cold with puddles everywhere. Eddie was walking towards the school's East entrance when a fat boy, fear on his face and running surprisingly fast, almost hit him. He leapt backwards and felt a double impact as a boy his own age, and a girl a little younger, ran into him. Eddie dived rather than fell and rolled himself upright. His pride in his agility evaporated when he realised he'd rolled into a puddle, soaking his new coat. Seconds later he narrowly avoided another collision when three of enforcers pounded by chasing their quarry, the fat boy.

Eddie recognised the boy who'd run into him – he was in his year, but not his class. Broad Street had five classes per year arranged alphabetically; Eddie was in S-Z so the boy's surname must start with a letter between A and R. Now what, A- R boy looked as frightened as the fat boy and was keeping himself between Eddie and the girl.

"It was my fault, hit me if you like but leave her alone."

Eddie was appalled – what sort of monster would hit the pretty girl smiling shyly at him from edge of the puddle?

"I'm not going to hit anyone, I just want to get out of this puddle." Eddie stepped forward, water splashing from his shoes and dripping from his coat. "Were you running from those thugs?" A-R boy nodded and Eddie added, "No need, I don't think they were chasing you and the girl."

Jimmy Orton hated school in general and Broad Street in particular because of the bullies. Now he and his sister had run into the psycho who'd battered the Lomax brothers and knocked him into a puddle. Surprisingly, he didn't seem fierce, more comical in his oversized coat and shiny black shoes, and he was apologising to his sister for frightening her.

An opportunity: if he befriended the psycho he could get protection from the bullies. He didn't have to try, the psycho was smiling at his sister and offering to escort them home. What could he talk about, he had to say something? The subject filling his mind was schoolwork – today was maths homework night and Jimmy hated maths. Better and better, Eddie the psycho liked maths.

Eddie couldn't believe it: he was sitting at the Ortons' kitchen table drinking tea and eating cake. The house smelled of baking, unlike home which smelled of vodka. He couldn't understand why his mother thought vodka didn't smell – it did, and when her friends called the house smelled of sherry and gin as well. Eddie hurried his tea and cake – he had to be useful, start Jimmy's homework quickly. Jimmy wasn't a natural scholar, he had to write everything down slowly to assimilate it.

As Jimmy wrote, Eddie helped Jilly, not that she needed help, but she seemed to like listening to his best slow, controlled voice.

Eddie was dictating an answer for Jimmy when Mrs Orton bustled up. "It's getting late, Eddie, don't you need to go home?"

He jumped to his feet, embarrassed at outstaying his welcome. "I'm sorry, I didn't notice the time."

She smiled. "I'm not trying to get rid of you, I just thought your mother would be worried."

She wouldn't.

As Eddie visited regularly to help Jimmy with his homework, he found that the Ortons had tea and cake at four o'clock every day. He met Mr Orton and didn't like him – he reminded Eddie of Pete Lomax, full of arrogant self-confidence and too stupid to know he was stupid.

Christmas Eve, Eddie's mother had gone to stay with Charles and wouldn't be back until Boxing Day. Eddie had the house to himself, he could do what he liked, eat what he liked, watch television, play music, anything. Better still, he had an invitation to lunch with Jimmy the day after Boxing Day.

The big day and Eddie approached the Ortons' house with trepidation – it appeared deserted. He didn't bother to knock – a glance through the curtainless window confirmed his worst fears.

"They've gone," a neighbour shouted over the fence. "They left in a hurry on Christmas Eve."

"I'm Eddie, did they leave a message for me?"

The neighbour gave a knowing smile. "They didn't leave any messages, that Stan Orton's a bad lot, he wouldn't want to be found."

The bitter cold was striking through Eddie's new coat, even huddled as he was in the corner of the bus shelter. For weeks he'd hoped for a letter or telephone call, but now he had reality. Eddie didn't blame Jimmy or Jilly, he blamed Mr Orton for taking them away. He'd been thinking about the girl, trying to identify the expression on her face when she sat and watched him. It was trust and she'd become 'The girl with trust in her eyes'. Eddie gave a forlorn smile; he could be romantic on the inside even if he was violent and emotionless on the outside.

The fight with Pete had brought repercussions after all, surprise attacks from boys seeking instant reputation as the boys who beat the boy who beat the Lomax brothers. Even in twos and threes they were no match for his maturing talent, and as the attacks came without warning he had no time to be frightened.

April, it was light enough to read in the bus shelter and Eddie had found a new author and a new hero. Fitzwilliam Darcy from Jane Austen's 'Pride and Prejudice' was cool, aloof and in control – but still got the girl. And not just any girl, he got Lizzie Bennet, a girl with spirit, humour and fine eyes.

There was a disappointment too, his new coat was showing signs of wear. New things didn't stay new, so Eddie had decided to buy his clothes from charity shops in future to save money and disappointment. He was back in his old routine, visiting his shops and sitting in the bus shelter. Eddie liked routine, and apart from the escalating violence his life hadn't changed much. So why was he so unhappy? Probably because he'd experienced a better life in his time with the Ortons. That could be why his mother was so bitter – she had a better life before he was born. He would try harder with her.

Eddie loved the summer, warm days and light evenings, plenty of time to work and read. He now spent his spare time at weekends in the garage; he'd bought a table, a chair, a kettle and some crockery and at four o'clock he had tea and cake like the Ortons.

His birthday had passed unnoticed again, proof if he needed it that his efforts with his mother had failed. He celebrated alone in the garage, a candle on his cake and a present to himself, an old electric guitar found in a junk shop. One day he would form a band and play Sixties music, Rock and Roll music, one day!

His mother had noticed his efforts, Eddie overheard her talking to Charles on the telephone. "The devious little bastard is up to something…"

Eddie wasn't up to anything and hated how his mother always called him 'the little bastard'.

August, a drinking binge had put his mother in hospital. Charles refused to have Eddie in his house and foster care was proving difficult. Eddie liked the words 'aberrant' and 'propensity', but disliked the two being combined and applied to him. Broad Street School's report to Social Services described Eddie as 'displaying aberrant behavior with a propensity towards unpredictable violent outbursts'. Eddie was incredulous that a school that ignored a hideous bullying regime could label him 'aberrant' and not be aware that his violent outbursts were him defending himself against unprovoked attacks.

Eventually Eddie was placed with Gerry Burchnall, a specialist in 'aberrant' children and his report surprised Social Services.

'I found nothing aberrant in Eddie's behaviour. The main thing I noticed is that he is almost obsessively tidy – leaving him alone in the house left me at risk of having my CD collection placed in alphabetical order, but little else'.

JANICE AND MIKE

Daisy Newton was distraught; she'd lost her husband and older son in a car accident, and now her younger son had been ensnared by a scheming strumpet. Arthur had the world at his feet, he was tall, handsome and had a good job, but his eye for a pretty face lingered too long on that of the vain and selfish Barbara Proud. He was smitten and she thought him a good catch.

Mrs Newton's gloom abated temporarily when the twins were born – Catherine and Elinor were blonde and pretty, but destined to be their mother's daughters in every way. A year later a sister brought enduring happiness to Daisy and enduring disappointment to Barbie: Janice took after her father. Barbie made her life miserable, the twins could do no wrong, Janice could do no right and Arthur shouldn't interfere. Janice turned to her Nan for support and was devastated when an ambitious Barbie persuaded Arthur to seek promotion in Leicester. Four years later, a desperately unhappy Janice was thrilled when he chased the rainbow of promotion back to Canley.

Arthur enrolled his daughters at Broad Street School unaware of its problems. The twins fitted in easily, their looks gaining them a host of admirers. Janice didn't – at fifteen she was very tall and painfully thin.

Music was an unpopular optional subject at Broad Street with one class for each year. Eddie enjoyed the class despite Mr Weston describing Rock as pornography in music and Chopin as lightweight. Today Mr Weston was late; Eddie was daydreaming when he heard a hesitant female voice.

"Is this seat taken?"

Eddie had modelled his manners on those in Jane Austen's novels – two centuries didn't prevent good manners remaining good manners. The girl was slender and elegant, she was talking to him and he was seated. He leapt to his feet and saw one of Vinnie's enforcers nudge a crony and snigger. Eddie looked at the girl again; she was slender, elegant and very tall.

Eddie quelled the sniggering with a ferocious glare, pulled back the chair then eased it forward as the girl sat down. Janice was animated, articulate, interested in music and Eddie was pleased that Mr Weston failed to arrive. They talked continuously, or rather, Janice talked and Eddie listened. He was entranced: she was a girl with spirit, humour and fine eyes, she was Lizzie Bennet come to life.

Lessons over, Eddie was heading for the shops on Hereward Street, taking a shortcut across the recreation ground. As he turned onto a path bordering a drainage ditch, he heard screams and saw a boy holding Janice by the wrists, twisting her round, trying to stop her kicking him. A second boy was rummaging through her schoolbag, throwing the contents into the ditch while Ray Powers stood by, egging them on.

Janice had been selected as a target – only a madman would openly challenge Ray and Vinnie and their team. Eddie was engulfed with shame, the coward in him had taken control again. Then a brainwave: he would create a monster so violent that everyone would fear him. He dropped his bag and ran forward before his courage failed.

The boy holding Janice shouted, "Fuck off, this is none of your business."

"Janice is my friend." Then another inspired idea. "And my bass player, I'll only give you one chance, let her go."

The boy threw Janice to the ground and sneered. "I'm not frightened, you wouldn't dare hit me!"

Seconds later he was on the ground, head ringing, right eye closing, the big left hand had done its work. The second boy dropped Janice's bag and stared at Eddie in amazement.

"You're fucking mad."

Eddie gave a benign smile. "Of course I'm fucking mad, I'm the psycho!"

"You're in deep shit now, Ray will sort you out."

Eddie glanced disdainfully at a motionless Ray. "I don't think so." His heart was pounding but his voice was controlled. "Now piss off before I lose my temper."

He turned his back, a deliberate gesture of contempt. After helping Janice to her feet, he turned and glanced back.

"Are you still here?"

Moments later they were gone, and Janice had a question. "What's this about me being your bass player?"

Friday afternoon and a really bad end to a really bad day for Mike. He knew starting a new school would be difficult, but Broad Street was a nightmare. The first few days weren't too bad, it was hard to find his way around and he hadn't made any friends, but nothing more. But the nightmare had begun this morning: a group of boys waiting for him by the school gates. They'd decided that as he took pride in his appearance he was gay, and at Broad Street gay boys had their heads shoved down a toilet. He made the mistake of complaining to his form master, the man ignored him, and at morning break it was head down the toilet time again for daring to complain. He spent lunchtime trying to avoid being seen but was not successful – his third encounter with an odorous toilet came just before afternoon classes started.

Classes over and Mike detoured by the boys' changing rooms to avoid the dreaded toilet block; once past there the school gates and safety would be in sight. He groaned with despair – his tormentors had outwitted him; they were waiting in the changing room doorway. Their gloating leader confirmed he was to experience a refinement to the hair washing experience in the changing room toilets. Seconds later, Mike's head was down a toilet and, directed by their leader, two boys packed paper towels round his head. When the toilet was flushed the pan filled and he was drowning in stinking water.

Eddie was walking towards the school gates hoping to see Janice. As he passed the boys' changing rooms he heard shouting and recognised Ray's voice – someone was having a bad time. He regretted allowing Ray to escape yesterday, Janice's wrists were badly bruised, only her spirit held back her tears. It would be easier this time, he was the monster, a boy with a terrifying reputation. It wasn't: Eddie threw back the changing room door, saw Ray directing two boys who were pushing a small boy's head down a toilet and felt sick with fear. But shame overtook the fear; Eddie gritted his teeth and strode forward.

"First you mess with my bass player and now you mess with my drummer – are you retarded or what?"

Ray swung round into a sequence of crunching blows and fell to the ground.

Eddie regarded the other boys dispassionately. "Want to try your luck?" They backed away in silence. "Then pick Ray up and fuck off."

Mike pulled his head out of the toilet, shook stinking water from his face and hair and spluttered. "We'd better run before they come back."

His rescuer shrugged with apparent unconcern. "They won't."

Later a puzzled Mike had a question. "What's this about me being your drummer?"

Janice had always been bullied because she was different – tall and thin, or in her case very tall and very thin. Her sisters bullied her at home and encouraged others to bully her at school. Now the bullying had stopped and she was living with her Nan. Her parents said it would ease the tension between her and her sisters caused by her unpleasant new friend. Janice didn't care what it did, she loved her Nan and loved living with her.

All Mike's family were small, but his father and brother compensated for their size with aggression. Mike wasn't aggressive and he'd been bullied at school and the butt of his brother's practical jokes all his life. Now his life was transformed, Eddie had stopped the bullying and warned his brother off too. Mike felt indebted to Eddie and was disappointed that Janice was more interested in enjoying her freedom than getting to know the boy who'd risked so much to protect them.

Eddie had protected two targets and hurt Ray into the bargain; retaliation was inevitable. When the attacks started, Eddie was ready, hitting first and hard, felling challengers without mercy or remorse. He knew he would be condemned as a monster but knew he had no choice – he couldn't take a punch, not even a little one.

Jim's Gym catered for the rough end of the tough end of the market; Eddie went there because it was cheap, unaware it was a registered charity. Jim Lutkin was an ex-streetfighter and ex-jailbird gone straight, running 'Box – don't Fight' to stop boys fighting on the streets. His students came from homes where fathers routinely fought outside pubs on Saturday nights before going home and beating their wives and children.

In this violent, twilight world the maturing Eddie was special, staggeringly fast with massive punching power from his big left hand. Jim was furious when Eddie admitted kicking the Lomax brothers.

"Kicking is for back alleys, carry on with that and you'll end up in prison." He paused. "And be careful with that left hand too, it's a sleeper – you hit someone with that and they go to sleep." He scowled. "And you don't want it to be the big sleep, do you?"

July and Eddie's sixteenth birthday brought an embarrassment of riches: two birthday cards, one from Janice and one from her Nan. Mrs Newton seemed to like him, but he'd learned that lesson, her old terraced house was falling to pieces so he was developing DIY skills. Janice was friendly but didn't take him seriously, not how he wanted her to. It didn't help that she was nine months older than him; not much, but important at sixteen.

August brought a new worry. Eddie took his motorcycle test and struggled to meet the minimum eyesight requirement. His peripheral vision was good, but his central vision was blurred. Why?

September brought news that eclipsed Eddie's personal problems: Neville Webster had hanged himself in his father's garage rather than return to Broad Street School. Eddie was consumed with guilt – Neville was the fat boy who'd run past, sweating and fearful, the day he met Jimmy and Jilly. He'd seen him since, skulking and hiding, but hadn't offered to protect him. What had Eddie done with his monstrous talent? Protected Jimmy because his sister was pretty, protected Janice because she was Lizzie Bennet come to life, and protected Mike because he wanted to pick a fight with Ray. That had to change!

HARD TIMES

Eddie's seventeenth birthday brought hope, a present as well as a card from Janice, then disappointment when she avoided him. He knew why: she couldn't separate him from the monster who'd fought a vicious running battle with Ray and Vinnie's enforcers for the past year, and getting caught up in his blood spattered final showdown with them had been the final straw. Insisting she was busy with her holiday job at a solicitor's was an excuse.

His mother was ill again, another drink-induced asthma attack, but this time her skin had an unhealthy yellow pallor. After speaking to the doctors at Canley Hospital, Charles stopped visiting and the look of loathing on his mother's face when Eddie appeared made it clear she blamed him for Charles' absence. Eventually the doctors spoke to Eddie – the yellowing of her skin was caused by advanced cirrhosis, the steroids she took for her asthma had masked the symptoms, her liver and abdomen were full of cancer. Charles had stopped visiting because his mother was dying and of no further use to him. Eddie closed his mind to her hatred and sat by her bed, hoping for reconciliation.

Early one Sunday afternoon Margaret turned to him. "You won't let me die alone, will you, Eddie?"

It was the first time she'd used his name for years and he shook his head. "No, Mum, of course not, I promise."

It was the first time he'd called her Mum for years too, normally using the less personal mother. She slept the rest of the afternoon and evening with Eddie sitting in a chair by her bed. At midnight he woke with a start and stared at the shrunken figure in the bed. She was no longer the woman who'd beaten him, terrorised him with her drunken rages and thrown his carefully prepared meals across the room because they were too hot or too cold or not what she'd wanted. For a moment he hoped, she was twisted across the bed with a hand reaching out towards him. As he grasped the lifeless hand, he realised it was too late, he'd broken his promise, she'd died alone.

Charles arranged a meagre funeral, few mourners at the crematorium and no funeral tea, but he insisted on Eddie meeting him at the house directly afterwards. Oddly, he brought Charlotte, his daughter, with him.

"Father's will said we were to have half each of his estate on Mother's death." Charles made no attempt to disguise his anger and Eddie guessed that something bad was coming. "As you're under eighteen I'm both the sole executor and your legal guardian." He leaned forward. "I sold this house at auction last week and I've invested your half in long term bonds – you won't see a penny until you're about thirty." Charles was gloating. "House clearers are coming tomorrow; you've got until then to move your crap."

He thrust a piece of paper at Eddie. "That's Social Services' number, you'll need it."

Eddie wanted to hit him with the sleeper, but couldn't, not in front of Charlotte.

Eddie now knew what an HMO was – he was in one. A House in Multiple Occupation had no private facilities; bathrooms, toilets and kitchens were all shared. He was there because he was under eighteen, legally a minor and unable to form a contract to rent a room even if he had the money, which he didn't. The newsagent had sacked him the same day they repaired the tower block lifts and since then he'd lived on his dealing profits and housekeeping money. Yesterday Charles had taken his home, today was in an HMO provided by Social Services, and tomorrow he would have to find a job.

With Mike's help he'd rescued those items he could prove were his and paid a sympathetic van driver to drop them outside the HMO in Cromwell Court. Somehow, they'd crammed everything into the tiny room, but the place was a shambles and Eddie hated untidiness. Cromwell Court was off Cromwell Road, the worst road in West Town with West Town being the worst area in Canley. Eddie was living among the unemployed and the unemployable, among drug addicts, glue sniffers, winos and prostitutes.

Eddie didn't know if Janice was aware his mother had died. She'd missed the last rehearsal of their fledgling band 'The Roadrunners' and not replied to his telephone calls or notes he'd sent from the hospital. He'd called at her Nan's house on the way to Cromwell Court, found no-one at home and slipped a note with his new address under the back door. In his heart he knew it was pointless.

It was impossible to make his room tidy, Eddie stopped trying in despair; he would make some tea and think what to do next. He couldn't, he didn't have any milk! As he picked up his wallet, his birthday present from Janice, he heard footsteps on the stairs and a tentative tap on the door. He swore horribly – it was probably some arsehole wanting to borrow some milk. It wasn't; he threw the door open to reveal a startled Janice.

"I found your note." She gaped at the grubby shambles that was his room. "What are you doing here?"

Eddie tried to explain. "Didn't you read my texts…"

Janice interrupted. "No, I thought…" She hesitated. "Nan's away and I've been staying with Ian." She hesitated again, embarrassed but defiant. "We met at work, we're in love." She turned as a car horn sounded outside. "That's Ian, he's taking me for a pizza, I've got to go."

She hesitated for a moment, surprised by the shock on Eddie's normally impassive face. "We'll talk another day." The horn sounded again and she was gone.

Despite years of practice, Eddie was no good at rejection, and this was rejection on a grand scale. The sense of loss was appalling, but rejection made it infinitely worse. He sat in his battered armchair and tried to think logically: Janice wasn't unkind, so why had she rejected him so callously. Perhaps he hadn't been rejected, he simply hadn't been considered. It didn't help much, the sense of loss alone was more than he could bear. Any chance of them getting together was gone, if she hadn't considered him before then she wouldn't consider him now, unemployed and living in an HMO.

Eddie needed a cup of tea; he couldn't think clearly but he could make tea. No milk, he didn't have any milk! His wallet was still in his pocket, he would go and find a shop. As he skirted round an overflowing skip and a row of stinking dustbins, Eddie saw a shop. He walked towards it, mind full of Janice, and was startled by a harsh voice.

"The wallet, give it here!"

There were two men, both filthy, and the shaven headed one shouting at him was waving a knife. The other, a big man with a mop of greasy black hair, was reaching into the skip. It was too much, Charles' revenge, the grubby room, Janice and now two winos were trying to rob him. The man with the knife moved closer, too close to a very angry Eddie who thrust the knife aside with his left hand and banged the man squarely in the face with his right. Baldy staggered back and fell, blood spurting from a broken nose; he was down but not out.

In his peripheral vision Eddie saw the mop haired man coming at him, swinging a piece of wood he'd taken from the skip. Eddie knew he had to finish him before Baldy was back in action, so swayed backwards, evaded the man's clumsy blow and let go with the sleeper. As it made contact, Eddie felt the shock all the way up his arm. That hadn't happened for a while, not since he'd improved his timing and identified the softer places to hit. He'd hurried the punch, hit high and early, striking the man's cheekbone instead of the soft side of his jaw. No matter, the power was there and the man's legs went from under him like a building dynamited from the bottom; he was down and out.

Baldy was scrabbling about on the ground trying to reach his knife. Eddie walked towards him, the heels of his shiny black shoes clicking on the pavement. Baldy's arm was stretched across the gutter, Eddie stamped hard and felt the arm break through the sole of his shoe.

Eddie still couldn't have a cup of tea, he'd come straight back to his room after the fight. All he could think of was Janice – she was off somewhere with Ian, and he was fighting winos in the gutter!

There was no point trying to sleep, he had nightmares enough at the best of times and hated to think what tonight would bring. He had to plan his future and his first priority was a job, any job, money was essential for everything. It would be difficult – when he'd visited the Job Centre the bespectacled clerk's first action was to telephone Broad Street School for a reference. He'd gulped as he replaced the receiver.

"We'll have a problem finding something for you!"

Unsurprisingly the reference wasn't good, his only hope was to take any job that was offered, start before references arrived and try to prove he was employable. He'd wrapped his fragile collectables in back copies of the Canley Herald and unwrapped some, looking for the jobs pages. It galled him that his mother took the Herald owned by the Proctor family, Vinnie's family, rather than the Advertiser; but their jobs section was good.

The advert on page 10 read 'Fultons – Auctioneers and Valuers since 1895, require a porter/handyman. Apply in person between 7.45 and 8.00 am Tues-Sat'.

Fultons Auction Hall was located in what used to be the Broadway Cinema at the south end of Canley High Street. Eddie was shown into an untidy room by a balding, overweight man who was puffing and sweating in the cool of the early morning. The shape of the room identified it as having once been the Cinema's box office.

"The manager will be here in a minute, you can sit down if you like."

The portly man disappeared out of one door, leaving Eddie alone. He was conscious of his charity shop clothes and his left hand hurt, even bound tightly in strips cut from an old tee shirt.

"Hello, Eddie?" The voice came from behind him; someone had come in the other door.

Eddie swung round. "Gerry, what are you doing here?" It was hard not to be pleased to see Gerry, despite everything that had happened.

"I was about to ask you the same thing." Gerald Burchnall looked puzzled. "Albert said there was someone here for the job." Eddie saw his expression change. "It's not you, is it?"

Eddie's face fell. "You're the manager?"

Gerry nodded and Eddie forced a smile. "I'm sorry, if I'd known, I wouldn't have come."

"What have you done to your hand?" Gerry sounded concerned.

"Fighting."

One word that said everything and nothing. Eddie hated seeing the disappointment on Gerry's face, he held up his bandaged hand and forced another smile.

"I'm really good at it, I think I'll put it on my CV in case someone wants a minder." He shrugged, the smile gone. "I'd better go, I don't think that Fultons – Auctioneers and Valuers since 1895 would want you to hire the local psycho."

Gerry shook his head wearily. "Stay and have a cup of tea, there's no-one else here for the job."

The tea was hot and there were biscuits. Both were welcome – Eddie still didn't have any milk and had missed breakfast.

Gerry hesitated before asking his question. "Why aren't you at school doing your 'A' levels?"

Between sips of tea Eddie told him dispassionately about his mother's death, Charles' revenge and the room in Cromwell Court. He didn't look at Gerry, he was bound to be kind and Eddie couldn't cope with kindness at the moment.

Instead Gerry's tone was harsh. "Who have you been fighting?"

The truth was easy. "I went out for some milk and two winos tried to rob me." He grimaced. "They wanted my wallet and I wouldn't give it to them. We fought and I won, but I hurt my hand."

Gerry visualised the scene, Cromwell Road was a human cesspit, and… "Eddie, tell me that these men weren't armed?"

"I'll tell you that if you like…"

Gerry shook Eddie's shoulder fiercely. "Why didn't you just give them the wallet? Money's not that important."

"Money isn't, but the wallet was a present."

"Who from?"

Eddie's voice cracked. "Janice, she's a friend, you met her once."

"Your girlfriend?"

"No." Eddie shook his head. "She's got a boyfriend, she told me last night."

"Before the fight?"

"Yes." Eddie stared at Gerry. "I hurt them, Gerry, I really hurt them, but one had a knife and I couldn't let them have the wallet." He turned away. "I'd better go."

Gerry took a deep breath. "The job's yours if you want it, the pay's poor, the work's hard and no-one else wants it, starting now."

Eddie's first day as a porter/handyman had been hard, Albert had developed idleness into an art form and Eddie's damaged hand hurt horribly after doing most of the lifting and carrying. He wasn't complaining, he had a job, step one on the way up. The job would suit him too, at Fultons he would have first sight of everything that came into the saleroom, attend auctions as a porter and help in the restoration workshops. He was being paid to learn the business and he would learn quickly, work hard, deal hard, make something of himself.

Now he had to rationalise his thoughts of last night. He was in his present predicament because he hadn't planned ahead, he needed a business plan and rules to ensure he worked hard and didn't make more stupid mistakes.

The business plan first, evening classes to finish his 'A' levels and a daytime course on his Mondays off to learn building skills. Renting was dead money, the day he was eighteen Eddie would buy the biggest house he could afford in the worst condition. He would renovate it, sell it and buy another. His hopes rose; buying a house was a dream but tomorrow he could start looking for a privately rented room, Gerry had agreed to act as guarantor. Step two on the way up.

The rules next, they would have to be exceptionally rigorous because he was exceptionally weak, lazy and stupid. Rule one would be to eradicate emotion – simply controlling his emotional display wasn't enough, he should have realised that years ago. He would start with the big one, bury any thought of him and Janice getting together in the deepest, darkest corner of his mind so it could never escape and hurt him again. As of now, Eddie Stagg was in control, he was the iceman.

He stared at his pen, he wanted to cry just once before burying his emotions forever, but couldn't. If he did, he would be crying for himself and he wasn't worth crying for, never had been, never would be.

CHAPTER 3

Halcyon days

THREE STEPS TO HEAVEN

L edbury Road was at the good end of Canley's prestigious Norwood Estate, the end furthest from West Town. It had established trees and carefully tended gardens in front of substantial detached and semi-detached Sixties houses. On Sunday mornings respectable husbands connected their hosepipes and washed their cars before taking their respectable able wives and children for rides in the country. Sometimes these husbands and wives would watch proudly as their children earned extra pocket money by washing the cars using buckets of soapy water and sponges.

In the Fifties Eddie Cochran sang about 'Three Steps to Heaven'. Ledbury Road wasn't heaven and it wasn't the Fifties, but Eddie Stagg had taken three steps to get there. Cromwell Court was a human cesspit where prostitutes complained about muggers and drug addicts. Step one was moving to a converted loft above a lock-up garage in Gladstone Street. In Gladstone Street tattooed men in vests walked Rottweilers and grinned defiantly as their animals crapped copiously in other people's gateways. These men and their wives complained about prostitutes plying their trade on street corners. Step two was to a derelict Victorian terraced house in Princes Street that Eddie renovated from top to bottom. In Princes Street the tattooed men wore tee shirts and dragged their Labradors into the gutter to crap. These men and their wives complained about dog fouling. Step three was to a semi-detached house in Ledbury Road, a move only made possible because the house was a repossession trashed by the dispossessed before leaving. In Ledbury Road car washing men and their wives complained about Eddie, an unsmiling man with a bad reputation and his garden full of elderberry bushes that gave birds the ability to leave huge purple splashes on their freshly washed cars.

The anonymous letter came in the post – the residents of Ledbury Road felt strongly that Eddie and his garden lowered the tone of the neighbourhood. He wasn't surprised that no-one had spoken to him face to face, bad reputations grew with the telling, the worthy residents doubtless assumed that anyone confronting him would be battered senseless.

In the six months Eddie had owned the house, he'd done virtually nothing to it, he'd been too busy dealing, making money to pay the mortgage and rebuild his capital reserve. It was just as well he had – three weeks ago he'd arrived at work to find Gerry talking to Fultons Area Manager, Piers Farmer. With immediate effect Fultons were closing their Canley Branch, all staff were being made redundant with pay in lieu of notice. Mr Farmer, a man remarkable only for his luxuriant nasal hair, had given Eddie a bland reference and an insincere sweaty handshake. Later, Gerry had given Eddie a suspiciously glowing reference and an equally insincere sweaty handshake.

However, thanks to Gerry's reference, Eddie had a job, starting Monday, in the Building Control Department of Canley City Council. It was a Scale 2 post, one step above the school leavers and no-hopers, but it would pay the mortgage. He was lucky to get it, his good A levels and Diploma in Building Management only outweighed his bad reputation by virtue of the glowing words of Gerald Burchnall OBE, City Councillor and highly respected advisor to all manner of local and national children's charities. After his interview, Eddie met his new colleagues; chinless men in big suits and sturdy girls in comfortable cardigans. Few Rockers and definitely no streetfighters, but the latter was a good thing.

Eddie stirred in his chair, and the mug that had been threatening to spill its contents for hours finally did so, releasing a stream of cold tea down his chest. The waistband of his jeans dammed the stream, allowing a pool of tea to accumulate and soak through his tee shirt. He woke with a start and leapt to his feet, swearing profusely; he'd broken a rule – tea breaks were to be taken standing up or sitting on a hard chair. The reason was crushingly obvious – if he sat in an easy chair he would go to sleep.

Eddie examined his tee shirt and jeans, they were sodden, and they were his good ones! No, that wasn't right, he never worked in good clothes? He looked at his watch, then went to the window and drew the curtains. His watch showed seven o'clock and the window revealed a bright, clear summer morning – he hadn't fallen asleep during a tea break, he'd been asleep in the chair all night.

The memories he'd dismissed as an impossible dream came flooding back. He blinked hard, it wasn't an impossible dream, he hadn't dreamed for years, not since the nightmares had tightened their grip on his mind. Last night he'd called the prettiest girl in the world sweetheart and held her while she sobbed. Later she told Janice she was his girlfriend, kissed him goodnight and asked to see him again.

It wouldn't last, someone would tell her about him and there would be a telephone call, probably from her mum, telling him to stay away. And so he should: Jilly deserved better than a brutalised streetfighter with his head screwed up by endless nightmares.

SUNDAY TEA

Eddie changed into his work clothes and launched a ferocious assault on his garden. Three hours later he'd uprooted five elderberry bushes, torn out the biggest weeds, found the remains of a lawn and earned a tea break. Inside a flashing light on his answering machine indicated a message, hopefully not Mrs Orton telling him to stay away from Jilly. In reality it was probably business, SIKO (Oldies) and SIKO (Music), divisions of SIKO (Canley) Limited, both advertised in the Canley Advertiser.

He pressed the play button to hear 'Eddie, this is Jilly', as if she needed to say, he would recognise her voice anywhere 'Mum can't wait to meet you, can you come to tea this afternoon?'

The telephone only rang twice before Jilly answered. She sounded excited, talking to him and her mum at the same time, could he come at four o'clock?

Her voice dropped to a whisper. "I've told Mum and Jimmy about last night." Then she was excited again. "Jimmy's girlfriend's coming." Eddie hoped she wasn't local, or at least hadn't gone to Broad Street School. "Deborah moved here from Northampton about four years ago but she went to Broad Street, you might remember her."

That was about the time he left Broad Street, so Eddie hoped he didn't remember her, or rather she didn't remember him.

"What's her surname?"

"Aston."

Eddie's heart sank – of all the people for Jimmy to meet, the girl who'd witnessed his final showdown with Ray and Vinnie.

The ambush was on the piece of waste ground by the school's East entrance, the scene of Eddie's fights with Pete Lomax. Vinnie, Ray and four enforcers grabbed Janice as she was walking home and slapped her until she cried out for help. To make sure Eddie came, an enforcer was sent to tell him she was in trouble.

The planned odds of six to one reduced to five when Ray Powers conveniently sprained his ankle and hobbled away. They were soon four – the messenger didn't fool Eddie who felled him before running to the waste ground. Then it was two to one; when the two enforcers slapping Janice released her to attack Eddie, she tripped one and wrapped her shoulder bag strap round the neck of the other. Then they were even, Vinnie hung back, allowing Eddie to fell the enforcer and Vinnie in turn, before turning to the boy recovering his footing and his half strangled cohort.

Deborah was an unintended witness, and her screams alerted workmen on a nearby roof. Eddie heard them shouting as they disappeared down their ladder and realised they'd seen the ambush, six boys attacking him and Janice. It was his chance to hurt Vinnie and Ray so badly they would never dare bully again and call it self-defence. The workmen wouldn't see, they were halfway down their ladder. Eddie didn't think Deborah would see either, she was too busy vomiting after witnessing the crunching blows that felled the enforcer and Vinnie. But Janice would see, so Eddie didn't batter Vinnie senseless or go after the hobbling Ray.

When the workmen arrived, he was helping Janice to her feet, surveying the scene and being astonished by the amount of vomit one girl could produce when she was truly frightened. In fact, Deborah had watched as well as vomited, but her hysterical description of carnage didn't match the reality of a few broken noses. The workmen described what they'd seen from the roof, a boy fighting overwhelming odds to protect his girlfriend. Eddie wasn't charged, but nor was anyone else.

If Eddie had battered Vinnie and Ray to a pulp, Juliet might still be alive. Janice was right not to consider him as a suitable boyfriend, not because he was violent but because he was thoughtless and selfish. And it wasn't a fight against overwhelming odds either, a boy with a monstrous talent had taken on six amateurs one at a time – they hadn't stood a chance.

Eddie needed to arrive before Deborah condemned him in his absence. For once he was lucky – as he drew up outside Jilly's house he saw a sturdy figure with thick, dark blond hair disappearing down the path to the back door. As a newcomer, etiquette demanded that he should knock at the front door. No need, it flew open before he reached it and Jilly dragged him excitedly into the living room where Mrs Orton was waiting.

She was smaller than he remembered, and she was smiling, something people rarely did when they met him.

"Look at you, you're all grown up." Her smile disappeared when she heard Deborah's voice in the kitchen. "Stan's not here, he's sorting out the business with Pete Lomax." A pause. "I'd prefer Deborah didn't…"

She turned as Deborah appeared with Jimmy hanging back behind her. Deborah gave an audible gasp and stopped abruptly when she saw Eddie, giving Jilly time to pull Jimmy forward to shake his hand. That Jimmy seemed more embarrassed than pleased was no surprise; Eddie had always suspected he wanted a minder not a friend.

Conversation was stilted, Mrs Orton smiled uncertainly and said Eddie should call her Eileen; Deborah was in shock; Jimmy was apprehensive; and Jilly simply wanted to be happy.

Eileen tried to break the ice. "When we last saw you your mother was ill?"

"She died four years ago…"

Deborah interjected icily. "Do you live with your father?"

"No, he died a long time ago, I live on my own."

The expressions on the faces surrounding Eddie reflected their evolving agendas. Eileen wondered if he owned a house, Deborah wanted to introduce his past, Jimmy wanted the day to be over and Jilly was upset that his parents were both dead.

Eileen was first to react. "Where do you live?"

"Ledbury Road, it's on the Norwood Estate."

A nod from Eileen, she knew the area, nice houses, privately owned.

Deborah changed the subject – she and Jimmy lived with their parents. "Where do you work?"

Eddie saw satisfaction on her face as he replied. "I was made redundant from Fultons Auctioneers a short time ago…"

"You're unemployed then?"

"No." He shook his head. "I start work at Canley City Council tomorrow."

Jilly gave a squeal of delight. "I work for the council, and so does Deborah."

Enough small talk; Deborah went in for the kill. "Jimmy tells me you were involved in some trouble with Pete Lomax last night?"

Eddie saw Eileen glance at Deborah and gulp. He guessed at her dilemma – Deborah was a sensible girl who would be good for Jimmy, she didn't want Stan's foolishness to prejudice their relationship.

He shrugged. "Pete was being offensive, so I spoke to him about it."

Deborah persisted. "Why was he being offensive?"

"Pete doesn't generally need a reason to be offensive."

"I suppose you hit him, that's your way, isn't it?"

There was no point lying, the truth was probably public knowledge. "He wouldn't listen to reason, so yes, I hit him."

Eileen was rattling crockery, desperate to leave the subject. Deborah didn't want to upset her and still had the other woman card to play.

"Are you still friendly with that Janice Newton?"

Jilly was clearly worried as they walked to Eddie's car. He was depressed; Deborah would win in the end, she had plenty of time to condemn him as a violent madman.

"It's pointless, Jilly." Eddie was crushed by the thought of not seeing her again. "Deborah will tell you I'm a psycho, and…"

Jilly interrupted. "But you're not, are you?"

"No, but I've done some terrible things…"

She interrupted again. "I doubt it but…" She hesitated. "Deborah kept talking about you and Janice, are you sure she's never been your girlfriend?"

The truth was easy. "Of course I'm sure, we're just friends, we've only ever been friends."

Jilly's mood changed completely, she was bright and cheerful again. "I'll see you at lunchtime tomorrow then. I'll make sandwiches for us both and we'll eat them in the garden by St John's Church."

"But what about me being a psycho?"

"Don't be silly." Jilly reached up to kiss him goodbye. "And don't worry about Deborah, she'll like you when she gets to know you."

Eddie doubted it.

FRANKIES

Janice was worried – Jilly had asked to meet her for lunch at Frankies tea shop. Frankies sold wonderful cakes as well as sandwiches and snacks, but she guessed Jilly wasn't interested in food. Janice hadn't changed the way she behaved with Eddie, but her facade of indifference hadn't been examined by a girlfriend before. Today Jilly would tell her to stay away from Eddie, she was sure of it. It would be easier if she disliked Jilly, but she didn't, she was special enough even for Eddie.

Frankies smelled of coffee and freshly baked bread, but Janice didn't notice; she could see Jilly waiting for her at a quiet table by the window.

"We need to talk."

Janice felt a wave of despair wash over her and wanted Jilly to get it over with.

Instead, Jilly smiled and asked an odd question. "Do you know what's wrong with Eddie's eyes?"

Janice was confused and stammered a reply. "No, well not specifically, he doesn't like glare and…?"

"He has cataracts in both eyes, he was born with them." Jilly saw the surprise on Janice's face. "I made him see a specialist; did you ever think of doing that?"

Janice hadn't and Jilly changed the subject abruptly. "Four years ago, Deborah saw Eddie hurt some boys in a fight at school, what was it about?"

More confusion for Janice, where was this leading? "They were the leaders of a gang of bullies, it was like a final showdown…"

Jilly interrupted. "Why were you involved?"

"I was used to lure Eddie into an ambush."

"Did you know it was an ambush?" Jilly's voice took on an edge as Janice nodded. "How many of them were there?"

Janice hung her head. "Six, but one dropped out."

"And you still shouted for him to come and help!"

"I was frightened!"

Their coffees were untouched, and the edge left Jilly's voice as she began a new line of questioning.

"Did you know Juliet Morris?"

Janice snapped angrily, "Just tell me, Jilly, no more questions, just get it over with."

Jilly reached forward and touched her arm. "Please, I don't want us to be bad friends."

Not bad friends? Janice felt a surge of hope, but what did Jilly want to hear? Janice opted for the truth.

"Yes, of course I did, her suicide forced the enquiry that ended the bullying at Broad Street."

Jilly made eye contact for the next question. "Did you know that Juliet loved Eddie?"

Janice was puzzled by the question, not jealous. It was the right reaction.

"Yes, everybody knew except Eddie."

Then hesitation before a whispered question. "Did you know that Eddie has terrible nightmares? The worst one is about Juliet, he blames himself for her death."

A shake of the head. "Juliet's death wasn't his fault."

Jilly looked away, avoiding eye contact; she needed to lie convincingly. "Good." A long pause. "I want us to be friends because that would make Eddie happy, but we couldn't be if you loved him too."

Janice wanted to scream and tell this pretty girl that she loved Eddie so much it hurt. Instead, she smiled, but inside she was crying.

Jilly found no family that would own Eddie, Charles was rude on the telephone and vile face to face, but she found three friends. Mike, a perfect gentleman harbouring a secret that would surface one day. Jim, a kind man with a violent past, dedicating his life to helping boys like Eddie. Roxy, a clever girl with a horrific past and a future thanks to Eddie. Gerry Burchnall wasn't Eddie's friend – his good works were motivated by an overpowering desire for recognition and reward.

Janice loved Eddie; Jilly was surprised she hadn't noticed that first night at the dance. The charade at Frankies was to find out if Eddie knew or if Janice would tell him. He didn't and she wouldn't.

SNOW WHITE

St Nicholas Church Hall was an old, prefabricated building with a corrugated asbestos roof located on the outskirts of Canley, miles from St Nicholas Church. It was set back from the road with open fields to one side and the rear, with the other side adjoining The Bell public house car park. Its isolation made it an ideal place to rehearse a rock band and 'The Roadrunners' used it regularly. Dave always arrived first, with Andy a close second. Janice usually arrived a few minutes early, Eddie generally made it on time and Mike was always late.

Monday evening, rehearsal time and nothing seemed to have changed. Janice sat at a table surrounded by piles of music and put them through their paces, and in the break Dave, Andy and Mike stood and talked football, and Eddie sat with Janice and talked about whatever they usually talked about. But things had changed – three months ago Jilly had appeared among them like a fairy tale princess. Dave could only imagine the willpower it must have taken for Janice to change from the distraught girl who'd cried on his shoulder to how she was now. Incredibly, the two girls were friends; Dave couldn't understand it.

Today Dave had troubles of his own. He'd mortgaged, borrowed and called in every favour owed to him and his father to buy the family used car business. His seven-year expansion plan was a masterpiece, but it meant seven years of hard work and restricted leisure time. Something had to give, and Dave didn't want it to be the band, the golf club or his social life. To add to his problems, Sharon, his sister, was being difficult. She was a single mother who resented the constraints parenthood placed on her career, education and social life, and relied on their parents to subsidise her and babysit regularly. As he'd persuaded them to retire early and move to the coast, she expected him to take their place. Sophie was a plain, sickly and insecure child, and Dave didn't want to pay for babysitters or do the job himself.

Dave had been staring vacantly at Eddie's Rickenbacker for several minutes, thinking about Sophie. When the guitar finally came into focus, he thought about Jilly – she'd named it the jingle-jangle guitar after the words in 'Mr Tambourine Man'.

He smiled. "She's beautiful."

"What, the Rickenbacker?"

Dave shook his head. "No, Jilly."

A bad move, Dave saw Eddie transfer his weight onto his toes and turn side on, hands moving up to his chest. He'd seen the movement so many times before, the slightest challenge would trigger it: Eddie was ready to fight.

"No! No! No!" Dave shook his head furiously. "I didn't mean…"

He pictured Jilly, she really was like a fairytale princess. No, she wasn't; Jilly was Sophie's favourite Disney character. Dave gulped, unless he explained himself quickly the next few seconds could be painful.

He smiled. "Anyway, I couldn't cope with a Disney character."

Eddie relaxed slightly. "What are you talking about?"

Dave was laughing now, with relief as much as anything. "Your Jilly, she's Snow White, she looks like Snow White, she speaks like Snow White, she even walks like Snow White."

Not a flicker of emotion on Eddie's face, just the controlled voice. "How come you're such an expert on Snow White?"

Dave could solve two problems at once – Sharon was useless with her own relationships, her endless stream of boyfriends doubtless contributed to Sophie's insecurity, but she was good with other people's. Jilly couldn't possibly have a future with Eddie; Sharon would confirm it.

"Does Jilly like children?"

Saturdays were always busy, Dave had missed lunch and was hungry, but before going home he would visit Sharon. This afternoon Eddie and Jilly were meeting Sophie to see if babysitting was an option.

Sharon met him at the door with a face like thunder.

He put on a smile. "Any chance of coffee and a sandwich?"

Dave liked his coffee weak, milky and in a china cup. His particular dislike was strong coffee in an overfilled mug that dripped as he lifted it. He groaned as Sharon banged a thick earthenware mug down in front of him filled to the brim with a noxious black liquid that slopped over the side and trickled across the table.

"She's a nice girl, but Eddie's a bit odd until you get used to him." Sharon mimicked Dave's voice. "And don't look all innocent, you know who he is!"

Dave protested. "But she's nice…"

"I'm not talking about her, I'm talking about him. You play in his band, you must know he's the local nutcase…"

Dave did and…? "Oh shit! Did he frighten Sophie?"

Sharon had her back to him, making a show of wiping a work surface. "No, Sophie's like that amazing girl, she thinks he's wonderful."

"Are you sure?"

Sharon didn't turn round. "Of course I'm sure, Sophie says that Eddie's a big silly who pretends a lot, and he's good at colouring, but not very good at drawing."

"I didn't mean Sophie."

Sharon turned round slowly and gazed at her brother. "I haven't heard that voice for a long time." She sighed and walked over to him. "You're sweet on her, aren't you?" Dave stared at his coffee in silence. "You want me to tell you that they're not suited, that they'll split up, don't you?" Dave nodded. "Well, I can't understand it either, but they're a couple, they won't be splitting up."

"Perhaps if you saw them for a bit longer?"

"They were here for hours, Sophie wouldn't let them go, she wants to go and live with them."

"She liked Jilly then?"

"Of course she did, she thought she was Snow White!" Sharon smiled, suddenly cheerful. "I'll make you a coffee in a nice china cup, and there are some sandwiches left from tea, Jilly made them." Her smile broadened. "The good news is I've got free babysitters, and Sophie's going to stay with them when I go on my training course next month."

"Stay with them, where?"

"At their house, where do you think?"

"You mean they're living together!"

"That's what couples do, isn't it?"

THE RED ESTATE CAR

Kings of Canley and the Canley Herald had signed a seven-year advertising agreement. Dave was pleased with the deal he'd negotiated – Kings had priority advertising, guaranteed editorial updates on their expansion and one third of their advertising costs would be deferred until the end of the seven years. The more he thought about it, the more it seemed too good to be true.

He'd negotiated the deal Vincent Proctor, the Herald's new advertising manager. Vincent was fresh from university and doubtless had the job because his father owned the Herald, but that didn't detract from his ability. They'd spent the morning briefing Kings staff on the agreement, gaining an enthusiastic response from everyone except Carl Boyd, Kings' new trainee salesman. On reflection, Dave regretted hiring Carl – he was bright and enthusiastic but also overweight with large stick out ears, not the clean cut image Dave wanted for Kings.

Dave's office overlooked the forecourt and what he was seeing was wrong. As a trainee Carl only sold if their senior salesman was unavailable. Arthur was free, Dave had seen him by the coffee machine, but Carl was showing a customer a red estate car. Now she was walking away, two mistakes in one day!

Five minutes later, Carl was in Dave's office. "Did you know Arthur was free?"

Carl was apologetic. "Yes, boss, I'm sorry, but she wasn't going to buy the car, she was only looking." His voice changed. "She was the prettiest girl I've ever seen, I just wanted to talk to her."

"You know our policy." Dave's tone was crisp and businesslike. "She could have been viewing the car for a husband or boyfriend, there could have been a sale." He sat back, his decision made. "We need a service receptionist, and I want that to be you."

"I understand, boss." Carl gave a hollow laugh. "A fat boy with stick out ears doesn't present the right image in sales."

Dave continued quickly to hide his embarrassment. "If you have the ability, you could expand the post with the business."

Carl's next words were a shock. "At least I won't have to suck up to Vinnie..."

Dave interrupted sharply. "That's enough, you've taken the change of job well enough, but don't push your luck." He leaned forward, wagging his finger. "Take my advice, Vincent has influence so don't upset him, and I'm your boss so don't upset me." He sat back and adopted a more conciliatory tone. "On a personal level, chatting up pretty girls can be risky, they're usually spoken for. What school did you go to?"

Carl looked puzzled. "Broad Street, same as Vinnie?"

"Really!" Dave hesitated. "I didn't know Vincent went to Broad Street?"

The rancour on Carl's face was disconcerting, the bad blood between him and Vincent must be serious.

Dave returned to his original theme. "Did you know Eddie Stagg?"

"The psycho? Yes!"

"The girl you were chatting up is his girlfriend."

Another surprise for Dave, Carl wasn't frightened, the rancour left his face and he shrugged. "That's a shaker, but I'm not worried; Eddie only hurts the bad guys and I was being nice. Anyway, I knew she was spoken for, she was wearing an engagement ring, a whacking great diamond."

The telephone ringing hid Dave's dismay and he waved Carl away. When his call ended, he paused, sighed, dialled Canley City Council and asked for Eddie Stagg in the Building Control Department.

"Eddie, has Jilly mentioned a red estate car?"

The voice was as controlled as ever. "Yes, can you do us a good deal?"

"You can have it at trade, call it an engagement present."

HALCYON DAYS

Life was wonderful and Eddie started listening to music again, not just rock and folk, but Chopin and Schubert. He started reading again too, and Jilly persuaded him to read to her, but when he read Charlotte Bronte's Jane Eyre there was a surprise.

"Eddie, your eyes are closed."

He smiled gently. "I don't need to look, I know this part."

"But how…?"

"I can see the pages in my mind, I just read them."

Jilly took the book from him. "Read it to me again, please."

She followed the text as Eddie spoke; he was word perfect, even pausing to turn pages in his mind. After a few minutes, she stopped him, her head full of questions.

"Have you always been able to do that?"

"Yes." Eddie nodded. "My mind's full of things, pages of writing fade but pictures and memories don't."

Jilly was beginning to understand. "Your nightmares, are they real or…?"

Eddie shrugged. "Real, imaginary, sometimes a combination of both. I see the old man who comes for his shoes, but I never met him. I see Juliet in her best blue dress, but I never saw it." He was silent for a while then brightened up; it was impossible to be unhappy when he was with Jilly. "But it's how I make money dealing, I can remember prices, dating features, hallmarks, all sorts of things."

Janice was married and Eddie was troubled – she deserved better than Andrew Fox. In an undeserved stroke of luck, Andy had won a competition for a four-day break in Las Vegas. For the first and last time in her life, Janice drank too much, they visited an instant marriage parlour, and she was now Mrs Fox.

Eddie was married, a white Rolls-Royce, a beautiful ceremony and a reception at a good hotel. Stan Orton let Eddie pay for everything but resented his ability to do so. They honeymooned in Italy; a week touring Venice, Florence and Rome, and a second week on the beach in Lido di Jesolo, planning their future together.

Eileen had been pregnant and married to Stan Orton at seventeen, seduced by his confidence and superficial charm. A second child at eighteen trapped her in a loveless marriage and a life of perpetual debt, constantly moving to avoid his creditors. Her dream was to own a house like Ledbury Road, and she couldn't believe it when Jilly and Eddie moved to a larger house in Norwood Road.

Jimmy and Deborah were married, an unplanned pregnancy prompting a hurried ceremony at a Register Office. Their life was falling apart, and it was difficult not to feel bitter; they bought a starter home but lost it when Jimmy was made redundant. No financial help was possible from the Astons – Deborah's father was made redundant at the same time as Jimmy – and no help from the Ortons either: Stan and Eileen were separating. Deborah struggled to control her envy of Eddie and Jilly's beautiful home and easy lifestyle. She refused to believe his rapid promotion was down to ability – she ascribed it to his being a protégée of Councillor Gerald Burchnall OBE, now Chairman of the Social Services Committee. She was also deeply suspicious of where his money came from – no-one could possibly earn so much dealing part time. Even Eileen was a source of envy: she was on the brink of a career – Eddie had encouraged her to study and she was hoping to start teacher training.

Mike wouldn't be marrying, he'd met Gary and accepted the inevitable. They worked in the same accountancy firm and feared that colleagues would notice their closeness. So, in a bold move they started Chilvers & Co. Chartered Accountants, but attracting business was difficult.

Dave wouldn't be marrying yet either – the prettiest girl in the world had married a dehumanised psycho and no other girl compared. Thankfully, Kings of Canley was flourishing, but all work and no play was making Dave a dull boy. In reality, there was a great deal of play, Dave was simply unused to hard work. He was also beginning to regret his advertising agreement with the Canley Herald. Vincent handled everything personally, writing editorials and having his picture taken with Kings staff. Not a problem until unpleasant rumours about Vincent began surfacing, which if true Kings could suffer by association. Dave would speak to Vincent; the rumours were probably unfounded.

August, the next couple of weeks would be quiet. Janice had scraped together enough money to take her and Andy to Majorca for a fortnight's holiday, Mike and Gary were taking a short break whilst their new office was being decorated, and Eileen was in Bath looking for student accommodation.

Jilly was thrilled for her mother, Jimmy wanted to be thrilled, Deborah tried not to be envious, and Stan Orton hated Eddie and Eileen in equal measure. Eddie was genuinely pleased for Eileen, but worried about Janice, Mike and Jimmy. Janice and Andy were always bickering, and a holiday was unlikely to put things right. Mike and Gary were happy together, but frightened of going public and worried about making a success of their new business. Jimmy and Deborah had serious money problems but had refused his offers of help.

Thursday, Jilly's cookery class night, Eddie was preparing to take her when the telephone rang. It was business: Keith Harris with a 1964 Bronze panel Vox AC30 guitar amplifier for sale. Keith had the knack of finding rare vintage equipment, but also had the knack of knowing what it was worth.

"This is like rocking-horse shit, mate." He sounded enthusiastic. "Come and have a look, I'm sure we can do a deal."

Eddie suggested that Jilly take the car, he would use his old BSA motorbike and collect the amplifier later if he bought it.

Jilly hated the motorbike. "You take the car, I'll go on the bus."

She looked relieved and a little furtive – that usually meant she was planning a surprise and wanted him out of the way. Eddie smiled, kissed her goodbye and went amplifier hunting.

A wasted evening: Keith was totally unrealistic about price; he could keep the wretched amplifier. As Eddie drove home in the gathering dusk, his rearview mirror filled with light – someone was coming up behind him fast. Moments later a red four-wheel drive with bull bars on the front was alongside him. He recognised the passenger as Phil Windsor, son of Bendigo Windsor, a property racketeer who owned half of nearby Stanford. Eddie recognised the driver too, Ray Powers, the man he'd allowed to escape and hound Juliet to her death eight years ago. Ray shouldn't be behind the wheel – he had a drink-driving ban.

Eddie drove on wondering whether to report Ray to the police. No point, they wouldn't take his word against that of Ray Powers, son of Chief Superintendent John Powers, Head of Canley Police Division. Eddie shrugged and turned onto the well-lit Norwood Road; the substantial detached houses oozing solid respectability. Not that he was respectable, of course – the streetfighter had retired but his reputation lived on.

As Eddie reversed onto his drive, the headlights of the red estate swept across the road, briefly illuminating the bus shelter directly opposite. He thought he saw movement low on the ground, probably not important. The house was in darkness, Jilly wasn't home, so Eddie decided to investigate the movement before she arrived.

The streetlights were on, the hard sodium light throwing unforgiving shadows. Eddie ran across the road, hoping and expecting to find nothing. A moment later his heart was in his mouth, he could see a figure lying at the back of the bus shelter. Then fear like nothing he'd ever felt before – the figure was Jilly; in front of her a black shadow was slowly moving forward.

The impact of the speeding car had thrown her into the back of bus shelter among the cigarette ends and empty crisp packets. She was wedged under the concrete seat with her back twisted at an impossible angle. When Eddie reached the pavement he realised what the moving shadow was: blood looked black under sodium lighting and the pool was moving inexorably forward, slowing as blood seeped into cracks between paving slabs then surging forward again. The scene was so unreal he felt numb.

A neighbour screamed. "I've called an ambulance…"

Jilly was alive, she moved her head and tried to smile. "Oh Eddie, I knew you'd come."

Her hair was matted with blood, with more seeping from her nose and ears. Eddie knew he mustn't move her; instead, he knelt down, knees in the pool of blood, and took her hand.

"I'm here sweetheart, and the ambulance is coming."

She looked up at him, her voice pleading. "You won't leave me, will you Eddie."

Eddie tried to be calm, reassuring. "Of course I won't."

"Not ever, promise?"

"Not ever sweetheart, I promise."

The pain was coming in waves, and when it did Jilly writhed and screamed. When the wave of pain passed, she looked at him, speaking calmly.

"I saw the car, it was a big red four track thing with bars on the front." She paused, looking puzzled. "Eddie, why have you let go of my hand?"

He hadn't – the last convulsion must have broken her back, she was paralysed.

"I took my hand away to do this." He brushed her hair away from her eyes, leant forward and kissed her gently. "I love you, Jilly, everything will be OK, I can hear the ambulance coming."

"Eddie…" She hesitated, then the pain came again and she started to scream. Eddie wanted the screaming to stop, he would give anything for the screaming to stop, then it did.

CHAPTER 4

Aftermath

BETRAYAL

The paramedics looked grave, placing Jilly gently on a yellow spinal board with her head clamped between pads before lifting her into the ambulance. They were kind, one sat with him and Jilly, talking all the time.

Someone must have telephoned Jimmy, as a few minutes after Eddie arrived at the hospital he and Deborah appeared white faced and shaking. Kindly but firmly the doctor told them what he'd already told Eddie that Jilly was 'dead on arrival'. Eddie was numb, his mind wouldn't work, but it didn't need to work, nothing mattered any more. A police car arrived before the ambulance, he told them it was Ray and Phil and described their car. He told Jimmy, then Deborah was screaming, beating at him with her fists.

"You know who did this and you're still here! I saw you beat five boys to a pulp for just slapping that Janice and you're doing nothing about the bastards who killed Jilly!" Her face was inches from his. "We know who's important to you, don't we! We know what you've been up to for years, don't we!"

He wanted to scream back, tell her it wasn't true. It wasn't, it was beyond belief, but she went on and on and Jimmy joined in. Then Stan arrived, he was drunk and joined in too.

Eventually he took the car keys Deborah threw at him and went to look for Ray and Phil. He'd promised Jilly he wouldn't leave her, but...! He would find them quickly and go back, but where should he look, they could be anywhere. After a few minutes he decided to go back and face the music. No, that made it sound as if he had something to hide and he didn't, Janice was his friend, their friend, nothing more.

Fate intervened, as he turned into Midland Road by the twenty-four hour car wash he saw the red four-wheel drive – the bastards were trying to wash away evidence of the accident. Ray screeched to a halt as Eddie blocked the exit with Jimmy's old car, then he and Phil were out and running and Eddie couldn't get his door open, the handle had broken. By the time he scrambled out of the passenger door they'd disappeared.

The engine of the four-wheel drive was still running and the radio blaring. No, it wasn't a radio, it was a scanner tuned into the police control room. Eddie listened with disbelief as they described his red estate as having been involved in a fatal road traffic accident. They were covering for Ray Powers, son of Chief Superintendent John Powers, giving him time to destroy evidence. Anger took over from numbness; Eddie understood anger, he had to do something that couldn't be ignored.

It had been a long day for the reporter at the Canley Advertiser, a visit from a minor Royal was big news in Canley. He expected the telephone call to be from the Editor checking that he'd filed his copy. Instead, it was a maniac accusing the police of covering up a fatal accident and saying that in ten minutes he would block the front door of Canley Central Police Station with a car. Nine minutes later he was outside the Police Station, camera at the ready. Moments later a red four-wheel drive appeared, horn blasting, and drove slowly to within inches of the Police Station doors.

It was dark, so dark that even with his hand held in front of his face Eddie couldn't see it. The cells were underground and they'd turned off the cell and corridor lights. Eddie didn't like the dark at the best of times and this level of dark was frightening. A blinding flood of light and a clank as a hatch in the cell door opened.

A disembodied voice shouted, "Has your memory improved yet, who was driving?"

Eddie ran forward and screamed. "It was that bastard Ray Powers, how many more times do I have to tell you?"

"Wrong answer."

The hatch banged closed, the lights went off and it was dark again.

The custody sergeant made a token attempt at complying with The Police and Criminal Evidence Act (PACE) by allowing Eddie to make a telephone call before locking him in a cell. Eddie telephoned Jimmy at the hospital and told him what had happened, but that was hours ago.

Another blinding flood of light, the same disembodied voice, and a prompt. "Sign a statement saying Phil was driving and they weren't speeding, and we'll let you go."

"Never!"

As Eddie rushed towards the door, blind in the glare, the sergeant laughed and added, "We can hold you for twenty-four hours without charge, remember."

The lights went off again, the darkness was total and frightening. What was Jimmy doing, he should have been here hours ago.

Deborah was ashamed of herself, she'd always disliked Eddie, fearing the violence that lurked just below the surface, but neither her dislike nor her suspicion of a relationship with Janice excused her behaviour. Jilly loved Eddie, she would have wanted him with her and would have hated seeing Deborah screaming accusations.

Apologies would wait, Deborah's priorities were to Jilly, her family, Eileen and then Eddie in that order. She would have to do everything – Jimmy was no good in a crisis and Stan couldn't be trusted. First she would help the nurses prepare Jilly for the hospital Chapel of Rest, try to hide the evidence of her terrible injuries and make her fit for Eileen to see. Then she would leave Jimmy at the hospital and go home, check on baby Emma and telephone anywhere and everywhere to find Eileen. She didn't see Jimmy answer his telephone or hear the argument between him and his father.

The custody record stated that Eddie had been arrested for the theft of a motor vehicle and had been held for twenty-two hours with hourly welfare checks. The custody sergeant knew it was a travesty of the facts so when Eileen arrived with a solicitor in tow it took literally minutes to secure Eddie's release.

Eileen knew what Eddie would find at the hospital – Jilly had been moved from the Chapel of Rest to a slide out refrigerated cabinet in the mortuary on her father's instructions. Stan Orton had taken a terrible revenge, not only had he persuaded Jimmy to leave Eddie in a police cell, he'd denied Eddie and Eileen a last goodbye with Jilly in the Chapel of Rest. Jimmy hadn't stopped him, but when Eileen returned to the hospital with Eddie, he was full of remorse. He watched as a nurse took Eddie's arm and tell him that when Jilly was in the Chapel of Rest, she'd looked like a princess waiting for her prince to come. He saw Eddie die inside and wished he'd been stronger.

Eddie stood in the mortuary and watched Jimmy cry on his mother's shoulder, they comforted each other and he was ignored. Despite Jilly's efforts to integrate him, he wasn't family, he would always be on the outside looking in. He watched and wondered how bad a son had to be for his mother not to love him?

Eddie wanted to cry but couldn't. You couldn't cry for the dead because they couldn't hear, his mother had beaten that into him after his father died. If he cried, he would be crying for himself and he wasn't worth crying for – his parents had beaten that into him as well. No matter how much it hurt he had to remain in control, he would be of no use to anyone in pieces. When Eileen finally turned to him, he was impassive, the shields Jilly had worked so hard to tear away had all clicked back into place.

CONSPIRACY

The initial cover-up was amateurish, the police control room circulating incorrect vehicle details and failing to identify Ray and Phil only delayed their arrest. Eddie's telephone call to the

Canley Advertiser before reversing the four-wheel drive up to the police station doors placed the matter in the media spotlight and should have ensured a rigorous investigation. However, the press lost interest when Eddie was released without charge and professionals took over the cover-up.

Sir Charles Napier QC was a local boy made good. After thirty-five years living and working in London he'd returned to his roots, buying a former rectory on the outskirts of Canley. His reputation allowed him to pick and choose his work and he was now regretting a moment of weakness, accepting an instruction as a favour to a colleague without reading it first. The brief was to defend Raymond Powers and Philip Windsor on charges relating to a fatal hit and run incident. His colleague had assured him that the case was straightforward, but the more he read the more concerned he became.

Sir Charles specialised in defence, routinely finding procedural errors that weakened prosecution cases or caused them to collapse. He gained little pleasure securing acquittals in such a manner, but proper procedures were necessary to ensure rigorous investigation. However, as he examined the evidence in the Powers and Windsor case, the number of errors beggared belief.

The case should have been indefensible, a blood sample taken from Powers after he'd refused a breath test showed him to be three times over the legal alcohol limit. Statements from eyewitnesses described him driving at high speed and accident investigators estimated his speed as 55mph in a 30mph area. Furthermore, Powers was already disqualified from driving following a drink driving conviction in Leicester, and he and Windsor had failed to stop after the accident.

A cursory inspection of the paperwork showed the case to be riddled with gross and damning errors. Non-compliance with The Police and Criminal Evidence Act (PACE) was wholesale, witness statements were unsigned or incorrectly dated, and both defendants had been questioned prior to caution. Non-compliance with The Criminal Procedures and Investigations Act (CPIA) was equally pervasive. The Act required prosecutors to advise the defence of all material evidence at the time of indictment or as soon as practicable thereafter; failure to do so could result in evidence being ruled inadmissible. Sir Charles couldn't believe the amount of evidence that had been withheld and only advised days before the trial.

Basic investigation procedures had been ignored. The blood sample taken from Powers had not been sealed, it would be impossible to prove that the sample tested was taken from him. Their vehicle had been left overnight in an unguarded compound before being forensically examined, evidence linking it with the crime scene was thereby compromised. Even the tape measure used by the accident investigators to measure skid marks to assess speed had no calibration certificate.

The junior barrister instructed by the Crown Prosecution Service to present the prosecution case was hopelessly out of his depth. As Sir Charles had accepted the instruction, he had no choice but to expose the myriad breaches of PACE, CPIA and basic procedures. When he'd finished the only charges left were driving whilst disqualified and failing to stop after an accident.

Sir Charles was sickened by the triumphant smirks of the defendants and their odious supporters in the public gallery and left the final day to his junior, the colleague who'd sought the original favour. It was a second mistake he was to bitterly regret, paid handsomely by Bendigo Windsor, the junior presented evidence that Sir Charles had refused to countenance. He produced dubious statements from witnesses alleging the dead girl had been seen drinking in a public house and walking unsteadily to a bus stop. The junior suggested that the dead girl had strayed onto the road whilst intoxicated, that she was partly to blame for the accident. The truth was that Jilly had drunk an orange juice with her friends before hurrying home to Eddie.

Ray Powers was fined and banned from driving for a further three years. Philip Windsor was fined.

Sir Charles did not believe that the Powers and Windsor case failed through a coincidental series of gross errors. On occasion his London chambers employed Doug Bracken, an honest and diligent retired police officer, to investigate when they suspected corruption. Such was his anger that Sir Charles paid Bracken personally to research the backgrounds of the defendants.

Bracken quickly found that Ray Powers was the son of Chief Superintendent John Powers, Head of Canley Police Division, and that the Senior Investigating Officer, Chief Inspector Jackson, was from his Canley division. More disturbing was Bracken's assertion that the lifestyles of both men were unlikely to be supported by their police salaries.

Further enquiries showed that Bendigo Windsor was a close associate of Jerome Proctor, who in turn was a close associate of Powers senior. Rumours of corrupt and illegal practices used by Proctor and Windsor to gain business and deter rivals abounded, including trade cartels, bribery of officials and intimidation. Bracken believed that Powers intercepted and subverted complaints using Jackson and a number of junior officers. He also believed that Powers diverted police resources from deprived areas and used police officers to provide security cover for businesses owned by Proctor and Windsor.

Bracken was unable to discover why Powers' superiors at County Headquarters allowed him to continue his corrupt practices.

THE DEMON COMES

Four years of Jilly's love had made the nightmares go away, but now they were back, all of them. Eddie was running in the dark again, hiding from someone or something he couldn't see. Then he was falling, arms flailing, knowing he would soon hit the ground and die. He could hear himself screaming then wake just before impact. He saw Neville Webster in his father's garage, noose round his neck, eyes bulging and face turning black as Eddie pulled on the rope. Neville was trying to scream but no sound came, and when it did it wasn't Neville, it was him. The old man came for his shoes again, bursting through the door and clawing at the wardrobe. There were so many others, but they all faded when he woke.

Juliet's nightmare started with her lying on a plastic sheet in her best blue dress surrounded by her most precious things. She was clutching something and calling out to him, but he turned and walked away. He walked then ran and each time he looked back she was no further away, and her cries were louder and more plaintive. Then she was screaming, and he was running so fast he could hardly breathe and all he could see was the despair on her face. Eventually he would scream himself awake, but the images took hours to fade.

Now there was something new, Jilly in the Chapel of Rest looking like a princess, and he had to walk down a dark corridor to reach her. At the end of the corridor he came into a flood of light, but Jilly was further away and calling out to him. He walked then ran down more dark corridors and each time he came into a flood of light she was further away. Jilly was crying and pleading, and he kept shouting that he was coming but he wasn't, he was getting further away. It went on and on, endless dark corridors and bright lights, running so fast he couldn't breathe. Then a terrible transformation from a princess into the girl on the yellow spinal board, face broken, her hair matted with blood. More corridors, more lights then the final horrific change, her face decaying into that of the old man who came for his shoes.

The nightmare was over, he was awake; Eddie could see his room in the glare of the light he always left on, but the images wouldn't go away. He washed and dressed and tried to behave normally, but it was impossible. That night the images were still there, as soon as he fell asleep the images repeated over and over. Eddie was living in a nightmare, the horrific images of the night terrors were with him awake or asleep. He couldn't tell anyone, they would think he was mad and lock him away and that mustn't happen, he had retribution to plan now the law had failed. Anyway, the terrors were a punishment he deserved – if he'd crushed Ray Powers eight years ago, Jilly and Juliet would both be alive. He focused on one thing at a time, switched off every other thought or emotion, and slowly the iceman began to function.

He felt like an intruder in the Norwood Road house – it was Jilly's pride and joy and he couldn't live there without her. He couldn't continue working for the Council either, he needed a place to hide. The solution was to sell the house, buy something derelict to renovate and only emerge to face the world when he had to.

The deed was soon done, the proceeds from Norwood Road bought Eddie a modern starter home and a sprawling derelict house in Gladstone Street. Letting the starter home would provide an income whilst he hid in the derelict house, converting it into bed-sits.

Roxy and Mike helped him clear the house but didn't see the last item Eddie placed carefully in his box of precious mementoes. The plain white paper bag looked innocuous enough as did the words 'Don't open until I get home' written on it in Jilly's neat round handwriting. Inside the bag a pregnancy test kit had 'Congratulations' written on it.

Mike was out of his mind with worry, he'd returned from a wonderful holiday with Gary to find Jilly dead and Eddie a Zombie. The two things keeping Eddie going were his determination to take revenge and knowing that so many vulnerable people depended on him. Mike had to delay Eddie's revenge until he was rational enough to plan carefully.

Eileen had lost her daughter and was frightened she would lose her granddaughter too. Deborah had strong family values, she detested Stan Orton for his constant betrayals, so how would she react to Jimmy's terrible betrayal? Would she assume he was like his father, leave him and take Emma with her? At the hospital a dispassionate Eddie proposed a solution: Deborah should not be told Jimmy had left him locked in a police cell. She would assume he'd gone off somewhere and be so busy hating him she wouldn't suspect Jimmy of anything.

Ray and Phil had disfigured and killed Jilly and shown no remorse. Eileen wanted them disfigured in turn and wanted to see it happen. Eddie agreed, but insisted that no blame should attach to her. Eileen struggled with her conscience, Eddie had taken Jimmy's blame and earned Deborah's undying hatred, could she agree to his taking her blame as well? Yes, but she agreed to Mike's insistence on a delay.

Eileen looked grimly at Eddie as they sat with Mike on a park bench.

"I want you smash their faces, disfigure them like they did Jilly. I want them to feel some of the pain and despair she felt every time they look in a mirror." She paused; the next words were Mike's. "But you must take time and plan it very carefully, you have to get away with it like they did. You can't go to prison, too many people depend on you; Sophie, Roxy and all your girls…"

CHRISTMAS

Every day was wonderful with Jilly, but Christmas was special. Perhaps she was trying to make amends for the Christmas when Eddie peered into the Ortons' empty house, or trying to erase memories of all the Christmases he'd spent alone and unhappy. On their first Christmas in the spartan and empty Ledbury Road house, they had a real Christmas tree with lights and Jilly worked wonders with his ancient cooker making mince pies and sausage rolls. The house became a home with the smell of baking.

Eddie knew that Christmas without her would be unbearable, so he set himself a virtually impossible work target. He'd repaired the leaking roof and crumbling chimney stacks of the derelict house in Gladstone Street during a cold but dry November. Now the rain had come he'd moved inside and his Christmas target was to take down and replace the collapsed first floor ceilings. To complete his misery, the demon came on Christmas Eve – Eddie woke screaming at four in the morning, his mind full of horrifying images. He revised his work target upwards, he would replace the collapsed ceilings and strip away loose plasterwork in all first floor rooms.

Four o'clock Christmas Day afternoon, thirty-six hours since the demon had come, and Eddie was still on his feet. The images had gone but if he relaxed, he knew they would be back. He'd not had more than two or three days without them for months; exhaustion was a small price to pay to clear his mind. But he'd broken a promise he'd made to Jilly, all the old rules were back, work targets, performance targets, minimum productive hours...

As Eddie tired his work rate slowed, he wasn't meeting his performance targets. The rules were specific, failure to meet targets incurred penalties, longer work periods and shorter breaks. He began taking his tea breaks standing up and eating cold food from tins, also standing up. He had to – if he sat down he would go to sleep, and he didn't want to go to sleep.

Janice was having a miserable Christmas. This year she and Andy were spending Christmas Day with his family, and Fox family gatherings involved drinking too much and ridiculing anyone different to them. How many jokes could there be about being tall and thin and having a big nose? And why did Andy join in? Janice was beginning to wonder whether she even liked Andy, let alone loved him as she'd once thought.

In the spring they'd bought a house together, but what should have been a new beginning caused more problems. Their mortgage was based on joint salaries, but Andy promptly quit his job to start a get rich quick scheme that didn't work. It had been a monumental task scraping together enough money for a fortnight in Majorca and a complete waste of time. Any hope it might revitalise their marriage was dashed by Andy taking full advantage of the cheap drink on offer and being permanently drunk. He'd tried to make amends since, but today he was drunk again.

Four o'clock, Christmas Day afternoon, the pigs were full of food and drink, asleep and snoring. Eventually her pig would wake, drink some more, then she would drive him home. In the meantime, she would think about Eddie and the news that was waiting when they'd returned from Majorca.

It had been a long drive from the airport with Andy lolling drunkenly in the passenger seat and when she struggled through the door with their suitcases the telephone was ringing. It was her mother.

"Your father's ill, he collapsed vomiting blood, he's in hospital. You'll have to do something, you can't expect me to cope."

Her father had suffered with stomach problems for years, but this was different: he'd lost so much blood he was in intensive care. She rushed to the hospital, spoke to the doctors and calmed her mother and sisters. When his condition stabilised, she took them home to be told:

"Oh, I meant to say, your Nan's had a slight stroke, I suppose it was the shock of Arthur being taken ill."

Janice wanted to tear her mother limb from limb, Nan was in the same hospital! She rushed back to find Nan weak but still able tell her that Jilly had been killed.

She went to see Eddie, the Norwood Road house looked the same, the red estate car on the drive looked the same, but Eddie didn't. He tried to smile but his eyes were dead, the iceman was back, but this time he was for real.

It was painful thinking of Jilly, she'd always been incredibly kind, never stopping her seeing Eddie. Janice hated herself for her wickedness when Nan told her about the accident – she was pleased, Eddie was free! Then she knew she'd lost him again; if he ever recovered from losing Jilly he might, just might, grow to love a tall, thin girl with a big nose who'd tried so hard not to be easy, cheap and stupid. But how could he love a wicked girl who was pleased to hear Jilly had been killed? She and Eddie would never happen, no matter how much she loved him; Janice wanted to cry but couldn't, the pigs were waking.

Tomorrow they would be with her family. Her father looked terrible, her mother made him return to work before he went onto half-pay. It wouldn't be a happy day but at least Nan would be there. She was an old lady now, the stroke had aged her, but her mind was sharp. There would be no jokes about being tall and thin or having a big nose tomorrow.

The Chilvers were playing happy families, Mike had been summoned to join brother Paul and his new wife at their parents' house for Christmas Dinner. He wasn't happy;

Christine was like Paul and his father: small and aggressive. Mike's ideal Christmas would be a family day with children, but that wouldn't happen now. He didn't think of himself as gay, he didn't chase men like Dave chased women, he just loved Gary. His mother might understand, but Paul and his father definitely wouldn't, they were extremely homophobic, referring to Gary as 'that shirt-lifter'. One day he would tell them Gary was his life partner as well as his work partner, and that they were living together in the flat above the office.

Chilvers & Co Chartered Accountants were in trouble – securing a local authority contract could save them long term, but in the short term they had desperate cash-flow problems. The contract paid quarterly in arrears and Mike couldn't see how they could survive until the first payment date. He'd told Eddie about his problem, Eddie needed to be needed, he would find a solution.

"How's business, Mike?"

Paul was talking to him through a mouthful of turkey. He wasn't really interested, he just wanted to start a conversation so he could brag about his successful sports management business.

"It's building slowly, accountancy clients are slow to change…"

Mike was interrupted by his father waving a fork, complete with roast potato, at him. "You're not likely to attract clients while you work with that shirt-lifter!"

He paused as Mrs Chilvers came through from the kitchen. She sat down and dropped a bombshell. "Did you say you're sharing the office flat with Gary?"

Mr Chilvers choked on his roast potato, a dribble of gravy running down his chin as he tried to speak. "You're fucking what! Are you mad?"

Mike tried to sound unconcerned. "Gary sold his flat to put money into the business."

Mr Chilvers cleared his mouth and started again, spitting fragments of potato as he ranted.

"Jesus fucking Christ, my son's living with a bum bandit."

Mike flicked a Brussels sprout with his fork – now probably wasn't a good time to announce he was gay.

The Astons weren't playing happy families, they were a happy family, or as happy as they could be with the spectre of Jilly's death and money worries hanging over them. Deborah didn't know what had caused the rift between Jimmy and his mother, it wasn't his fault the hospital had moved Jilly from the Chapel of Rest to the mortuary before she arrived. Even less she couldn't understand why Jimmy and Eileen remained friendly with Eddie. It was ages before he returned to the hospital, but he wasn't with Janice as Deborah first thought – she was in Majorca – so he must have been with one of his trollops. It took Deborah all her time to be civil to him and that was better than he deserved.

Both Jimmy and Deborah's father were still out of work and their money worries were likely to get worse as Deborah was pregnant again. This time it was planned – Deborah was convinced that her failure to be close to her brother Julian was because she was ten years older than him, not because he had learning difficulties and she resented the care her parents lavished on him. She wanted her children to be close in every way, but finding an affordable place to rent was nigh on impossible.

Midnight, Christmas Day and Eddie had been on his feet for forty-four hours. The images of the terrors had long gone but he had cramp everywhere, the combination of pain and exhaustion was unbearable. No! Eddie threw down his hammer in disgust: lying in a bus shelter bleeding to death knowing that your child was dying with you was unbearable; this was nothing. The terrors were there to remind him that if he'd battered Ray Powers senseless eight years ago, Jilly and Juliet might still be alive.

Four o'clock Boxing Day morning and Eddie had finally done it, he'd blown his mind up. Two hours ago, he'd seen Neville Webster run by, sweating and fearful. Later he'd seen Lizzie Bennet walking to meet Mr Darcy, but it wasn't the girl from the television adaptation, it was Janice, his daydream at sixteen. And the penalties weren't working – he simply couldn't make his tired body move fast enough to meet his performance targets. The only option was to set an achievable target and re-impose the penalties another day. How about fifty hours on his feet?

More movement, this time it was Mike, hair dripping wet from his head-first trip down the changing room toilet, the hallucinations were coming every few minutes now. Then sound, a crash, his hammer had slipped from his nerveless grasp. Eddie kicked at it in despair and walked towards the room with a mattress in one corner. Fuck the fifty-hour target, fuck the nightmares and fuck the terrors; he'd had enough.

More sound, the telephone ringing. Eddie heard his answering machine cut in then Mike's worried voice asking how he was. He scrambled to the telephone as quickly as his aching body would allow. He was OK, but what time was it? And what day was it? Mike sounded more worried than ever, it was four o'clock Boxing Day afternoon, would he come to tea, just him and Gary.

A miracle, Eddie had slept for twelve hours, no nightmares and no terrors. That night the nightmares were back, four nights and the terrors were back, but now he could fight them and there was so much to do.

He had to plan his revenge, he didn't want to wait or disfigure Phil as well as Ray, but that's what Eileen wanted so that's what he would do. Eileen had believed in him, she made Jimmy tell the truth and came to the police station to get him out, he could refuse her nothing.

Mike needed money, Eddie had pressured Gerry Burchnall into giving Mike a local authority contract and would bankroll him until the first payment date. The fact that it would take every penny of his reserve would give Eddie an incentive to work harder.

Sophie needed stability – four years of Jilly's love had transformed an insecure, bed-wetting infant into the beautiful, well-adjusted child she was now. Sharon could destroy that in months by ignoring her to pursue her career, education and social life.

Janice needed help, Nan and her father were ill, and she was struggling with her evening class course work.

Jimmy and Deborah needed a home. Deborah was a good wife, a good mother and a good daughter. Jimmy was weak not bad, and Emma was Jilly's Goddaughter – he would find a way to help them.

Roxy and the girls needed protection, the pimps and pushers were back in Gladstone Street. Eight years on and Powers' and Proctor's policy of diverting police and council resources away from West Town hadn't changed. Eddie hadn't noticed because he was too busy being happy with Jilly, and

Roxy hadn't told him because she wanted him to be happy with Jilly. Well, now he knew, he was back and he was angry.

Finally, Eddie looked at himself, Jilly would hate to see the way was living. He would clean himself up, live decently, and every day at four o'clock would drink tea, eat cake and think of her.

CHAPTER 5

Retribution

RETRIBUTION

Eileen listened intently as Eddie showed her a knife. "On your way back to Bath, I want you to buy a knife identical to this one, they're available in good hardware shops." Eddie smiled grimly. "I bought this one in Canley, the sales assistant will remember me as I haggled for a discount, but you must be unobtrusive, then post it to me."

Next, modern technology. "You need to learn all about mobile telephones, in particular how to program a telephone to dial remotely." A pause and another grim smile. "The last thing is some lessons from Roxy."

August and 'The Roadrunners' had a gig playing at a Sixties revival night at The Heron Public House. The first set had finished, and everyone was crowding round the bar, clamouring for drinks. It wasn't a polite clamour, The Heron was a rough pub where minor drug dealers and prostitutes plied their trade. Ray and Phil used it as their local, they enjoyed the seamy side of life and considered themselves invulnerable, so dealing a bit of cannabis and cocaine was lucrative and fun.

It wasn't a coincidence that Eddie bumped into Ray on his way to the bar. He backed away as Ray's beer slopped down his tee-shirt and saw Ray and others in the throng around the bar, smirk knowingly. Nor was it a coincidence that he broke a guitar string tuning up before the second set.

He turned to Dave. "My spare strings are in the car; I won't be long."

Phil liked tarts, particularly red-haired tarts, and the one he was talking to was showing an interest in his new mobile telephone. Distracted by Ray slopping beer over Eddie, he left it with her and was relieved when she returned it. Shortly afterwards his newly programmed telephone dialled remotely. Not far away Ray's telephone rang – he was expecting a call, he usually had one around this time on a Saturday. He didn't answer it, he assumed it was his prompt to go to the car park to do a deal. He gestured to Phil to follow; their stash was in Phil's car.

Eddie was waiting on the path to the carpark, holding the knife Eileen had bought for him by the blade with his hand inside a supermarket bag. Ray appeared, responding to the call programmed into Phil's phone by Eileen, temporarily a red-haired tart. Ray wasn't frightened, Eddie had already backed away from him once this evening, and put his hand out automatically when Eddie thrust something towards him. As Ray touched the handle of the knife Eddie grasped Ray's hand and let the supermarket bag blow away. He then dragged the knife forwards, stabbed himself in the chest and slashed downwards. Ray was slow and heavy with drink and gaped stupidly at his hand holding the knife and the blood soaking through Eddie's tee-shirt.

Eddie's first punch wasn't hard, its purpose was to push Ray's head back and set him up for a blow to his midriff. It was the sleeper at its best and drove every ounce of breath from Ray's body. The fight as such was over, now it was simply punishment. As Ray's head came forward, Eddie caught it, much as he'd caught the back of Pete Lomax's shirt in the Broad Street School toilets five years earlier. This time his motive was very different – then he wanted to protect Pete's head; now he wanted to ensure that Ray's head met the concrete path face down. Assisted by Eddie's firm hand it did so, and the crack on impact confirmed the damage to be much more than a broken nose. Ray's chin hit first, breaking his jaw and teeth, followed by his nose. Handsome Ray was handsome no more, but it wasn't enough. A year ago, he'd killed Jilly and smirked, nine years ago he'd hounded Juliet to her death and laughed.

Ray's right arm was stretched along the path. Eddie moved it so that his hand, still gripping the knife, was on the raised edge. A shiny black shoe stamped to the sound of breaking bone. Eddie saw a flash of light as the pub door opened, doubtless Phil on his way, but he had time for more punishment. The rigid leather sole of Eddie's Barker shoe almost tore away Ray's right knee-cap. This should be making Eddie feel good, but it didn't, he felt sick.

Phil was on the path, he saw Ray on the ground with Eddie standing over him and picked up a wooden stool that Eddie had conveniently left on a nearby picnic table, placing it using another anonymous supermarket bag. Phil was slower than Ray, it was laughably easy to avoid the swinging stool. The second sleeper of the night crunched home under Phil's ribs. He dropped the stool and folded over. Eddie's firm hand caught his head and guided it to smash, face down, onto the wooden seat of a second picnic table. Another crack, not as bad as Ray's but bad enough.

The sound of the fight had alerted drinkers in the pub, Eddie only had seconds before they piled out to see what was happening. Ray was a mess, he'd had enough. As Eddie moved towards Phil a group of drinkers burst through the pub door, temporarily blinding him with flashes of light. He caught his foot on the edge of the path and fell, striking his head on the stool that Phil had dropped. He felt blood running from the cut on his head and couldn't believe his luck. The supermarket bags he'd used to keep his fingerprints from the knife and stool had blown away, leaving a knife bearing his blood and Ray's fingerprints and a stool bearing his blood and Phil's fingerprints.

The pain from the knife slash was getting worse though and there was blood everywhere. A tall, slender figure was running towards him, thrusting aside anyone in her way. Then she was holding him, it was incredibly comforting. In the confusion a small dark-haired woman, still wearing a red wig, slipped unobtrusively away.

PRISON

The inmates of HM Prison Padmoor operated a complex hierarchy system based on many factors including type of crime committed, number of crimes and success rate. Bank robbers were given more respect than burglars, who were given more respect than shop-lifters. However, a burglar caught on his hundredth crime would be given more respect than a bank robber caught on his first outing. Violence was respected, armed robbers were given more respect than ordinary robbers, and muggers more respect than pickpockets. Surprisingly, or perhaps not as criminals are still human beings, conventional morality also played a part – for example, those who mugged old ladies were not respected.

Sex offenders were reviled by other inmates and excluded from the mainstream hierarchy, but had a system of their own with paedophiles at the bottom. Eddie was amazed to find that pimps were not regarded as sex offenders.

Revenge, particularly violent revenge, was respected and respect made prison life bearable.

It wasn't a coincidence that undercover drugs officers from a regional crime squad, not the local Canley force, were at The Heron on the night of the fight as Eddie had anonymously tipped then off about drug dealers operating there. Their officers saw Eddie back away from Ray after the beer spilling incident and saw him leave the pub first, followed by Ray then Phil. They took initial control of the crime scene, secured the evidence and sent it all properly sealed to the regional forensic science laboratory.

The Canley mafia closed in on the remainder of the investigation. Eddie hoped that he, Ray and Phil would be charged with affray as the evidence he'd planted indicated he was defending himself against attack. Realistically, he expected to be charged with grievous bodily harm as he'd hurt them so badly. In the event Eddie was charged with grievous bodily harm, malicious wounding with intent and attempted murder, and remanded in custody. Ray and Phil were not charged.

Eddie had respect – attempted murder and violent revenge were near the top of the criminal pile. Prison life was bearable, but prison wasn't part of his plan. His solicitor was confident that a good barrister would make short work of the attempted murder charges, less optimistic about malicious wounding and certain of conviction for grievous bodily harm. He advised Eddie to expect a prison sentence of around eighteen months.

"Stagg, your brief's here."

Eddie wasn't expecting his solicitor, but the prison officer was definite. "You are Edward George Alonzo Stagg, aren't you?" Eddie nodded. "Then it's you he wants, get a move on."

The interview room had been freshly decorated, the smell of paint partly obscuring the normal prison stench of boiled cabbage and stale urine. Eddie heard two people walking along the corridor outside. One was a prison officer; they wore rubber soled shoes that squeaked on the tiled floors. The other was wearing good shoes with heels that clicked and soles that clacked on the same floor. A rattle of keys, the door swung open to reveal Sir Charles Napier.

"There's no mistake, I'm here to see you." Sir Charles smiled cheerfully. "I was visiting a recidivistic regular who spoke of a new inmate with 'respect' and I recognised your name." The smile disappeared. "I'll come straight to the point, my conscience has troubled me deeply since the trial of Powers and Windsor, I'm here to make amends."

Eddie couldn't accept his offer. "I did it, Sir Charles, I attacked them, but I intend to lie and plead not guilty."

Sir Charles leaned back in his chair. "Are you saying you intended to kill them?" He saw the shock on Eddie's face. "I thought not. Reg the recidivist said that you were not 'tooled up', that you 'done them with your bare hands', is that so?"

Eddie winced at Sir Charles' mimicry. "My intention was to hurt them, not kill them."

"Revenge for the death of your wife?"

Eddie stared at him. "It's more complicated than that, it's a long story."

Sir Charles smiled gently. "Tell me, I'm in no hurry."

SOPHIE

Eddie didn't consider himself particularly chauvinistic, but would have known he was near a school by the dreadful standard of parking and the preponderance of small hatchbacks lining the roadside. In contrast, he parked the red estate neatly and was soon standing near a group of mothers outside the school gates.

Sharon had four priorities in life: her career, her social life, her education, and Sophie. They weren't always in that order, but Sophie usually came last. The telephone call had come fifteen minutes ago, Sharon on her mobile outside a meeting room. A new job, a new boss to impress, an unavoidable meeting and would he pick Sophie up from school? Yes, of course he would! Would he get her tea, the meeting could be a long one? Yes! Yes! Yes! Eddie's fears that his latest escapade would stop Sharon using him as a babysitter were clearly unfounded.

The natives were getting restless, a strange man standing outside a school was unlikely to be popular with a group of mothers, Eddie would be glad when Sophie appeared.

"Eddie-e-e-e-e."

Sophie was running across the playground, the little rucksack she used to carry her books flapping about on her back. She was tall for her age and had a fair turn of speed; Eddie felt choked to see her sprinting towards him. Sophie came through the gates without slackening speed and launched herself at him, just as she used to when he and Jilly met her and Sharon in the park. He caught her and swung her round, squealing with pleasure, legs kicking the air, before placing her gently on her feet.

"Pleased to see me?"

There was a tremor in her voice, less than a month since Eddie had seen her and the insecurity was back. Just as well Charlie had organised bail so quickly.

"Of course I am, seeing you has made my day."

Eddie felt angry, it should be him feeling insecure not a beautiful child like Sophie. She smiled and stuck out her hand, he took it and they walked towards the car with Sophie swinging his arm backwards and forwards.

Suddenly she stopped. "Why were they looking at you funny?"

Eddie knew who she meant, the mothers. He'd warned her before, but a reminder was no bad thing.

"Well, you remember me telling you about bad men…"

Sophie interrupted. "You mean pervs?"

Yes, Eddie did mean perverts. He opened his mouth to continue but Sophie released his hand, stood back and pointed at the group of mothers.

"Do they think you're a perv?"

Eddie had no time to reply, Sophie was off. Moments later she was standing in front of the mothers in the classic pose of defiance, legs apart, arms wide, head thrust forward.

"My mum asked Eddie to pick me up. I know he's a bit scruffy but he's not a perv. Do you hear me, he's not a perv."

She emphasised the last words by stamping her foot on the ground, then she was back.

"That told them!"

Eddie couldn't take Sophie home – neither of them had a key. He couldn't take her to the half-finished bed-sit conversion either, the local psycho fresh out of prison on bail for attempted murder turning up with a nine-year-old girl might attract telephone calls to social services.

"Can we go to McDonald's? I won't tell Mum."

Sharon didn't approve of junk food. A different uncle every month was OK, putting her career, social life and education before Sophie was OK, but not junk food.

Eddie was stern. "You know better than that."

A shame-faced Sophie repeated the phrase he'd told her so many times. "Girls mustn't keep secrets from their mums." Then she brightened up. "If I promise to tell Mum, can we go to McDonald's, please-e-?"

Eddie groaned inwardly, McDonald's was heaving so they would have to share a table and Eddie hated asking; Jilly always did that sort of thing.

Sophie tugged at his hand. "You stand in the queue, I'll get us a table and I'll wave when you turn round."

That's what Jilly did, Sophie had seen her do it many times. Eddie was relieved, he was fine with queues, you just stood and waited. A few minutes later he turned from the counter, tray laden with burgers, fries and soft drinks to see Sophie waving her arms above her head.

They were sharing a table with Mark and his Gran. She gave him a concerned smile and asked if he would look after

Mark while she spoke to her friend Mrs Thomas. Mark and Sophie were soon chattering happily while Eddie listened to a succession of 'Oh, I knows' and 'Well, I nevers' from Gran and Mrs Thomas. After a final explosive 'Well, I never' Gran was back, but before leaving she gave him another concerned smile and hoped he would soon be better.

"What did you tell Mark's Gran?"

Sophie was brazen. "I said you were my dad and you look awful because you've been ill."

A chaperone would be arriving at his building site at five o'clock. Wednesday was Janice's evening class night; she'd passed her administration and accountancy examinations and was now studying for a legal qualification. Her ambition was to be a practice manager for a firm of solicitors, but she was struggling with some of the more arcane principles of English law. Eddie's three weeks in prison at the start of term had thrown her and they were trying to catch up – between five and seven every Wednesday was coursework time.

A blue hatchback appeared as they pulled onto the drive, Sophie waved furiously at the driver and Janice waved furiously back. The same car and driver had been waiting for Eddie outside HM Prison Padmoor the day after his meeting with Sir Charles Napier. Charlie was a man with prodigious influence, a word with a Judge in Chambers and Eddie's remand in custody had been changed to bail.

Sharon was having a minor attack of guilt. Women didn't have to be maternal to be good mothers, they just needed to be happy, as happy mothers meant happy children. Jilly and Eddie made her life easy by babysitting regularly and having

Sophie to stay every other weekend. Everyone thought Sophie wanted to be with Jilly – she did, of course, everyone loved Jilly – but Sophie really wanted to be with Eddie. It was him she ran to first in the park, him who read the bedtime stories and him she cried for when she was sick. Eddie loved Sophie and obviously wanted to keep seeing her and now he'd been to prison and might be going back Sharon could take dictate terms. Her guilt quickly evaporated – if she was happy, Sophie would be happy and taking advantage of a monster was not something to feel guilty about.

Sharon's next module in her Open University sociology course was child-care auditing. Research showed that child abuse was mostly carried out by relatives, close friends or neighbours, not strangers. She wasn't worried about Eddie – he was weird and frightening, but not a pervert. Sophie had never been frightened of him, not even on the days when he seemed completely off his head. However, Sharon was a good mother, she would ask the questions suggested in the module and record the answers in her manual.

Her tutor had advised her to start positively. "You like Eddie a lot, don't you?"

Sophie was writing, holding her pen right at the bottom, and didn't look up. "Yes!"

"I like Eddie as well."

"No you don't, you're frightened of him."

Sharon was prepared, her tutor had discussed interview recovery. "If I understood him better, I would like him better." Sophie looked up, interested. "Now Jilly's gone to heaven, does Eddie have a special girl?"

The answer should be a puzzled no, instead Sophie ignored the question, put her head down and started writing again.

Sharon felt a spark of alarm, her voice was sharp. "Sophie, you must tell me."

"I know." Sophie was whispering. "Eddie says girls mustn't have any secrets from their Mums."

Sharon was confused and repeated the question. "Does Eddie have a special girl?"

Sophie's reply was scarcely audible. "Janice."

Were the rumours true? Sharon didn't care, but asked how Sophie knew.

"He does her homework."

Sharon wanted to laugh. "But he does your homework."

"No." Sophie shook her head. "He helps me, but I have to do it myself. He tells Janice the answers and she writes them down."

Another day, another meeting and could he pick Sophie up from school? This time the mothers smiled at Eddie as Sophie raced through the school gates, and Mark and Gran beckoned them to share their table at McDonald's. Gran's smile was concerned again, she would have to be told the truth.

Later, in the car outside the bed-sits, Sophie pulled out a piece of paper and handed it to Eddie. He and Sharon rarely spoke, they communicated through Sophie. The piece of paper listed five items written on it in Sophie's best handwriting: singles club, key, tea, Janice and roof.

"Mum says can you babysit when she goes to her singles club on Sunday nights?" She looked imploringly at Eddie who nodded. "Mum's getting a key cut for you so we can go home when you pick me up and not to your awful slum." Eddie smiled, Sharon probably didn't expect Sophie to repeat the last part. "Will you cook my tea, and Mum doesn't mind if you do

Janice's homework at our house." This was getting bizarre, and what was roof? "There's a wet patch on my bedroom ceiling, can you mend our roof?"

THE TRIAL

Prosecuting barrister Miles Austin QC felt smug; the great man had made a mistake. In his opening address Sir Charles Napier had launched a stinging attack on the character of the main prosecution witnesses, Powers and Windsor. He'd quoted drugs possession convictions and questioned why neither had been charged with dealing or possession after cannabis and cocaine was found in their car after the fight at The Heron. He also quoted Powers' drink driving conviction and the involvement of both men in the death of Mrs Stagg. Miles Austin could now attack the character of the defendant in rebuttal and he was well prepared – the Powers, Windsor and Proctor families had contributed funds to ensure witnesses were eager to testify.

The procession of men who'd been beaten by Eddie Stagg seemed endless – could anyone doubt he was a violent madman? Miles Austin's confidence grew, he smirked at Sir Charles and received a cheerful smile in return. However, Sir Charles hadn't made a mistake, he rarely made mistakes; Doug Bracken had diligently researched the backgrounds of dozens of men Eddie remembered beating over the years.

Prosecution and defence witnesses had been and gone, advocacy was finished, now it was time to sum up, time for Pinstripe Charlie to take the stage.

"Members of the jury, the prosecution would have you believe that my client–" Sir Charles waved theatrically at Eddie– "was desperate for revenge and attacked Powers and Windsor with a knife, intending to stab them to death." He stood, hands on hips, staring at Ray and Phil. "This version of events beggars belief, it flies against the facts, it flies against the forensic evidence, in fact it flies against everything except the determination of Canley police to convict Mr Stagg." He turned to glare at police officers in the public gallery. "Earlier I told you that Ray Powers' father is John Powers, Head of Canley Police Division, and asked if this fact could have prejudiced the investigation." He turned sharply back to the jury. "Of course it did, the investigators were told Mr Stagg was guilty and set out to prove it. That is not their job, their job is to investigate with open minds, discover the facts and present them dispassionately. This they did not do, this case is flawed, it is a shameful travesty."

Sir Charles clasped his hands behind his back and beamed at the jury. "For my part I am eternally grateful to the Criminal Procedures and Investigations Act and my reputation as a stickler for its correct implementation." He expected puzzled looks and had his explanation ready. "This Act requires that all evidence discovered by the prosecution must be made known to the defence. The reason for this is to ensure that all evidence reaches you, the jury, whether or not it helps the prosecution case. Failure to comply can cause a case to fail.

"Let us start with the Atlas Major all purpose knife found at the scene. The prosecution presented Darren Albright, a respectable young man who honestly remembered Mr Stagg buying such a knife from his hardware shop. They also presented two delivery drivers who recalled seeing such a knife at a bed-sit conversion presently being undertaken by Mr Stagg in Gladstone Street. The prosecution would have you believe that Mr Stagg attempted to stab Powers with that very knife. Powers' memory of the fight is hazy, not surprising in view of his injuries, but what is indisputable is that the only person stabbed that night was Mr Stagg!"

Sir Charles leaned forward, as if sharing a secret with the jury. "Unlike the prosecution I paid close attention to the forensic evidence. The knife found at the scene bore a partial palm print on its handle, it was too smudged to provide a definite match, but under cross examination the experts accepted that whilst the print could belong to Powers, it definitely could not belong to Mr Stagg. The knife also had blood on the blade, all of it belonging to Mr Stagg." Sir Charles leaned forward again. "Can you believe it? Even with this information available to them the investigators persisted in their belief that Mr Stagg was the aggressor. So, what happened next?" He snatched a plastic bag containing a knife from the table in front of him. "I insisted that the police search Mr Stagg's bed-sit conversion in my presence where they found this, my client's Atlas Major knife, the one he bought from Darren Albright."

He threw the knife contemptuously onto the table. "And what of the second weapon, the stool? Again, the prosecution showed scant interest in the forensic evidence, so let me remind you. There were many fingerprints on the stool, including those of Windsor, but not those of Mr Stagg. But his blood was on it, just as his blood was on the knife!"

Sir Charles shuffled some papers before moving to a new subject. "Now to the parade of the pummelled." He turned and bowed to Miles Austin. "My learned friend thought he would ambush me, he thought he would show Mr Stagg to be a gratuitously violent man by presenting these wretched people. Instead, thanks to Mr Stagg's remarkable memory and the diligent enquiries of Mr Bracken, we have seen these men in their true light." He made a show of examining a sheet of paper. "Ten of the eighteen have convictions for living off immoral earnings, fourteen have convictions for dealing or possession of Class A drugs and all have multiple convictions for violence. These wretches are convicted pimps, drug pushers and thugs…"

Miles Austin was on his feet, spluttering with rage. "Your Honour, I protest most strongly."

Sir Charles turned and spat out his words. "His Honour will not hear you because I speak the truth. Compare the records of these men with that of Mr Stagg: prior to this matter he has neither been charged with nor convicted of any offence. The facts speak for themselves, these men did not complain to the authorities after being beaten because they had something to hide!"

A pause for the jury to absorb his comments. "I must remind you of an important fact I elicited from the battered ones: in none of these encounters did Mr Stagg use a weapon. I did not bully these men to obtain this fact, I was easy with them, they gave their testimony freely. Whilst fighting these dreadful people my client never used a weapon, whatever the odds."

Sir Charles paced up and down then glanced at the jury; he had their rapt attention, he was working them like an audience.

"But that isn't true, is it?" He looked enquiringly at them. "Surely you are testing me, I can see it on your faces. What about the shoes!" The jurors were leaning forward, hanging on his words. "How could I forget the shoes, the prosecution made great play of the fact that Mr Stagg was wearing robust, leather soled shoes. They suggested he bought them to fight with, to use as a weapon." He snorted with derision. "Alice Popplewell didn't think so, she said 'that nice boy Eddie has bought shoes from my charity shop for fifteen years, always lovely shoes, the last pair were Barkers'."

A moment of drama, Pinstripe Charlie, with agility belying his years, kicked out his right leg and brought his foot crashing down on the table in front of him. "This is a Barker shoe, I've worn Barker shoes for forty years. I buy mine in Bond Street not charity shops – does that make me an up-market weapon-carrying thug?"

He slid his foot from the table and straightened his gown. "We must view facts dispassionately, we must not adjust them to suit our preconceptions. When we do this the only scenario that fits the facts is that Powers and Windsor armed themselves with a knife and a stool and attacked Mr Stagg."

The afternoon brought a beaming Charlie to a new subject.

"Logistics! We know the meaning of the word, it means positioning, where people are. The drugs squad officers confirm that Mr Stagg left the public house first, followed by Powers then Windsor." Sir Charles adopted a boxer's stance. "It may surprise you to discover that I am not a pugilist." He lowered his hands. "But if I were, if I wanted to pick a fight, I would follow my intended victims from a public house, not go outside and hope he would emerge. And remember, shortly before the fight Powers spilled beer over Mr Stagg who backed away, hardly the action of a man seeking trouble."

"Now to mobile telephones!" Sir Charles picked up a mobile telephone and waved it at the jurors. "Powers said that he left the public house after receiving a telephone call. He didn't answer the call, the telephone ringing was a prompt, he had an assignation. He would not confirm the nature of his assignation, but the presence of drugs squad officers..."

As Miles Austin leapt to his feet, Sir Charles shouted. "Mr Austin, it is a fact that quantities of cocaine and cannabis were found in Windsor's car!" Miles Austin sat down as Sir Charles continued. "Telephone company records confirm that a call was made from Windsor's telephone to Powers' telephone at around this time." He shrugged. "Windsor denies making the call, he would have us believe he met a woman, or to be precise 'a red haired tart', in the public house who showed great interest in his telephone. His preposterous suggestion is that she programmed his telephone to call his friend Powers. Now, I will admit that I am not overly familiar with tarts, so it is possible that, as a general rule, they are particularly adept at programming mobile telephones, but I think it unlikely."

Sir Charles paused whilst the jury sniggered, then changed tack. "We're back with the CPIA, you remember, full disclosure of evidence whether or not it is useful to the prosecution. This disclosure shows that Canley police issued an arrest warrant for a Roxanne Bailey immediately after the fight. This lady operates an escort business and, in her professional capacity, wears a red wig. It is no secret that Miss Bailey and Mr Stagg are close friends, so the investigators convinced themselves they had identified Mr Stagg's accomplice, the 'red haired tart'. But they couldn't find her; it was a week before she was arrested and charged. Eventually they discovered why she had been so difficult to find, at the time she was allegedly programming

Windsor's phone she was a thousand miles away, on holiday in Spain!"

Pinstripe Charlie gazed vituperatively at police officers in the courtroom. "Despite a diligent search, Windsor's 'red haired tart' has not been found. In the light of Mr Stagg's overt friendship with Miss Bailey, would it be mischievous of me to suggest that someone tried to 'set her up' thinking that no-one would believe the word of a tart?

"Now I must dispel a misconception, the prosecution would have you believe that Powers and Windsor had no motive for an attack. They produced witnesses who testified they had seen Mr Stagg observing Powers and Windsor on a regular basis and suggested that this was part of a planning process for his attack. Utter nonsense! When Powers knocked down and killed Mrs Stagg, he was a banned driver. He is still a banned driver and Mr Stagg's surveillance was to determine whether or not he was continuing to drive. When I obtained a court order and compelled Canley police to produce their control room records, they showed eight telephone calls from Mr Stagg reporting seeing Powers driving a car! Mr Stagg wasn't planning an attack, he was openly trying to stop a banned driver from taking the wheel of a car. Powers and Windsor became tired of being watched and attacked Mr Stagg to stop him doing so.

"And let me dispel another assertion by the prosecution, they stated that Powers and Windsor would not be so foolish as to mount a blatant attack on Mr Stagg." Sir Charles paused before shouting at the jury. "Well, why not? They killed Mrs Stagg and got away with it! They doubtless thought they could attack Mr Stagg and get away with that as well! And they have, haven't they? Despite compelling evidence and Mr Stagg's serious knife wound, neither man has been charged with anything." He injected incredulity into his voice. "But Mr Stagg was charged with grievous bodily harm, malicious wounding and attempted murder!"

Time for contrition. "Mr Stagg's defence was very robust, but for God's sake these men killed his wife! Jim Lutkin and Billy Wells paid tribute to his truly remarkable fighting ability – if he'd wanted these men dead they would be. If he wanted to cut them to pieces, he would have done so with ease. It is to be regretted that during the fracas both men fell, face down, onto hard surfaces. Dr Norman would have you believe that their facial injuries were inconsistent with a fall. He suggested that Mr Stagg thrust their faces onto the hard surfaces with tremendous force, but then I have shown that Dr Norman is a close friend of Powers senior.

"Mr Stagg cannot be blamed for breaking the arm that held a knife that had stabbed him. He cannot be blamed for responding violently to being attacked. He cannot be blamed for being very angry indeed and hurting the men who attacked him."

The jury didn't take long to deliver their verdict. Not guilty of attempted murder, not guilty of malicious wounding but guilty of mitigated grievous bodily harm. Detailed evidence of the extensive injuries suffered by Powers and Windsor made a custodial sentence likely and Eddie stood impassively as sentence was pronounced.

"A custodial sentence is appropriate in this case." The judge paused to read his notes. "You spent 21 days in prison on remand, that is your sentence, you are therefore free to go."

POST RETRIBUTION BLUES

For four days at Birmingham Crown Court Pinstripe Charlie held Judge and Jury in his thrall. He persuaded them that Eddie was not a gratuitously violent man, that he was a guardian angel to vulnerable girls or, at worst, a vigilante. He also persuaded them that Eddie was a victim, a man who'd lost his wife in tragic circumstances only to be attacked by those responsible for her death.

The reports that filtered back to Canley were very different. The Canley Herald filled their pages with Miles Austin's lurid allegations and gave away free copies for the period of the trial. Very few bought the Canley Advertiser to read their balanced view, and Eddie was condemned as a monster who battered, maimed and got away with it. The Herald openly declared that he'd planned and executed a brutal revenge, shown no remorse and hired one of the most expensive barristers in England to defend him. The fact that Charlie had represented Eddie free of charge and had joined him in his quest to root out the rampant corruption in Canley was their secret.

It was over and Eddie was alone with his guilt and reality. Would it be Broad Street and Juliet all over again, would everyone forget Jilly and only remember the psycho who'd battered and maimed two men? Eddie wasn't worried about being branded a psycho – the monster had walked too often for him to play the innocent – but he couldn't bear the thought of Jilly being forgotten.

When he was seventeen in the grubby room in Cromwell Court and Janice had run down the stairs to Ian, he'd thought the sense of loss and rejection would overwhelm him. An hour later he was fighting winos in the gutter and thought he'd reached the bottom. A week later Mrs Morris came to his room in Gladstone Street to tell him about Juliet and he realised he wasn't even close to the bottom.

When he found the pregnancy test kit, he thought there could be no greater despair. Then he thought of Jilly in the bus shelter, she knew she was pregnant and must have known how badly she was hurt. Eddie couldn't even guess at the depths of her despair, but she'd talked to him and tried to be brave. And it was his fault, he hadn't hunted Ray down after the fight with Vinnie and the others because he didn't want Janice to think he was a monster. He hadn't hunted him down after Juliet's suicide because he was too busy with his own petty problems. He was two deaths too late, Jilly and Juliet need not have died, everyone should hate him, but not as much as he hated himself.

CHAPTER 6

Money for nothing?

MONEY FOR NOTHING?

August, and a change that was first a shock, then a relief and finally a disappointment: the old wooden bus shelter on Mayors Road had been replaced by a modern glass and tubular steel structure. Eddie had often driven by, intending to stop and sit there one more time, but hadn't. This time he did stop, too late as always, and stood by the new structure. The demolition was recent, there were fragments of wood on the ground and a piece of green felt lodged under a nearby hedge. He was tempted to retrieve and keep it, but that would be pointless.

After the initial shock, Eddie was relieved the bus shelter had gone; they had not been happy times. Relief soon changed to disappointment; he'd sat in the bus shelter after visiting the Ortons for the first time, savouring his memories before going home to his mother's drink-fuelled dislike. He'd sat there for hours the Christmas he'd stared through the window into the Ortons' empty house, not wanting to go home and admit that his friends had left without telling him. Good memories and bad, but all memories of Jilly.

He'd sat there with Juliet and talked about music. She wasn't embarrassed to be seen with him; he saw pleasure on her face whenever they met. Why didn't he know what everyone else knew? Juliet was a lovely girl, not pretty like Jilly or elegant like Janice, but she had that glow inside that all really good people had. He was proud to have her as his friend, he wished he could sit with her one more time and tell her so.

Eddie knew he was avoiding the issue; he'd not stopped and sat in the bus shelter because most of the memories were of Janice. She'd never sat there with him, Janice was more forthright than Juliet, she would have asked why he didn't take her home. Instead, he'd sat and daydreamed and pined for her.

He was worried about Janice; it wasn't the old feelings coming back, he was simply concerned for a friend. She was depressed, her father and Nan were ill, and Barbie and the twins let her do everything. To make matters worse, Eddie was convinced that Andy was deliberately undermining her self-confidence. Janice was a clever girl who became more and more attractive as she got older; with a little self-belief she would realise she was too good for Andy and leave him. An unattached Janice would have to fight the suitors off – not him of course, Janice was his friend, nothing more.

In two weeks it would be the third anniversary of Jilly's death and Eddie had a better life than he had any right to. That first Christmas without her he'd learned how to tame the terrors and had since refined the technique. The trick was to work hard and deprive himself of sleep so he could push himself to hallucinate and clear his mind in less than a day. Unless triggered by something, the terrors came much less often now, but he had to be ready. The upside was that he could maintain a semblance of normality most of the time; the downside was that he was horribly tired all of the time.

Just as it became with Juliet, so it had become with Jilly; most people had forgotten the beautiful girl who'd died so terribly but remembered his violence. How could people close their minds to the fact that Ray and Phil had mown Jilly down, left her to bleed to death in a bus shelter and shown no remorse? Eddie wasn't trying to justify his brutal revenge, but he couldn't understand the endless sympathy that still came their way. The Canley Herald kept the story running for months with editorials and articles on plastic surgery. They were clever too, printing pictures of Ray and Phil as youngsters, making it look as though he'd disfigured boys not men. Eventually the public tired of the gruesome details, but not of talking about the psycho.

Eddie had exploited his knowledge of planning and building regulations to complete the bed-sit conversion quickly; he had needy tenants waiting. His dealing profits plus a loan had bought him a derelict three storey house and a similarly derelict adjoining short parade of shops at the better end of West Town. The renovated shops were now individual small businesses, and the three-storey house would soon be three flats. Two were complete and tenanted, the third, the top flat, was his temporary home.

SIKO (music) and SIKO (oldies) were flourishing and had been joined by SIKO (PA), a Public Address hire business. Eddie had permanent and semi-permanent PA set-ups in pubs, clubs and schools all over Canley. Combined with his dealing and rental income, he was making a prodigious amount of money. Was it money for nothing? No chance, money was a means to an end, not an end in itself.

SEEDS OF CHANGE

Heavy overnight rain had left a wet patch on the bedroom ceiling in the top flat. Eddie's roofing work was usually good, but something had clearly failed, probably the lead flashing around the chimney stack. It would take ages to build a scaffold tower three storeys high, so he would repair it from a ladder.

His longest ladder just reached the chimney stack and Eddie could see the loose flashing. A few minutes later he was sitting astride the apex of the roof, dressing the lead back into place with a mallet. One piece was hard to reach so Eddie hooked his leg round the chimney stack and hung down; the rules did not permit fear of heights. Perhaps the rain had made the roof particularly slippery, perhaps he was more tired than usual, perhaps anything, but he was sliding down the roof. A moment of temptation, three storeys down to a concrete courtyard – in seconds he could be with Jilly.

No! No! No! What about his girls! Eddie twisted violently, tucked his head under and executed a forward roll down the roof. As his feet touched the guttering he thrust with all his might. Now he was falling, like in his nightmares, his thrusting legs projecting him towards the huge ash tree in the courtyard that he'd spent so much time root pruning to prevent damage to the foundations of the flats. He hit it spread-eagled, the thin upper branches breaking and slowing his fall. Further down a thicker branch bent but didn't break and Eddie felt a searing pain in his side. As he twisted his head to look another branch struck his face and everything was dark.

St Nicholas Church Hall had changed little over the years. The re-decoration four years ago had lasted well, just a few scuffs on the paintwork and the odd faded patch where the sun had caught the walls marked the passage of time. There were improvements too, each year the village hall committee replaced a couple of rotting wooden windows with plastic double glazed units; with care the old hall would last for years.

Rehearsal time again and Dave arrived first as usual. He was in a bad mood and knew why: it was almost three years to the day since Jilly was killed. On the way over he'd called in to see Sharon and found her in a foul mood. Nothing to do with Jilly, Sharon was feeling sorry for herself, and angry with the world for treating her badly.

"I never thought it would be like this, I was going to be a successful single mother with a beautiful, talented daughter." She'd paused before continuing angrily. "But she's not, is she? She's plain and she's ordinary."

Dave was shocked. "Sophie's a sweet girl, well-adjusted with a nice personality…"

Sharon snapped back, "No-one admires sweet and well-adjusted, they admire talent, achievement, beauty! I've wasted eleven years on her and I don't want to go to speech days to see other girls get prizes." She was in tears. "The Kings have always been a clever, attractive family and Kenny was like a Greek God – why hasn't Sophie inherited any of it?" Then she'd turned on him, pointing her finger. "And don't look at me like that, the only thing you're interested in is your bloody business. You turn up once a month for half an hour then bugger off again. Well, you can bugger off now, I'm not getting you any tea."

Dave used to share one of Sharon's weaknesses, being uncomfortable with unattractive people. If Sophie had been pretty, he wouldn't have encouraged Sharon to foist her off on Jilly and Eddie. Nor would he have demoted Carl Boyd from salesman to service receptionist if he hadn't been fat with stick out ears. Carl had become an exceptional service manager; if Dave had given him a chance he would have been an exceptional sales manager. Dave was ashamed of his obsession with appearance; a procession of pretty girls hadn't made him happy. The new mature Dave was looking for a nice girl, being pretty would be a bonus not a requirement. Jilly was the nicest girl in the world as well as the prettiest, he wouldn't have gone off dealing like Eddie and let her get knocked down and killed.

"Always you and me first." Andy had arrived looking smart. "What do you think of my new shirt, impressive or what?"

It was impressive, designer and expensive, but Dave struggled to be complimentary. He'd always liked Janice but never taken her seriously, not attractive enough, or that's what the old Dave thought. The new Dave was worried about her and angry with Andy for buying expensive shirts when they were obviously short of money. Janice was depressed, doubtless worn out by a combination of Andy's extravagance and worrying about the psycho. The vivacious girl of seven years ago was gone, and it didn't help that Andy was always picking fault with her. Dave was still trying to find a compliment when he heard footsteps. It should have been Janice but, for once, Eddie was early.

Dave turned and gasped. "What's happened to you?"

The right hand side of Eddie's face was one huge bruise, the eye was closed with stitches in among the swelling. There was something wrong with his left side too, he was twisted over guarding it, but the voice was as controlled as ever.

"I fell off a roof."

Andy sniggered. "Finally met your match, someone better than you."

Eddie fixed Andy with his good eye. "In your dreams; I fell off a roof."

Andy was gloating. "Come on, tell us, who sorted you out?"

Then the movement Dave had seen so many times, Eddie transferring his weight to his toes, turning side on with his hands moving up to his chest. Eddie was ready to fight, but was presenting southpaw like a left-hander, protecting his damaged side.

His voice had a real edge. "I think I'll wipe that smile off your face."

Dave stepped forward. "Pack it in or..."

He was still angry with himself and Sharon, and his anger showed in his voice. A mistake, Eddie fixed them both with his good eye.

"Or what! Come on, I'll take the both of you."

Andy was no longer gloating, he knew that even with one eye and a damaged side Eddie was still horribly dangerous. Dave gaped at Eddie, he was out of control.

"Eddie, stop it!"

They'd missed the sound of the door. Three words and Eddie's heels were down and he was backing away. As he turned to face the girl who'd controlled him so easily, Dave saw despair on his face. Eddie was frightened he would upset

Janice, or frightened he wouldn't, that was why he was so easily provoked.

The scream seemed to go on for ever and Dave wanted to hold Janice and comfort her as he'd done seven years ago at the dance in Broad Street School Hall.

The top flat was finished, and Eddie was looking for a new property to renovate. It would have to be small – the huge loans he'd taken out to fund improvement projects in West Town and buy the West Town café had strained his credit limit. He would have to work harder than ever to pay off the loans at his target rate, but was phlegmatic about it – he'd only ever been really good at two things: fighting and working. The fighting was more or less over, three years of uncompromising brutality had cleared the pimps and pushers, not just from Gladsone Street but from most of West Town, which left working.

Eddie and Janice were having lunch at Frankies, as friends, nothing more. Janice was worried about Eddie, he'd always been afraid of heights so specialised in repairing roofs to prove he wasn't. Working himself into an early grave was bad enough but falling off roofs…? A flash of inspiration had set her searching through property advertisements.

"When you were twenty, what did you want the most?"

She glanced at Eddie; his right eye was beginning to open, the side of his face a massive purple, yellow and red bruise. Try as she might, she could never guess what he was thinking, but it should be that he wanted his own restoration workshop. Eddie wasn't thinking that at all, at twenty what he wanted most was to get together with Janice. The moment came and went as Janice explained.

"A workshop for the SIKO businesses."

Janice didn't understand Eddie's flicker of surprise – what else had he wanted? She produced the property details with a flourish and smiled as he read them. When he'd finished, she took them back and read aloud.

"Cedar Walk, Canley. Detached workshop with fully glazed shop/display area to front and enclosed yard to rear. Previously a monumental masons, but permission for most trades."

MAY

Rehearsal time again and Mike was driving to St Nicholas Church Hall, late as usual. He didn't notice that the rows of drab houses gave way to hedgerows filled with cheerful May blossom; he was worried about Janice and Eddie.

Mike was happy, business was steady, and he and Gary were living together in the flat above the office. Ostensibly they were business partners sharing costs, but his father and brother had still disowned him, living in the same building as a shirt-lifter was enough. He wanted to tell the world he loved Gary, but wondered who else would disown him if he did.

Janice was nothing like the spirited girl she used to be. Her Nan and father were ill, and she was worried about Eddie, but there was more to it than that. Mike agreed with Eddie that Andy was deliberately undermining her confidence, frightened he would lose his meal ticket if she realised what a clever, attractive girl she was. That brought Mike to a new worry: he suspected that Dave was taking an interest in her. Mike would have to keep an eye on him, Janice was vulnerable at the moment and the only person right for her was Eddie.

Eddie was a pariah; dislike of him had grown rather than abated. For some it was pathetic revenge-taking, paying Eddie back for having to be nice to him to please Jilly. Others, including Dave, blamed him for Jilly's death, for going out dealing rather than taking her to her evening class. Blaming Eddie might ease their hurt, but why not blame the real culprit, Ray Powers? In addition, his amazing ability to make money excited resentment not admiration, and seemed to reinforce the idea that he was cold and uncaring. Eddie wasn't uncaring, he hid his hurt away because that was the only way he could function, and made good use of his money. And yet almost everyone believed him to be a violent maniac, a belief aided by the number of men being found face down in alleys after Eddie retuned to West Town. Fair enough, Eddie was responsible but he wasn't a maniac; he was protecting his girls.

Eddie provoked some of the dislike by busking in Canley High Street on Saturday afternoons. He said he wanted to show the world he wasn't ashamed of hurting Ray and Phil, but Mike suspected a deeper motive; Eddie wanted everyone to hate him as much as he hated himself.

Janice's hope that buying the workshop would make Eddie ease up a little hadn't worked. Eddie had converted the loft into a rudimentary living space and was working harder than ever. The only good news was that he had a companion, a huge grey tabby cat called Desmond who was given to attacking anyone he didn't like, which seemed to be everyone except Eddie.

Odd, as Mike drew into the car park, he saw Jimmy's car but not Eddie's estate or Janice's hatchback. His concern increased when he pushed through the doors into the hall to see Andy, Dave, Jimmy and Deborah huddled round a table. He'd wondered why Andy, not Janice, had telephoned to arrange the rehearsal, and why were Jimmy and Deborah there?

Andy was on his feet with a smile of welcome. "We've got a proposal for you."

Mike looked at the others, Dave seemed embarrassed, Deborah defiant and Jimmy worried.

He snapped, "Where's Eddie and Janice?"

Andy was unabashed. "Sit down, hear us out." Mike remained standing and Andy shrugged. "We should be the band, without Eddie we could be popular again, no more being banned from half the pubs and clubs in Canley. We're sick of him, we want Eddie out and Jimmy in." Andy slapped him on the back. "Come on, Mike, you know it makes sense. You don't owe him anything, all he cares about is making money and building his fucking empire."

He looked to the others for support, Dave and Deborah nodded grimly, but Jimmy's head was down.

Mike stared at them in turn, sickened by their disloyalty. Andy interpreted his hesitation as indecision and smiled again.

"Are you with us then?"

"No." Mike spat the word out. "Eddie's my friend, he'll always be my friend, I owe him more than you'll ever know."

Mike paused; dare he tell them some of what he knew? No, not with Andy there.

Andy wrongly interpreted his hesitation as a change of mind. "Come on, Jimmy in and the psycho out?"

"No, you're the psycho, not him!" Mike glared at Jimmy and Dave. "I can understand this drink sodden moron wanting Eddie out but.."

Mike got no further, Andy grabbed his arms and shook him angrily. "Eddie wouldn't be your friend if he knew your dirty little secret, would he? Go on, tell them if you dare!" He pushed Mike towards the others, nose wrinkling with distaste. "Tell them you're a tail gunner, that you and Gary sleep together, that you're queers." He pushed Mike again. "Cleaners see things, two bedrooms but only one bed slept in, two cosy mugs on the bedside table!"

He looked at Dave, Jimmy and Deborah for support, but didn't get it.

Mike shrugged his shoulders, embarrassed but not apologetic. "Yes, I live with Gary, so why not have all the other names: shirt lifter, bum bandit, turd burglar…? Eddie guessed when I was fifteen, he accepted it then and he accepts it now, he likes Gary." He paused. "And Janice knows, she likes Gary as well."

A crestfallen Andy stepped back, his crude personal attack had backfired.

Mike offered an olive branch. "'The Roadrunners' can carry on as before if you want?"

Andy gave an almost imperceptible nod, turned on his heel and strode towards the door.

Deborah stood up. "Why do you always defend that maniac…?"

Mike took a deep breath, this was his chance; Andy was beyond hope but the others weren't. It meant betraying confidences but…

"Please sit down, I need to talk to you."

Deborah sniffed. "There's nothing to say, Andy told the truth, we wanted Eddie out and Jimmy in."

"No." Jimmy shook his head. "I thought I was going to join the band, not replace Eddie."

Deborah snapped at him,. "You thought wrong, I want you away from that monster!"

Mike saw Jimmy jump guiltily at Deborah's words – was he hiding something? He decided to probe. "You look guilty, Jimmy, what are you hiding?"

Deborah stepped in. "He's not hiding anything, Eddie's a disloyal monster and that's the end of it."

"He's not disloyal and he's not a monster." Mike glared at her. "You've had a down on him ever since you saw him give a few boys a well-deserved bloody nose years ago, but have you ever asked yourself why he did it?" He paused for effect. "Because he wanted to put an end to a vile bullying regime. Not for his own sake – they were no threat to him – but to protect those who couldn't protect themselves." Mike went right up to Deborah's face. "Ray Powers hounded Juliet to her death and nobody did anything. Juliet named him and Vinnie in her suicide note and nobody did anything. The enquiry report criticised them and the teachers and the governers, and still nobody did anything. Ray mowed Jilly down and left her to die in agony in a bus shelter and all everyone talks about is Eddie hurting him!"

Dave had heard rumours about Vincent being a school bully and liking S&M sessions with call girls after he'd signed his seven-year advertising partnership with the Canley Herald. The contract was due to end soon but if he didn't extend it he would have to pay seven years deferred advertising costs immediately.

Deborah remembered seeing Eddie batter four boys in front of her, but her mind was on more recent events.

"I'll tell you something about Eddie that will make you realise what he is…!"

Jimmy leapt to his feet. "No, Deborah, leave it!"

"No, I won't leave it." It was her turn to take a deep breath. "At the hospital, after Jilly was killed, I wanted Eddie to find the men who did it. I shouted at him, accused him of having an affair with Janice and kept shouting until he went. I know it was the wrong time to make accusations, but he didn't come back for a whole day, he was off taking comfort with one of his trollops." She sneered at Mike. "Well, what do you think of him now?"

Mike saw Dave nodding slowly, clearly ready to believe anything bad about Eddie, but Jimmy looked desperate to leave. Why?.

He bluffed. "That's not true, is it, Jimmy?" he shouted. "Is it?"

Jimmy's voice sounded strangled. "He wasn't with anyone."

Deborah turned on him. "You don't know where he was, but he wasn't with Jilly. I left her in the Chapel of Rest looking like an Angel and he didn't come."

Mike bluffed again. "The truth, Jimmy, tell the truth!"

The strangled voice continued. "Eddie didn't come because he couldn't, he was in a police cell. They locked him up after he backed the car into the police station doors. He telephoned me at the hospital, asked me to get him out." He paused. "Dad persuaded me to leave him there."

Deborah gaped at her husband. "No, you're lying!"

"I'm not." Jimmy shook his head. "Ask Mum if you like..." His voice tailed away.

Mike found his voice. "You bastard!"

Jimmy stared at him, distraught. "But, I thought you knew? Did you know..."

"No, I didn't." Mike cleared his throat. "Did he hit you?"

Jimmy whispered. "No, he just stood in the mortuary and sort of shrivelled up. It was like he sort of switched off."

Mike had to go on the offensive, even though he was breaking his word. "My turn to tell a secret." He stared at Jimmy and Deborah. "Your house, the one you've lived in for the last three years where the rent's so cheap it must seem too good to be true..."

Deborah interrupted, "What's that got to do..."

Mike shouted her down. "It's Eddie's house, for Christ's sake, didn't you ever wonder why it was so cheap, why you've never had a rent increase?"

She protested, "But we got it through a proper letting agent."

"The West Town Letting Agency?"

"Yes?"

Mike laughed. "The one Eddie recommended to Jimmy?" Jimmy nodded then hung his head as Mike continued. "Eddie owns the business, two of his girls run it." He turned to Deborah. "Well, who's disloyal now then? Jimmy betrays Eddie in an unspeakable way and gets forgiveness and a cheap house to live in."

More for them later, Mike turned on Dave. "Why do you want Eddie out of the band?"

Dave shrugged. "Some days he's so far off his head I think he's on drugs..."

Mike interrupted viciously, "Don't lie to me! Eddie's a teetotal non-smoker, he's never touched a drug in his life, and you know it." Mike didn't have to bluff this time, he'd guessed Dave's motive. "Tell the truth or I'll tell it for you."

Dave was tired of pretending, perhaps the truth would exorcise some ghosts. "I want to get Janice away from him, she's a nice girl, she deserves better."

Mike snorted. "Like who, you perhaps?"

Too personal, Mike changed subjects abruptly. "You're happy to mix with a pervert and sadist like Vinnie Proctor, yet criticise Eddie?"

A good call – Dave was eager to avoid talking about Janice. "Vincent said Ray Powers ran Broad Street School and Eddie fought anyone and everyone because he enjoyed it."

Mike hissed, "Only a fool would believe that, think about it while I tell you all another secret." He stepped back and glared at them. "None of you were at Eddie's trial, but I bet you read the newspaper reports." Nodding heads all round. "Do you remember the allegation that a red-haired tart had helped him, and that Roxy was arrested then released?" More nods. "Well, the red haired tart did exist, but she wasn't Roxy, she was Eileen, dressed up like a tart and trained by Roxy." Mike stared at a stunned Jimmy. "Your Mum asked Eddie to disfigure Ray and Phil and be part of it, so that's what happened. If you don't believe me, ask her."

Mike made his demands while they were in shock. "You're going to help me prove Eddie isn't a monster, and you're going to help me get him and Janice together." He saw the outrage on Deborah's face and snapped, "Use your eyes, for Christ's sake, Janice is wasting away and Eddie's like a dead man walking about – do they look like a happy couple? Now, here's what you are going to do…"

JANICE

Janice had broken an unwritten rule by visiting Eddie without telephoning first. It wasn't planned, Andy had gone out without saying where he was going, and she'd just done it. Eddie was working too hard and she wanted to see how he looked when he hadn't had time to prepare himself. Her worst fears were realised, he answered her knock on the workshop door looking haggard and exhausted. She couldn't hide her concern and then it came from nowhere, the look that had melted her inside when she was seventeen, but better. This time Eddie opened his eyes right up and openly smiled before they were half closed again.

Her intention to berate him for working too hard disappeared in her confusion and she stammered out a story about an incomprehensible piece of legislation she needed to master for an urgent essay. Eddie smiled again, found the Regulations on the HMSO website, explained them in plain English and suggested an essay structure. She scribbled some notes then fled before she made a fool of herself.

Andy was home early, sober and belligerent. Drunk and belligerent was normal, but sober and belligerent was a bad sign.

"You've been out, your car radiator's hot, where have you been?"

"You went out first, where have you been?"

Janice was glad she'd answered back, but knew what would happen. Andy grabbed her by the arms and shook her. He was a powerful man and it hurt, it always hurt, she didn't wear long sleeves to hide her thin arms, she wore them to hide her bruises.

"I said where have you been?" His face was inches from hers. "You've been to see that fucking Eddie, haven't you?"

Years ago when Eddie taught her self-defence, he said that amateurs often fought square on with their legs apart and how vulnerable it made them. Andy was a drunk and a bully, she deserved better, he deserved a lesson and his legs were apart. A bony knee in the groin gave the lesson, Andy's hands fell away and he staggered back, his face a mask of pain.

"Yes, I've been to see Eddie and if you ever hurt me again, I'll tell him," Janice screamed at him. "And he'll come and hurt you!"

The wardrobes in the main bedroom were full of Andy's suits, sweaters and endless designer shirts. Janice kept her clothes in the spare room so moving the rest of her things in there didn't take long. Andy didn't retaliate; he stayed in the sitting room moaning and feeling sorry for himself.

Tomorrow she would do what she should have done years ago:, close their joint bank account and stop her payments to Andy's credit cards, store cards and loans. She would pay the mortgage and utility bills but from now on Andy would have to manage his own debt problems. They would lead separate lives in the same house, and she would do what she wanted when she wanted.

Their spare room was long and narrow with a window at one end and a single bed against the wall, just like her old room in Nan's house. Janice lay on the bed, closed her eyes, held her locket and dreamed she was back in the little terraced house with Nan. Tonight she would cry herself to sleep thinking about Eddie like she used to, but now there was a glimmer of hope. Janice opened the locket and looked at the pictures inside, one day she would tell everyone it wasn't Nan's pendant, that it was a locket that Eddie gave her. Downstairs, Andy was quiet; he would never touch her again.

CHAPTER 7

Rehabilitation

UNPALATABLE TRUTHS

"Jimmy, what else are you hiding?"

Deborah was fuming, Mike had made her look a fool and she suspected Jimmy hadn't told her everything. Slowly a shamefaced Jimmy admitted his part in a second act of betrayal.

"Dad told them to move Jilly to the mortuary as revenge against Mum for leaving him. I didn't try to stop him, I was angry with her for leaving us..." He paused, shaken by the contempt in Deborah's eyes. "Mum said you'd hate me for what I'd done, she was frightened you'd leave me and take Emma with you." He hung his head. "Eddie said I should let you think he'd gone off somewhere, he said you'd be so busy hating him you wouldn't ask any questions."

It was an unpalatable truth, Deborah wanted to hate Eddie, blame him for anything and everything to ease her grief. But now she wanted facts before complying with Mike's demand to talk to Eileen about Janice, Roxy and Eddie's girls. A Land

Registry search confirmed that their house was owned by SIKO (Canley) Ltd and a Company Search confirmed SIKO was Eddie's company. Deborah wasn't surprised that Eddie declared directorships in other companies, but was shocked to find that Daisy Newton and Eileen Orton were co-directors with him of Catering Services (Canley) Ltd and Care at Home (Canley) Ltd.

Eileen met Deborah at Bath railway station and they walked to the house she shared with four other students. The photographs on Eileen's desk showed she had no quarrel with Eddie – there were pictures of him and Jilly together, alongside those of Jimmy and Jilly as children and her and Jimmy with Emma and Jack.

"Eddie didn't want to hurt Phil, but I insisted, so what does that make me?" Eileen's eyes flashed. "I also insisted in being involved, I wanted to see them being hurt! He's not a monster, Deborah, but he'll do anything to protect his girls."

Deborah spoke harshly. "Mike said I should ask you about his trollops and…"

Eileen interrupted angrily. "Don't call them trollops! There but for the grace of God could be me, or even you!"

Deborah hid her surprise by asking about Eileen's directorships. "I nearly didn't go to university because I couldn't cope with the idea of student loans and getting into debt, so Eddie said he'd start dealing seriously again and help me." Eileen's voice cracked. "That's why he was out the night Jilly was killed." She cleared her throat. "Anyway, after Jilly died, he made me an executive director of the two companies and I get monthly pay cheques. They do some sub-contracting but mostly they're a front to manufacture employment histories and references for his girls. Mrs Newton used to do most of it, but I've taken over now she's unwell. His girls cost him a fortune."

"I've been such a fool." Deborah stared at Eileen. "Eddie offered to help us so many times, but I always refused because I thought..." She paused and stared at Eileen again.

"You thought he earned money from his girls?" Eileen gave Deborah a withering look and continued. "Janice is as silly as you, she has a real problem with Roxy and the girls and doesn't know her grandmother has been helping them for years. And before you ask, Jilly quite liked Janice, they must have talked and reached an understanding." Eileen's voice cracked again. "Eddie and Janice have never been an item, but now Jilly's gone they're a love story waiting to happen. At one time I couldn't have coped with the idea, but now I think he's earned another chance at happiness."

Dave was feeling guilty, he'd promised Mike he would talk to Carl Boyd about Vincent, but hadn't. He hadn't renewed his contract with the Canley Herald either, he'd resigned himself to another year in his poky flat and paid the deferred advertising costs. He would talk to Carl tomorrow, or perhaps...? The telephone ringing rescued him from his indecision; it was Sharon sounding flustered.

"I've got to go out, it's a fantastic job opportunity but Sophie's sick again, I can't find anyone else, you'll have to come."

She hung up, giving him no chance to refuse. Dave thought that Sophie's weak stomach was a thing of the past, but apparently not. He ordered a taxi, he didn't fancy leaving his new car outside Sharon's house in the Lower Eltham Road after dark.

Sophie answered the door to his knock, wearing an old dressing gown. As Dave stepped into the hall the smell of vomit wafting from the open cloakroom door almost made him gag. He gulped, forced a smile and walked quickly through to the sitting room. Sophie followed, bringing the smell of vomit with her, and Dave almost gagged again. He saw the disappointment on her face and felt ashamed of himself, he forced another smile and risked soiling a good sweater by giving her a hug.

They sat on the sofa with Dave discreetly inspecting his sweater. "You want your mum, don't you?"

Sophie was trying hard not to cry. "I don't want Mum, I want Eddie."

Dave forgot his sweater, he must have misheard. "Eddie?"

She nodded and stared at him, wide eyed. "Eddie always looks after me when I'm sick. Mum couldn't find him tonight, she left a message, I want him to come."

Sophie hiccupped, and as Dave moved out of the line of fire, he heard the squeal of car tyres, someone had stopped outside in a hurry. Moments later a car door slammed and he heard the sound of running footsteps. Sophie jumped to her feet and ran towards the door as a key rattled in the lock. Dave followed to see Eddie burst through, bend down and scoop her up. Then she was clinging to him in floods of tears; Sophie didn't have to be brave any more.

Saturdays were always busy and Dave liked to be at work early. Today he was earlier than usual, he'd not slept well, too much on his mind. Sophie was sick again before he left, mostly down the front of Eddie's shirt. Dave was horrified, fearful of how Eddie would react to being covered in vomit. He needn't have worried, there was no anger, no revulsion and no iceman either, for all the world Eddie was a doting parent totally unfazed by it all. When Dave left, Sophie was sitting in an armchair, pale faced but happy, chattering to Eddie as he washed her hands and face from a bowl of warm water.

Work was impossible, Dave put a note on Carl Boyd's desk and went to visit Sharon. She looked the worse for wear, the supposed job opportunity had degenerated into a drinking session. At eight-thirty she was in her dressing gown, surprised to see him and suspicious.

"What brings you here so early on a Saturday morning?"

"I wanted to make sure Sophie was OK."

"No, you didn't!" Sharon snapped at him. "You want to stick your nose into my business."

Dave's retort was equally sharp. "Yes, how come Eddie's got a key to your front door?"

He saw surprise turn to horror as Sharon spluttered, "For Christ's sake, you don't think there's something going on between me and that awful man, do you?"

Dave didn't, but... "No I don't, but Sophie tells me that he always looks after her when she's sick, then he turns up and lets himself in with a key!"

"The bloody fool shouldn't have, not with your car outside."

Dave was beginning to understand. "I came in a taxi, I was worried about leaving my car outside at night."

Sharon didn't want to antagonise Dave, she needed a new car and wanted him to subsidise it.

"OK, I'll tell you, but keep it to yourself. And don't look so bloody smug, I bet you didn't hang around long once he arrived." Sharon was angry again. "The stupid girl doesn't want me, she wants him; even when Jilly was alive she wanted him, can you imagine that? He looks after her on Sundays when I go to my singles club, and the key is for when he picks her up from school so he can let himself in and cook her tea."

"I thought you had a childminder?"

Sharon sneered. "Have you any idea how much childminders cost? I have a childminder pick her up three days a week and the other two I pick her up myself. If I get stuck in a meeting I call him, he's free and reliable. He's useful too – my roof doesn't leak any more, the doors don't stick, the taps don't drip, he even decorates." She snorted with derision. "And you needn't have worried about your precious car! There's no graffiti on my walls, no rubbish in my garden and nobody vandalises my car. Everyone knows him round here – would you scratch my car and risk having that madman come after you?"

Derision turned to bitterness. "You and your flash new car, Mum and Dad told me you bought their business too cheap, they used to help me financially but now they can't afford to."

Back to sneering: "Do you know who picks Sophie up from school if Eddie's busy?" Dave shook his head. "His tart, that awful Roxy, and Sophie thinks she's wonderful!"

Carl Boyd was frightened, he'd come in late to find a note from Dave on his desk asking him to go to his office at eleven o'clock. He had no illusions about being clever, he'd dragged himself up from service receptionist to service manager by dogged hard work. However, since the birth of his son he'd reduced his hours and been late a couple of times. Dave had obviously noticed, he'd been giving him sideways glances for a while, and now this.

Carl checked and re-checked his performance figures – at their last meeting he'd predicted meeting his ambitious targets, but hadn't quite done so. Combine that with his timekeeping lapses and he was in trouble. At two minutes to eleven he was outside Dave's office, files in hand. The door was ajar; Dave was a modern boss – he only closed the door if he had a private meeting or was about to bollock someone. Carl went in and closed the door firmly behind him.

Dave's confidence was at rock bottom. Last month Mike had exposed him as a hypocrite and a bad friend. Last night Sophie had exposed him as a bad uncle. This morning Sharon had exposed him as a bad son, pointing out that he'd bought Kings of Canley on the cheap, effectively taking money his parents needed for their retirement. She'd also exposed him as a bad brother, not caring if she was coping as a single mother. Now Carl Boyd had exposed him as a bad boss too.

Carl had come into his office, stuttering with fear, promising to do anything to meet his targets. It had taken Dave a while to realise that Carl genuinely believed his job was at risk. It was ludicrous, Carl was an exceptional service manager – how could he possibly believe he was in trouble? A few moments' thought revealed the obvious: Dave occasionally mixed socially with his sales manager, but had never met Carl outside work, he didn't fit his preferred social stereotype. Carl was a superb manager, but he didn't know his wife's name or that they'd just had a baby.

One comment hit Dave hard. "I know I have to work harder, perform better because…"

His voice had tailed away, but Dave knew what he was thinking.

A chastened Dave reassured Carl that his work was beyond reproach and that the meeting was to ask about Vincent and an alleged reign of terror at Broad Street School.

"Forget alleged, Vinnie Proctor and Ray Powers were sadists, they loved seeing people being hurt and humiliated. God knows how they got away with it for as long as they did, even with their fathers being Chairman and Deputy Chairman of the school governors. Mind you, they were clever, they got others to do the dirty work, they just stood back and enjoyed it."

As he relived the past, Carl started to shake. "Occasionally some hard cases would get together and challenge them, but Vinnie had loads of enforcers, a few beatings and resistance soon stopped. Then word went round that Eddie Stagg had protected a couple of targets and thumped Vinnie into the bargain, but no-one thought he would last long.

"Then Neville Webster hung himself." Carl looked away. "We all knew why; Vinnie and Ray made his life a misery. We were sure there'd be an enquiry but there wasn't, everything went quiet for a while then they started up again worse than before. Next thing Eddie offered to protect anyone who needed it, and all he wanted in return was for us to speak up when it was over, tell the world he wasn't a monster."

He stared at Dave. "Don't get me wrong, he was incredibly violent, but what choice did he have, just him against Vinnie and his team? Nobody helped, we were sure he'd eventually get beaten and we'd be in deep shit." Carl lowered his head. "He wasn't beaten, but afterwards no-one spoke up for him, we just wanted to pretend it never happened. I don't avoid Eddie because I'm frightened of him, I avoid him because I'm ashamed."

SEPTEMBER

The sun was shining directly into his eyes, Eddie hated glare and moved his head so the frame of the window blocked it out. Respite was brief, the late afternoon sun was dropping quickly, minutes later the glare was back. He needed to adjust the canopy over the workshop window but that would mean stopping and he didn't want to stop, he'd finally perfected two-handed sanding, and the concentration required to work his hands independently at speed blocked out the images of the terrors. It was remarkably quick, but stooping over his work with his back unsupported was remarkably uncomfortable. No matter, uncomfortable was OK, the images had faded, and he'd worked through his latest batch of furniture at amazing speed.

Relief, the sun dropped behind a scrap of cloud, the glare disappeared, and Eddie upped his pace a little. God he was quick now, no not just quick he was hot, he was on fire! A laugh welled up in his throat but the sound that emerged was the cackle of a madman, shrill and high pitched. Eddie was shocked into immobility, he knew he was off his head but didn't like it to show quite so obviously. He leaned forward to start again, but the glare was back and he couldn't see. His congenital focal plane cataracts were relatively mild and non-progressive, but bad enough to fill his eyes with an explosion of light in the glare of the sun. Eddie stepped back and tried to straighten up. He couldn't, his back was so stiff he could hardly move and his arms hurt, and his shoulders, and his legs; in fact, everything hurt.

He peered slowly round the workshop; the clock on the wall showed two minutes to four and he was pretty sure it was Thursday. In the early hours of the morning he'd seen

John Wayne striding across the workshop. Later he'd seen his mother asleep in her armchair with her daily bottle of vodka. Other hallucinations had been popping and banging around ever since; he'd probably done enough. He gazed at the picture of Jilly on his workbench and his mind filled with pictures of her happy and smiling, and pretty, so incredibly pretty. The pictures didn't decay into the horrific images of the terrors; he had done enough, it was over, it was four o'clock, it was tea time.

Eddie switched on the kettle and opened the fridge door looking for milk. The smell that hit him was like the sweaty crutch of a Turkish wrestler. Not that he was overly familiar with the perspiring genitalia of far eastern European sporting combatants, but he could imagine that on a hot day in Istanbul such a smell might well be similar to that presently emanating from his fridge. A wry smile disappeared in an instant, Jilly always laughed at his jokes, even the bad ones ...

He stood, frozen in time, until the click of the kettle switching off roused him. The fridge door was still open and Eddie reached inside for the milk. A tentative sniff showed it to be good, so he bent painfully forward to search the fridge for decaying matter. Good news, not only was the fridge clean but he found an elderly Eccles cake to have with his tea. Eddie glanced towards the window where Desmond was catching the sun on the workbench and suddenly recognised the smell. He tipped the fridge forward and discovered three rotting mice laid neatly beside the motor. Smell problem over and disposal of the carcasses would wait, Eddie walked wearily towards the door that opened into the yard and stepped out into the remains of a warm September afternoon.

It took two mugs of tea to wash down the stale Eccles cake, and afterwards Eddie sat at the table in the yard for a long time thinking of Jilly and how she loved the summer. He shivered slightly, it was cooling rapidly and the shadows were long, summer was nearly over, he'd missed another one. But that was how it should be, it wouldn't be right to enjoy summers without her.

Back in the workshop Eddie examined the table he'd been working on and the others stacked against the wall. His work quality was adequate rather than good – he'd do a better job when they returned from the chicken shed. Eddie's latest venture was having Georgian-style furniture made from solid timber in Malaysia and shipped to him for assembly and hand finishing. The skill was to remove all evidence of the belt sanders and other machinery used in modern manufacture. Finish quality was more important when the items returned from the 'ageing' process, six months in a damp chicken shed complete with chickens. Eddie would re-polish the furniture the same way he restored antiques, leaving the minor blemishes that were ostensibly the signs of age. He sold them to dealers as 'Aged Reproductions', but suspected that many reached the retail market as the real thing.

The finished items of furniture had to be moved to the storage area at the back of the workshop. Eddie braced himself, he knew what else was there – the vintage Vox AC30 guitar amplifier he'd been looking at the evening Jilly was killed. He'd bought it unseen on the telephone from a regular contact but recognised it as soon as the carrier dropped it off. It had taken him thirty-six hours to tame the terrors that came that night.

Eddie's tidy mind was reflected in a tidy and well organised workshop. Furniture and collectables were restored at a large bench under the window overlooking the yard, with a smaller side bench used for guitar and amplifier repairs. Storage areas for pending and completed work were on either side of the door leading to the unused shop front with guitars, amplifiers and furniture in separate bays.

After taming the terrors, Eddie sometimes thought about the future, the long-term future, not just a few days ahead. The trouble was that when he did, he thought about Janice, and guilt hit him like a wall. How could he possibly think about another woman when he loved Jilly? Even if he could get past the guilt Janice deserved better, someone who hadn't done so many terrible things and wasn't off his head. But Jilly deserved better and she'd loved him! Then fear mixed in with the guilt, apart from Jilly's death Janice had hurt him more than anyone or anything. Soon guilt and fear combined to overwhelm him, it would be wicked to love Jilly and Janice at the same time, and even if it wasn't he couldn't go through all that hurt again.

Eddie worked steadily for a while then started to think again. A few months ago, Deborah started talking to him again and being nice to Janice. Mike must be behind it; he was usually behind any good that happened. It doubtless helped that her life had improved, Jimmy had found regular employment and he and Deborah were about to buy a house. Eddie was pleased that his ruse with his starter home had helped them get back on their feet, Jilly would have approved. They were looking at a former council house on the edge of West Town, not a great area, but it would give them the space they needed.

Back to thinking about Janice, her father shouldn't be at work, but now the twins were back living at home following broken marriages Arthur was the sole breadwinner. Nan was a little better but worrying about Arthur was dragging her down. The good news was that something had happened between Janice and Andy, she was regaining some of her self-confidence. She wasn't the spirited girl she used to be but nothing, not the drab, shapeless clothes nor the awful short haircut could hide what an attractive girl she was. With that thought an avalanche of guilt washed over him.

A CALL TO ARMS

The dry weather continued into October, but now there was a distinct chill in the air and little warmth in the watery sun. At ten past four Eddie was sitting at the table in his yard, examining the helicopter seed pods from the sycamore tree in the garden behind the disused Methodist Chapel next to his workshop. He was trying to convince himself he wasn't cold; fetching a coat would mean disturbing Desmond who was keeping his lap warm.

Mike must be working very hard, Jimmy and Deborah had come to the last two Roadrunners gigs and sat with them at the band table. They were proud of their new house and Jimmy had made friends with the son of a neighbour. Eddie was pleased: Jimmy needed a friend and Deborah said Bob was likeable and easy going.

Eddie heard the telephone ringing in the workshop but ignored it, he was comfortable having convinced himself he wasn't cold. Shortly afterwards it rang again, Eddie walked wearily through to the workshop and picked up the receiver. Deborah was in a panic.

"Jimmy's new friend is Bob Lomax!" She gasped for breath. "Pete's been released from prison and he's making trouble, something to do with parking. Jimmy tried to sort it out, he talked to Pete last night, but I'm worried he'll get hurt."

Eddie parked the red estate neatly outside Jimmy's house and sat on the warm bonnet, swinging his shiny black shoes back and forth. It wasn't long before he heard footsteps, two people walking towards him. He didn't look up until they were close and was surprised to see Bob Lomax and a scrawny little man in front of him. Bob hadn't changed much over the years, a bit taller and leaner than he remembered, but that was all.

"Hello Bob, remember me?"

Bob did and stopped abruptly. Scrawny man carried on two paces before stopping and scrambling back. Bob stared at Eddie for a few moments before stammering.

"Yes, but…I mean…"

Scrawny man nudged Bob. "Tell him, Bob, tell him he can't park here unless he pays Pete. Tell him to pay up or fuck off."

Bob stepped forward, pulled his shoulders back and spoke clearly. "I'm really sorry about what happened to your wife." He flapped his hands. "I'm not saying it to stop you hitting me, I knew her, she was really nice to me, and to Mum…"

Eddie cut him short. "How did you know Jilly?"

"The Housing Benefit office, she knew who we were but she was nice, she treated us like normal people."

Two thoughts coursed through Eddie's mind – guilt for kicking Bob all those years ago and his trial; Pete was in the parade of the pummelled but not Bob.

"You didn't give evidence at my trial?"

Bob looked surprised and shook his head. "No."

Eddie was confused; he'd come to confront Pete, not Bob. He asked sharply, "What did Pete say?"

Bob opened his mouth in a sort of smile – his front teeth were missing. "It was the first time I'd refused to do what he told me, he wanted to make sure it was the last."

One word from Eddie: "Shit!"

More memories, the fight years ago with Bob hanging back not wanting to be involved but not daring to defy his brother. Once Pete had been sent to a Young Offenders Institution, Bob had kept his head down and behaved himself. Bob was a victim not the bad guy!

Scrawny man nudged Bob. "Tell him to fuck off, tell him, or Pete will sort you out."

Bob nudged him back. "Shut up, Darren, I'm talking."

Eddie glared at Darren before turning back to Bob. "Jimmy, the guy who lives here." He gestured at Jimmy's house. "Do you know who he is?" Bob shook his head. "He's Jilly's brother, and Deborah was her friend."

This time one word from Bob. "Shit!"

"Tell him, Bob!" Darren was getting agitated. "Tell him or we're in trouble."

Bob pushed Darren roughly in the direction of his house. "Go and tell Pete that Eddie Stagg's out here waiting for him, see how brave he is then. Go on, fuck off and tell him!"

Darren backed away slowly, then turned and ran towards the house. Bob took a pace forward.

"If Pete comes out it won't be three on to one, I'll be with you, if that's OK?"

Eddie nodded grimly before pointing at Bob's leg. "How's the knee?"

Bob gave a gap-toothed smile. "Recovering."

"I'm sorry about that." Eddie grimaced. "I owe you for it, and for not giving evidence at my trial. And for today for that matter, but I'd still like to ask a favour."

Bob shrugged. "Ask away."

"Keep an eye on Jimmy and Deborah for me. Make sure people don't throw rubbish over their fence or let their dogs crap in their gateway."

Bob grinned. "Or park red estate cars outside their house?"

Eddie grinned back; Bob had a sense of humour. "Yes, that sort of thing." He paused. "In return, if you have any trouble…"

Bob interrupted, "From people called Pete, for example?"

"Yes." Eddie nodded slowly. "Particularly from people called Pete. Any trouble, you contact me and I'll sort it." He peered at Bob's house. "I don't think Pete's coming out to play." Another gap-toothed smile from Bob as Eddie continued. "I'd like Jimmy to think it was him talking to Pete last night that did the trick, I was never here, OK?"

Bob held out his hand. "That's a deal."

Eddie shook the proffered hand firmly, then watched Bob walk briskly back to his house. He had a spring in his step, Pete's reign of terror was over.

Eddie heard a door bang as he walked to his car and turned to see Deborah running down her garden path wearing a dressing gown and slippers. They were sturdy, sensible slippers and it was a warm, sensible dressing gown, but it was five o'clock in the afternoon! Rather more remarkable was that she was clutching a small axe in her left hand. That it was in her left hand wasn't remarkable – Deborah was left-handed – by why an axe? Eddie inclined his head towards it and used his best slow, controlled voice.

"Hello Debs, do you want me to chop some sticks or something?"

She gazed aghast at the axe and thrust it into her dressing gown pocket. "What happened with Bob?"

"We had a nice chat about old times."

Her tone was sharp. "Tell me what happened!"

"Bob's a good guy and Pete won't trouble you again. We've agreed I was never here, Jimmy sorted the problem talking to Pete last night."

Eddie changed the subject by pointing at the axe. "That looks really clean, have you been scrubbing it?"

Deborah didn't reply but Eddie hadn't finished. "Not at work this afternoon?"

"I called in sick."

Deborah saw a flicker of a smile on Eddie's face. "Cunning plan, Debs, if Jimmy was in trouble you'd leap out of your bed of pain, pick up the nice clean axe that just happened to be on your bedside table, run outside, and Pete's history."

Her voice was hushed. "I didn't know if you'd come."

"You know me, Debs, never one to miss out on a fight."

She shook her head. "No, that's not how it is, but if Jimmy's to believe this was his doing, you'd better go before he comes home."

Then, the biggest surprise of the afternoon, Deborah leaned forward and kissed Eddie on the cheek. A moment later the sensible girl in sensible slippers ran back down the path and her door banged closed.

A SENSIBLE GIRL

It was a fallacy that well covered girls felt the cold less than slim ones; Deborah was perished, whereas Angie and Sue seemed impervious to it. Being asked to join them on a Saturday afternoon shopping trip was flattering but, on reflection, a mistake. She was now their manager, and as they'd never asked her before, Deborah was wondering about their motives. Perhaps she was being overly suspicious, or frustrated by the fact that they were both slim, didn't feel the cold and all the clothes they tried on fitted them. Deborah's only purchase was an electric drill for Jimmy, and carrying it was making her arm ache.

At four o'clock Canley High Street was crowded with Christmas shoppers, less than a month to the big day. Deborah could smell Frankies tea shop, but Angie and Sue said they couldn't stop, they had to be home early. If she'd brought her own car she could have stopped for tea and cake, and why had Angie parked in the expensive car park at the bottom of the High Street?

Angie and Sue did have an ulterior motive. Last week, whilst hurrying to avoid a sudden shower, they'd literally run into the mad busker. Rumour had it that he'd nearly beaten to death the two men who'd killed his wife in a hit and run accident and was now quite mad. To their surprise he seemed ordinary, apologising even though it was clearly their fault and offering to play a request. No-one would believe their story if they told it, but everyone would believe sensible Deborah. They needed to be at the bottom of Canley High Street where he played in an alley beside W H Smith's bookshop by four o'clock, the time he finished.

They raced ahead with Deborah struggling along behind. The drill was heavy, it was cordless with a hammer action and six torque settings; Deborah was sure Jimmy would be pleased with it. He'd always been a good husband but after Jilly's death he'd become edgy and depressed as if he was carrying a huge burden. He was, of course, and now he'd told her the truth and she'd forgiven him, he was back to his old self. Unfortunately, Jimmy and his mother weren't completely reconciled, but at least they were talking again. Eileen had completed her university course and intended returning to Canley in the New Year; she'd applied for teaching posts and was awaiting interviews.

Angie and Sue had timed it just right, the mad busker was coming to the end of a song – if they paused for a few seconds, Deborah would turn the corner and see them talking to him. His guitar rang out as he finished his song with a flourish, he looked up and gave a smile of recognition, but as Angie stepped forward to speak, he looked past her at Deborah.

"Hello Eddie, I thought it sounded like you."

The girls swung round, mouths dropping open as the busker spoke. "Would you excuse me for a moment?"

"It's OK, Eddie, we're together."

Angie and Sue stared with disbelief as Deborah walked forward and offered her cheek. The busker kissed it and pointed to her heavy bag.

"What have you got in there, Debs, it looks heavy?"

"It's a drill for Jimmy, a Christmas present."

The busker took off his guitar. "I was about to finish, we could go for tea and cake at Frankies?"

The girls were mortified by Deborah's reply. "We can't, we're in Angie's car, and she and Sue have to be home early."

Eddie shrugged. "No problem, I could take you home afterwards, and I'd better carry the drill."

Angie and Sue gaped at each other as Deborah and the mad busker walked off towards Frankies. There would be a story to tell round the coffee machine on Monday morning, but not the one they'd planned. Boring Deborah, the sensible girl in sensible shoes, knew the mad busker. He called her Debs, kissed her on the cheek in front of everyone on the High Street, and took her for tea and cake at Frankies.

TEA AND CAKES

Even carrying the heavy drill and his guitar, Eddie set a brisk pace. Deborah puffed a little as she asked, "How do you know Angie and Sue?"

"I don't." Eddie wasn't out of breath. "Last Saturday it started to rain and they bumped into me running for shelter and ended up on the floor. My reputation's bad enough without being accused of tripping young ladies, so I tried to be friendly. How about you?"

Deborah was still puffing. "I work with them, I'm their manager."

Eddie stopped and faced her. "Oh God, I'm sorry, that's your reputation ruined."

"Never mind." She sniffed disdainfully. "I'm tired of being boring and sensible."

Frankies was full of shoppers relaxing after an afternoon's shopping. The only free table was at the front in the window.

Eddie pointed with his guitar case. "If we sit there in full view your reputation will never recover."

Deborah walked wearily towards the table. "I'll live with it."

At peak times Frankie employed senior citizens and an elderly waitress arrived quickly, out of turn quickly and Deborah felt eyes boring into the back of her head. Her first words were spoken to Eddie in a conspiratorial whisper.

"A lovely pair of Barkers came into the shop yesterday, they're your size so I've kept them for you." She straightened up and continued in a normal tone, "And what can I get you?"

Eddie introduced Alice Popplewell who helped in a charity shop and managed the West Town Day Centre in addition to her part-time job as a waitress. Deborah noticed her discreetly take the bag containing Eddie's busking earnings, despite him distracting her with a question.

"How's Jimmy getting on with Bob?"

"Good, Bob's back to his old self now Pete's gone. He didn't stay long after…"

Their order arrived quickly with a smiled thank you to Eddie from Alice. He hid a hint of self-consciousness with another question.

"Have you met Mrs Lomax?"

Deborah put her cake down. "Yes, she's really nice but worn out and old before her time. I suppose having a husband and son in and out of prison would wear anyone down and Bob can't get regular work – everyone assumes he's like Pete and his father. Hilda, that's Mrs Lomax, has a cleaning job, but I'm sure they're short of money." She gazed longingly at her cake. "Bob restores and sells old furniture he buys at car boot sales, but I don't think he makes much at it."

Eddie bit into his Eccles cake conscious of the fact that if he kept Deborah from her fresh cream Belgian bun for much longer his life would be at risk. As they munched away, he noticed Deborah shooting him sidelong glances. They weren't the glances she used to give him, the ones that should have turned him into stone, they were more like concern. It had been going on for months, it was time to ask why.

"What's going on, Debs? You and Dave are being nice to me and Janice? I can understand Janice, but why me?"

Deborah came straight out with it. "Jimmy told us."

No reaction from Eddie, just a slow, controlled reply. "Jimmy told you what?"

She tried again. "He told us what he did after Jilly died."

"Why, what did he do?"

"For Christ sake, Eddie, I know."

Still no reaction. "Know what?"

"This is ridiculous." An exasperated Deborah leaned forward in her chair. "He told us that he left you in the police cell. Later he told me, just me, that he let Stan move Jilly before you and Eileen arrived. I've spoken to Eileen and she told me that she asked you to disfigure Phil as well as Ray and she told me the truth about your girls. You're not the bad guy, Eddie."

Eddie shook his head, his voice controlled and emotionless. "What I did to Ray and Phil was bad, but I've done much worse before and since. I can make as many excuses as I like, but the simple fact is that only a monster could do it over and over again."

CHAPTER 8

A glimmer of hope

CHRISTMAS AGAIN.

When he thought about it dispassionately, Eddie knew he wasn't inherently wicked even though his parents told him repeatedly that he was. He'd done wicked things because he was thoughtless and selfish, but had always tried to learn from his mistakes and make amends. His friends accepted him for what he was because they understood, but now Deborah was treating him like the good guy. At Frankies he'd told her he wasn't, but there was only so much he could say in a café where people might overhear. Anyway, it had made no difference: she'd invited him to Christmas dinner. Thankfully he was able to refuse graciously – he was helping Alice Popplewell and her St Nicholas Church ladies at the West Town Day Centre.

Alice was a remarkable lady; at seventy-six she helped in the St Nicholas Church charity shop and managed the West Town Day Centre. Her only paid employment was in Frankies' tea shop on Saturday afternoons, the money used to take her and her beloved Percy on holiday to Cornwall every year. The Christmas after Jilly's death saw the first St Nicholas Church Christmas Feast at the Day Centre for the elderly and disadvantaged of West Town. Unfortunately, its success was marred by the disgraceful behaviour of some of the guests, Alice and her ladies needed a minder, Eddie volunteered his services and had worked there ever since.

Mike knew Eddie's Christmas routine and had asked him to lunch on Boxing Day. Eddie couldn't accept that invitation either – Mike's mother and Gary's parents would be there and the rules did not permit his intruding on family occasions.

Christmas Day was good, the Feast went well with even the winos thanking Alice and her ladies for their hard work. The evening was even better, Sophie was at her grandparents for Christmas but called him on the mobile telephone he'd bought her. The trend continued into Boxing Day, Mike and Gary called at the workshop after taking their parents home, and Mike persuaded him to ring Janice. She was spending Christmas with Nan and her parents; unless there was an improvement in Nan and Arthur's health it could be their last together. She seemed genuinely pleased to hear from him and they chatted for ages. Eddie knew he was a lucky man and spent the remainder of Christmas thinking of those less fortunate.

Eddie had been dwelling on Deborah's comments about Bob and Mrs Lomax. He still felt guilty about hurting Bob all those years ago and had thought of a way of making amends. Bob needed work and Eddie needed a full-time employee – he was spending a fortune on sub-contractors and carriers. In reality he needed several employees, but hadn't considered them before because the workshop was his place to hide when the terrors came. Eddie also reflected on his mortality: if he fell ill or had an accident or met his match in a fight, his businesses wouldn't run themselves. The final piece of the jigsaw was finding a new place to hide, he'd scraped together the money to buy a row of derelict lock-up garages not far from the flats.

Evening on the 27th December was not a good time to visit uninvited, but Eddie needed to act before his nerve failed. He parked the red estate some distance from the Lomaxes' house – he didn't want Jimmy or Deborah to see it – and the walk made him wish he'd brought a coat to keep out the bitter cold. Someone was in, Eddie saw light through the curtains and heard a television. He shivered on the doorstep for a few seconds before knocking, and it was some time before the door opened slowly. Deborah was right, Mrs Lomax looked worn out, and nervous when she saw him. He tried to look friendly, something he'd always had difficulty with.

"Hello, I'm Eddie Stagg..."

She interrupted quickly. "I know who you are. We don't want any trouble, Pete's gone and Bob's a good boy."

Eddie moved back slightly. "I'm not looking for trouble, I'd like to speak to Bob if I may?"

The word that struck Eddie as he peered round the Lomaxes' sitting room was impoverished. It was spotlessly clean, but the sparse furnishings were poor quality and worn out. The exception was an antique mahogany dining chair by the door which Eddie examined while Mrs Lomax went to fetch Bob from his shed. Eight o'clock the day after Boxing Day and Bob was still working! It wasn't much warmer inside than out and Eddie heard the gas fire clicking and cracking as it warmed up. The radiants weren't glowing, the fire could only have been on for a couple of minutes. He saw a bundle behind an armchair and stepped forward to investigate. It was an overcoat – Mrs Lomax had been watching television in her coat to save on the gas bill and had turned the fire on and thrown her coat behind a chair when he'd knocked.

Bob appeared, his face a mixture of nervous and friendly. Mrs Lomax hovered nearby, clearly worried. Eddie had rehearsed his words, he shook Bob's hand and started.

"I've come to ask a favour."

He saw them visibly relax, the change in Mrs Lomax was particularly striking, he was now a guest.

"Where are my manners? I haven't offered you a cup of tea."

Eddie detected distress in her voice and guessed why – he'd learned a great deal about pride from Alice and the ladies in the charity shops. Mrs Lomax was of a generation older than her years, her pride required that guests were offered tea in good china and she wouldn't have any; Pete or his father would have sold or broken it years ago.

He tried to look apologetic. "It's a cold night, I'd like a mug if that's possible?"

His reward was the relief on Mrs Lomax's face.

Eddie wanted Mrs Lomax to be there when he asked his favour. Stalling for time was easy, they talked about the antique chair.

"Nice chair, Bob, what period would you say it is?"

The chair had been beautifully restored, Bob was obviously clever with his hands, but did he know his furniture? Bob looked at the chair, looked at Eddie and shrugged before replying.

"I'd say William IV." He gave a lazy smile. "It's 1830 to 1840, it could be George IV, William IV or early Victorian. It's possibly Victorian, but I'll sell it as William IV."

Eddie smiled back. "It would sell better as Georgian."

"It would, but I don't think it is." Bob had a conscience.

Mrs Lomax returned with three mugs of tea and the last of the Christmas mince pies. She still looked nervous as did Bob, his voice cracking as he asked: "You mentioned a favour?"

Eddie was well rehearsed. "I've more work than I can cope with and I'm spending a fortune with sub-contractors and carriers." He paused. "I need permanent help, but finding someone reliable who's prepared to work for the likes of me is a problem." He made eye contact. "So that's the favour, would you work for me?"

Eddie dropped his gaze, unable to cope with the gratitude in Bob's eyes. A fourteen-year-old piece of guilt began to fade then rebounded; why had he waited so long to put things right?

BOB AND ELLIE

It was good discipline having someone else in the workshop – Eddie couldn't live within himself and dwell on his past misdemeanours. Bob was good company, he didn't say a great deal but what he said was usually worth hearing. Eddie kept thinking about Mrs Lomax, a woman old before her time. When he eventually spoke out, the risked rebuff didn't come, just gratitude for his concern.

"A white van picks her up a five in the morning to go and clean stinking toilets and greasy kitchens before the dirty bastards who make them stink and cover them in grease get there. It's a filthy, rotten job but it's all she can get, she's a Lomax. It was the same for me, I could only get casual work; but now Pete's gone and Dad's back in prison we're slowly getting straight. We're paying off the rent arrears and trying to buy back some of the things they pawned to buy beer or bet on the horses."

As Bob spoke, Eddie had an idea – Mike hadn't found a reliable cleaner since sacking Mrs Clarke last May. And Charlie and his son Stephen hadn't come to terms with housework since the death of Lady Napier six years ago. Eddie would make a few calls then ask a favour of Mrs Lomax.

A snag: Eddie filed receipts, invoices and delivery notes in chronological order, everything else was in his head or on computer, and Bob was neither telepathic nor computer literate. Eddie wasn't disappointed, more relieved to find something that the versatile Bob couldn't do. They discussed the problem, Eddie admitted resenting the time he spent on administration, and Bob made a suggestion.

"You need someone to organise us."

Eddie smiled, Bob took nothing for granted, he said 'you' not 'we' and he was right, they needed someone to organise the general book-keeping and stock control, answer the telephone and organise collections and deliveries in their new van.

"Did you have someone in mind?"

Eddie's gentle question elicited the fact that Bob had met Ellie, a single mother struggling to find work that fitted round caring for her young son, at his upholstery class. Ellie was a born organiser, had bookkeeping experience and drove their van with panache.

The inevitable had happened, the terrors came early in the night, only an hour after Eddie's head hit the pillow. He was in the workshop, the immense concentration needed to sand two handed at high speed was starting to clear his mind.

"Working yourself into the ground won't bring her back."

It was Bob's voice – what was he doing in the workshop in the middle of the night? Simple: it wasn't the middle of the night, Eddie had lost track of time. Eddie was angry, he should be hiding in the lock-ups and Bob should mind his own business. The movement was automatic and immediately regretted, weight transferring to his toes, turning side on, hands coming up to his chest.

Bob shook his head sadly. "Don't be silly, sit down and I'll make us some tea."

The images came back as soon as Eddie stopped, but they'd been worse, he could function.

"Nightmares?" Bob's tone was matter of fact.

That was definitely none of Bob's business, but Eddie's anger evaporated as Bob explained. Ever since he could remember, his father had routinely beaten the whole family. Later, Bob also became Pete's personal punch bag, so he knew about nightmares.

"You've got to talk about them, not hide away feeling guilty."

That depended on how guilty you were; Eddie needed to hide.

VALENTINE'S DANCE

The Roadrunners had a charity gig, a Valentine's dance in Broad Street School Hall with proceeds going to CCCC, the Canley Confederation of Children's Charities, revitalised under the leadership of new chairman Gerald Burchnall OBE. Deborah helped Janice organise the dance but was unable to attend, she and Jimmy had influenza. Sharon was otherwise engaged, but had given permission for Sophie to attend so long as she was chaperoned at all times.

Andy was miserable, he believed that charity began at home and was the first to leave the stage at the end of the first set, heading for the bar. The buffet opening put Sophie in a quandary – the young lady in her wanted to walk demurely back and forth collecting plates of food for her, Eddie and Janice; but the girl in her wanted to run. In the end she did some of both and soon the band table was groaning under the weight of food. At the bar Dave thought Andy needed some food to soak up all the beer he was drinking and persuaded him to visit the buffet. A bad move: Andy saw Janice, Eddie and Sophie together and snapped.

"Look at them, Mummy Bear, Daddy Bear and Baby Bear, I'm going to get pissed."

Mike returned to the band table before the second set to find Dave, Eddie and Janice huddled together looking worried.

"Andy's so drunk he can hardly stand."

Mike's mind went into overdrive. "Janice can play bass?"

She shook her head vigorously. "I can't, I has to stay with Sophie."

Her comment stirred Dave's memory – before Andy left the buffet for the bar he had asked if Deborah, Jimmy or Sharon were coming later. Dave confirmed they weren't, and Andy had smiled, the bastard wanted to drop them in it but not give Janice the chance to save the day.

Decision time for Mike; he took a deep breath. "Gary's here, he'll look after Sophie."

Soon Dave was on the outside looking in and didn't like the experience. Eddie was explaining to an amazed Sophie that Janice was a good bass player, that she was The Roadrunners' original bass player. Janice was shaking with nerves and only had eyes for Eddie. Mike appeared with a very smart, fair-haired young man who Janice kissed on the cheek and Sophie hugged like an old friend. Eddie was his usual laconic self, a nod and a single word 'Gazz'. Dave had to be introduced.

A problem: Andy hated anyone touching his precious bass, but Eddie had the answer.

"My old red Fender Precision is in the car, the one Janice used to play."

Mike took charge, Eddie was to come out of the shadows and stand facing Janice so she could follow his chord changes. Dave watched as Mike led them gently into position, Janice was still shaking and Eddie seemed to have switched off. The crowd guessed something was happening, Dave could hear a buzz of voices behind him.

He approached the microphone. "Good news and bad news." The buzz stopped. "The bad news is that Andy, our bass player, was taken ill during the interval." He turned and bowed to Janice. "The good news is that Janice, The Roadrunners' original bass player, is taking his place."

The buzz started again, followed by a round of applause; the crowd were with them.

Then Dave heard Mike's voice behind him, firm and authoritative. "Bad Moon Rising, and we're playing in D."

A good choice, a song with a simple bass part that would work without bass at a push, all it needed was the wall of sound from Eddie's big Marshall.

Four clicks on Mike's drumsticks and they were off. The wall of sound was there but the bass wasn't loud enough – Eddie's old Fender didn't have the power of Andy's modern bass. No matter, it was audible and after a few shaky notes Janice settled into a rhythm. Dave had turned his amplifier up ready to lend a hand if things went wrong but hoped they didn't, he couldn't remember the complete chord sequences to some of their numbers, too many years hiding behind Eddie's wall of sound. By the third verse they were sounding pretty good and some dancers were taking to the floor, they needed a rocker next to keep them there.

Song over and Mike shot off his drum stool like a rocket to adjust the bass amplifier. Janice and Eddie didn't move, they just stared at each other. Dave turned back to the microphone as Mike shouted.

"Rock and Roll Music, the Beatles version, in E."

Another good choice, a song that rocked with a solid walking bass part. Four clicks from Mike, a huge flourish on an E chord from Eddie, a moment's silence, then Dave began.

"Let me hear some of that…"

The next words were 'Rock and Roll Music', and guitar, bass and drums should come in together. They did, the bass was walking, the band was rocking and more dancers were taking to the floor. Dave wanted to turn and look at Janice but didn't; he might unnerve her.

Mike's third choice was Blue Suede Shoes, another rocker, and suddenly everything clicked. Mike and Eddie were always together, but now it was more than that, the three friends had a rhythm sound to die for. If they had a guitarist to add fills and riffs, they would have a band to die for, but Dave knew his limitations, he couldn't sing and play anything complicated at the same time. The dance floor was crowded, the dancers weren't concerned with fills and riffs, they wanted rhythm and were getting it! Then Sophie appeared in front of him dancing with Gary, Dave tried to catch her eye but she was looking past him, her head going back and forth between Eddie and Janice.

Dave risked a glance at Janice; for the first time in years she was wearing a bright colour and the fashionable red top suited her. Years ago, he remembered thinking that if you could get beyond the fact that she was so tall and thin, she wasn't unattractive. They were stupid words then and even more stupid now, Janice was a very attractive girl and Dave would never understand why she only had eyes for a weirdo like Eddie.

They'd been playing for an hour and Dave couldn't remember when he'd enjoyed singing so much. Andy was a virtuoso bass player but given to filling every space between the vocals with improvised bass solos. If he was bored, he would solo with the vocals, which annoyed Dave and disconcerted the dancers. No such problems now, since their third number the dance floor had been packed, the dancers enjoying themselves as much as him.

Dave was an Eagles fan and was disappointed that Mike hadn't called for his favourite song 'Lying Eyes'. Perhaps Janice didn't know it, so Dave decided to ask her. She was miles away, he had to call three times to attract her attention. When she eventually reacted, she didn't seem to recognise him, then nearly jumped out of her skin when she looked past him and saw the dancers. For the past hour Janice was seventeen again, rehearsing in Mike's garage and Dave had broken the spell.

Janice did know Lying Eyes but why was Mike shaking his head? Dave shrugged and turned back to the microphone.

Eddie was playing his Rickenbacker twelve-string, the huge jangle filling the hall, and Dave was drifting, enjoying himself. As they approached the third verse, Mike began hitting his drums like a blacksmith striking an anvil then struck a huge crash on a cymbal. What was his problem? Dave tried to think, he knew the chord sequence to Lying Eyes all the way through and third verse was the same as the others. At the moment he was just strumming the odd chord, pretending to play, hiding behind Eddie's twelve-string, but he knew where he was. Then Mike did it again, another huge crash on a cymbal.

Was it the words? Dave thought ahead and there it was: 'She wonders how it ever got this crazy, she thinks about a boy she knew in school'.

Shit! Shit! Shit! That was why Mike shook his head. Dave started playing hard, getting his rhythm going as he sang 'She wonders how it ever got this crazy'. As he did so Janice fumbled a note and stopped. As Dave continued 'She thinks about a boy she knew in school', Eddie missed a chord change and stopped, but it was OK, he and Mike were driving it along.

Behind him Dave heard Mike counting his friends back in. "After four, on a G. One, two, three, four."

The twelve-string was back, a bar later the bass was back but the spark had gone and Dave was sorry.

Mike and Gary helped Eddie put the semi-comatose Andy in the passenger seat of the red estate and getting him out by himself was difficult. Janice held the front door open as he carried Andy down the path, draped over his shoulder.

"Lay him on the carpet in the sitting room."

Eddie struggled through to where Janice had spread a dust sheet on the carpet. He laid Andy down none too gently, moved him into the recovery position and watched as Janice put a cushion under his head and spread newspaper in front of his face. This had happened before – the newspaper was there to catch the inevitable stream of vomit.

Eddie hadn't been in the house before and glanced round while Janice was busy with the newspaper. It was clean and tidy, Janice would see to that, but it wasn't a home, there were no flowers, no photographs, no signs of love.

On the doorstep as Eddie was about to leave, Janice hesitated and gave a nervous smile.

"I'm going to my room." Another hesitation. "When Andy wakes he can go to his."

NAN

The four and a half years since Jilly's death had been filled with grief, guilt, violence and grinding hard work. Eddie was tired of being so tired it was hard to think logically. Rather more, he was tired of pretending he wasn't tired, that he didn't mind being alone, that he didn't mind being reviled by almost everyone, that he didn't feel guilty about Jilly and Juliet... Eddie paused, said the last words out loud and waited for a wall of guilt to hit him 'and I'm tired of pretending I don't love Janice'.

Was there a chink in the wall of guilt? At the dance, the moment they'd put their instruments down, Sophie had run past him and her Uncle Dave and thrown her arms around Janice. Immediately afterwards she made him give Janice a hug and tell her how well she'd played. Sophie loved Jilly but didn't seem to have a problem with him and Janice being close, but being close and being together were different.

Back to reality: Arthur Newton died a week after the Valentine's dance. Barbie wouldn't let him retire and his heart had given out under the strain of his chronic illness. The burden of the funeral arrangements fell entirely on Janice as Barbie and the twins declared themselves too upset to help. Eddie supported Janice and a frail Nan at the funeral and realised the time had come to talk.

The little terraced house looked very smart, the coat of paint Eddie applied last year shone brightly in the watery sunlight. Nan was a long time coming to the door, she moved very slowly nowadays, and welcomed the help of the carers that called three times a day.

The sitting room was warm and cosy, Eddie made a pot of tea and they made small talk whilst eating the cream cakes he'd brought.

Then Nan put her cup down firmly and asked, "What did the consultant tell you at the hospital last week, you were talking to him for ages?"

Eddie tried not to look worried. "He said that you'd probably live to be a hundred."

Nan patted his arm. "You're a good boy, Eddie, but a bad liar, I know how bad it is." She paused. "So, do you love my Janice?"

Eddie was shocked into a stammering reply. "Well… yes… but, it's complicated." He lowered his head and stared at the floor. "I loved Janice when we were at school, I still loved her when she met Andy, but when she wanted him to take her place in the band it was too much and I stopped." There was a long pause. "I must have stopped because I fell in love with Jilly. I still love Jilly so how can I love Janice as well?"

Nan sighed. "You don't have to stop loving Jilly to love Janice; it's not a competition."

Another chink in the wall of guilt, Nan didn't seem unhappy about the local psycho loving her granddaughter.

"And don't you worry about that Andy." Eddie saw open dislike on her face. "She never loved that horrible man."

"I'm not worried about him, but…" Eddie voice petered away.

Nan's voice was surprisingly firm. "It's taken me fifteen years to get you to talk about Janice so don't stop now." She shook his arm. "There's something else, isn't there? Tell me, it can't be that bad."

Eddie smiled bleakly. "Guilt, Nan, lots of it. Did I make Jilly unhappy because Janice was always around? Could I make Janice happy when she knows how happy I was with Jilly? Am I being disloyal to both of them?"

"Anything else?" Nan was shaking her head.

Eddie was bitter again. "I destroy people's lives, if Janice gets involved with me she could end up being destroyed as well."

Nan was getting annoyed. "Now you're talking rubbish?"

"It's not rubbish, my parents told me I destroyed their lives. Juliet and Jilly loved me and they're both dead and I've hurt more people than I care to remember."

Nan sat back and her armchair creaked. Eddie remembered the sound well from the happy evenings he and Janice had spent together with the old lady.

"From what I can make out your parents destroyed their own lives with drink." She leaned forward, her armchair creaking again. "You mustn't blame yourself for Jilly's death, or Juliet's, blame Ray Powers! And what about your successes, Roxanne and all those poor girls, where would they be without you?"

"Janice has always hated the girls, even Roxy..."

Nan gave a tired smile. "I know, but perhaps..." She stopped, grabbed his hand and squeezed it with a sudden intensity. "Eddie, will you do something for me?"

"Of course, Nan, anything."

"I want you to go away for a long time, and don't worry about your girls, Roxanne and Mike will look after them." Her grip on his hand tightened. "When you were in prison Janice was tearing her hair out after three weeks. Go away for a couple of months and find out if you can live without each other." She smiled confidently. "Believe me, when you come back it won't be complicated anymore."

Bob and Ellie had gone home, Eddie caught up on his dealing telephone calls and emails then ate a hurried sandwich. If he pushed on hard, he could meet his evening work target before midnight and have time to review his account files before going to bed. Ellie was complaining that she couldn't do her job properly because most computer files were password protected. She sounded resentful, Eddie understood her point but...

Eddie heard footsteps, someone had let themselves in with a key; he turned to find Ellie fixing him with a glare that brooked no argument.

"We need to talk." She paused. "I was desperate for a job and Bob persuaded me to work for you, he said you weren't a monster despite your evil reputation. Well, maybe or maybe not, but something's going on, you're making huge amounts of money and most of it disappears into two black holes. I won't work for you if you don't trust me, and I can't work for you if you're dishonest. Your choice: tell me the passwords to the black holes or I'm off."

Eddie hesitated but she was right, either he trusted her or he didn't. "Artemis and Agamemnon, the other files are confidential, and the only person you tell is Bob."

Bob had screened off part of the workshop to create an office and Ellie had been in there for nearly three hours. Eddie straightened up from his work as she pushed through the door into the workshop.

She peered at him as if she'd never seen him before in her life. "Look at the state of you!"

Eddie was puzzled. "I looked much the same this morning..."

"This morning I thought you were a money-obsessed monster and I didn't care.

"Who says I'm not?"

"I do, you stupid man! Ajax and Achilles, I guessed two more passwords, Greek mythology and names of warships beginning with 'A' isn't that difficult." Then she was screaming at him. "You spend small fortunes renovating properties then rent them to charities and God knows who else for peanuts. You're subsidising half the population of West Town!"

Eddie shrugged. "Just a monster then."

Ellie shook her head. "I found telephone numbers for some of the businesses you subsidise, I called them on your private line and found I was talking to some of your girls. They all think you're some sort of saint!" She paused, visibly upset. "You make huge amounts of money, give most of it away, work like a slave and live in a loft!"

Eddie shrugged again. "It helps with the guilt, it's no fun being a monster."

Ellie was screaming again. "It's not your fault Neville Webster, Juliet and Jilly are dead, and those bastards deserved what they got."

"How do you know about Neville and Juliet?"

"I spoke to a girl called Roxy. Is she as scary as she sounds? She said she would tear my head off if I ever did anything to hurt you!"

Eddie gave an amused smile. "She scares me." He paused. "I have no regrets about hurting the monsters who hurt my girls, which probably makes me a monster, but could you or any sane person batter and maim time and time again, well could you?"

"No, probably not, but it's just as well for your girls that you can. I don't approve of violence but sometimes..."

Then she was screaming again. "What's done is done and me and Bob are going to stop you working yourself into an early grave, and the first thing is a labourer to do the heavy work."

Saved by the bell, the telephone was ringing – was it fate or had Jim been primed?

"He's a good lad, he just needs a chance."

Darryl was a gentle giant, immensely strong and intensely loyal. His convictions for petty theft were a result of his being abandoned at crime scenes to allow the real culprits to escape.

His convictions for violence were him lashing out after being taunted beyond endurance. Bob and Ellie liked him – Darryl joined the family.

"Why don't you use the shop front?"

A sensible question with an obvious answer and now an obvious solution. Customers were unlikely to buy from a shop manned by the local psycho and he could earn more working and dealing sitting in a shop. Having personable staff changed that and an added incentive was giving part-time work to Dawn and Amy, two of his girls struggling to earn a living from their pet supplies business in his parade of shops by the flats. Some shopfitting by the incredibly versatile Bob, and Canley Collectables was in business with furniture and collectables on one side of the door and band equipment on the other.

ROXY

The tenant in the top flat had reported a damp patch on the bedroom ceiling. At six in the morning Eddie was examining, through binoculars, the roof he'd fallen from eighteen months earlier. A missing ridge tile was the culprit, an unpleasant job that he would contract out.

Eddie's flight to New York departed from Heathrow in two days' time. He remembered the pleasure on Nan's face when he showed her the ticket; he remembered her words too.

"Don't you worry about me when you're away, you've made me happier than you can ever imagine." Her smile had faded. "A mother shouldn't outlive her children, and both my boys have gone. When I go don't grieve, just look after Janice."

Eddie was thankful he'd delayed his departure for a few weeks to organise things. Nan's consultant had told Eddie that a shock could bring on a stroke that she probably wouldn't survive. It had happened, a combination of Arthur's weakness and Barbie's desire to gloat. Nan had asked Arthur to make a will to prevent Barbie squandering everything and he'd promised he would. He lied: Barbie made one of her rare visits to her mother-in-law to tell her that she and the twins had sold the house and were going on a world cruise to find rich husbands. A day later Nan was dead but Eddie was there to mourn her and support Janice.

Eddie heard the rattle of a taxi engine behind him. A few moments later a door slammed, the taxi drove away and he heard footsteps; it was who he expected and the joke he expected.

"Fancy something different, dearie?"

Eddie turned slowly, making sure his face was expressionless. The girl standing a few feet away holding her long coat open with her hands on her hips was small and slim with bright red hair. She was smiling, anticipating his reply.

"Why, what have you got, leprosy?"

Roxy walked forward with the curious strutting gait of small girls in very high heels. She wrapped her arms around him and leaned her head on his shoulder before standing back and glaring accusingly at him.

"You're as thin as a stick and you look like shit!"

Eddie smiled; Roxy said something similar every time they met. "But you, on the other hand, look very well."

She prodded him viciously. "You're a bloody fool, Eddie Stagg, you work too hard." She sniffed. "And you're not here by coincidence, are you?"

"No, I thought I'd buy you breakfast at the cafe."

Access to the converted loft over the garage in Gladstone Street was down a short alley, across a concrete courtyard and up a metal staircase, only the garage door opened into the street. Whilst walking to his room Eddie occasionally saw a red-haired girl, about his age or slightly older, going to a room that opened into the yard. Late one evening Eddie heard screams coming from the room and saw a man attacking the girl through partly open curtains. As he ran down the staircase and across the yard, he noticed that the curtains in the other windows overlooking the yard were resolutely drawn.

When he burst through her door, Eddie thought he was preventing a rape, but he wasn't. The rape had happened three years earlier, a runaway flattered, seduced then put on the street by Jed. Girls aged quickly on the street, Roxy could no longer pass for fourteen and attract a premium price, so Jed wanted her to service a different pervert market, sadists who enjoyed hurting girls. Roxy refused, her spirit wasn't entirely broken, and Jed intended proving he could and would hurt her more than any punter. Jed and his minder Errol controlled Gladstone Street with a regime of uncompromising violence, but tonight Jed was alone, he enjoyed hurting girls.

Eddie crossed the room in four strides, two blows and Jed was down. He glanced at the girl and was startled to see short dark hair and a red wig on the floor. When he looked back Jed was making for the door; he had no stomach for even odds.

The world of pimps and prostitutes was alien to Eddie; he listened aghast as Roxy explained it to him. She was frightened for him, desperate for him to escape before Jed returned with Errol. In a few short weeks Eddie had abandoned Juliet to her death, lost Janice, watched his mother die, been thrown out of his home by his brother and attacked by winos. Enough was enough, Eddie walked out into the grimy yard lit by diffused light from curtained windows, sat on an upturned oil drum and waited.

Errol was a part-time bouncer, part-time minder and full-time sadist. He was casual about his ability to punish Roxy's upstart friend and grinned as Jed waved him forward into a left hand that would have felled an ox. In the next few minutes Eddie realised the true extent of his monstrous talent as he beat and kicked the two men into a bloody shambles without taking a single blow in return.

Eddie and Roxy were attacking the prodigious platefuls of fried food that constituted the West Town Café's full English breakfast. Eddie had always been amazed by Roxy's ability to combine an enormous appetite with being petite, but today he had other things on his mind.

"When are you going to give up this escort game, Roxy?"

She waved a piece of fried bread at him. "It's a legitimate business, the girls don't turn tricks, we vet all applicants and always send minders to parties and with stripograms. I'll go respectable when I've paid off my mortgage."

"But it's not safe!"

"It is with you around."

"But I'm going to America on Monday for two months?"

Roxy swallowed a mouthful of egg before replying. "No-one's going to miss you that quickly."

"Oh." Eddie grimaced. "Don't you think so?"

Roxy put down her knife and fork. "So that's what all this is about! You're going for the absence makes the heart grow fonder bollocks with the tall, thin girl. Go on, admit it!" She picked up her knife and waved it at him. "You're a bigger fool than I thought, you're too good for the likes of her."

"Janice, her name's Janice and I don't understand why you two can't get on."

Roxy shook her head despairingly. "OK, OK, I'll keep an eye on her as well as Mike, I don't want you worrying yourself to death while you're away."

"Thanks, Roxy, and make sure you look after yourself." Eddie hesitated. "Mike's got access to my bank accounts, so if you need money for anything…?" Another hesitation. "And if anything heavy happens, have a word with Jim." Roxy nodded and gave a self-conscious smile. "And remember, Charlie's a good friend."

Eddie sat back and looked round. A few working girls from outside West Town were having breakfast, including two youngsters he'd not seen before. One was sporting a black eye and the other a swollen mouth, Eddie gestured to them.

"Who are the girls, is there a banger in town?"

A banger was a punter who liked hurting girls, the type of punter Jed wanted Roxy to service all those years ago.

Roxy glanced at them. "They moved here from Leicester to escape a pimp who recruited for a wealthy banger, but rumour has it they've jumped out of the frying pan into the fire, the banger's from around here."

Eddie took an interest. "What's his name?"

Roxy shook her head. "Don't know, I'll see what I can find out."

Alarm bells were sounding in Eddie's head. He and Charlie still didn't understand why John Powers had stripped West

Town of police or why his superiors let him get away with it. Doug Bracken felt that Jerome Proctor was at the root of it but had no proof. Time for Roxy to write down an address Eddie gave her and heed his words of warning.

Roxy changed her clothes in the Café's back room before going home. She ran her escort business from her old room in Gladstone Street; home was a substantial semi-detached house on the Norwood Estate. On the face of it, Roxanne Bailey was a respectable businesswoman in a smart business suit but guessed her neighbours weren't fooled. None of them spoke to her but she didn't care, she had her friends and in three months' time her house would be paid for.

After a shower and a coffee, Roxy went to her computer. She'd always kept a diary and was writing a book based on her diaries. She liked to write a thousand words before going to bed and today the words came easily. The closing words of Chapter Four were much the same as her diary entry for the day.

'It's more than twelve years since the kind boy with beautiful blue eyes beat my pimp and his minder half to death in a grimy yard off a dirty back street in Canley. Today that same kind boy bought me breakfast and we talked. He still calls himself 'An unsmiling man with a bad reputation' and every time he says it, I wonder why as everything about the expression is wrong. He has always smiled a little for the tall, thin girl and smiled a great deal for his sweetheart. He's a boy, and will remain so if he lives to be a hundred. But most of all, to his girls and to the few people who really know him, he will always be a hero.'

CHAPTER 9

The Streetfighter

THE GUN

Dusk, and Eddie was lost in the back streets of New York. The receptionist at the smart hotel he'd stayed in for his first three nights in the city had given him directions to some tourist hotels, but he'd lost his way after detouring to visit a music shop. A newspaper seller had pointed out a short-cut, but either Eddie had misunderstood his directions, or the man didn't like Englishmen, because Eddie was now in a badly lit alley. Decaying tenement buildings arrayed with steel fire escape staircases created an aura of brooding menace, this area made Gladstone Street seem positively benevolent.

At the end of the dark alley Eddie could see a wider one with better lights, but his view was obscured by a row of large lidded skips, dumpsters – Eddie was learning a new language. As he approached them, he heard the unmistakable sounds of a fight: grunts, thuds and shouts. He had no desire to be a hero so put down his bag, moved slowly forward and peered round the side of a dumpster. The fight was to his left, a big man on the ground, rolling expertly trying to evade the flailing boots of three protagonists all wearing dark jackets with red emblems. To the right of the fight a fourth red emblem man lay on the ground writhing in pain, with a fifth draped unconscious over an abandoned car.

Good guys didn't use odds of five to one, the temptation to intervene was strong, but this was New York not Canley. Then he saw it, in the gutter just past the dumpster: a handgun. Eddie had never seen a real handgun before and the one in front of him looked like something out of a John Wayne Western. He peered at the fight again, the man on the ground didn't stand a chance, he couldn't gather enough momentum to roll himself upright. Before long one of the flailing boots would hit something vital and he would be finished. Eddie crept forward and picked up the gun; it was heavy and looked real, but was it? Across the road, between the fighting group and the two injured men, were a row of metal dustbins. Eddie grasped the gun with both hands, pointed it at a dustbin in the middle of the row and pulled the trigger.

Nothing, he was pulling the trigger and nothing was happening! Did elderly guns have safety catches? No idea! Perhaps it was single action, John Wayne's characters often pulled the hammer back two clicks before firing. He raised the gun again, pulled the hammer back one click, two clicks and squeezed the trigger hard. The hammer fell and Eddie noticed a perceptible delay before the gun fired. When it did Eddie was pleased he'd used both hands as the recoil was massive. The sound was a huge dull clap, nothing like the sharp cracks heard in films. A cloud of acrid blue smoke spurted from the barrel, then another perceptible delay before the bullet hit the dustbin he'd aimed at. Eddie moved to one side to peer round the smoke to see the dustbin spinning from the impact of the heavy bullet, spraying rubbish and rats. The red emblem men froze but didn't run so Eddie raised the gun again, aimed to their left, pulled the hammer back two clicks again and squeezed the trigger. His reward was a second huge dull clap and cloud of acrid smoke. The recoil knocked him off balance, and as he recovered he heard the bullet whining into the distance after ricocheting from the pavement.

The red emblem men burst into action, grabbing their fallen comrades and running towards a dark coloured van Eddie hadn't noticed hidden behind another dumpster. Moments later there was the roar of an engine, a squeal of tyres and they were gone.

THE GIRL WITH THE SMILE

Eddie had booked the smart hotel on the internet and had made good use of his stay scouring music shops, pawn shops and junk shops in good, bad and indifferent areas seeking bargain priced guitars. He'd found them too – high quality Fender, Gibson and Rickenbacker guitars were much cheaper than in England and Eddie had shipped a batch back to the workshop in Cedar Walk. Before leaving he'd given the immensely skilful Bob a crash course in guitar renovation; he would soon have them in pristine condition and displayed in their shop window.

However, his attempts to convince himself he was enjoying himself were unsuccessful; he didn't have a problem with his own company, but he did have a problem with unfamiliar surroundings. Occupying himself for two months would be next to impossible – he'd already shipped enough guitars to stock his shop for weeks; he needed to find a job.

Mike had insisted on driving him to the airport and they'd managed to retain their composure as they shook hands at the departure gate. He would keep a watchful eye on the businesses; Eddie trusted Bob and Ellie but they were inexperienced. Eddie had also given Mike a difficult commission: tracking down the long-term investments Charles had made in Eddie's name when he was seventeen. He remembered Charles' mocking voice: 'I'm investing your half in long term bonds, you won't see a penny until you're about thirty'. In a few months' time Eddie would be thirty; if there was any money Mike would find it.

Initially Janice had been shocked when he said he was going away, but later seemed unconcerned, almost pleased. Perhaps he'd misread her comments 'my room' and 'his room', he hoped she'd be upset. Now Eddie felt guilty, it was bad enough leaving so soon after Nan's death without wanting her to be upset as well. Maybe she needed time away from him to think; Eddie hoped Nan was right, that Janice would miss him as much as he was missing her.

The big man stood up, glanced at the departing van then at the gun in Eddie's hand. A wisp of smoke drifted from the barrel as Eddie lowered it; he didn't want to appear threatening. The man walked forward slowly, arms held away from his sides, palms flat and pointing forward. He was in non-threatening mode as well.

Despite the noise of the fight and the shots, no-one had come to investigate, shades of the resolutely drawn curtains in Gladstone Street all those years ago. The big man stopped a few paces from Eddie and gave a slow nod, the universal gesture of thanks. He was a fraction shorter than Eddie but very wide. His flat features and jet black hair suggested a far eastern origin, but the voice was unmistakably American.

"Hell, man, you took a risk, I could be a bad guy."

Eddie shrugged. "Good guys don't use odds of five to one."

The big man smiled and pointed at the gun. "I see you found my gun?"

He moved back slightly, another classic non-threatening move. "Perhaps I could have it back?" He paused. "If that's OK with you?"

"Sure." Eddie handed over the gun. "It looks old, the sort of thing I used to see in Western films."

The big man glanced round nervously, but his voice remained calm. "It's well over a hundred years old; I'll tell you about it later, we'd better go before those guys come back."

Chin picked up Eddie's heavy bag as if it weighed nothing and jogged off quickly. They zig-zagged through a maze of alleys until they found streetlights, then dived down another alley and zig-zagged again until they came to a brightly lit street.

Chin slowed to a walk and turned to Eddie. "Have you eaten?"

Eddie hadn't, it was one of his many failings – if he was busy or distracted he forgot to eat. The diner was quiet, the waiter knew Chin and gave Eddie a friendly smile. They sat in a cubicle waiting for their hamburgers and fries with Eddie wondering why Americans offered cream with coffee then brought milk.

"You a tourist?"

Eddie explained that he was in New York combining business with pleasure, a sort of working holiday.

"I got lost, saw the fight, then the gun and you know the rest."

No, Chin didn't know the rest – in New York no-one helped or got involved. He explained that he had a legitimate sideline dealing in antique firearms and someone must have thought he was supplying guns to a rival gang. He wasn't and the misunderstanding could have cost him his life.

They ate their burgers and talked. Chin was intrigued: tourists didn't get involved in fights in New York back streets, and if they did, they definitely wouldn't be blasé about it afterwards. He made his offer on impulse and wasn't sure who was the most surprised.

"Have you got a place to stay?"

Home was a compact ground floor apartment in an anonymous block.

"My wife's visiting her sister, she'll be back in the morning, but you can stay as long as you like."

Chin reminded Eddie of Jim – not his appearance but his demeanour, a reassuring mix of confidence and concern. Nonetheless, Eddie had no intention of staying more than one night, the risk of a nightmare or the terrors coming to embarrass him was too great. For one night he would set his headphone alarm on a thirty-minute repeat.

In the meantime, he was surprised by the big man's facial scarring and mutilated nose. The words came out before he could stop them.

"You're really quick for a big man but…"

Chin was smiling. "But what?"

"But?" Eddie paused then continued. "Your face is all messed up?"

Chin was bemused, unless they were incredibly good or incredibly lucky all fighters had messed up faces. The Englishman talked like a fighter but apart from a thin scar under his right eye his face was unmarked.

He asked tentatively. "You a fighter?"

Eddie shrugged. "Yes, sort of."

"Boxing, martial arts...?"

Eddie shook his head, his tone matter of fact. "Whatever wins."

Statisticians say that coincidences are so common that no-one should be surprised when they occur, but Eddie was still surprised. Not only did Chin remind Eddie of Jim, he was Jim's American equivalent. Chin's Gym taught self-defence and fitness to fund its primary purpose: teaching youngsters to box to stop them fighting on the streets. Yesterday the gym had a staffing problem; now it hadn't and Eddie had a job.

Morning found Eddie more tired than usual after his alarm waking him every thirty minutes throughout the night. Tomorrow night would be different, the first aid room at Chin's Gym would be Eddie's home until he returned to Canley. Showing remarkable trust, Chin left Eddie alone in the apartment while he went to collect Ellen. Eddie was fighting a losing battle with the coffee maker when he heard the door open and a swishing noise, then they were in front of him. The apartment had little natural light and Chin and Ellen clearly preferred low lighting. Eddie preferred fluorescents – his cataracts impaired his vision in low light as well as in glare.

He knew he was staring and heard a sigh of disappointment from Chin.

"Hell Eddie, I thought you were different."

Eddie couldn't tear his eyes away from the girl in the wheelchair. She had dark hair, pale skin and huge, dark blue eyes. She wasn't as pretty as Jilly – nobody was – but in the poor light...

Chin's words struck him, he thought Eddie was staring at the wheelchair. He wasn't; he'd guessed last night after seeing the wide doorways and power points positioned at waist height.

"No!" Eddie shook his head.

He scrabbled about in his wallet, pulling out the photograph of Jilly and spilling the remaining contents onto the floor.

"A few years ago that could have been you."

Ellen studied the picture, smiled gently and handed it to Chin. "You're a kind man, Eddie, even a lot of years ago I wasn't that pretty. Who is she?"

As she spoke the likeness disappeared, her accent was American, her voice deeper and her mannerisms quite different.

"My wife, she was killed nearly five years ago."

Chin had picked up the contents of Eddie's wallet and was looking at the second picture. "Who's the girl with the smile?"

It was an old picture, back then when Janice smiled her whole face lit up. "She's a friend, it's complicated."

BACK HOME

The two men had finally met and were eyeing each other warily. In his capacity as chairman of the Canley Confederation of

Children's Charities Gerald Burchnall OBE was meeting Jim Lutkin, organiser of 'Box – don't Fight'. The previous chairman was as anti-violence as Gerry and had consistently vetoed Jim's applications to join CCCC. Gerry was determined to be open minded and the statistics in Box – don't Fight's annual report were impressive. The report itself was a masterpiece, compelling and persuasive with annexes containing tables and graphs comparing the re-offending rates of boys attending Jim's Gym with all manner of other rehabilitation schemes. Over a five-year period the record of 'Box – don't Fight' was consistently outstanding. Gerry recognised the author's style, he'd seen plenty of Eddie's work at Fultons.

CCCC members received Local Authority funding and access to central government grants for special projects. Jim made it clear that 'Box - don't Fight' needed money, despite the upbeat business plan in the annual report.

"Don't be fooled by the new changing rooms and toilets, our landlord's very generous, but we can't expect him to subsidise us for ever, we need our own money."

The edge had gone from Jim's voice, but his look of mild contempt lingered. Gerry was unused to such looks, twenty years working with children's charities had earned him respect and an OBE, so what was Jim's problem? Gerry asked and received a blunt reply, Jim resented suggestions that he encouraged boys to fight.

"The other bloke didn't want to know, he just gave me a mouthful and pissed off."

Gerry grunted. "Try me, I'm different!"

"What are the two major violence problems we deal with?" Gerry didn't answer, he wasn't expected to, it was a rhetorical question. "Domestic and street, men knocking their wives and kids about, and lads in gangs fighting on the streets." Jim jumped to his feet, he talked better moving about. "Now, what does men hitting their wives and lads in gangs fighting have in common?" Another rhetorical question. "Unfair odds, that's what, a bloke hitting a woman or a child, or a group of lads kicking the shit out of some poor sod by himself." He glared at Gerry. "Now, think about boxing."

Gerry shrugged and Jim threw his hands in the air in despair.

"That's the trouble, everyone misses the bleeding obvious. Picture a boxing match, you must have seen one on the TV, go on, describe it."

Gerry tried. "Two men knocking the hell out of each other."

Jim's voice was full of contempt. "You're still missing the bleeding obvious." He slowed right down as if he was talking to an idiot. "It's one bloke fighting one other bloke of a similar size and ability, that's why it's called a match." Jim speeded up again. "My boys fight matches and after a while it becomes a matter of pride; they don't want to fight somebody smaller or less experienced, or hit a woman, or use odds of three or four to one. For Christ's sake, it works, you've seen the figures, our re-offending rate beats any of your lot. And those figures are straight, Eddie did them."

Jim made some tea and as they sipped the strong, sweet brew from chipped mugs, Gerry saw Jim's expression change; the little fighter was upset.

"The lads from violent homes where everybody gets a beating aren't too bad, they think it's normal. Eventually someone outside the home picks on them and they fight back and feel proud of themselves, even if they lose. My job is to get them to fight matches in a boxing ring and only in a boxing ring."

Gerry could see Jim studying him closely, watching for a reaction. "The bad ones are those that get singled out for beatings, they're always loaded down with guilt, they think it's their fault. You know the ones I mean, the ones like Eddie."

Gerry couldn't disguise his surprise, and Jim was shouting at him. "There, I bleeding knew it, you and those fucking arseholes from Social Services thought he was naturally violent and I made him worse. Well he isn't and I didn't, his parents used him as a fucking punch bag and no-one knew or cared, so now he can't bear the thought of anyone being as frightened and alone as he was, and he fights for them."

Gerry covered his confusion by asking to see Jim's accounts – the previous chairman's lax auditing procedures had allowed some charity organisers to misuse funds. Gerry had been involved in a few shady deals in his time so had an eye for dubious bookkeeping. But Jim's accounts were exemplary, the only odd thing was that the rent for his gym was unrealistically low. Gerry probed hard and eventually Jim exploded.

"Oh fuck it, it's about time Eddie got the credit he deserves. Three years ago the lease on this place expired, the landlord doubled the rent and we were in deep shit. Then all of a sudden the place was sold and the new landlord put the rent down, much lower than before. I didn't think much about it until he started renovating the place, with new changing rooms and toilets and not putting the rent up. Eventually I got the truth out of my assistant – our new landlord is Artemis Properties, and if you dig deep enough you'll find that's Eddie."

Gerry was puzzled. "How did your assistant know?"

"She's a long-time friend of Eddie's, Roxanne Bailey." Jim sensed Gerry's reaction to the name. "Yes, the supposed red-haired tart from Eddie's trial." He leaned forward. "She's a really clever girl with proper qualifications, she'll be looking for a proper job soon, so if you hear of anything let me know."

Gerry was about to advertise for a full-time coordinator for CCCC, and a man with the vision to recruit an ex-prostitute would be noticed. Gerry wanted to be noticed, an OBE was good, but a knighthood...?

ARTEMIS AND AGAMEMNON

Eddie wasn't into Greek mythology, but reading C S Forrester's Hornblower novels meant he was into warships and the Royal Navy had a tradition of naming their vessels after Greek Gods.

HMS Agamemnon was a real Napoleonic wars two-decked wooden warship mounting sixty-four guns when the norm for a ship of the line at the time was seventy-four, and much larger ships were not uncommon. The Agamemnon's most famous captain was Horatio Nelson who used the ship to devastating effect, regularly defeating much larger vessels. For him the Agamemnon was 'Bigger than anything faster; faster than anything bigger'.

HMS Artemis was a fictional Second World War Light Cruiser made famous in 'The Ship', a novel by C S Forrester. In reality, most warships are small, so much so that Frigates and Destroyers are regarded as powerful weapons of war. Light Cruisers are significantly larger than Destroyers, similar in physical size to Heavy Cruisers. HMS Artemis, and the real Light Cruiser on which it was based, carried massive six-inch guns the same as many Heavy Cruisers, the difference between them being in the thickness of their armour. Light Cruisers were prodigiously fast and massively armed but pitifully thin armour left them unable to take punishment, they were 'eggshells armed with sledgehammers'.

Eddie read 'The Ship' many times, and read a great deal about Nelson's exploits in the Agamemnon. He likened himself to the Agamemnon and Artemis, bigger than anything faster; faster than anything bigger, massively armed but unable to take punishment. Eddie knew how good he was, unless he met the street-fighting equivalent of a battleship he was unlikely to be beaten. There were no battleships in Canley, but this was New York.

Jim was giving Gerry another lesson on battered children.

"Once lads like Eddie start to fight, they want to take on really big lads or two or three at a time to prove they're not cowards. They're trying to get rid of the guilt but they can't, they're all twisted up with it, everything's their fault." Jim gazed at Gerry in despair. "For Christ's sake, anybody with a brain bigger that a peanut should spot them."

Gerry 'Peanut Brain' Burchnall felt uncomfortable and was relieved when Jim decided to give him a boxing lesson. Minutes later he was standing in a boxing ring holding hand pads in front of his chest with Jim wearing boxing gloves and talking excitedly.

"Don't worry, I won't hit you, I'll hit the pads, but I'll aim a bit to one side so you'll have to move to catch the punch in the middle."

Jim looked old but the punches came so fast that Gerry hardly had time to move the pads before they landed.

Jim shouted, "Look for the signs, I told you to look for the signs."

Gerry looked and eventually noticed that Jim bowed his head slightly before throwing a right. It gave him a split second to anticipate and to move the pad into position. Before throwing a left, he dropped his shoulder and leant backwards slightly, two movements giving him extra time to move into position.

Jim grinned. "Good, you're getting the idea."

He might be, but Gerry was exhausted, and not just physically, the concentration needed to watch and anticipate was astonishing.

Another first for Gerry: he was sitting on the edge of a boxing ring drinking beer from a bottle. Jim lit a cigarette and smoked it right down to the filter tip before stubbing it out. He saw Gerry's look of disapproval and shrugged.

"Eddie and Roxy are always moaning about my fags, I'll give up one day." Suddenly he beamed at Gerry. "You got there in the end, you started to read the signs."

Gerry took swig of beer before replying. "Yes, but I still can't believe how fast it happens. I hardly saw your hand start to move before it was on the pad. It was a bit easier when I read the signs, but even then…"

Jim stared at him. "Shall I tell you why Eddie's so good?" Gerry nodded as Jim continued. "To start with he looks ordinary, it's like having the local librarian square up to you so no-one takes him seriously. Then he switches off and there's fuck all there, no signs, no emotion, nothing. Before you know it there's a hand in your face, usually a right. It's not that hard and you think, that's OK, but then he hits you again and again and you don't see them coming either. So you decide to step back, a mistake because everyone glances before they move. That's when he hits you with the big left hand, it's telegraphed a bit, but you miss it because you're looking backwards. That punch is a fucking monster and you go down." Jim scowled. "Then you'd better hope you haven't pissed him off or hurt one of his girls or he goes in with the boot and you're meat paste."

"Girls, what girls …?"

Jim interrupted sharply. "I mean fifteen and sixteen year old girls that have been put on the street by pimps and drug pushers and neither your lot nor the police give a shit …"

Gerry interrupted in turn. "CCCC doesn't deal with prostitution…"

Jim shouted him down. "These girls are children, not prostitutes!"

Chin was worried; out of gratitude he'd given someone he hardly knew a job, a place to live and access to his home. Ellen liked Eddie, insisting that he ate with them some evenings and spent hours talking to him about England and the girls in the photographs. Chin wasn't so sure, he found Eddie impossible to read and people that closed were often psychopaths.

The gangs ruled the streets where Chin grew up. At twelve he was running with them, at sixteen he was a respected gang member, and at nineteen he was an enforcer with a fearsome reputation. Violence ruled his life until a girl was caught in the crossfire of a shootout. It probably wasn't a bullet from his gun that hit her, but it could have been; Chin still had a spark of humanity left so stayed to comfort her. The police thought he was an innocent bystander; the girl knew he wasn't but said nothing. He visited her in hospital to ask why and it just happened for both of them. Ellen would never walk again and Chin would never understand why she wasn't bitter. Now he taught boxing to try and stop boys joining the gangs and fighting on the streets.

Ellen taught sociology and when she talked to Chin about body language, he knew what she meant – all fighters read their opponents looking for signals that could predict a knife being pulled or a punch being thrown. Chin had to fight the unreadable man who gave no signals to see if was a real fighter or a self-deluding fake.

The ladies' self-defence class had finished, Eddie was stacking the floor mats when Chin took a pace forward and threw a punch. It wasn't a huge blow and it was telegraphed – any good fighter would be able to parry it. The blow wasn't parried, the Englishman simply wasn't there, a second blow also missed by miles, the Englishman was astonishingly fast, and a punch was coming towards him. It was in Chin's face before he could move, then a second and a third thumped home and he still hadn't moved. Chin glanced behind him before stepping back and didn't see the massive left hand until it crunched in under his ribs. He'd been hit that hard before by really big men when he'd been overconfident or careless. No big man had ever hit him twice, they weren't fast enough, but the Englishman was, and he shouldn't be able to hit that hard.

The punch drove all the breath from Chin's body and he tipped forward. As he folded over, Chin swung to his right, moving away from the knee that was surely coming. Milliseconds later Eddie's knee crashed into Chin's face; moving away reduced the impact but Chin was in serious trouble, he had to go down. Fighters hated going down – once on the floor you could end up staying there – but if you were good you could dive and roll away from trouble.

As Chin gathered momentum a shiny black shoe hooked behind his knee, pulling him across and back. His momentum gone, Chin could neither roll away from trouble nor roll himself back upright, he was in a heap on the floor. A rigid leather sole was about to stamp on his arm; this was going to hurt.

"Shit!" Suddenly Eddie was on his hands and knees beside him, his face full of concern. "Shit, I'm sorry, I went into autopilot, I should have known it was just a bit of fun."

Chin had his answer – for a few seconds the icy control disappeared but the only emotion there was concern, no triumph or surprise at beating a much bigger man.

"You expected to beat me!" Chin couldn't keep the surprise from his voice.

Eddie shrugged, the control was back, his shields had clicked back into place. "I'm much quicker than you; unless you got close enough to grapple I'd always win."

Chin shook his head and gave a bemused smile. "And you'd never let me get that close?"

"No." It wasn't a boast, it was a statement of fact.

CHAPTER 10

A girl from Brooklyn

FOLK SONGS

Eddie liked folk music, not traditional folk where bushy-bearded men in corduroy trousers placed a finger in one ear before singing unaccompanied dirges to the delight of pasty-faced vegetarian girls in cotton print dresses. Eddie liked contemporary folk and, in particular, sixties contemporary electric folk.

In his early teens passing time in charity shops after school, Eddie searched through endless boxes of vinyl records seeking inspiration. If a record cover caught his eye he would buy the album, usually for less than a pound, and listen to it. He started with Bob Dylan before moving on to British folk heroes such as Donovan, Al Stewart and Fairport Convention. Later he found records from Fairport Convention's solo offshoots, Richard Thompson and Sandy Denny, but always returned to Al Stewart.

Juliet liked folk music and she and Eddie sometimes sat in the bus shelter on Mayors Road and talked about artists they liked. He would give her the records he'd tried and didn't like, loan her the records he did like, and search for duplicates or make tapes if she liked them as well. Juliet loved Al Stewart's early albums where young love and romance dominated his lyrics. She found a review of an early Al Stewart album in an old magazine where the reviewer compared him to another sixties folk singer, Mike Heron. Eventually Eddie found a Mike Heron record in a charity shop, but didn't like the music so gave it to Juliet. She didn't like the music either but loved the title 'Smiling men with bad reputations'. Eddie became her 'Unsmiling man with a bad reputation'; it wasn't meant unkindly – Juliet was never unkind.

In the letter Mrs Morris brought to Eddie in his room in Gladstone Street, Juliet described some of the precious things she had with her on her plastic sheet. Top of the list was the Mike Heron record, Juliet was thinking of an unsmiling man with a bad reputation as she waited patiently to die.

Chin's first aid room was small and dingy with a narrow barred window overlooking an even dingier alley. Eddie wasn't complaining, his converted loft over the workshop in Cedar Walk had no window, no view and no natural light. He liked his job and could talk to both Ellen and Chin. Bob said he should talk, not hide away feeling guilty and he was right, there had been no sign of the terrors in the two weeks he'd spent in New York. Nightmares, yes, but there had always been nightmares.

Eddie wanted a permanent cure for the terrors; a madman was no use to Janice. The thought brought an immediate avalanche of guilt – was he trying to forget Jilly and move on to destroy Janice?

Food for thought, but food for sustenance was on Eddie's mind as he stepped into the twenty-four hour diner two minutes' walk from Chin's gym. The diner served enormous portions and Eddie struggled to clear his breakfast plate. He felt bloated and decided to walk back past the Gym to a music shop two blocks further on, but outside the gym he found folk music in his head, words from an Al Stewart song explained.

Al Stewart's first album in 1967 was 'Bed-Sitter Images'. Eddie liked the album, it was melodic, had superb finger-picked guitar playing and was filled with rose tinted images of bed-sitter land. However, he had difficulty understanding some of the lyrics, for example 'Swiss Cottage Manoeuvres' started *'On a Christmas cake day one Friday in August'*. Eddie had no idea what that meant and the song went on to describe meeting a girl: *'She had eyes like a poet and hair like a rainbow'*. Understanding *'eyes like a poet'* was easy, Janice had eyes like a poet, eyes that had seen a great deal of other people's happiness but very little of her own. Picturing *'hair like a rainbow' was* difficult until now!

As the early morning sun caught the hair of the girl standing outside Chin's gym, it reflected oranges and golds and red and yellows, the colours of a rainbow. Eddie thought of Juliet and smiled sadly, the girl thought he was smiling at her and smiled back.

"What time does the gym open?" Her accent was tainted, but unmistakably English, and she was clutching one of Chin's advertising leaflets for a ladies' self defence course. The leaflet had an address and a map, but no opening times.

Eddie tried a better smile and asked the obvious question. "Where are you from?"

The girl pointed vaguely. "Brooklyn."

Eddie shook his head with amusement. "No, I mean where are you from originally."

The girl laughed, recognising Eddie's measured English accent. "Chelmsford."

Eddie was back in the diner, he'd told the girl from Brooklyn that the Gym only opened afternoons and evenings and she'd suggested having coffee.

Most people prefer talking to listening, Eddie preferred listening but rarely did either with strangers. However, girl with rainbow hair was the first English person he'd met in a fortnight, and countrymen meeting in a foreign lands should talk, shouldn't they?

She wouldn't tell him her name; instead she leant back in her chair and smiled.

"I hate my real name, choose one for me."

Eddie did his best to smile back, but his thoughts were many miles and years away. He was relieved when she liked his anonymous choice.

"How about Brooklyn?"

Brooklyn's story started happily: Mum, Dad, Brooklyn, a younger brother and sister; then went horribly wrong. Mum died and a dutiful Brooklyn took her place, leaving school at sixteen and taking menial jobs to help support the family. As is the way of things, her efforts were taken for granted and her objections to her hard-earned money being used to buy treats for her sister and beer for her father were ignored.

One fine June morning an angry Brooklyn woke up, packed a bag and hitch-hiked to Spain. It wasn't the romantic adventure she'd hoped for, it was lonely and frightening, but she persisted and took a job in a bar for the summer. In late autumn she returned home expecting to be greeted like a returning prodigal with her family now appreciative of the sacrifices she'd made. Instead, she found nothing but resentment – unless she apologised and reverted to her previous uncomplaining role she wasn't wanted. Even a fool can have a day off, so Brooklyn turned round and hitchhiked back to Spain.

This time it was romantic; within a month she met Lawrence, an American in Spain on business. When he returned to America she went with him, and ten years later they were still together, just about. Lawrence had a liking for recreational drugs, eventually recreation degenerated into habit and gave Brooklyn a new career. After retraining and a year working in the field, she was a qualified drugs rehabilitation counsellor. Unfortunately, Lawrence wasn't one of her successes, he was presently in residential rehabilitation in San Francisco and she was working in a rehabilitation day centre in Brooklyn.

"I couldn't take it any more so I gave him an ultimatum, no more broken promises and no more lies, go into residential rehab. He'll be out in five weeks and we've agreed to meet at noon on Pier 39 in San Francisco. If he's not there, or he's not clean, it's over."

PEOPLE, FRIENDS AND ADDICTS

Eddie had a job he liked in a fascinating city with a place to stay and friends to talk to. He even had a place to hide if the terrors came – the twenty-four hour New York subway was full of spaced-out people. Despite this he was homesick, not for Canley or the workshop, but for the people that made Canley home. Eddie couldn't get Janice out of his mind and was consumed with guilt because he missed her even more than Sophie or Mike or Roxy.

Mike was a better friend than Eddie had any right to and was the kingpin in the complex arrangements Eddie had made to keep everyone safe while he was away. Eddie was concerned about Roxy, she was overseeing the girls but who was overseeing her? Mike, of course, but he was overseeing everyone. When Eddie voiced his concerns to Mike he received a knowing smile in response. Why was he always the last to notice? Roxy and Jim were more than colleagues making 'Box – don't Fight' an effective charity, they were an item.

Jim wasn't as old as Eddie thought, he was forty-four. When Eddie went to Jim's Gym fifteen years ago Jim was the same age that Eddie was now. At twenty-nine he'd dragged himself out of the gutter, including two years in prison for grievous bodily harm, and dedicated his life to stopping boys making the mistakes he'd made. It was a pity Eddie had to come to New York to realise just how special Jim was.

Brooklyn was disturbingly naïve for someone involved with addicts. Eddie knew about pimps, men without scruples of any kind who happily procured girls for perverts. Pimps were often pushers as well, addicted girls were easier to control than non-addicted girls, and Eddie's remedy for both was to beat them so badly that they would never dare return to West Town. He was a realist, being victims didn't necessarily mean that prostitutes and addicts were trustworthy, he left that incredibly difficult value judgment to the exceptionally perceptive Roxy. Unfortunately, Brooklyn believed that victims should be trusted unless the contrary was proved, a view doubtless influenced by her experience with Lawrence.

Addicts rarely rose early, theirs was a twilight world, so Brooklyn worked afternoons and evenings, the same as Eddie.

They started breakfasting together, talking of England and music and books before starting work. Eddie introduced her to Chin and Ellen with moderate success; they liked her, but shared Eddie's worries about combining naivety with drug culture.

Within days Eddie, Chin and Ellen were proved right – they had arranged to meet Brooklyn for a late evening meal at an Italian restaurant a few blocks from the gym and she arrived late, flustered and excited. A pusher and his minder had forced their way into the rehab centre seeking ex-customers who owed them money. A fight had broken out and in the ensuing mêlée the pusher had dropped a notebook containing details of his suppliers and customers. Brooklyn had found it, copied it, and taken the original to the police.

"Did you tell the police you'd taken a copy?" Chin sounded worried; he knew from bitter experience that not all police officers were honest.

Brooklyn was still excited. "Yes, I told them I'd made a copy, he said he needed it and I said I'd hidden it. He asked again but when another man came in, he lost interest."

"Shit!"

Now Chin was seriously worried – as Brooklyn talked 'them' had turned into 'he'. She'd dealt with one officer who'd stopped talking when a second arrived.

His tone was icily calm. "Does anyone else know you have a copy?"

"A couple of patients saw me at the photocopier, but they wouldn't tell anyone."

Chin shook his head despairingly; Brooklyn's idealism was unreal. For patient read addict in rehab, a person who would sell his grandmother for a fix.

Overnight bad turned to worse, the rehab centre was broken into, searched and the hidden copy of the notebook taken. Ignoring Chin's warning, Brooklyn contacted the police officer she'd initially spoken to who seemed more interested in whether she'd read the copy than the fact it had been taken.

"He told me not to go anywhere."

Eddie and Brooklyn met Chin in an anonymous diner three subway stops from the gym. The word on the street confirmed that Brooklyn was in serious trouble, the book belonged to a minion of Cal Baduci, a sadistic and unforgiving crack cocaine dealer. The minion had disappeared, probably killed for being careless, and Chin feared that the same fate awaited Brooklyn.

"There's no point going to the police, even if you get an honest one they wouldn't be able to protect you twenty-four hours a day." Chin was emphatic. "You've got to go, and quickly. It doesn't have to be forever, dealers like Cal rarely last long, in a year or so he'll be dead and gone."

Brooklyn shook her head with disbelief. "No, it can't be that serious."

Chin was angry. "It can and it is! It's not just you, anyone around you could end up dead and I don't want these maniacs near Ellen." He turned to Eddie. "Take her, drag her if you have to, but take her a very long way away, and do it now."

NO PLACE TO HIDE

Eddie returned to the gym, threw his belongings into his bag and jogged to the nearest subway station. He'd left Brooklyn at the subway station next to the anonymous diner, making her promise to take a long ride before checking in to a hotel. They would stay overnight then leave early, mingling with morning commuters. He'd given her the number of a public telephone next to his subway entrance and waited there for her call giving the address of the hotel.

Brooklyn still wasn't taking the matter seriously; the hotel was the sort of place that rented rooms by the hour and was only three subway stops from the rehab centre. The only thing she'd done right was to pay cash and check in under a false name. Security at the hotel was non-existent, open doors, no CCTV cameras and when Eddie arrived the desk clerk was asleep, face down on the counter. Brooklyn had booked room 113 which Eddie assumed was room 13 on the first floor. He ran up the dark stairway to find that room 113 was at the end of a gloomy corridor next to a fire escape. He tapped on the door and tried the handle in one movement. The unlocked flimsy door swung open to reveal Brooklyn standing by the window peering into an alley filled with rubbish, dumpsters and rats. She gave him a rueful smile.

"This is all a bit melodramatic; I think Chin's been watching too many gangster movies."

Eddie was angry, Chin didn't frighten easily and definitely wasn't given to melodrama. Less than six blocks from where they were standing, a group of thugs would have kicked Chin to death if Eddie hadn't intervened.

She recoiled as he snapped. "For Christ sake, Brooklyn, you're in serious trouble, drug dealers kill people!"

"I'm sorry, Eddie, I'm really sorry." Then, childlike, she smiled and brightened up. "If I promise to lock the door, will you go out for some food, I'm starving."

Eddie had passed a McDonald's as he'd jogged from the subway to the hotel. Thankfully the queue was short and he was soon back outside the hotel clutching a bag of burgers, fries and coffee. He paused and looked round – in daylight with bustling people and flashing neon signs the area didn't seem that dangerous; perhaps Chin had overreacted.

Or perhaps not. The first thing Eddie noticed as he pushed through the hotel doors was that the desk clerk had disappeared. He felt a sense of foreboding – in this sort of hotel, desk clerks didn't leave their rows of keys unattended. A picture of Brooklyn in the room flashed into his mind: she was wearing a leather jacket. Shit and double shit, she wasn't wearing that jacket in the anonymous diner, she must have gone back to her room to get it.

The gloomy corridor had bare floorboards – that was why Brooklyn wasn't startled when he'd opened the door earlier, she'd heard his heels clicking on the boards. This time he scooted down the corridor on the soles of his shoes, hoping he was wrong. He wasn't: the flimsy door was closed but the wood around the lock was splintered. Eddie dropped the bag of food and thrust the door open.

Brooklyn was cowering on the floor by the window with her arms over her head in a forlorn attempt at defence. The grossly fat man standing next to her turned with elaborate unconcern as Eddie burst through the door. He wasn't particularly tall, a little shorter than Eddie, and a casual observer might dismiss him as harmless because of his bulk. But Eddie wasn't a casual observer; the fat man moved easily and had a boxer's upper torso, his head met his shoulders without the courtesy of a neck. Fat man was calm and confident, he was dangerous and knew it.

A second man standing closer to Eddie was Mr Average, but he was sweating and moved slower than the fat man. Sweaty man was nervous, he wasn't dangerous but didn't know it.

"Beat it, sonny!"

Eddie wasn't overly fond of being called sonny, but it meant that the fat man didn't see him as a threat. The paralysing fear that was the lot of snivelling cowards evaporated as Eddie heard Brooklyn whimper. He moved slowly forward, within striking distance of the sweaty man.

Fat man had seen enough. "No second chances here, sonny, take him, Weasel."

Sweaty man grinned, he may be nervous but he enjoyed his work. He looked down and pressed his thumb on an object clasped in his right hand. Eddie heard a click and saw a flash of movement as a long, wicked blade appeared. Unbelievable: sweaty man was supposed to be a professional but was moving towards Eddie square on with his legs slightly apart and still looking at his knife! His sloppiness would soon become his painful undoing.

Eddie went up on his toes and kicked, his foot reaching sweaty man before his eyes left his knife. It wasn't a perfect testicle spreader, Eddie's aim was slightly to his right, the man's left, with his shiny black shoe scraping the sweaty man's left thigh before striking his left testicle. The next few moments were like a comedy sketch: the sweaty man rose onto tiptoe hoping that the movement would reduce the impact on his testicle. It didn't and he pursed his lips, sucked in a huge gasp of air and gave a strangled scream.

The fat man was overconfident; as he waved Weasel forward he dropped his knife into his jacket pocket and reached for a cigarette. As Eddie's shiny black shoe was doing its work on sweaty man's left testicle, the fat man's hand was closing round his cigarette lighter. When Eddie turned to him, the fat man's reflex was to jab his thumb on what he was holding, but the action produced a jet flame from his lighter not a blade from his knife. The few moments he spent gazing stupidly at the flame gave Eddie time to wind up the sleeper. It was a good one, well timed and landing flush on the side of fat man's head.

Eddie didn't wait for the fat man to fall before turning back to the sweaty man struggling back onto his feet. His face was contorted with pain and fury as he lurched towards Eddie but, incredibly, he hadn't learned his lesson, he was still square on. Eddie went up onto his toes and kicked again. This time his aim was better, only very slightly to his left, the man's right. His shoe gently grazed sweaty man's right thigh before impacting massively on his, as yet, undamaged right testicle. No comedy scene this time, sweaty man pitched forward vomiting, he was down and out.

Back to the fat man and for a moment Eddie feared that his light cruiser had met a battleship; the fat man was clambering to his feet. No-one had ever got up from a well-timed sleeper to the head before, but Eddie stopped worrying when he saw how laboured the fat man's movements were. He wasn't a battleship, he was an old, slow, badly damaged heavy cruiser. All Eddie needed was a weapon to finish him and his eyes lit on a nearby wooden chair. As he turned back holding the chair, the fat man's right thumb jabbed down on his knife; no choice left, Eddie swung the chair at the fat man's head.

Chairs are cumbersome weapons, easier to swing back first than front first. That was how Eddie used it, striking the fat man solidly on his head and shoulder. The blow had the same effect as the sleeper, the fat man was down but not out. Eddie had to improve his weapon and flipped the chair over in the air so he could swing it with the front of the solid wooden seat as the leading edge. It was all or nothing, Eddie aimed carefully and accelerated the chair through a long arc.

The crunch as the seat hit the fat man's temple reminded Eddie of the sound Ray and Phil's faces made as he smashed them. The effect was immediate, the fat man crashed to the floor and lay twitching with blood spurting from a great gouge in his head.

Eddie looked back at the sweaty man lying semi-conscious in a pool of vomit; he wasn't a danger but was a witness to murder, the fat man must be dead. Eddie lifted the chair and moved forward.

"Eddie!"

Eddie swung round to see Brooklyn recoil as the fat man convulsed in a death throe, spraying blood everywhere. He dropped the chair and knelt beside the fallen man, the seat edge had driven his skull inwards creating a massive wound stretching from his temple to his ear. The bleeding had stopped but Eddie could see slow pulsing inside the wound; a few seconds later the pulsing stopped and the man lay still.

The fight was over, Eddie was back in real time, not the slow motion that always happened when he fought. He heard whimpering behind him, Brooklyn was crouched on the floor, her eyes tightly closed.

He shook her gently. "Brooklyn, we have to go, now!"

There was no response. Eddie had no time for niceties – there could be other maniacs looking for them; he shook her firmly.

"Brooklyn! Open your eyes."

The whimpering stopped, her eyes opened slowly and she stared alternately at the semi-conscious sweaty man and the dead fat man. She was too shocked to scream, her mouth opened and closed noiselessly as Eddie pulled her to her feet.

"Don't look at them! Just follow me."

Eddie ran to the splintered door and dragged it open. A glance along the corridor showed that all the other doors were firmly closed. He shouldn't be surprised; hotels that rented rooms by the hour were unlikely to attract public spirited citizens. He left Brooklyn inside the room and sprinted down the corridor to peer down the stairs at the check-in desk. The clerk was still conspicuous by his absence – Eddie guessed he'd been told to go and establish an alibi for himself somewhere.

The fire escape at the end of the corridor was a type Eddie had seen in films; the last ten feet or so was a ladder on a counterweight. He stepped on it, swung quickly to the ground then held the ladder for a trembling Brooklyn to follow.

Ground was a badly lit alley that was deserted apart from a couple of brave rats foraging in bags of rubbish. To Eddie's left were more dark alleys, to his right were bright lights. They followed the bright lights to a subway station but walked past it, dodging back and forth across the street and in and out of shops. Eddie had no idea how effective this would be in losing a tail if they had one, but he'd seen it done in films. After half an hour they reached a busy subway station bustling with people. They spent the next hour on a succession of subway trains, jumping on and off just before the doors closed – he'd seen that in films too.

Brooklyn was tired, the shock was wearing off. Eddie hoped they were now safe and got off at the next station. A wino sitting with his back against a newspaper stand was surprisingly well spoken and gave them directions to a respectable hotel two blocks away.

CHAPTER 11

Back home

SELECTION AND RECRUITMENT

C anley's Norwood Estate was built in the early sixties on the site of an old wartime airfield. The sole surviving wartime building was the administration block situated on what had once been the airfield's northern perimeter. Despite its unprepossessing appearance and the huddle of elderly prefabricated buildings surrounding it, the block was a Grade II listed building. The entirety represented Canley City Council's commitment to staff training, the Canley Professional Development Centre (CPDC).

Deborah was sitting in room K1, the oldest and most decrepit of the prefabricated buildings on the site. She knew that the standard of training depended on the quality of the lecturers not the quality of the accommodation in which it was undertaken, but for the last two days the quality of both had been similar. Selection and recruitment policy was never going to stir the soul, but the two lecturers had taken tedium to new heights. It had taken grit and determination to stay motivated, but Deborah had both; she was a manager, a junior one but a manager nonetheless.

Following his promotion from Head of Service to Director, Eddie's old boss Steve Carter had restructured his Directorate. The process had included rewarding Deborah's dogged hard work by assigning additional responsibilities to her post and designating it as managerial not supervisory. As managers would be involved in staff appointments, Deborah was required to attend a three-day selection and recruitment course. Lunchtime on day three brought the good news that the afternoon lecturer was to be Steve Carter. His subject was 'Spotting the fakes' and Steve did not speak in a grinding monotone.

For two and a half days male grinding monotone and female grinding monotone had taken alternate lectures. They'd taught her that all posts must have job descriptions that identified key tasks and responsibilities. There had been endless, dreary examples of what did or did not constitute a key task. The unrelenting tedium continued with how to devise a person specification from a job description. This part was important and could have been made interesting, but the lecturer's intention was to instruct, not entertain. Person specifications had to identify essential and desirable criteria to match applicants to posts. The procedure was very precise, applicants had to 'demonstrate' they satisfied essential criteria to be offered an interview. Male grinding monotone had made it clear that 'demonstrate' meant prove not claim.

Deborah's reward for surviving the morning was a calorie-laden lunch, beef casserole followed by steamed treacle pudding and custard. Back in room K1 she regretted eating so heartily – for the past two days she'd had trouble keeping awake after lunch and Steve Carter was very observant, he would notice if she flagged.

An hour later Deborah was sitting on the edge of her seat, wide awake and enthralled. 'Spotting the fakes' was a robust exposé on doing precisely that, spotting charlatans, liars and self-deceivers. Later in the afternoon Steve would be expanding on the definition of 'demonstrate', but for the moment he was talking about body language. For two days Deborah had looked at her watch every few minutes after lunch, willing the tea break forward, today she was willing it back, not wanting Steve to stop. She recognised many of the signals Steve described and was beginning to grasp how much these signals affected how she related to people.

Question time and a gruff voice asked, "How easy is it to disguise body language?"

Steve smiled. "It's possible to learn a few tricks to fool a casual observer in the short term, but long-term disguise is virtually impossible. Do not underestimate the importance of body language; eventually fakes will give themselves away."

Gruff voice continued his questioning, he was convinced he could disguise his body language and question time became role play time with Steve playing interviewer. Gruff voice performed poorly with everyone recognising his fake signals. Their tea break was long overdue, but no-one wanted to stop, all eager to try their hand at fooling the observers. Eventually, Steve closed the session with a warning.

"In twenty years of careful observation I've only ever met one person who had almost complete control of his body language, and it made him virtually impossible to read or evaluate. He was a very disturbing person to be around and to make it worse he seemed to have no problem evaluating me." Steve shrugged.

"This man succeeded because he had amazing control and an exceptionally brilliant mind; don't try it yourself, you'll fail."

ANDY AND JIMMY

Music had never played a great part in Deborah's life; she listened to the popular music of her youth but even that she could take or leave. Jimmy was different: he loved music and oddly for such a gentle man his particular favourite was rock music. He played guitar at home and the debacle at the St Nicholas church hall last May hadn't stopped him rehearsing occasionally with 'The Roadrunners'. Deborah was surprised by Eddie's sudden decision to take a long break in America, but thrilled when he asked Jimmy to take his place in the band while he was away.

It wasn't going well and Jimmy was unhappy. He said he found it difficult holding his own against Andy's loud and determined bass playing and hadn't acquired the knack of keeping going when he made a mistake. Deborah suspected there was more to it than that, he'd reverted to the worried man he used to be, as if he was carrying a new burden.

Eileen wasn't the problem; Jimmy and his mother weren't completely reconciled, but their relationship was greatly improved. She'd returned to Canley in January to take up a teaching post at Southfields Primary School and bought a flat less than a mile away from them. They visited regularly and Eileen was a willing babysitter. Was it the furniture? Eddie had given Eileen all the furniture he'd put in storage after Jilly's death and she'd turned her sitting room into a facsimile of Jilly's room in Norwood Road.

Bob wasn't the problem either. Since he'd been working for Eddie, Bob's confidence had grown enormously and he was making a great success of running SIKO in Eddie's absence, but Jimmy wasn't the jealous type, that was her province. Nothing had changed at work either, no promotion but Jimmy didn't want promotion, he enjoyed his job as a storeman.

Deborah had gone full circle; it had to be something to do with the band, not his playing, someone was upsetting him. She'd worried enough, it was time for a direct question.

"What's wrong, Jimmy? You're all upset again, who's upsetting you?"

"No one."

Jimmy was shaking his head, but avoiding eye contact at the same time. Deborah had learned a great deal from Steve Carter's lecture, Jimmy's body language indicated someone, not something, was the problem.

Her tone was sharp. "Jimmy! Tell me! You promised no more secrets."

Andy Fox was feeling bitter; he didn't care that his marriage to Janice was over, but he wanted to come out of it with some money. There was virtually no collateral in their house so he'd hung on to Janice hoping Arthur or her Nan would die and leave her something he could have half of. Arthur had left everything to Barbie, which just left the old dragon.

The day after Eddie left for America, Andy cornered Janice and demanded to know what was in her Nan's will.

Her satisfied smile infuriated him. "If you're hoping for a nice payout ,you can forget it. Nan didn't leave the house to me directly."

Why would Janice smile about that, and what did 'directly' mean? He couldn't make her tell him, she wasn't frightened of him anymore, not with the psycho lurking ever closer; so he went to see a solicitor.

"The terms of this document are most unusual but has been drafted by someone very skilled in Wills and Trusts." The solicitor was a humourless man who had obtained a copy of Mrs Newton's will from the Probate Registry. "In simple terms Mrs Newton's real property, the house, has been left in Trust for a single beneficiary. The Trustees have the absolute power to sell or rent the property at any time of their choosing and at whatever price they see fit. If Mrs Newton's intention was that you should not benefit in any way from the sale of the property, then the Trustees have the power to make that happen. Her goods and chattels have been left directly to Mrs Fox, so you could claim half of their value, but I assume it is the house that excites your interest."

Andy knew the answer to his question. "Who's the beneficiary?"

"Mrs Fox."

"And the Trustees?"

The solicitor studied the document. "Edward Stagg and Michael Chilvers." The solicitor raised his head from the will and stared at Andy. "I believe this was drafted by Stephen Napier, a very competent man who specialised in Wills and Trusts. In addition, his father is Sir Charles Napier QC so I would not recommend challenging its terms."

Andy was angry, the bastards had stitched him up, so now he would cause trouble, and Eddie had provided a soft target.

Deborah had worn Jimmy down; it was Andy stirring up trouble.

"But what he says makes sense, we had a drink together after a rehearsal and…"

Deborah interrupted. "We listened to him last May and made fools of ourselves. Andy's like most salesmen, plausible but not to be believed."

Jimmy snapped, "You haven't even bothered to ask what he said!"

She hadn't, it would doubtless be some outrageous allegation about Eddie, but she would hear Jimmy out.

Andy had asked why Eddie and Jilly hadn't started a family straight away, they both loved children. He'd gleefully provided the answer – one of his friends frequented the West Town Café and had seen Eddie there with a small, dark haired girl. She was smart and well dressed, not one of the tarts he openly mixed with, and the friend swore he'd seen Eddie with the same girl for years. Andy was clever, he'd not made his usual lurid allegations about Eddie and Roxy or Janice, he'd concentrated on the unknown girl. He suggested that Jilly had found out about the girl, and they were about to separate when she was killed.

MCDONALD'S

Wednesday, 3.30pm, Dave had finished work early, picked Sophie up from school and was driving to McDonald's. The first and third Wednesdays in the month were McDonald's days for Eddie and Sophie; today was the third Wednesday, Eddie was in America and Uncle Dave had decided to buy the burgers.

Life was on the up for Dave, he'd found the woman of his dreams, probably? Sue was not a bimbo, she was a professional musician who gave private tuition, organised musical events and played violin in small orchestras and string quartets. They'd met when she'd organised an event at Sophie's school, Uncle Dave stepping in again while Eddie was away. Eventually he would have to introduce her to the band, but Dave was apprehensive about doing so – Sue liked his business and golf club friends but could be very dismissive to those she felt were not her equal.

McDonald's was busy but Sophie soon spotted Mark and his Gran and introduced Dave before dashing to the counter to order their burgers. Mark was very polite, shaking his hand and calling him Mr King. Gran called him David and asked if he would look after Mark while she spoke to her friend Mrs Thomas who was there with her daughter and granddaughters. Dave guessed that Mark was perfectly capable of looking after himself but smiled his agreement and they were soon listening to a barrage of 'Well I nevers' and 'Oh I knows' from Gran and Mrs Thomas.

Sophie returned with a tray laden with burgers, fries, fizzy drinks and coffees, gave him his change and sat down. Gran was eating later so Dave wondered why she had ordered so much – perhaps they were hungry? Burgers and fries were not Dave's favourite food but eating them with two very sociable youngsters made up for it. An upsetting moment came when Mark asked Sophie if she'd heard from Eddie recently and her pretence of being unaffected by his absence instantly evaporated and she was close to tears. Thankfully, a diversion was at hand: a dark blue Bentley drawing slowly into the car park.

Sophie disappeared at amazing speed, reappearing moments later in the car park, greeting the man stepping out of the Bentley. He was everyone's idea of a favourite grandfather, round and jolly with silver hair and twinkling blue eyes. Sophie introduced him as Charlie, Mark clearly expected him, pulling up a chair and presenting him with a burger, fries and coffee.

Charlie beamed at him. "Perhaps I could call you Dave rather than Uncle Dave?"

ROXY

Discussing Andy's ludicrous allegations seemed to have crystallised them in Jimmy's mind. Deborah's attempts to reassure him had failed miserably so eventually she braved Mike's fury, told him about Andy's allegations and asked if he knew anything about the alleged girl. To her surprise Mike was amused, not furious, said he knew the girl well and would speak to her.

It had been a hard week and Deborah was relishing the thought of a quiet Saturday afternoon, Jimmy had gone to the football with Bob, and Eileen had taken the children to the park. She flopped down in front of the television to watch a makeover program she'd recorded where the presenters were dressing the larger lady, not something she wanted Jimmy to see her watching. Almost immediately the doorbell's strident tone disturbed her peace, Deborah groaned and walked wearily to the door. She vaguely recognised the smartly dressed girl on her doorstep and smiled hesitantly.

"You're Jilly's friend." A long pause as she struggled to remember her name. "Roxanne?"

No return smile from the girl. "Yes, I was Jilly's friend Roxanne, but if I put on a short skirt and a red wig I'd be Eddie's friend Roxy and you'd slam the door in my face."

Deborah's smile became fixed. "No." She shook her head. "No, I wouldn't, please come in."

Deborah was bewildered – why hadn't she made the obvious association between Roxy and Jilly's friend Roxanne? The answer was equally obvious: Roxy should be a coarse and vulgar red haired tart whereas Roxanne was smart, dark haired, well spoken and very much in control. In fact, Roxanne was so controlled it would be easy to dismiss her as hard and emotionless, but Deborah had seen the master at work for years and Roxy wasn't that good.

"Mike said you wanted to see me, he said you were trying to help Eddie but had a problem?"

Simply by turning up Roxy had solved the problem – Deborah had seen Roxanne and Jilly together many times and envied their closeness.

Deborah thought quickly. "I need to know more about his girls if I'm to understand why he's so incredibly violent."

Roxy examined her carefully for a while before calmly and dispassionately describing a world Deborah could hardly believe existed. A world where vulnerable and runaway girls were seduced, raped and put on the streets. A world where pimps, perverts and sadists without morals or conscience operated without fear of police intervention. A world where Eddie fought psychopaths armed with knives and iron bars to protect girls he hardly knew.

"I was brought up a children's home." Roxy made eye contact. "I suppose some of them are OK but mine wasn't;

it was run by perverts who enjoyed fiddling with little girls. Eventually I ran away and met Jed, but it was out of the frying pan into the fire, I ended up a prostitute at fifteen." She gave a sad smile. "Two years later Jed was giving me a beating because I refused to go with a pervert who liked hurting girls when Eddie kicked open the door and thumped him. I told Eddie what I just told you and he should run as Jed would be back with his minder. He just shrugged and said two people were already dead because he was a selfish idiot, and he wasn't going to risk me being the third." Roxy's voice cracked as she continued. "I didn't understand, all I knew was that he was a nice boy, and I didn't want Jed and Errol to maim or kill him. Anyway, he refused to go and when they came I was paralysed with fear and could only watch as he walked across the yard, knocked them down and kicked them until they stopped moving.

"After the fight he took me to his room, made a cup of tea and we talked. I told him everything and he said he would never let anyone hurt me again." She gave a weary smile. "I'd heard that tale before and was frightened that in a day or two he might be like all the others, want me to meet a 'friend' and it would all start again." Roxy laughed out loud. "Anyway, the next day he did ask if I would like to meet a friend." She laughed again. "But it was Mike, I couldn't believe it, in the space of two days I'd gone from having nothing and no one, to having the two nicest men in the world looking after me."

Roxy was ice cool again. "A few days later a couple of thugs turned up with iron bars looking for the guy who had beaten Jed and Errol. They wanted to smash him up and take over their patch. Eddie was with me, but they assumed he was a punter and asked him if he knew where this Eddie was! In an instant Eddie had knocked them down and was kicking them. He gave me a despairing look and said it was Juliet all over again, the only way to stop the bastards coming was to be worse than them. He dragged them out onto the road and broke their legs with an iron bar he'd taken from them. Others did come, or girls asked him to help them, and each time he got more violent and inflicted some gruesome injuries and they stopped." Roxy grimaced. "That first time the shock on his face at what he'd done eventually faded. After the next fight the shock never went away, he was traumatised but we were safe.

"That's why so many girls have stayed in Canley, Eddie's here so they feel safe. And you can forget any idea of romantic attachments, you don't shag proper heroes, you put them on a pedestal and hope they don't fall off. Well, Eddie hasn't fallen off, he'll never fall off, he's the real thing."

She shrugged. "The girls think he's invincible but I'm more realistic, one day someone will get lucky and Eddie won't walk away from a fight; even he can't beat the odds for ever. That's why I loved Jilly so much, she stopped him fighting, looked after him and made him happy. He needs someone to look after him, and not that Janice!"

Deborah found her voice. "What about the police..."

Roxy snapped angrily. "There are no police in West Town, that bastard John Powers moved them out years ago. He calls it 'diverting resources to more appropriate areas' so the only time we see police in West Town is when he sends vanloads to knock down doors looking for stolen property. And they always find it, even if they have to plant it!"

Deborah's mind turned to Janice. At seventeen she had watched Eddie batter four boys and was spattered with their blood. Just watching from the sidelines had traumatised Deborah so badly she'd needed counselling. Was it surprising that Janice had turned to plausible flatterers for comfort. OK, Andy and his like were not Jed and Errol but...

"Now, about Janice..."

Jimmy was home and not looking much happier for his afternoon with Bob.

"Doesn't your model railway society meet on Tuesday evening?"

Deborah knew it did, but it was the only evening Roxy had free. She wanted to apply for a job as coordinator to the CCCC, a post funded by Canley City Council. She was confused by their selection and recruitment procedure and Deborah had offered to help.

Jimmy nodded morosely.

"You'll have to give it a miss, we've got a visitor."

MRS LOMAX

Mid-afternoon and Hilda Lomax wasn't working, she wasn't even considering working, she was waiting for her tea and cakes to arrive. Frankies had opened a cake shop in the small shopping precinct on Cedar Walk and on fine days they put tables and chairs outside for their customers to use. The table Hilda was sitting at was in partial shade, but from it she could see the top of Eddie's workshop peeping above the supermarket's trolley racks. She sniffed and dabbed her eyes with a tissue, she blamed it on hay fever, but in truth she was close to tears. Her Bob wasn't just working there, he was the manager.

The waitress brought her order and called her madam. That was a novelty, it must be her new clothes and the fact that she no longer smelled of chip fat and toilets. Hilda dabbed her eyes again, her life had been transformed, a white van no longer called for her in the early hours of the morning to clean filthy kitchens and toilets. Instead, she ate breakfast before catching a bus to clean homes and offices that were clean before she arrived. She was now working for Mr Chilvers, Sir Charles Napier, his son Stephen and several of their professional friends, and earning more money that she'd ever earned before. Mr Chilvers insisted that she call him Mike so she did to his face, but it wasn't right that she should call a gentleman like Mr Chilvers by his first name so when she spoke of him she called him Mr Chilvers.

Sir Charles said she should call him Charlie; it was shocking that she should address a Knight of the Realm in such a manner. Oddly, though, it seemed natural to call Stephen by his first name, he was a professional man with lovely manners but very quiet, understated and shy. He was clearly self-conscious about an awful scar on his neck and tried to hide it with high collars and cravats – perhaps one day he would tell her what had caused it.

Hilda stared at her cup, Frankies used good china not the thick earthenware that some places used, but it wasn't as good as her Royal Doulton. A week after Bob started working for Eddie, he'd come home with an antique Royal Doulton tea set in a cardboard box. It was identical to the one her mother had left her, the one Pete took and sold to buy beer. Bob told her he'd found it in a second-hand shop then left the room. A few moments later he'd come back and told the truth. He'd told Eddie about her tea set and Eddie had spent a day ringing round his contacts to find a replacement, then asked Bob to say he'd found it in a second-hand shop.

Eddie wouldn't have friends like Mr Chilvers, Sir Charles and Stephen if he wasn't a good man. The tea set showed that he understood the things that mattered to her and her mother's generation. She and Bob owed him a huge debt so why didn't she like him? Hilda sniffed again, she would always be polite to Eddie and praise him to anyone who would listen. He would have her loyalty for ever, but it would be so much easier if he wasn't so frightening.

SELECT AND RECRUIT

The grinding monotone voice was getting Gerry down; Brian might be extremely knowledgeable about Canley City Council's selection and recruitment procedure, but he was also extremely dull. Gerry was not allowed to select candidates for interview because he hadn't attended a course, so he had to observe whilst Brian selected.

Canley City Council heralded their selection and recruitment procedure as a pathway to fairness and equality. In reality its complexity ensured that those who had attended the training course, or had access to someone who had, were at an advantage. The most common mistake made by candidates was a failure to properly 'demonstrate' their ability to satisfy essential criteria. Brian liked the word 'demonstrate' and pointed Gerry towards article 4(ii)(a) where 'demonstrate' was closely defined. Applicants were sent copies of the procedure with application forms; he could see no excuse for getting it wrong.

Gerry disagreed, the procedure ran to eight closely typed A4 pages and was unspeakably tedious. He prided himself on his determination but had only made it to page five, Article 4(ii)(a) was on page seven.

Brian wrote the ten essential criteria identified in the person specification on the left side of his checklist and the names of the forty-three applicants across the top. A tick in a box meant the applicant had 'demonstrated' their ability to satisfy the appropriate essential criteria and a cross meant they hadn't. Article (4)(ii)(e) allowed a 'P' to be used where demonstration could be 'deduced easily from information on the application form'. Brian was enjoying himself, ticking and crossing and occasionally sucking his pencil before entering a 'P'.

"Article 5(i)(a) is quite specific, you know." Gerry detected a minute change in Brian's monotone. "Applicants with ten ticks must be interviewed and offered the job unless someone does demonstrably better at interview."

Much more of Brian's sniffing and sucking his pencil and Gerry would lose the will to live. Suddenly Brian wiped his pencil on a grubby handkerchief and placed it neatly beside the checklist.

"We're halfway through, time for coffee."

Gerry groaned inwardly; that meant he would have to make small talk and Brian was bound to be a stamp collector or bird watcher. No, God help him, Brian was a steam railway enthusiast and launched into details of his hobby with gusto. Gerry had nothing against train spotters, they were invariably harmless individuals and he'd never heard of anyone being stabbed with a Great Western Railways cap badge or battered to death with a leather bound copy of a1906 London Midland

Scottish timetable. In fact, train spotters were more likely to be victims of violence from people bored beyond endurance by talk of bogeys and minute design differences between the Mk III and Mk IIIa steam pressure relief valves. Gerry gulped his coffee and turned back to the application forms, even 'demonstrate' was more interesting than Brian.

The first twenty-two application forms had yielded three potential interviewees, all eight tick internal candidates. The two essential criteria defeating them were 'understanding how control and exploitation can be exerted by fear of reprisal' and 'knowledge of domestic and street violence', both recommended by Gerry. After another interminable hour of Brian ticking, crossing and sucking his pencil, the pile was almost gone and they had three eight tick interviewees plus one with eight ticks and a P. All were internal candidates, the system had defeated the outsiders. When Gerry had glanced through the application forms earlier, he'd recognised a name and put her form at the bottom of the pile, hoping that Brian would become more lenient as he progressed.

Brian was on the last form, he'd ticked seven boxes and was now judging whether or not the applicant had satisfied the eighth essential criteria. He nodded sagely and placed an eighth tick on the checklist. Essential criteria nine received a surprised nod and another tick. Gerry considered essential criteria number ten to be unfair, character references had to be from three 'recognised professionals'. The head of Human Resources justified this decision by explaining that the CCCC coordinator would have access to child abuse files. A list giving examples of who would and would not be regarded as 'recognised professionals' was included with application details.

Gerry had placed Roxanne Bailey's application form at the bottom of the pile; she was already a nine tick applicant, could she make it ten?

Brian gasped and handed the form to Gerry. The first 'recognised professional' was no surprise, Michael Chilvers – Chartered Accountant. The second and third were a shock: Stephen Napier – Solicitor and Sir Charles Napier QC – Barrister at Law.

CHAPTER 12

New York to San Francisco

EDDIE'S GIRLS

Eddie liked analogue watches with black hands on a clear white face because they were easy to read. Not only did his cataracts fill his eyes with an explosion of light in the glare of the sun, they blurred his central vision and compromised his contrast perception even in good light. The watch he was studying had black hands on a large white face and engraved on the back were the words 'To Eddie with love Janice'. When she bought it, Janice didn't know Eddie had cataracts, she simply knew that his eyesight wasn't very good.

Eddie had been studying the engraving on the back of the watch a few minutes before meeting Jilly in the fire escape corridor at the dance in Broad Street School hall. The next day she'd invited him to Sunday tea, kissed him, told him she'd make him better and arranged to meet him for lunch the next day in the garden by St John's church. As they ate their sandwiches, he told her about the watch and said he wouldn't wear it any more. Before leaving for America, he'd taken the watch from its box and worn it when he'd said goodbye to Janice, hoping she'd notice.

The Greyhound bus hit a bump in the road and Brooklyn stirred in the seat beside him. They hadn't taken a room in the tourist hotel in New York; instead, they'd caught a westbound Greyhound about to leave from a stop opposite the hotel. Their second night on the road was almost over, a succession of Greyhounds speeding them towards San Francisco. Brooklyn had dozed fitfully most of the way, doubtless traumatised by the horror of the fight. Eddie hadn't slept and was horribly tired; he wasn't traumatised of course, you couldn't traumatise a monster, but he couldn't risk, sleep, nightmares and the night terrors.

His hopes and plans were in ruins, he wasn't much of a catch before leaving for America, but now he was a killer on the run from drug dealers and the police. When they next stopped, he'd ring Chin from a public telephone to check that he and Ellen were safe.

Eddie had to concentrate on something to keep awake. So often music had been his saviour and so it was now, the lyrics of Al Stewart's song 'Swiss Cottage Manoeuvres' reminding him of his girls.

On a Christmas cake day one Friday in August
in a bookshop in Charing Cross Road
I first set eyes on a girl
and at once I did know
She had eyes like a poet and hair like a rainbow
reflecting the lights that did glow
And the sadness she kept in her eyes
struck my senses a blow.

All Al Stewart songs reminded him of Juliet, of sitting with her in the bus shelter on Mayors Road. Lines three and four reminded him of Jilly, he knew she was special the first time he saw her. The first part of line five *'She had eyes like a poet'* was Janice, her eyes had seen too much of other people's happiness and too little of her own. The second part of line five was Brooklyn and lines seven and eight were Roxy, the sadness in her eyes reflected a childhood stolen by beasts like Jed.

Sophie wasn't in the song, but she was seldom far from Eddie's thoughts. Not long before Jilly died they'd spoken to Sharon about Sophie coming to live with them permanently; that hope had died with Jilly. He wished he was home with her now, he wished he'd never left.

HIGH NOON

Chin was trying to mingle unobtrusively with the early morning joggers. He looked the part in a tracksuit, but jogging wasn't his thing – he was a fighter not a runner. Ten minutes ago, he'd received a bizarre telephone call from Eddie giving a false name and pretending to be a prospective customer.

"I'm using the public telephone at the subway station, is it far from your Gym?"

Chin had gone along with the charade, eventually realising that Eddie wanted him to go the subway station telephone. He slowed to a walk before stopping by the telephone and looking round. No sign of Eddie – perhaps he was hiding somewhere, making sure the coast was clear before showing himself. Chin felt conspicuous and bent down to tie the laces on his trainers. Now the telephone was ringing, it was the one that Eddie had used for his call from Brooklyn, and he'd remembered the number. It rang for some time before Chin realised what was happening and lifted the receiver.

"Chin, is that you?" Eddie sounded worried. "Are you OK?"

It was like something from a spy movie – Eddie wanted him to catch a train to another public telephone.

"Hell Eddie everything's cool, she's got away with it, they're all so busy fighting each other she's forgotten."

Chin couldn't understand why Eddie had gone quiet. Then he was talking again, choosing his words carefully.

"Two representatives called on us, our discussion was robust, have you heard about it?"

Chin was confused. "Eddie, speak plain English, there's no need for this cloak and dagger stuff."

Another pause, then the controlled voice again. "The two representatives must have followed Brooklyn. One was grossly fat, the other was a regular guy and we disagreed violently."

It was Chin's turn to go quiet, he heard Eddie asking if he was still there. "Yes, Eddie, I'm still here, I just can't believe it. Describe the men again and don't worry, nobody's listening."

"They were professionals, the regular guy was called Weasel."

Chin swallowed hard before replying. "Word in the street is that Fat Eddie and Weasel were jumped by a rival gang two nights ago. Fat Eddie's dead and Weasel's got real bad balls ache. Cal's out for revenge, there are bodies everywhere." He gulped again. "Was that really you, those guys were a legend?"

"Yes."

"Shit! I knew you were good, but I didn't know you were that good."

"Nor did I."

Good news: if Weasel stuck to his face saving lie, Eddie might literally have got away with murder, but his priority now was to find a place for Brooklyn to sleep. He half carried her to a motel opposite the Greyhound stop but luck wasn't with him, they only had one room available. Sharing a room wasn't a problem as such, the problem was that the terrors were lurking and he couldn't be sure that his alarm would keep him awake.

Brooklyn curled up on the bed fully clothed and fell asleep immediately. She hadn't looked him in the eye since they'd left New York; hardly surprising, it must be difficult to make eye contact with a monster prepared to kill a defenceless man.

Eddie drew the curtains, positioned an armchair directly under a lamp in the corner, set his headphone alarm to repeat every ten minutes and sat back.

Eddie was trying to scream but couldn't. His mind was detached from his body, he could see his mouth open and close, and no sound emerge. He'd run up and down dark corridors and into bright lights time and time again with Jilly becoming more and more distressed before screaming and transforming into the broken girl on the yellow spinal board. Why couldn't he scream, it would be better if he could scream!

He was awake, he was sure he was awake, but he couldn't be; it was dark and he always left a light on. And someone was screaming, but Eddie couldn't see who it was. He thrashed about in blind panic then there was a flood of light and someone was shouting at him.

"Eddie! Eddie!"

Brooklyn was shaking his shoulder, she'd woken up, disconnected his alarm and switched off the light. The screaming stopped abruptly, it was him, Eddie felt his mouth snap closed.

232

"Eddie I'm sorry, what have I done?"

She dragged him out of the armchair and cuddled him like a child, trying to comfort him. The bright light was helping, Eddie managed to push the images far enough back in his mind to function.

"I've got to go, Brooklyn. I've got to be by myself."

He struggled to get away, but Brooklyn was strong. "Eddie! Please tell me what you're seeing!"

He couldn't tell her, he couldn't tell anyone.

The railway line hadn't been used for years, there were weeds and small bushes sprouting between the rotting wooden sleepers. Eddie followed the line out of town, jogging between the lines, matching the length of his pace to the spacing of the sleepers. Now he was in the middle of nowhere, the weeds and bushes were denser than ever and he was alone. He didn't feel the scorching heat of the midday sun, his only thought was to devise something that needed enormous concentration and activity. He wanted to be back in the workshop doing his two-handed sanding.

It was contrived, but much of his life was contrived and it was beginning to work. He had to jog along the track from sleeper to sleeper crossing back and forth over the metal rail every third pace. Every tenth sequence he had to stop and jog backwards seven paces, still crossing the rail every third pace. Eddie had no idea of the time but guessed it to be early evening, the heat had gone from the sun. He'd not seen or heard anyone by the desolate track all day but suddenly he saw movement: Fat Eddie and Weasel talking and smoking in the scrub away to his right. A bad sign: the hallucinations had started with recent events; they worked quicker and better when they were old or fictional.

More jogging and counting and it seemed like an eternity before Eddie saw more movement. This time it was immediately beside the track, three men standing in the shade of a building, arguing and pointing down the track. They were dressed in western clothes and wearing guns; this was better, this was fictional. One turned his head and Eddie recognised the battered, swarthy face of Jack Elam, the archetypal baddie in countless westerns. Eddie recognised the movie as well, the men were the gunfighters waiting for the noon train bringing their leader in 'High Noon'. Eddie shook his head, Jack Elam wasn't in 'High Noon' – was it a good thing or a bad thing his hallucination was wrong?

The scene disappeared, whisked away in a swirl of dust, and Eddie reminded himself of the story. Gary Cooper played a town marshal whose wedding to a girl played by Grace Kelly was interrupted by the gunfighters coming to kill him. Years before, he'd fought the men to save the town and sent their leader to prison. Now, without deputies and needing help, the townspeople didn't want to know, he was on his own. In a moving scene at the end of the movie the girl played by Grace Kelly picked up a gun and shot one of the gunfighters.

Another eternity then movement in the scrub to the left of the track, a girl in a long, old-fashioned dress was standing with her back to him, holding a gun. The gun had been fired recently, Eddie could see a wisp of smoke drifting from the barrel. He gave a start, reality and fiction were mixing together; it was Chin's gun, the wisp of smoke identical to the one Eddie had seen after he'd fired it. And the girl wasn't Grace Kelly, she was too tall! As she turned to face him Eddie's heart almost stopped; it was Janice wearing Grace

Kelly's lace-collared dress, gripping the gun and smiling at him. Eddie smiled and waved, hoping she'd smile back, but she'd gone.

He'd probably done enough, but even if he hadn't he had to lie down before he fell down. Eddie knew he mustn't make himself comfortable – if he did he would sleep for hours and he needed to get back to Brooklyn; she was frightened and alone. A barren, stony patch in open ground looked suitable, he lay on his side with his head unsupported; discomfort or cold would soon wake him.

What was happening, the hallucinations should be over? Eddie was drifting into sleep but could see more movement and feel himself being pulled and lifted. Now he was warm and his head was comfortable, Eddie didn't know what was happening but was too tired to care.

Eddie was awake, he could see stars in the clear night sky and a dull glow of light from the nearby town filtering through bushes on the ridge above the railway line. He couldn't understand why he was warm and struggled to get up. His right arm was numb where he'd been lying on it and someone was talking to him.

Brooklyn had followed him from the motel and watched him jog back and forth along the railway line all day. When he fell asleep she put his head on her lap and covered him with her coat. Eddie had got it wrong as always, Brooklyn didn't think he was a monster, she couldn't look at him because she was ashamed that she'd risked their lives for the sake of a leather jacket.

TACOMA FLATS

Another day took them deep into cowboy country, vast open flatlands covered with thin scrub and cactus plants with grey smudges on the horizon that hinted of distant mountains. The only change in a hundred years was the thin ribbon of tarmac stretching as far as the eye could see. Afternoon brought substance to the grey smudges and the foreground had turned red. Huge towering red mesas, red flatlands, red dust blowing everywhere and Sedona, beautiful in its quiet desolation. Even the tourist shops brimming with dream-catchers, blocks of iron pyrites and other tourist trinkets seemed interesting rather than tacky. They found a diner with red and white chequered tablecloths and matching cushions on bentwood chairs and ordered coffee and apple pie.

Brooklyn insisted she wasn't traumatised, but that Eddie was. No chance, he didn't do traumatised, or if he did it was so long ago it didn't matter anymore.

"Eddie, you've got to talk to me." She leaned forward and gripped his arm. "If it wasn't for you, I'd be dead so talk to me, let me help."

"The nightmare wasn't about the fight…" Eddie stopped, even an anonymous diner thousands of miles from home wasn't the place to talk openly about murder.

Brooklyn gripped his arm again. "I have four weeks before I meet Lawrence in San Francisco. You can tell me anything, you've nothing to lose, once we part we'll never see each other again. I trained as a trauma counsellor, I only changed to dugs counselling because of Lawrence."

The next day found them in the American equivalent of an English greasy spoon transport café. Their plan was to rent a cabin somewhere, but first they needed food – apart from the Sedona apple pie they'd eaten little since leaving New York. Plates piled with eggs, bacon, hash browns and beans temporarily removed the need for conversation and as their plates cleared they talked about books and music; serious stuff was for later. Eddie tried to be positive, Janice was older and wiser, this time she might, just might, understand.

"Hey! You guys are English, well you are anyway." The man pointing a mug of coffee at Eddie was small, weather beaten and bow legged. "Can I join you, this place is kind of full."

Lamarr Potts looked like a battered ex jockey and appearances were not deceptive. He'd enjoyed moderate success before one fall too many left him unable to ride competitively; now he drove trucks for a living and bred horses as a hobby. Lamarr was amiable, funny and openly fascinated by Eddie's controlled English accent.

"My Mabel reads English books, proper books, literature and all. Have you heard of Jane Austen?"

Eddie struggled with Lamarr's accent, Mrs Potts was Maybelle not Mabel and Jane Oarstin was Jane Austen. Apparently Maybelle was a serious Anglophile and Lamarr was immensely proud of the fact that she organised an Annual Literary Festival in their home town of Tacoma Flats.

This year the festival was to feature early nineteenth century female English authors and Maybelle had a problem: the ex-patriot she'd booked as a reader had been taken ill. The festival started tomorrow and she'd not found a replacement.

Brooklyn made the offer before Eddie could demur, starting tomorrow he was Maybelle's reader. In fact, she could do much worse, Eddie had read Jane Austen, Fanny Burney, Ann Radcliffe and the Bronte sisters voraciously in his youth. Their reward was three weeks rent-free in a holiday cabin on Lamarr's ranch.

An American truck driver's concept of a short drive was different to Eddie's – it took four hours to reach Lamarr's ranch house. The promised cabin wasn't even in sight, but the arrangement included the loan of an elderly Ford pickup.

Lamarr had telephoned ahead and a nervous Maybelle greeted them on the front porch and ushered them inside to a laden table. Eddie was horribly tired but tried hard to be friendly by smiling and talking of England in his best slow controlled voice. As the meal progressed, he saw Maybelle giving him sidelong glances; perhaps it was time to sing for his supper.

"Would you like me to read for you?" Eddie had decided on a passage he knew so well he wouldn't stumble over the words in his tiredness. "How about Mr Darcy's letter to Lizzie Bennet?"

"I have a copy..."

Eddie shook his head gently. "No need."

He closed his eyes and page 227 of the battered paperback he'd read so avidly in the bus shelter appeared in his mind and he began to read. 'Be not alarmed, Madam, on receiving this letter, by the apprehension of its containing any repetition of those sentiments, or renewal of those offers, which were last night so disgusting to you.'

The only person Eddie had ever read to regularly was Jilly; he thought of her as he followed the text and was filled with intense sadness. He gulped and continued. 'I write without any intention of paining you, or humbling myself, by dwelling on wishes, which, for the happiness of both cannot be too soon forgotten…'

Those words made him think of Janice and the combination of guilt and sadness tore the page from his mind. Eddie heard Maybelle sniff and opened his eyes to face the music.

"You and this young lady are not a couple, your Lizzie's back home in England, isn't she?"

Eddie knew he was staring, but was too tired to stammer any sort of response.

The quiet desolation of Sedona was beautiful, but the complete isolation on the cabin's veranda was even better – here you could scream and no-one would hear.

"You told me you were an antique dealer and part-time musician!" Brooklyn hesitated. "Antique dealers and musicians don't usually fight and beat knife wielding thugs, do they?"

"I don't lie, Brooklyn, I miss things out, but I don't lie."

Eddie reached into the side pocket of his bag and handed her a business card. It had 'SIKO (Canley) Ltd. Antiques, Collectables, Band Equipment and PA Hire' in bold type with 'E G A Stagg - Director' below it in smaller type. He thrust the card back in his bag and continued.

"I have staff running the businesses while I'm away and my band's called 'The Roadrunners', I've probably got a card for them somewhere." He grimaced. "I know how bad it looks, I would have killed Weasel if you hadn't stopped me, but I'm not a psychopath."

Brooklyn hung her head. "I never thought you were, and I didn't shout out to stop you, I shouted because I thought the fat man was still alive."

"Oh."

"What I can't get my head round is that when Weasel pulled a knife you seemed relieved!"

"I was – if he'd a pulled a gun we'd be dead. Knives are OK, I'm pretty good with knives."

"How many knife fights have you had?" Brooklyn sounded incredulous.

"None as such, I don't carry a knife."

"OK, OK, how many fights have you had where your opponents had knives?"

"Too many."

"Why, for God's sake?"

Eddie took a deep breath. "When I was seventeen I met a girl called Roxy and the people who raped her, beat her and turned her and girls like her into prostitutes carried knives."

"And you fought them to protect these girls?"

"Yes."

Brooklyn nodded sagely. "And that's when the nightmares started!"

Eddie shook his head. "No, the fighting and seeing girls with their teeth knocked out or their faces cut open by the bastards didn't help, but they started a long time before that."

"We'd better start right at the beginning then."

Eddie liked anonymity, a life in the shadows, but had no chance of it in Canley. There he was an unsmiling man with a bad reputation who battered, maimed and disfigured and, apart from a short spell in prison, had got away with it. Within a very short time in Tacoma Flats, he wasn't an anonymous reader at Maybelle Potts' Literary Festival he was her boy Eddie. Maybelle liked him, and Eddie could no more understand it than why Janice's Nan liked him so much, insisting that he call her Nan not Mrs Newton. Nor could he understand why Alice Popplewell liked him, repeatedly calling him 'that nice boy Eddie' in the witness box at his trial.

Being onstage at the literary festival wasn't daunting; the audience weren't interested in him, they were interested in what he was reading. Moreover, with the lights in his eyes he couldn't see them, he could be reading to an empty hall. The question-and-answer sessions were equally painless with disembodied voices politely asking questions and absorbing his answers. The guest speakers didn't query his credentials either, Maybelle said he was an expert and that was that, preconception ruled.

In their endless hours talking on the quiet veranda, Brooklyn reflected at length on his preconceptions of others and their preconceptions of him. She also reflected on guilt; Brooklyn was big on guilt, and guilt was a more difficult subject than preconception. Life in the limelight was infinitely easier than talking to Brooklyn about preconceptions and guilt.

SAN FRANCISCO

San Francisco was cosmopolitan, liberated, bustling with tourists and, like most such places, anonymous. Canley was too small and parochial for anonymity – once acquired a bad reputation would last for ever. But Eddie didn't want to live in a big city, he liked and needed the reassurance of familiar surroundings more than he needed anonymity.

Three weeks of intensive counselling hadn't cured Eddie; the damage wrought by years of abuse, fighting, guilt and horror couldn't be reversed that easily. Brooklyn's greatest achievement was persuading him that guilt and culpability were not conjoined, that unbearable guilt didn't necessarily mean he'd done something terribly wrong.

Despite the horrors of his adult years, Brooklyn was convinced that Eddie's problems, including the terrors, were rooted in his childhood. Apart from the routine beatings, his parents' punishment of choice was to lock him in a windowless boxroom. It was quite big, but with the door closed it was so, so dark he could hardly see his hand in front of his face. Every now and again one or other of his parents would wrench the door open, admit a flood of light and demand he apologise for what he'd done. Mostly he had no idea what he'd done so couldn't apologise and often spent whole days and/or nights in boxroom. Being locked in the dark police cell after Jilly's death with the hourly floods of light and demands for him to change his statement re-awoke and reinforced the childhood memories.

They spent a day together in San Francisco taking in the sights: the piers, the seals basking in the sun on the pontoons, the cable cars, and the grey smudge of Alcatraz beyond the Golden Gate Bridge. In the evening they checked into separate hotels on Sutter Street and rode down to the bay on a cable car for a last meal together.

The next day Eddie spent the morning touring music shops looking for a few more items to send back to Canley. At lunchtime he sat down in a burger bar and reached into his pocket for a dime for the juke box. He read the list on the counter display, selected 'At the Hop' by Danny and the Juniors, and pressed the button. The unmistakable beat started and the waiter smiled and slid a plate of chips, a bowl of tomato ketchup and a huge burger towards him. Johnny Rockets' burgers dwarfed the burgers Eddie bought in McDonald's in Canley; they tasted different too, not better, not worse, just different.

By now Brooklyn should have met Lawrence at Pier 39. If he wasn't there or wasn't clean, she would meet Eddie at Johnny Rockets at one o'clock. Either way it would be goodbye, they would travel to the airport together, take different flights and never see each other again. It was for the best, their time together had been too painful, too personal, too everything!

Two o'clock and no Brooklyn, Eddie was pleased for her and hoped that Lawrence would have the sense to stay clean this time. Why did nice girls fall for addicts, drunkards, men who knocked them about or cheated on them? But then Eddie wanted a nice girl to fall for a monster who'd battered and maimed, had been to prison and was now a killer! Eddie felt the confidence Brooklyn had instilled in him draining away, he was tired and homesick and still in love with two girls at the same time.

CHAPTER 13

A letter from America

THE PRIZE

Speech Day at Robert Stephenson School and Sophie had an achievement to celebrate, a Hay Prize for Literature junior commendation certificate. The annual senior Hay Prize for literature was very prestigious, entries being ten-thousand-word essays on a chosen literary subject and Professor Hay was notoriously hard on plagiarism or work that owed more to the tutor than the pupil.

Three years ago, in an attempt to stimulate interest in younger pupils, Professor Hay had introduced an under-fourteen category. Entries were three-thousand-word essays with the five best entries in each of six regions being awarded a commendation certificate. This year not only had Sophie won a commendation certificate, but Professor Hay had volunteered to attend their Speech Day in person to present Sophie's certificate and all the other prizes.

A major disappointment for Sophie was that Eddie wouldn't be there to witness her success. The fact that her mother insisted she was too busy to attend was so normal that Sophie hardly noticed. All pupils were given two tickets for Speech Day, but prize winners could request a third. Usually, Eddie came to Speech Days and Sports Days with Roxy or Janice; today Uncle Dave was coming with Roxy and Janice!

At one time Dave and Sharon were close, but lately their relationship had been soured by bitter arguments. The new mature Dave saw his sister's weaknesses all too clearly because he'd displayed most of them himself before he'd grown up. A particular bone of contention was her continued disappointment in Sophie, refusing to attend school functions unless she won a prize, and a commendation certificate didn't count.

Dave was thirty-seven, a successful businessman and experienced in life, but today he felt nervous. It wasn't the prospect of being in a strange environment, it was the prospect of stepping into Eddie's shoes and meeting Roxy. He'd known about her for years, everyone had, but they'd never met. How should he address or react to an ex-prostitute just appointed as coordinator for the Canley Confederation of Children's Charities?

Janice was easy to find, girls that tall stood out, and she'd already found Roxy and Sophie. Stupidly, Dave expected to meet a blowsy red-haired tart; instead, Roxy was small, dark-haired, smartly dressed, well-spoken and very much in control. Her precise way of speaking reminded him of Eddie, his influence was everywhere. With her new longer hairstyle, Janice looked more attractive than ever; it was hard not to keep looking at her.

They were quickly joined by Mark and his Gran, and they sat together in a group near the front of the hall. Soon everyone fell silent as Professor Hay, a heavily built man with a deep, booming voice, rose to his feet. His first task was to award the school prizes and Dave saw parents glow with pride as their children walked forward to receive a firm handshake, an encouraging word and their prize. Finally, Professor Hay held aloft the senior Hay Prize, a large silver cup on a stand engraved with the names of previous winners, and spoke enthusiastically about the joy of reading before calling Sophie forward. It was Dave's turn to glow with pride as she walked forward to receive her commendation certificate, then, suddenly, it was over.

Dave was admiring Sophie's certificate when he heard a booming voice at his elbow. "Well done I say and very well deserved, an excellent essay."

Professor Hay shook his hand and looked enquiringly at their small group. Dave hesitated, he was Sophie's only actual relation and only knew Gran as Gran.

Sophie didn't hesitate. "This is my Uncle Dave, this is Roxy and this is Janice." She smiled. "And this is my best friend Mark and his Gran."

Professor Hay was unconcerned, he'd attended countless presentations and encountered countless complicated family groups. He was charming and approachable, but Dave sensed he was leading up to a question. A smile at Sophie, a deep breath and the question.

"Do you have private coaching in English?"

Sophie looked puzzled and shook her head, but Professor Hay persisted. "I'm not suggesting for one moment that your essay isn't original work, but a gifted tutor can introduce unusual concepts for a pupil to explore." He hesitated. "I, I only say this because the concept underlying your work reminds me of an essay that won the National Hay Prize some twelve or thirteen years ago."

Sophie shrugged. "Eddie helps me with my homework?"

"Eddie!" Professor Hay stood back and smiled broadly. "Would that be Eddie Stagg?"

Sophie had gone for a burger with Janice, Roxy, Mark and Gran. Dave was annoyed with himself. If he'd cancelled his business meeting instead of just delaying it to attend Speech Day, he could have joined them. It didn't help knowing that he wasn't as mature as he thought, in some ways less so than young Mark. Dave asked him why his parents weren't at Speech Day and an insensitive question brought a considered response.

"My parents and my other Gran have full-time jobs, I didn't win anything and their time is precious. I'm just pleased that you and Roxy and Janice could come to support Sophie, it would have been even better if Eddie was here."

Dave was irritated that Eddie's name had cropped up again and asked, "Do you know who he really is?"

Again Mark's response was considered. "Yes, we know who he is, and we know he's been to prison. We know who Roxy is as well and we like them both very much."

JANICE

Janice was still tingling with excitement after an amazing day. First Roxy had telephoned to say that Sophie had three tickets for Speech Day and would she go with herself and Dave. More surprisingly she'd gone on to say that they needed to talk and try and bridge the gulf that had always existed between them. The astonishing truth was that Mike had persuaded Roxy to talk to Deborah, and Deborah had persuaded Roxy to talk to her.

They sat together in the school hall, shared Sophie's pride in her certificate and saw her obvious pleasure in seeing them together. Then a bombshell: Eddie was a previous winner of the National Hay Prize and Professor Hay said his essay was a work of genius. That Eddie was a genius came as no surprise to Janice, he'd guided her through her 'A' Levels, administration, accountancy and law qualifications with nonchalant ease. Successive tutors had admired the quality of her coursework and successive examiners had questioned the disparity between her coursework and examination grades. Each time they'd accepted her explanation of examination nerves as the coursework quality didn't change when she changed tutors. The simple truth was that the professional tutors were not giving her unfair help; Eddie was.

Eddie didn't know he'd won the Hay Prize, Professor Hay had read his essay, refused to believe that material of such insight and maturity could be the original work of a sixteen-year-old and delayed the award. After extensive research and consultation, he realised that the material was original, Eddie was exceptionally gifted and approached Broad Street School to be told that Eddie had left the area leaving no forwarding address.

Janice was living in her Nan's house; her only contact with Andy was through the band. For the first time in years she felt optimistic, not because her finances were back under control or because the house evoked so many happy memories, but because she was away from Andy. Living separate lives in the same house had weakened his control; living apart had broken it.

With hindsight she realised that Andy had started undermining her self-confidence on day one. Eventually he made her believe she was worthless and unattractive, lucky to have him and that no-one else would want her. Her renaissance had begun the evening she'd seen Eddie in his workshop and fought back when Andy attacked her.

She slept in the small, narrow back bedroom; the larger front bedroom would always be Nan's. The sitting room was familiar and comforting, she and Nan always sat there in the evenings, it was full of happy memories. The front room was for special occasions or homework, Eddie had installed her computer there and programmed it to copy e-mails back and forth between home and work. The room was full of memories of Eddie.

At the time Janice couldn't understand why Nan seemed so contented in the last few weeks of her life, and why she wasn't upset when Eddie announced he was going to America for two months. Then she remembered her only major quarrel with Nan, the one about Eddie's locket. Immediately afterwards Nan suggested she take a long holiday and even offered to pay for it.

"You two need to be apart for a while, it will make you realise how much you mean to each other."

Janice never had the chance – two days later Eddie met Jilly at the dance in Broad Street School hall.

It was a month to the day before Eddie telephoned, a month in which she'd almost gone mad with worry and made a decision.

She would always be a tall, thin girl with a big nose, but she was no longer cheap, easy and stupid. She couldn't change her wicked thoughts when she heard about Jilly's death but would always regret them. Eddie needed someone to love him and look after him, Janice knew she wasn't special like Jilly, but no-one could love him more than her. When he came home, she would try to make him love her back.

There was a chance, the last time she saw Eddie he was wearing her watch, the one she'd bought him for his twenty-first birthday. And as they'd said goodbye, he'd asked if she'd thought about growing her hair, saying it suited her better longer. Were these signs, or was she deluding herself?

THE LETTER

Brooklyn didn't want to forget Eddie but did want to forget the horrors that inhabited his mind and the memories of the fight in the New York hotel room. She owed Eddie her life and had tried to repay the debt by exposing his demons and making him talk about guilt, blame and preconceptions. He seemed to respond but she knew that if he went home and stopped talking, he would regress very quickly. Brooklyn had done what she could, it was time to pass the buck.

During their last night in Tacoma Flats, Brooklyn searched Eddie's wallet as he slept and found two pictures. The impossibly pretty girl had to be Jilly, so the girl with the smile had to be the girl from school. After jogging up and down the disused railway line for hours Eddie had stopped, smiled and waved at an empty desert and mouthed a name that sounded like Janice. In the wallet she also found a creased business card for 'The Roadrunners' with a contact mane of Janice Fox and a business e-mail address. Then confirmation, as she'd replaced Eddie's wallet, his watch tipped over to reveal an engraving on the back.

Janice saw a flag flashing on her computer, an e-mail had arrived. The sender was in a cyber café in the USA and the message was brief and cryptic.

'I got your e-mail address from a Roadrunners business card. I think you are Eddie's friend but need to be sure. Please answer the following questions.

1. Complete the following 'An unsmiling...
2. What's on the back of his watch?

Janice felt rising panic, the person sending the message obviously knew Eddie, but who was he or she? The only way to find out was to reply.

1. An unsmiling man with a bad reputation.
2. An engraving 'To Eddie with love Janice'.

The reply was immediate. 'Thank you, please send a secure postal address for a letter.'

It had arrived, a letter from America was on the floor when Janice returned from work. She tore the envelope open and pulled out the contents. It had been written in a hurry, the pages were stained with coffee and the handwriting was untidy, and female!

'I don't have much time so I'll be brief. Your friend Eddie is ill, not physically but mentally. Post Traumatic Stress Disorder (PTSD) doesn't just affect soldiers, it can affect anyone subjected to trauma(s). As Eddie is sensitive and his traumas extensive and severe, he is very ill. I trained as a trauma counsellor and I've tried to help but he's NOT cured, he MUST have someone to talk to and confide in when he comes home or he WILL be very ill again.'

Janice read on, her heart pounding, who was this girl, how had she met Eddie and were they...? Ten minutes later she felt physically sick, the girl had summarised Eddie's life in three close written pages. A sensitive child systematically beaten and locked in a dark boxroom for no discernible reason other than daring to look at his parents. 'That's why he developed his disconcerting habit of having his eyes half closed all the time!' Drunken rages, rejection, endless nightmares and unbearable emptiness. Then a boy fighting back and creating a monster to protect her and so many others, only to be rejected again by everyone except the unwaveringly loyal Mike. Later a deeply unhappy youth, meeting child prostitute Roxy and taking the monster to the edge of madness fighting brutal, lonely battles in alleys and back streets before going to his room to fight the loneliest battle of all with his guilt and self-hatred.

'The final unendurable trauma was watching his wife die screaming in agony only to be betrayed and rejected rather than supported ...'

The bastard, Janice stuffed the letter in her pocket and ran for the door.

Deborah collapsed gratefully into an armchair; Jimmy had insisted she sit down and watch television while he washed up.

The children were asleep, all she could hear was the television and the clank of dishes.

Damn! The front doorbell was ringing insistently, Deborah groaned, put on her slippers and trudged wearily towards the door.

"Where's that bastard Jimmy?"

Janice thrust her aside and strode towards the sound of clanking dishes. Deborah ran across the room and placed herself squarely between Janice and the kitchen door.

"What's wrong, Janice, what's happened?"

Janice hissed at her. "Get him in here and I'll tell you."

Jimmy appeared in the doorway, startled by the commotion.

Janice glared at him over Deborah's head. "How could you and your bastard father leave Eddie in a cell and make them move Jilly?" She knew she was shouting but didn't care. "Why do you hate him so much?"

Deborah's reply was the final straw. "Shush, you'll wake the children."

When Eddie taught Janice self-defence he told her she moved quickly. Not as quickly as him – no one moved like Eddie, he was like a shadow. In comparison, Deborah was hopelessly slow and it was her own fault for placing herself in front of Jimmy. Janice hit her squarely in the face with a proper punch like Eddie had taught her. He said no-one liked being hit in the face and you didn't have to hit very hard to knock someone over. He was right, Deborah toppled backwards, tripped over a chair and was down.

Jimmy stood gaping with astonishment and Janice hit him before he could raise his hands to protect himself. As he staggered back, she hit him again and he was down. Punches weren't enough, Janice aimed a scything kick at his groin, this would hurt!

It didn't; Deborah was down but not out, she grabbed Janice from behind, pulling her backwards so the kick missed. Jimmy scrambled to his feet, lurched forward clumsily then fell on top of Janice, driving all the breath from her body. She tried to wriggle free, beside herself with anger and frustration but also ashamed of her lack of control.

Life wasn't fair, after years without hope, Janice had almost come to believe that one day she and Eddie might get together. Now her hopes were in ruins, he was in America with another woman and she was fighting like an alley cat in Deborah's sitting room. She curled up in a ball on the floor sobbing, it wasn't the pain from Jimmy falling on her, the pain was inside and it wouldn't go away. She could hear Deborah's angry voice, but she was shouting at Jimmy not her.

"For Christ sake, Jimmy, stop moaning, think yourself lucky it wasn't Eddie who hit you. Go to the kitchen and clean yourself up."

She heard Jimmy's plaintive voice. "But my nose is bleeding."

Deborah's retort was unsympathetic. "Shove a tissue up it. Now go away and leave us alone."

This shouldn't be happening – Deborah wasn't angry, she was being kind and reassuring. "I've sent Jimmy away, I'm not surprised you're angry, but who told you?"

Janice opened her mouth, but words wouldn't come.

Deborah grimaced then forced a smile. "I can guess who taught you to fight, I've never seen a girl punch before."

Janice gulped, talking between sobs. "Eddie taught me... but now I've lost him again..."

Deborah tried again. "Who told you about Jimmy?"

On impulse Janice pulled the letter out of her pocket and thrust it at Deborah.

"See what we've done, not just you and Jimmy, all of us."

Deborah sat down and read the letter slowly. All her research, even the long talks with Roxy hadn't prepared her for what was in the letter.

"Why didn't he talk to me, Deborah? Now he's talked to this woman, her, and I've lost him."

Deborah couldn't stop her voice shaking. "Did you read the last page?"

Janice stared at her. "I read about Jimmy then..."

"Let me read it to you: 'Eddie talks about his close friends as if they were family, but he talks about you differently, you're not family you're closer, more personal which can only mean one thing. I think the problem is that he can't cope with the guilt of loving two girls at the same time, even though one of them is dead'."

Deborah took a deep breath and asked the obvious question. "Do you love Eddie?"

"Of course I do..." Janice stopped abruptly, she'd broken the ultimate taboo.

She could hear Jimmy in the kitchen running a tap and moaning. Deborah was talking calmly to her with one eye closed and blood trickling from her nose. If that wasn't bizarre enough, Janice had just shown her an intensely private letter and told her she loved Eddie.

The words burst out. "I remember girls staring at me full of envy when he used to pick me up from school on his motorbike." She gave a sudden smile. "He's like James Dean, but with nicer eyes?"

Deborah took Janice's arm. "I've never seen his eyes because they're half closed all the time." She paused. "But the girls at school weren't staring out of envy, they couldn't understand why any sensible girl would choose to mix with a lunatic like Eddie." She paused again. "The only rival you ever had was Jilly."

Janice was staring at her, open mouthed with astonishment.

Deborah gave a deep sigh. "We need to talk."

A SERVICE

The service reception area at Kings of Canley was bright and welcoming with comfortable sage green chairs on a beige carpet, the intention being to make visits an enjoyable experience. The staff were cheerful as well as polite, appearing genuinely happy in their work.

Janice had booked her car in for a basic service and an MoT, but wasn't sitting in the service reception area, she was being treated like a VIP in the plush sales area. Carl Boyd had met her at the service reception desk, escorted her to the sales area and given her coffee and biscuits. She glanced uneasily at the customers waiting for the courtesy minibus into the town centre, hoping that Carl's hospitality wouldn't make her late for work. It wouldn't, a toot on a car horn and Dave was outside holding open the passenger door of his BMW.

Two days since the letter and Janice felt ashamed of herself, not for hitting Jimmy but for hitting Deborah – she was simply being a loyal wife. Deborah telephoned last night and they'd talked for ages about the past and the contents of the letter. She told Janice about Mike's attack on them at St Nicholas Church Hall last May and some of what she'd discovered since. It didn't make Janice feel any better – why hadn't she found what Deborah had found?

"Penny for them?" Dave had been talking to her and she hadn't heard a word.

"Sorry, Dave, I was miles away."

He gave a wry smile. "Several thousand miles away at a guess – did you say he telephoned last night?"

Eddie was telephoning regularly now, always with an excuse as if he had to justify calling her. Last night it was to say that he would be home in time to arrange her car service and MoT as usual. He'd organised both since she'd picked him up from HM Prison Padmoor, he'd driven her car home and been appalled at the state of the brakes on her car. This time Janice was ahead of him, she'd already booked it into Kings of Canley's workshop. She didn't want or expect special treatment, she'd telephoned like any other customer, but Carl Boyd was ahead of her.

Eleven o'clock and Carl was having coffee with Dave. It was their regular weekly meeting, but today there was an additional agenda item that brought a rueful smile to Carl's face.

"I asked Dick Boon to look at Janice's car, you know how thorough he is." Dave nodded, puzzled by Carl's smile. "Do you have the invoices Janice gave you?" Dave did and Carl studied them before continuing. "These confirm what she said, three basic services, a set of brake pads, an exhaust tail pipe and a clutch adjustment." He laughed outright. "I told Dick the car was probably in a right state…"

"And…?"

Carl shook his head. "He was a bit fed up, he thought I was trying to trick him. Apparently, the car's in excellent condition, it's been fully serviced to a very high standard. It's also had a complete brake overhaul, not just pads but discs, callipers and hoses, drums; a top quality exhaust system front to back and a complete new clutch assembly." He paused. "Someone's spent a pile of money on that car."

Dave needed a drink; watching nice girls cry was right up there in his top ten of unpleasant experiences, and being the unwitting cause made it worse. He thought Janice would be flattered that someone, doubtless Eddie, had spent 'a pile of money' on her car. Obviously, he didn't understand girls as well as he thought he did, or perhaps he just didn't understand nice girls.

Comparing Sue with Janice was inevitable. Sue should be the girl of his dreams; attractive, intelligent, talented and vivacious. He'd closed his mind to the unpleasant side of her character, wanting her to be the nice girl of his dreams, but the reality was that Sue could be gratuitously unkind to those she considered unattractive, unintelligent or untalented. It was a familiar character trait; he was like that once. In contrast, Janice was attractive, intelligent and talented, but never unkind.

Years ago, Dave had watched Eddie walk out of Broad Street School hall hand in hand with the nicest girl in the world. Today he sat in his car and watched the second nicest girl in the world cry knowing she loved the same man. Dave threw his drink across the room and sat with his head in his hands. He didn't love Sue and probably never would, he didn't love Janice either, he just loved the idea of being in love with a nice girl. Life wasn't fair – if it was, nice girls wouldn't love dehumanised weirdos like Eddie Stagg.

Janice was sitting in her Nan's armchair; upset and confused. Dave wasn't the slightest bit surprised that Eddie had spent a pile of money on her car, but she was. Did everyone know something she didn't? Was Nan right, did Eddie love her all those years ago? Did Eddie love her before he went to America? The thought of all those lost years was heartbreaking, and the thought of losing him to this girl in America was unbearable. The glimmer of hope she'd clung to since he'd gone away was fading away.

The telephone was ringing when she came through the door, Eddie saying that he was catching a flight to Italy but would be home at the weekend. That was typical of her luck, she would be away, her final examinations were in a fortnight and she'd booked a weekend residential refresher course. She had to go – if she passed her final examinations she could apply for the practice manager's job. The present manager retired in three months, but Janice hadn't expected to be considered for the job, the partners wanted someone with connections and a degree. However, Eddie's choice of replacement tutor whilst he was away had changed their minds. Every week for the last two months, Sir Charles Napier QC had picked her up from work in his Bentley to tutor her on the law. The obsequiousness of the partners to Charlie and their sudden respect for her abilities was rather nauseating.

Eddie kept asking her if she was upset. She was, but had denied it convincingly. Now she was crying and there was somebody banging on the door.

She threw it open angrily. "Roxy!"

Roxy eyed her disdainfully. "Well, aren't you going to ask me in?"

Apart from being bullied and manipulated by Andy, Janice thought herself in control of her life, but according to Roxy she was in control of nothing and needed sorting out.

"Mike's out somewhere so Eddie telephoned me in a right state; he's worried about you, so I said I'd call round. He's going to telephone me later and when he does, I'm going to tell him you're fine and you are damn well going to be!" Roxy shrugged. "It's partly my fault, I never thought you were good enough for him and said so. Anyway, if you want him you've got to do something about it, not sit here weeping and wailing."

"But he's met someone else."

Roxy snorted derisively. "Rubbish! It's only ever been you or Jilly, but he's so twisted up with guilt about her death and frightened that you'll hurt him again, he doesn't know what to do." She turned deadly serious. "One question, and you'd better tell the truth: do you love him?"

Janice heard herself screaming. "Yes! Yes! Of course I do!"

"Stand up!"

The words were said with such authority that Janice jumped to her feet. Roxy circled her, looking her up and down, tugging at her baggy sweatshirt.

"Eddie's got absolutely no self-confidence so we've got to be careful, but the shrinking violet approach isn't going to work either. Now, do you actually have a shape under your baggy sweatshirts and huge jackets?"

"I wear big jackets because I have wide shoulders."

"Big and baggy are not the same thing, take that sweatshirt off!" Roxy circled her again. "You've got a shape, a good shape, so why all the baggy stuff?"

Janice heard her voice cracking. "Andy said I had to hide the fact I was so thin."

A sniff from Roxy. "I bet the short, cropped hairstyle was his idea as well."

Janice nodded. "He said longer hair made my face look smaller and my nose even bigger."

Roxy peered at her. "Who said you had a big nose?"

"My first boyfriend. I told Andy and he agreed, and has made jokes about it ever since."

"That bastard would have made a good pimp." She stood back. "Trust me, your nose is not big, not small, just ordinary, they were trying to undermine you. Anyway, back to business, Eddie generally goes for tall, skinny blondes so two out of three's not bad. The longer hair's good, all you need now are clothes that fit and some decent underwear to enhance things a bit."

Janice interrupted, grappling with what Roxy had just said. "But Jilly…"

Roxy interrupted in turn. "Eddie loved Jilly because she was Jilly, generally he goes for tall, skinny blondes. For Christ's sake he's a man, he looks, haven't you noticed?"

No, Janice hadn't, then another question. "Who's your best friend?"

"Eddie."

Roxy looked skywards in despair. "Apart from Eddie."

"Mike."

"I mean a female friend, someone to go shopping with."

Janice waved her hands helplessly. "I haven't really got one."

"It will have to be me then." Then Roxy was deadly serious again. "When did it happen?"

"When did what happen?"

"When did you fall in love with Eddie?"

Janice was in tears again. "In that horrible little room above the garage in Gladstone Street. He opened his eyes and looked at me and…"

Roxy was incredulous. "That was years ago. Why…"

She didn't finish her question, Janice was screaming at her. "Because I wanted him to find someone special."

BREAKING NEWS

In common with most police forces, Canley Police Division held a press conference every morning to disseminate information. They were usually tedious affairs and the media sent junior reporters unless they anticipated important breaking news. It didn't matter if the junior reporters were dull witted, Canley Police Division provided a printed list of items arranged in order of importance.

Wednesday morning saw a junior reporter from the Canley Herald at the press conference, whereas the Canley Advertiser sent their editor. As usual the list was presented by a sergeant; a senior officer only attended if there was an important matter to report.

Item one of five and therefore by implication the most important matter was 'Woman (72) injured in City Centre mugging'. Item two was 'Serial shop-lifter arrested'. Item three was 'Men questioned after incident at a party'. Item four was 'Theft of cash by bogus meter reader' and item five was 'Theft of lawnmower from garden shed'. Its position in the list suggested that item three 'Men questioned after incident at a party' was not a serious matter.

The full text of item three read 'Acting on information from a reliable source and supported by an officer from another force, Canley Police visited an address in the Canley area. Two men were questioned regarding an alleged assault on two women. A search of the property produced items that are being examined. Two men have been bailed and released. The women are being questioned and enquiries are continuing'.

Thursday's Canley Herald carried the front-page story 'Elderly woman injured in City Centre mugging'. The remainder of the front page and part of page two were dedicated to the arrest of a troublesome serial shoplifter. Page four carried a paragraph headed 'Local men questioned' which reproduced the Canley Police press release word for word.

The Advertiser's front-page story was radically different; their headline read 'Sex and drugs shame of local man' and presented the story in two parts. Part one outlined the facts, identifying the men as Vincent Proctor (31) and Mark Tinkler (46) and the 'reliable source' as Roxanne Bailey, Co-ordinator for the Canley Confederation of Children's Charities. They included a quote from Gerald Burchnall OBE, Chairman of CCCC, giving fulsome praise to his co-ordinator for protecting two vulnerable girls. He clarified CCCC's position, their brief was to protect all persons under the age of eighteen and the 'women' concerned were in fact girls of sixteen and seventeen.

Mark Tinkler was identified as a pimp who procured two girls for the depraved attentions of Proctor. Their initial willingness to participate evaporated when they discovered the extent of Proctor's sadistic desires, but their objections were ignored. Boldly, the Advertiser revealed that the 'items being examined' included Class 'A' drugs, a video cassette tape and a number of DVDs.

The second part of the story was a damning analysis of the police press release. They compared it with other press releases where individuals were identified if they had been charged. Proctor and Tinkler were charged before being bailed so could and should have been named. Why were girls of sixteen and seventeen described as 'women' and why was it not made clear that the girls were questioned as witnesses not defendants? Why did the press release say 'supported by an officer from another force' when the officer in question was in fact an senior observer from the Independent Police Complaints Authority?

The girls were the ones Eddie had seen in the West Town Café the day he'd bought Roxy breakfast before leaving for America. Later, Roxy had spoken to them and suggested they take her mobile number in case of emergency. One girl managed to telephone whilst Proctor was concentrating his attentions on her friend and Roxy recognised him from her description. Eddie had given her Proctor's home address, Roxy had her man!

She guessed that Canley Police would either refuse to raid Vinnie's home, tip him off before doing so and/or destroy evidence found at the scene. Therefore, her first telephone call was to Charlie who had initiated an enquiry into Canley Police after the trial of Powers and Windsor. The enquiry had been obstructed at every turn and bogged down in red tape for years and Roxy hoped this event would provide the breakthrough they needed. It required every ounce of Charlie's influence to get a Detective Chief Inspector from the Independent Police Complaints Authority to Vinnie Proctor's house as observer before the arrival of the Canley officers. Neither he nor the Canley officers realised the significance of the video cassette.

CHAPTER 14

Venice

FLIGHTS OF FANCY

Eddie didn't enjoy air travel, long haul was tedious and even short haul was marred by endless queuing and security checks. His attitude was shared by many Europeans who only encountered air travel on their annual holiday. However, as America was such a large country, for many Americans air travel was routine, and so when Eddie telephoned Chin to say he was flying from San Francisco to Rome via Chicago his immediate response was that they should meet there.

Parting from Maybelle Potts in Tacoma Flats was a tearful affair and Eddie still couldn't understand why she was so fond of him. He was 'my boy Eddie' and he'd promised to telephone and e-mail regularly and read for her at next year's Literary Festival. Both promises would be easy and a pleasure to keep, but a third that he would bring his Lizzie to the Festival was impossible to make, his newfound optimism didn't aim that high. Parting from Brooklyn in San Francisco was much easier, she was eager to see Lawrence and happy to part with Eddie's demons.

The windy city was neither windy nor interesting. Not that either mattered, Eddie was meeting friends not sightseeing, and was humbled that they'd made such an effort to see him. Over lunch Chin told him the news, Weasel's claim that he and Fat Eddie had been jumped by a rival gang had provoked open warfare. Whilst occasional gang related deaths were both expected and tolerated, wholesale slaughter wasn't, and the FBI had intervened, reopening investigations into recent gangland killings. Good news for local residents but bad news for Eddie – the hotel room containing Fat Eddie's body also contained his fingerprints and DNA. If Weasel ever identified Fat Eddie's killer as English, the British Police National Computer held Eddie's fingerprints and DNA.

The eleven-hour flight to Rome gave Eddie time to think. Brooklyn had been very clear, he wasn't cured and probably never would be. Going back to his old ways would bring rapid regression, he had to keep his demons out in the open where he could see and fight them. With curious reverse logic, she'd concentrated on questions rather than answers. Some were obvious, some less so, and many used double negatives to make positives. His task was to answer the questions honestly and accept her interpretation of the results.

Did he genuinely feel guilty about falling asleep and allowing his mother to die alone, or was he angry at losing his opportunity to discover why she hated him and guilty because he was angry?

Why did he feel it was his duty to protect everyone? Complicated, but essentially those that could protect should protect.

Why did protection have to involve violence? It didn't; since he'd met Charlie they'd been working hard to find a better way.

Had his regular beatings harmed him? Not permanently, his mother didn't punch her weight and when his father joined in his heart didn't seem to be in it. What did hurt was a rare conversation with Charles when he was eight or nine year old. He'd asked when the beatings would stop and Eddie could still picture Charles' gloating face as he told him that for him and other normal children they never started. 'You get beaten because you're a wicked little bastard.'

Was Chin a good man? Of course he was…! Brooklyn had interrupted quickly to remind him that Chin had run with the gangs for years, maiming and killing for money. Why forgive Chin and not yourself?

Did he blame Janice for Juliet's death, or Jilly's? An outraged no was interrupted by Brooklyn reminding him of his bitter regret at not going after Ray Powers after the fight on the waste ground or hunting him down after Juliet's suicide. He'd not done either because he didn't want Janice to think he was a monster!

She had one answer: extreme mental and physical tiredness dulled his unhappiness and sense of loss but also impaired his ability to think clearly. A valid reason for some of his mistakes or just another excuse?

Their honeymoon tour of Italy had started in Rome with the first day filled with organised tours of the Colosseum, St Peter's Square, the Trevi Fountain and the Spanish Steps. The second day was free time and he and Jilly explored the centre of Rome on foot, walking along narrow streets that opened into beautiful piazzas surrounded by amazing buildings. In the afternoon they stopped at a pavement café where they were by served by an English girl. She and her boyfriend were spending a year in Italy with her working as a waitress and him busking outside cafés.

Later, sitting on the tiny balcony of their hotel room in Lido di Jesolo during their second week of their holiday, they had planned to emulate the girl in the café, quitting their secure jobs and the house in Norwood Road to live in Rome. They didn't of course, some dreams were meant to remain dreams – a week later they were eating their sandwiches in the garden by St John's church planning the redecoration of their sitting room.

Other dreams were real, a family, a future and Sophie was always part of the future, there had even been talk of her living with them permanently. Ray Powers had destroyed those dreams, and the guilt Eddie felt at disfiguring him evaporated when he thought of Jilly. That didn't mean he escaped guilt entirely – Phil Windsor was more stupid than wicked, Eddie shouldn't have hurt him as badly as he did.

VENICE

Eddie was sitting on a train thinking about preconceptions. Most Canley residents didn't know how corrupt Canley Police Division and Canley Council were as they did a pretty good job in all areas other than West Town. Little surprise therefore that non-West Town residents condemned his vigilante antics, particularly so when his name was regularly splashed over the front page of the Canley Herald with pictures of Ray and Phil's reconstructed faces.

The problem with Canley Police Division was that Chief Superintendent John Powers' corrupt activities were never challenged by his superiors at County Headquarters. The Independent Police Complaints Authority enquiry initiated by Sir Charles Napier QC years ago had been obstructed at every step, the protection afforded to Powers had to extend to the very top. Eventually, Eddie, Charlie and Doug Bracken would get a breakthrough and once they had rooted out the corruption the streetfighter could retire.

The problem with Canley Council was similar with Jerome Proctor as Council leader and many of his cronies and minions as committee heads. Powers and Proctor were known to be close associates so there had to be a link between the influence that protected both from challenge. Finding the link or the source of either man's influence was proving very difficult. Sex and/or drugs had to be there somewhere, that was usually where the big money was made, but even the diligent Doug Bracken couldn't directly connect either to Powers or Proctor.

Italian public transport was cheap and reliable, and Eddie enjoyed the journey from Rome to Lido di Jesolo rather more than the flight from Chicago to Rome. Lido di Jesolo sprawled in a narrow band down the Adriatic coast south of Venice. At night the main shopping road was closed to traffic and locals mingled with tourists, promenading in family groups and stopping for coffee or a glass of wine. Despite the ready availability of alcohol there was little or no trouble; instead, the bustling streets reflected family values and relaxed enjoyment. Eddie checked in at a Hotel on Piazza Mazzini, a stone's throw from the hotel he'd stayed in with Jilly.

The next morning he started early, travelling on local buses to the ferry terminus at Punta Sabbioni via Playa Drago. The ferry crossed the Venetian Lagoon, stirring heart-stopping memories of Jilly before mooring within sight of the twin columns at the end of St Mark's Square. By eleven-thirty Eddie had visited the Cathedral, walked to the Rialto Bridge and started back looking for the antique shop where Jilly had bought an antique print of the Carnival of Venice. Another heart-stopping moment came when he found the low bridge over the narrow canal and the stone steps leading via an alley to the shop. He stepped onto the bridge and leaned on the metal handrail to gather his thoughts.

"Excuse me, do you speak English?"

The voice was hesitant, and Eddie turned to see two girls away to his left clinging to each other for support. They were nervous, frightened even, but Eddie was used to frightened girls and attempted a smile.

"I am English!"

The girl's faces showed a mixture of surprise and relief, eyeing his lower half with mild suspicion. Eddie glanced down – he was dressed as he usually dressed, tee shirt, blue jeans and shiny black shoes. His smile widened with genuine amusement: tourists seldom wore blue jeans, and never wore shiny black shoes.

"Are you lost?"

The girls nodded nervously and Eddie smiled again. "I'm a tourist like you, but I know where we are."

Kelly and Donna were no longer frightened, relieved that Eddie spoke English and knew the way to the Rialto bridge. They'd spent an hour trying to find their way there from St Mark's

Square but had gone round and round in circles through narrow streets. Both looked a trifle pink, a combination of exertion, stress and too much sun; they needed a cold drink. So did Eddie, he'd had nothing since breakfast.

The girls were on holiday with their boyfriends much against the wishes of their parents who neither liked the boys nor thought the girls old enough to holiday by themselves. They were staying in Lido and had come to Venice on an organised trip. The guide had shown them St Mark's Square and told them to rendezvous back there at three o'clock for the return ferry to Lido. The boyfriends had stayed in Lido and Eddie guessed there was a problem – when he suggested a drink the girls hands had fluttered nervously towards their handbags; they were short of money. Offering cash to young girls could easily be misinterpreted, but buying them all a drink in a nearby café was not a problem. Eddie spent a pleasant half hour listening to their chatter, paid for the drinks, drew them a map and pointed out the signs to Rialto.

Venice was beautiful, but after sharing it with Jilly everything was a disappointment. After leaving the girls Eddie went down the steps and walked through the alley into the courtyard by the antique shop. The courtyard hadn't changed, the metal dome covering the well in the centre still reminded him of a submarine hatch, but the antique shop was now a restaurant. He retraced his steps and walked through the endless back streets he'd explored with Jilly, becoming more and more despondent, he couldn't feel her presence. By three o'clock he'd had enough, Jilly wasn't there, it was stupid of him to think she could be. His last stop was at the stone bridge over the narrow canal; he felt empty, coming to Venice had been a mistake.

"Eddie, Eddie!"

Kelly and Donna were running towards him, faces full of relief. They'd followed his map to the Rialto bridge, then wandered down a side street and got lost again. Eventually they'd found their way back to Rialto and followed his map back to the stone bridge. They were desperate to know the time, neither had a watch and their mobile phones had run out of charge.

Eddie knew the time, it was well past three o'clock, the girls had missed their guide and their ferry. He felt as relaxed as the girls were agitated, helping frightened girls who shouldn't really be allowed out on their own took his mind off his own unhappiness. Eddie had missed lunch and was hungry, but his offer to buy them all pizza and chips met resistance.

Eddie protested. "It's not a stranger, we met earlier, we're friends."

As the girls emptied their plates their mood descended into gloom and honesty.

"We've missed our ferry and we haven't got any money."

Donna looked away and Kelly was in tears, something unpleasant was going on – they hadn't just forgotten their purses. Eddie smiled sadly and talked as he would have talked to Sophie.

"Tell me what's happening, I won't be shocked?"

The girls hadn't known Dean and Jack long but the idea of going on holiday together seemed very adult and exciting. Things started to go wrong on the first day when Dean insisted they hand over most of their cash 'to keep it safe'. It soon became clear that neither boy had brought any money and intended to use theirs as their credit cards were maxed out.

They'd paid for the Venice trip with Donna's credit card but left it at the hotel as it was maxed out as well.

Eddie was angry, his first instinct was to find the boys and batter them senseless, make them bitterly regret abusing two nice girls. But no, Lido di Jesolo wasn't West Town stripped of police at the behest of Chief Superintendent Powers. In fact, few places were, and Eddie monster and streetfighter had no place here. He pictured two policemen he'd seen in Lido yesterday posing in their crisp uniforms with batons and holstered pistols on their belts. Authority, power and vanity dissolved into benign smiles when they saw children walk by escorted by proud parents and grandparents. No way would they tolerate Kelly and Donna being abused by two stupid, selfish young men?

"Eddie, are you OK?"

Donna sounded worried and Eddie forced a smile. "Of course I am, I was thinking." He paused. "I'll find a cash machine and draw out enough to last you for the rest of your holiday." Eddie saw the shock on their faces and threw up his hands. "It's a loan, I'll give you my address so you can repay me when you get home."

The girls stared at each other then nodded in unison.

"We'll go back to Lido together." Eddie sounded as cheerful as he felt. "I'll show you where my hotel is and then I'll walk with you to your hotel, they're quite close. I want you to find the boys and tell them that you're finished with them. Be firm, tell them that if they touch you again, you'll go to the police. Tell them to move all their stuff into one room and you move all yours into the other. If there's any trouble you come to me at my hotel and I'll sort it. OK?"

FOOD FOR THOUGHT

Eddie's hotel had a café bar opening directly onto the Piazza Mazzini. Most of the tables were empty, nine in the evening wasn't particularly late to eat, but it was early season. Eddie was sitting very visibly right at the front of the café bar eating pasta. It was good, slightly al dente with a delicate flavour, but Eddie had little appetite, he was worried about the girls. Two hours ago he'd left them in the foyer of their hotel and hadn't seen or heard from them since.

"Eddie! Eddie!"

Kelly and Donna were running through the empty café bar, bursting with excitement. The flopped into chairs at his table.

"We did it! We did it! We did what you said, and we've got the best room, the one overlooking the pool." They were hardly pausing for breath. "They argued but we weren't having any of it. We made them give us some of our money back, and said they had to give the rest back when they get home."

They paused, beaming and flushed, then looked at each other. "We don't know anything about you. All the time in Venice and on the ferry, we talked about ourselves. Why were you in Venice by yourself and why are you by yourself now?"

Early morning, Eddie had a seat on the first flight out of Venice Airport. With a tail wind, no delays and an airport taxi, he could be back in Canley before lunch.

The girls didn't return to their hotel until after midnight. For once he'd got it right, no violence, no victims, he'd simply helped two girls to help themselves. Their desire to know more about him seemed motivated by genuine interest not morbid curiosity, so he expurgated and modified the facts a little and answered not evaded their questions. He told them he'd been married and that his wife had been killed in a road accident five years ago. Their next question took him by surprise 'did he have a girlfriend?'. Was it so normal to want someone else only five years after a loved one's death that these girls could ask the question so casually.

They asked what he was doing in Venice and he told the truth, they'd honeymooned there and he was trying to find Jilly.

"But people aren't in places…"

Two young girls knew what it had taken him five years to discover. Jilly wasn't in Venice staring in wonder at St Mark's Basilica, or in Lido sitting on the tiny balcony where they'd planned to live in Rome. She wasn't in the quiet church yard shaded from the sun by a giant chestnut tree, or in the house in Norwood Road that she'd been so proud of. Jilly was inside his head, and if he could ever make peace with himself, he could make peace with her. Eddie thought of Jilly dying in agony in the bus shelter and wanted to cry, but couldn't. If he did, he would be crying for himself and he wasn't worth crying for, never had been, never would be.

CHAPTER 15

Home is the hero?

THE HOMECOMING

The early cloud had lifted to reveal a bright, clear July morning. Eddie asked the airport taxi driver to drop him on the main road, he needed the walk to the workshop to gather his thoughts. He grew increasingly apprehensive as he rounded the shallow bend and saw the sun glinting off the 'A' frame sign on the pavement proclaiming 'SIKO - Antiques, Collectables and Band Equipment' – would his homecoming be as good as he hoped?

A 'For Sale' board outside the Methodist Chapel next to the workshop gave him an excuse to stop. He'd heard rumours that the chapel was to be deconsecrated and sold before he left for America, obviously they were true. The board was screwed to a post under a small sycamore tree, doubtless a seedling from the huge one at the rear of the chapel. Extensive bird fouling on the pavement around the sign evidenced the popularity of the tree, but the sign itself was clean; it must have been erected recently.

Eddie saw movement in the shop doorway and was startled to see Sophie appear carrying a bucket and squeegee. She disappeared back into the shop, reappearing a moment later carrying a short stepladder. He stood motionless as she dunked the squeegee into the bucket in preparation for cleaning the windows. Eddie smiled and stepped forward and an instant later Sophie swivelled round, dropped the squeegee and ran towards him.

She wasn't! Oh yes she was! Two paces away she launched herself at him. Sophie wasn't a child anymore and Eddie didn't try to catch and swing her round like he used to. The impact nearly bowled him over, then she was clinging to him in floods of tears. Eddie felt a surge of relief, children cried when they were upset, young ladies also cried when they were happy, Sophie had grown up.

"I heard your clip-clop shoes."

Sophie wiped her eyes, smiled, and the words gushed out. "I'm working for Bob, I told Roxy I wanted to earn my own money, it's not fair that you give me pocket money all the time and she said I should ask Bob. I had to come for an interview with him and Ellie, and I'm on a month's trial."

She was taking tiny gasps of air at the end of each phrase, desperate to move on to each new fact.

"I come on my bike and start at half past nine, Bob says I can't come earlier because of the traffic. I clean the sign and put it out, polish the furniture and dust the guitars and amplifiers and clean the windows. Then I get the tea and the coffee and the milk and the biscuits for the week from the shop. I have to get coffee as well because Darryl doesn't drink tea. Bob says that if they run out of anything it's my fault, so I've got to get it right."

Bob was an instinctive manager, Sophie felt she'd earned the job and was proud of her responsibilities, it would be good to see him again.

Thankfully one thing hadn't changed: Sophie put out her hand for him to hold on the short walk to the workshop.

"And I order Desmond's food and cat litter from Dawn and Amy's shop, Bob says we have to keep the business in the family." She paused briefly and looked at him. "Has Dawn always had a poorly hand?"

No, she hadn't, her pimp's favourite punishment for recalcitrant girls was to have his minder hold them down whilst he broke their fingers one at a time with a pair of pliers. Eddie was not under the illusion that the ferocious beating he'd given both men would make them better people, but it would stop them and others like them hurting his girls.

"How do you get on with Desmond?" Eddie was curious, but the main reason for his question was to divert Sophie's attention from Dawn's hand.

She gave him a knowing look. "He's a big softy really, he pretends to be fierce because he doesn't want people to know he's lonely. But what about Dawn's…"

Bob appearing in the shop doorway interrupted her question, he and Eddie shook hands quietly, neither were given to emotional displays.

"Early tea break today, Sophie and you'd better go to the shop and get some cakes." Bob took out his wallet and handed her a note. "Today, and just today, mind, you needn't sign a petty cash chit first. And make sure you look both ways before you cross the road."

Sophie gazed skywards, ran to the edge of the pavement, looked carefully both ways and was gone.

Bob had made changes: he'd placed the guitar and amplifier repair benches together and partitioned them off to keep out the dust from the furniture restoration. He'd also recruited another full-time worker on a temporary contract because they were so busy. Ben was a serious and rather taciturn young man with a bad reputation, but came highly recommended by Jim. He helped Bob in the workshop as Darryl had developed a remarkable ability for setting up PA systems and now ran the PA Hire business under Ellie's supervision. She'd canvassed delivery work from local furniture and band equipment dealers, and Darryl now had more work than he could cope with, SIKO would soon need another van and another driver. Eddie didn't quite feel a stranger in his own workshop, but its days as a place to hide were long gone.

The converted loft over the workshop was more dismal than Eddie remembered. If Mike had been successful in recovering money from Charles regarding the long term bonds he'd supposedly bought with Eddie's share of their father's estate all those years ago, Eddie might be able to look for a house. If the news was very good, he might be impossibly optimistic and buy something Janice would like.

Back in the workshop Ellie gave him a meaningful look, ushered him towards her small office, pointed at the telephone and closed the door firmly behind her. To Eddie's surprise all his calls were answered, even Janice's mobile was switched on in the college refectory where she was having lunch during her weekend revision course. He desperately wanted to see her, two months away had made him realise that he didn't want to live without her. Unfortunately, that didn't mean she didn't want to live without him.

He would see her on Monday evening, she'd arranged a band rehearsal at St Nicholas Church Hall; it would be the regular Roadrunners line up – Jimmy was unable to make it. Eddie and everyone else were unaware that his indisposition was a black eye given to him by Janice. His diary filled quickly, on Monday morning he was meeting Charlie and Doug Bracken, apparently there had been important developments in the Canley Police Division corruption enquiry. On Tuesday he was decorating Sophie's bedroom and Wednesday was McDonald's day, it would be good to see Mark and Gran again. On Thursday he was having lunch with Jim and Roxy, Jim sounded worried when he telephoned, surely he didn't think Eddie disapproved of him and Roxy being together?

Sunday brought lunch with Mike and Gary; afterwards, the ever-discreet Gary discovered an urgent need to wash his car.

Mike beamed at Eddie. "Well, do you want the good news, or the even better news?" He was almost jumping up and down with excitement. "I've found piles of money, and screwed that devious, mercenary bastard Charles into the bargain." Mike saw concern on Eddie's face. "Don't worry, Angela divorced Charles two years ago, Charlotte and Philip won't be affected."

Charles' attempt to disinherit Eddie thirteen years ago had backfired. He'd put all Eddie's money in high risk, long term bonds expecting the company to fold, leaving him with his commission and Eddie with nothing. Instead, the company had prospered; Charles had unwittingly made Eddie a small fortune.

There was more. "Even when he was screwing you, he didn't do it straight." Mike was angry. "About thirty percent of the bonds were fake, he forged them and kept your money.

He thought they'd be worthless in a few years and no-one would know?"

Mike had given Charles a choice: pay Eddie the full value of the forged bonds or face fraud charges. Charles now had a huge mortgage on his house.

THE ROADRUNNERS

Sue wasn't having a mid-life crisis, only weak people who didn't know what they wanted had mid-life crises. She knew what she wanted, she'd always known what she wanted, the problem was stupid people getting in the way. Dave wasn't stupid, but he was seriously misguided. His business friends and golf club friends were her sort of people, she liked them and they liked her, but the people in his band …?

They'd been together for two months before he admitted singing in a rock band, and it was another month before she heard them play. Sue disliked the music as much as the people. Dave misunderstood, he thought she was unhappy with the quality of their playing and insisted that everything would be fine when Eddie came back, it was Eddie's band, not his. Well, this Eddie might improve the quality of the playing, but he wouldn't improve the quality of the music or the dreadful people.

Dave shouldn't mix with nobodies or weirdos, and her saying so had caused their first major argument which quickly led on to their second. Sue liked Sharon, she understood life's priorities and was realistic about her daughter's lack of any sort of talent. On the other hand, Dave was convinced that Sophie was simply late developing her full potential. Wrong, Sophie was as tediously average as the vast majority of the children Sue taught at her music workshops.

Sue was fed up teaching the talentless offspring of shopkeepers and civil servants, she wanted to play in professional orchestras and take master classes for talented youngsters. She couldn't, as most of her money came from the simpering shopkeepers and civil servants who drooled over their children's mediocre efforts. Dave could change that, he had the money and she had the talent.

St Nicholas Church Hall was a grubby little place, surely Dave could find a more prepossessing rehearsal venue? That question nearly provoked another argument, The Roadrunners had always rehearsed there and he liked it. A Monday evening in a grubby hall listening to a mediocre band playing vulgar music wasn't Sue's idea of a good time, but Eddie was back and Dave wanted her to hear the band as it should be. Sue knew she would dislike this Eddie, he was bound to be another amateur with an exaggerated idea of his ability.

A previous rehearsal had brought a new emotion for Sue, jealousy. She'd always been the centre of attention, the one in control who ended relationships and dumped friends. Dave was going off the boil and it was unnerving for Sue to realise that she was more keen on him than he was on her. Even more unnerving was the realisation that she was jealous of Janice – why did Dave and Mike make such a fuss of a boring stick insect? And whilst Janice and Andy were hardly on speaking terms now, they must have been once, they were still married.

For Sue punctuality meant being on time, not late or early. Dave tended to be early and today he was excessively so; he'd set up his amplifier and tuned his guitar before she arrived. In contrast to his usual irritating lateness, Mike was also there, drums set up ready. Andy, normally early like Dave, was nowhere to be seen.

Dave seemed nervous, he'd been deep in conversation with Mike when Sue arrived. She heard the door open and close then light footsteps, obviously Janice not Andy. Now what was going on? Janice had been shopping, she was wearing tailored pale blue trousers and a fitted white top, totally different to her normal shapeless sweatshirt and jeans. And she'd found a bust from somewhere too, it doubtless owed more to the underwear manufacturer's art than nature, but Dave had noticed, he could hardly tear his eyes away. Surely Janice wasn't stupid enough to make a play for Dave?

She wasn't; Janice's eyes were fixed on the door and she was fluttering like a schoolgirl on her first date. Moments later Sue heard car tyres crunching on the gravel outside. Dave peered out of the window then turned and smiled at Janice who jumped from the chair and hurried towards the door.

The man who appeared carrying a guitar case wouldn't stand out in a crowd, in fact he would struggle to stand out in a room by himself.

"Hello Eddie…"

There was a crash as the man dropped his guitar case and stood motionless, staring at Janice like an idiot. Then Dave and Mike were there, gently pushing the two together. Sue stared in disbelief, the wretched girl had the full set, this Eddie was clearly obsessed with her. Or was he, after a brief hug the two sprang apart as if they'd just done something intensely wicked.

Andy arrived late and gave the curtest of nods to Eddie before setting up his gear, hardly surprising given the chemistry between Eddie and his estranged wife. Janice rapped on the table in front of her.

"As Eddie's back we'll start with some open tuned stuff, we'll play 'Rocking all over the World' Roadrunners style in open G. Eddie starts."

Four clicks on his drumsticks from Mike then wall of sound leapt from the guitar player's amplifier, hard edged, aggressive and LOUD! And Mike was following the guitar player – totally wrong, drummers should lead not follow. After the intro Andy pitched and his bass wasn't overwhelmed, the guitar player wasn't excessively loud, he just sounded loud. Then Sue knew why: she'd attended a sound engineering course where the lecturer had lauded the benefits of high quality sound compression. She listened carefully, the guitar player's sound was huge, heavily compressed and rich in second order harmonics. This was valve compression – where did a small town hick learn about high quality valve compression?

Dave hadn't started singing, he was flapping his arms about and smiling at Janice. If the bastard wanted to smile at anyone he should smile at her not bloody Janice. Then he took a pace forward and started.

"Well here we go and here we go and…"

Gone were the bass heavy tones of before with Jimmy struggling to compete with Andy's determined bass playing. Sue waited for the instrumental, both a strength and weakness for the band. Andy might be a failed salesman with a serious drink problem, but he was an inspired musician who played amazing improvised bass solos, with Dave playing a simple repeating riff over the top. Occasionally he would lose his way and stop and as neither Mike nor Jimmy had the authority to keep it going, leaving Dave to step in to plug the gap. It clearly worried him and his singing had suffered, but today he seemed relaxed.

It happened, after a spectacular series of hammer-ons and pull-offs, Andy lost himself and stopped. The guitar player didn't flinch, he simply picked some notes within his chord shape, accented the first beat of the next bar, Andy picked up on it and was away again. Dave did nothing, he obviously knew what was coming. It was virtually seamless, only a musician would realise something had happened. The band may have improved, but this Eddie was seriously weird and vaguely familiar.

Next they played 'Honky Tonk Woman' by the Rolling Stones with Dave pouting and stamping, doing a passable imitation of Mick Jagger. It was too much, this wasn't the mature, wealthy and responsible Dave Sue wanted; the next time they were alone she would tell him how stupid he was.

Dave's flat was small, cramped and badly in need of decoration – the smart new house in Eltham that Sue had persuaded him to buy wouldn't be ready for months. It was more expensive than he'd budgeted for, but Sue had high expectations. Dave regretted buying the house, in fact he regretted quite a few things and Sue was clearly spoiling for a fight.

"I thought I recognised his face, it was all over the front page of the Herald for weeks!" Sue was shouting at him and Dave hated being shouted at. "It was bad enough having to mix with an alcoholic salesman and that half-wit store man and his frump of a wife, but a violent criminal!" She strode forward, jabbing at him with her finger. "And those three were like a freak show: a violent maniac, a gay midget and a stick insect." Sue paused before screaming. "And you were leering at her!" She paused again. "You have to make a choice."

Dave wasn't leering, he didn't leer at nice girls, and he'd already made a choice.

CORRUPTION

The morning post brought a pretty note from Kelly and Donna enclosing a cheque from their parents to prove they'd told them everything as he'd urged them to do. They also enclosed a picture taken by the waiter at his hotel, Eddie with a smiling girl on either side. Eddie thought about the girls, hoping they had a good life in front of them as he made the tea. At Bob's instigation, SIKO now had a staff meeting during Monday morning tea break, all staff were expected to attend to share their thoughts and ideas, and that included him.

"They were at it again; I mean no-one actually nicks that sort of stuff anymore." Darryl sipped his coffee before continuing. "I took the new batch of furniture to the lock-ups behind West Town Police Station like Bob said and there they were unloading the stuff they'd dumped a few months ago."

Eddie looked up sharply. "Dumped?"

Darryl hesitated then continued as Bob gave a reassuring smile. "Yes, dumped. Big old desktop PCs, cheap 35mm cameras, CD players and crappy old phones. That stuff's obsolete, everyone's gone to laptops, digital cameras, MP3 players, streaming and smart phones that do the net."

Ben grunted and stared at his feet.

"Ben?" Bob's voice was kind but firm. "Do you know something?"

"Who's going to believe me?" He shrugged. "I've got form as a thief."

Bob lifted Ben's head. "You know better than that, Jim believed you or he wouldn't have recommended you, we believe you or you wouldn't still be here!"

Ben started hesitantly. "You're in business and you've got stock you can't shift…?"

"Go on."

"So, you get someone to steal it. Not a problem if you know the right people, and you don't have to worry about the police because they are in on it. You dump it in West Town because there are no CCTV cameras there, wait for the insurance to pay out then tell police where it is and they pick it up and make their figures look good. If anyone is stupid enough to speak out, they get fitted up for handling."

Everyone, including Eddie, Charlie and Doug Bracken, thought it had to be sex or drugs or both to fund the extent of the corruption. Successive investigations failed to find any direct connection between Powers, Proctor and Windsor and trafficking drugs or girls because there was no connection. Eddie was sickened that Ben, Darryl and God knows how many others guessed what was going on, but he hadn't. Stripping West Town of resources wasn't done to allow pimps and drug pushers to flourish, it was done to facilitate wholesale insurance fraud. It was Broad Street on steroids – once a target had stolen for Vinnie's team he or she was forever a target for blackmail. That was doubtless how it became with those businessmen who asked for their stock to be taken: one false claim and they were blackmail targets for ever.

To divert suspicion from the dumping of obsolete stock on occasion, good saleable items were stolen to order and sold out of the area. And it wasn't just Canley's West Town that was a CCTV camera wasteland, neighbouring Stanford and Eltham within the Canley Police Division had similar deprived areas used for the same purpose.

A question that remained was why Chief Superintendent Powers' masters at County Headquarters failed to investigate his activities. And how did Jerome Proctor and Bendigo Windsor exert so much control over Canley, Stanford and Eltham City and Town councils that they could divert resources without challenge?

Gerry Burchnall didn't think of it as corruption, more a way to allow him to concentrate full-time on child protection issues. When Fultons closed their Canley Auction Rooms, they said it was because the branch was losing money and no longer viable. True, but Gerry had deliberately mismanaged the branch at their behest. As the old cinema that constituted the Auction Rooms was a listed Art Deco building, most people believed it could not be demolished and its prime Town Centre site redeveloped. Untrue, Gerry was confident that with appropriate funds at his disposal he could persuade fellow planning committee members to de-list the building. Fultons provided the funds, the building was de-listed, the site redeveloped and Gerry's reward was a pile of cash in a brown envelope plus a very generous redundancy payout.

It was bad luck that Gerry's glowing reference secured Eddie a job in Canley City Council's Building Control

Department. Even worse luck found Eddie working on the Cinema redevelopment project wondering how a listed building could be de-listed and demolished without a Public Enquiry. He trawled through a maze of holding companies and trading names and found Fultons and Gerry.

His gratitude to Gerry for giving him a job when no one else would secured his silence, but the incident soured their relationship. It was soured further when shortly after Jilly's death Eddie asked for a favour. Mike Chilvers had started his own company and was desperate for business, he'd tendered for a Local Authority Contract and Eddie asked Gerry to help him get it. It wasn't an outrageous request, Mike's tender was good and his work exemplary, but corruption was corruption. Eddie felt guilty and ashamed, Gerry didn't, and Mike never knew.

Canley was alive with rumours that Messrs Proctor and Windsor were insurance fraudsters on a grand scale. Even more damning in the eyes of the public were suggestions that they were using their influence to award Local Authority contracts to businesses they controlled or had interests in, and mismanaged finds awarded to local charities they allegedly supported. Gerry was safe, no-one had time to investigate bygone planning irregularities, but he was angry, he genuinely cared about local charities.

The Canley Advertiser was struggling to keep pace with demand. Its rival, the Canley Herald, was losing circulation and advertising revenue now its owner was suspected of being a fraudster. Worse was to come, the son of the owner and Herald Editor Vincent Proctor was about to make the front page of the Advertiser and the inner pages of the nationals.

EDDIE'S GIRLS

Despite overwhelming evidence of indecent assault, false imprisonment and possession of Class A drugs, Vincent Proctor entered pleas of not guilty. He was convinced that the two girls would fail to give evidence or crack under cross examination, and Chief Superintendent Powers would be able to introduce procedural errors that would prejudice the investigation. He was wrong on both counts, properly counselled and supported by Gerry Burchnall and Roxy, now coordinator to the CCCC, the girls stuck to their stories and the investigating officers knew better than to tamper with evidence under the watchful eyes of the officer from Independent Police Complaints Authority and Sir Charles Napier QC.

The front-page headline 'Sex and drugs shame of Canley Herald Editor' boosted the circulation of the Canley Advertiser to an all-time high. Proctor's surprise at being convicted was only equalled by his horror at his two-year prison sentence. The girl's pimp, Mark Tinkler, had the good sense to plead guilty and show remorse and received a three-month prison sentence. The DVDs found at the scene were recordings of Proctor abusing girls on previous occasions, but could not be produced as evidence as the seal on the evidence bag they had been placed in was damaged. The old VHS video tape found at the scene was not viewed by the original investigators and was in the same bag as the DVDs. An application for the DVDs and VHS video to be returned to Proctor was refused by the trial judge.

CHAPTER 16

A place to hide

THE BSA A65 LIGHTNING

The old BSA motorcycle was going well, battering its way into a stiff head wind along the Canley bypass at a steady 70mph. Eddie had a date, and unless he hurried he was going to be late. He pressed on and the snarl from the exhausts began to fade, he was going quickly enough to leave the sound behind him, too quickly for a man with poor eyesight. A glance at the speedometer showed 85mph and he backed off; there was no point being caught for speeding, and even less point risking his neck.

Eddie had found the red BSA in a greenhouse during a house clearance in his second week at Fultons. Gerry put it in the next general auction, Eddie bought it for a song and pushed it back to Gladstone Street. Most old mechanical things had an elegant simplicity, getting the old BSA working and roadworthy had been easy, and within a week Eddie had transport. The machine was older than a 1967 654cc vertical twin cylinder BSA A65 Lightning, the sports version with twin Amal Concentric carburettors.

Fultons opened Tuesday to Saturday and on his Mondays off Eddie would pick Janice up from school on the BSA and take her back to her Nan's. Before tea they would go over the previous week's homework, and after tea they would prepare for the following week. When Janice left school and started work at the solicitors, he would pick her up from the office, take her to Nan's and spend the evening helping her with her evening class coursework.

Other than an annual trip to the MoT Testing Station, Eddie hadn't used the BSA since Jilly died. Bob found it under a sheet in the workshop and asked if he could work on it. Thankfully his work was successful, for the second time in a week the red estate had let him down, an obscure electrical fault draining the battery.

Eddie had plucked up the courage to ask Janice out and reassuringly she'd said yes before he'd finished asking. His prompt was finding a late Georgian farmhouse for sale, the era when Jane Austen was writing her novels. Tonight, he wanted to show Janice the details and try to see if there was a chance she might share it with him one day. Even if he was deluding himself, it could be a place to hide – the farmhouse was semi derelict and he could renovate it on his bad days. Eddie felt depression washing over him, Janice was more attractive than ever, she looked gorgeous at the rehearsal, she could and should do much better than a half mad streetfighter. And a killer as well, that wasn't something he could casually drop into a conversation.

The old BSA had gone quiet again, he was back up to 85mph, it had never gone so well; Bob was a wizard with all things mechanical. Eddie saw the slip road to Walmington ahead, braked hard and changed into third. The bend off the slip road was deceptive, it tightened back on itself leaving the unwary travelling too fast. Eddie wasn't unwary, he braked again, changed into second, ran wide and laid the bike over into the tightening curve. As soon as he was upright, Eddie banged the throttle back on the stop and the BSA surged forward – it may be thirty-five years old but it had throttle response to die for.

Janice had agreed to meet him at the Red Lion at Walmington at seven-thirty and Eddie was two miles of twisty country road away. He'd always enjoyed twisty roads and street racing, his eyesight wasn't good enough for fast open road stuff. Fast riding techniques were coming back, drifting to the left for right hand curves and pushing over to the central white line for left-handers. Soon the village sign was in sight and Eddie braked gently. He stayed in top gear, even at 30mph the BSA had torque to spare and Eddie loved the deep rumble from the exhausts at low speeds.

A quarter of a mile to the Red Lion, Eddie rumbled through the village, the sound echoing and fading as it bounced off walls or disappeared into driveways or hedges. Now the Red Lion car park was in front of him and Eddie blipped the throttle, changing down into third then second. Janice's blue hatch-back was parked near the entrance and Eddie pulled up alongside and stopped. He remembered to turn both petrol taps off before hauling the BSA onto its centre stand and taking off his helmet. A glance at his watch, Janice's watch, showed it to be seven-thirty exactly, he was just on time.

THE RED LION

As Eddie pushed through the door into the Red Lion the contrast between bright sunlight and gloom temporarily blinded him. He saw movement at a table at the end of the bar, Janice was waving at him. Eddie walked forward carrying his helmet and saw a man standing by Janice's table – some bastard was trying to pick her up. He quickened his pace and his motorcycle boot caught a stool, sending it spinning it noisily across the tiled floor. The man jumped, stared at Eddie and walked quickly away.

Janice smiled nervously. "He thought you were going to hit him when you kicked that stool."

"I didn't kick it deliberately, it was the changing light, I just didn't see it."

Then a golden moment for Janice – Eddie was annoyed that she'd gone into the Red Lion alone, the compliment was spontaneous and unintended.

"You're a very attractive girl, Janice, an obvious target for predatory men."

In his black leather motorcycle jacket, Eddie looked more like James Dean than ever, but even when he was annoyed the controlled voice hardly changed – he still sounded like Mr Darcy.

"What are you grinning at?"

Janice knew why she was grinning inanely: not just attractive but *very* attractive.

Janice ordered a salad and then regretted it – she'd lost weight because she was unhappy not because she didn't like food. Tonight she was very happy and hungry, she wished she'd ordered something with chips.

"Well, show me!" Janice was eager to see the property details.

Eddie had tucked them in the top of his boot. He unfolded them carefully and handed them hesitantly to Janice.

'For Sale by Public Auction. A substantial detached, five bedroomed, stone built, Georgian farmhouse. Situated in an excellent position on the Upper Eltham Road, 6 miles from Canley and 2 miles from Eltham Village. This Grade II listed building is in need of renovation.'

Janice read the details slowly, the house sounded wonderful with original fireplaces, window shutters, cornices and other internal features, it even had a back staircase. She stared at the guide price in the Auction Catalogue.

"Can you really afford it?"

There was a long pause, Eddie was gathering his thoughts, making a decision. Janice knew it must be a momentous one – Eddie's thought processes were usually instantaneous.

He took a deep breath. "When my mother died, I should have had half the money from my father's estate. As I was under eighteen, she'd appointed Charles my legal guardian and he invested my half in high risk long term bonds. He took his commission, expecting the company to fail, but it didn't. The bonds matured a few weeks ago and Mike recovered the money for me."

"Enough to buy all this?" The property included outbuildings and a small paddock.

Another long pause and another deep breath. "Yes, and I can spend it on a house because I have some other money coming that will pay off the loans I took out a while back." Eddie hurried on. "Stephen, Charlie's son, has been working for me ever since Charlie got me off the attempted murder charge." Janice was holding her breath; Eddie was opening up. "It's taken three and a half years but they've finally paid up on both counts."

"Who has?"

No deep breath this time, but Eddie looked uncomfortable. "Canley police." Then the words came spilling out as if Eddie wanted to tell all before he thought better of it. "During the fight at The Heron, I slashed myself to make it look like Ray and Phil were the aggressors and the drugs squad officers took me straight to hospital. After the doctors sewed me up, put on a dressing and said I was fit to be discharged, some of Superintendent Powers' cronies took me back to Canley Central Police Station. I was handcuffed and couldn't fight back, and they gave me a good kicking and threw me into a cell. My stitches burst open and I nearly bled to death before the Custody Sergeant looked in, saw the pool of blood and called an ambulance. Hospitals keep records, the first time I went in all I had was a knife slash, when I went back I had broken ribs and lumps and bumps everywhere."

Eddie went quiet and Janice prompted gently. "You said both counts?"

No reply, and Janice reached over and shook his arm. "Tell me, Eddie, please."

"After I backed Ray's car into the Police Station's doors they locked me up. They turned the lights off and left me in the dark for twenty hours. They wanted me to change my statement, say that Phil was driving and that they weren't speeding. Charlie helped Stephen get the custody records and had them forensically examined, they'd been falsified, they hadn't complied with PACE which made it false imprisonment…"

Janice waited quietly, she could see there was more to come.

"Ray and Phil tried to sue me for hurting them. They thought it would be easy and without Stephen and Charlie it might have been. Stephen reminded them that a criminal court held that they had attacked me and threatened to counter-sue for the knife slash. In the end we cried quits on that one, but I got compensation for the beating and the false imprisonment."

There was a clatter of plates, their food had arrived, Eddie looked up and smiled. "I should get the farmhouse for less than the guide price, it's almost derelict. I'll put anything left over towards buying the Methodist Chapel next to the workshop. I'm thinking of expanding the business, I want to give more people like Bob, Ellie, Darryl and Ben a chance."

EIGHTEEN AGAIN

Janice drove home with the headlight of Eddie's motorbike bright in her rear view mirror. It was like being eighteen again, with Eddie taking her home from work or rehearsals or whatever. She stopped at a red traffic light, the headlight closed in behind her and she heard the engine of the BSA settle down to a low rumble. It reminded her of something else she'd got wrong – she had thought her Nan would hate the noisy old motorbike, but she didn't.

"When I hear that rumble I know you're home safe, I don't have to come down and check."

She thought her Nan would hate Eddie too, a strange boy with half closed eyes and a bad reputation, but she didn't. Nan loved Eddie from the day he first walked through her door until the day she died.

The traffic light changed to green, two more junctions and she'd be home. Janice hadn't asked Eddie in for coffee, nice girls didn't ask boys in on their first date. And it was a proper date – Eddie's excuse that he wanted to show her the house details was just that, he could have shown her them to her anytime.

After the food arrived Eddie was light-hearted, chatting about the band and music and how Sophie had grown in two months. Janice hadn't seen him like it for years, but she desperately wanted him to talk about America, tell her about Brooklyn so she could gauge whether or not she was a threat. She also wanted to know about the loans he'd mentioned, what he'd bought and why. He didn't mention either and she didn't ask.

She'd been hungry, the salad was good but not filling and she just did it, took chips off Eddie's plate. He'd saved the biggest, crispest chips until last, and she'd giggled and taken them. Janice thought herself too old to giggle, but tonight she was eighteen again.

Janice drew up outside Nan's house, got out of her car and smiled at the old motorbike rumbling quietly at the junction that led to the bypass. Just as she used to do all those years ago, Janice unlocked the door, switched on the light and waved. Eddie waved back, the engine note rose gently and he was gone.

The quickest way to Cedar Walk wasn't via the bypass, but hadn't been the quickest way to Gladstone Street either, Eddie simply liked riding the BSA along the bypass at night. Janice closed the front door and ran up the stairs to the back bedroom. One benefit of being tall was that she could see the slip road and the beginning of the bypass from her bedroom window. After a few seconds she saw the headlight of Eddie's motorbike appear from behind a row of houses. She heard the rumble change to a snarl, the big headlight dipping up and down as Eddie changed gear. Seconds later he was gone – was he eighteen again as well?

Eddie felt ashamed of himself, he was a man with 70mph eyesight in daylight so pushing the old BSA past 85mph at night was juvenile and stupid. No matter, he'd got away with it and would soon be home, two sets of traffic lights on a wide road then a sharp left into Cedar Walk. The first set of lights was red, Eddie stopped and put his right foot down to balance the bike. Moments later there was a 'boom, boom, boom' as two lads in a hot hatch drew up alongside him, stereo system pounding. They peered at the old BSA and sniggered, doubtless assuming it to be a museum piece. Perhaps it was, but big sixties motorcycles were still seriously quick.

Fuck it! Eddie was eighteen again, he wasn't going to be blown away by two shitheads. He'd slipped the bike into first gear as he'd come to a stop, now he put his left foot firmly on the rear brake and eased the clutch out until it bit. A touch of throttle, a firm pull on the front brake and the engine was straining against both brakes. Contrary to the highway code, Eddie watched the red light – waiting for the green light to come on rather than the red light to go out lost a split second. Alongside him driver shithead revved his engine furiously.

The red light faded, Eddie released the brakes, twisted the throttle and was off like a rocket. A touch on the clutch as the rev counter needle approached the red and he was into second, the needle sweeping round again. His museum piece would do 70mph in second, the shitheads were nowhere to be seen. Third gear and the second set of traffic lights were looming and red. Eddie braked to a halt and waited for the hot hatch to squeal to a halt alongside. Once was enough, Eddie smiled inside his helmet, raised his right hand and gestured the hot hatch forward as the lights changed to green. This eighteen was very different to the last one.

THE FARMHOUSE

Another nightmare, another morning in the workshop watching the dawn come up with Desmond for company and Eddie was struggling to remain positive. Yes, he hated the crushing tiredness and terrible loneliness of his old life, but it worked, he earned huge amounts of money and made good use of it. The terrors had gone away for the moment, but if they came back he could live with them. Being a pariah wasn't a major problem either, it was hard to remember when he hadn't been one.

The problem was Janice – could he live with being rejected by her again? Conversely, could he live with the guilt of being accepted by her knowing she deserved better? Could he live with the guilt of being disloyal to Jilly? Brooklyn said that moving on wasn't being disloyal, that closure would ease the guilt he felt. But how could he get closure, he'd lost his chance to say goodbye the night she died chasing Ray and Phil then stubbornly refusing to change his statement. Even if he could overcome these problems, did Janice love him? He didn't want her to accept him out of pity or misplaced loyalty, that would destroy both of them.

Eddie focussed his mind on business: his offer for the Methodist Chapel had been accepted and Bob and Ellie were already planning the expansion. The shop front of the workshop would be given over entirely to band equipment, and the antiques and collectables would be moved to the Chapel. Bob was a superb manager, and Ellie had an excellent business brain; together they were a redoubtable couple, Eddie was lucky to have them. Ellie had made it clear that Eddie's days in the workshop were over – no matter how hard or fast he worked, he could earn much more by dealing, so he was to 'go out and buy stuff for us to restore and sell'. The only work he was allowed to do was repairing the big PA and guitar amplifiers.

Carole had worked for Copeman & Partners, Solicitors, since the dawn of time. She was of indeterminate middle age, single, fiercely independent and exceptionally efficient. Unfairly, her very efficiency had militated against her being promoted, succeeding managers being eager to keep her in a position where she could mask their administrative deficiencies. Carole was tired of her job as a receptionist/secretary and desperate for promotion to secretary/PA. The only way it would happen was if Janice took over as Practice and Compliance Manager, thereby gaining her own office and secretary/PA.

Janice presently occupied a corner of the open plan administration room where partitions and filing cabinets were arranged to give the occupants a level of privacy. She would have preferred more privacy for the telephone call from Mr Copeman – at 2.30pm tomorrow she was to present herself in the boardroom to be interviewed for the post of Practice and Compliance Manager. Mr Copeman had given his usual supercilious laugh and confirmed that success in her final examinations was a prerequisite.

The telephone rang again as soon she replaced the receiver. This time it was Carole's slow grinding voice. "Janice, it's your boyfriend."

Carole had always referred to Eddie as her boyfriend and Janice's attempts to convince her to the contrary were always met with a knowing smile. Marrying Andy had made no difference – Carole didn't like him, referring to him as Mr Fox when transferring a call.

Eddie's controlled voice was unmistakable. "We've completed a day early, I get the keys tomorrow and I would like you to be the first to see it."

Janice knew where the farmhouse was, they'd detoured by it on their way to the cinema, her second proper date with a nervous Eddie who had no idea what film to choose. She'd suggested that they use her car – the red estate was too closely associated with Jilly.

In the bright midday sun the old house looked beautiful, the mellow limestone walls contrasting with the darker Collyweston slate roof. It had been terribly neglected, Janice could see holes in the roof, paint peeling from windows and doors, and guttering hanging drunkenly from rusting iron brackets. Despite the dereliction the house had an air of solidity and timeless serenity; she loved it. Eddie had cut back part of overgrown side lawn clearing a path to the side door, the imposing front door with its Georgian crescent fanlight had been sealed up for years.

There was no sign of him and Janice approached the side door with trepidation. In the four weeks Eddie had been back she'd alternated between wild optimism and total despair, and today was a despair day. The combined worry of her interview in the afternoon and meeting Eddie at lunchtime meant she'd hardly slept last night. Being awake had given her too much time to think – nothing had really changed, Eddie was still special and she was still a tall, thin girl with a big nose.

Janice was wearing the black business suit Roxy had persuaded her to buy. It was the most expensive item of clothing she'd ever bought and she felt self-conscious in it. She felt self-conscious in the other clothes Roxy had persuaded her to buy too. Andy's formula of short hair, drab colours and shapeless clothes allowed her to fade into the background. Roxy's formula of bright, fitted casual clothes and well-cut business suits made anonymity difficult.

Eddie answered the door to her knock wearing smart black trousers and a stylish cornflower blue shirt that matched his eyes. He was more nervous than she'd ever seen him, he seemed embarrassed, or worried, or something.

The side door opened directly into a large sitting-room with a flagstone floor and a wide inglenook fireplace. The room seemed to be full of doors leading to the front and back of the house, side rooms and a walk-in understairs cupboard. The kitchen was at the back of the house and had a cast iron kitchen range, a beamed ceiling, an external door to the right, and two internal doors to the left. The first door was tall and opened to reveal a narrow, twisting back staircase, the shorter door hid a wide pantry. Janice followed Eddie up the staircase to see contrasting bedrooms at the rear and front of the house. The rear ones were cottage like with low, beamed ceilings, whereas the front ones were grand with high ceilings and decorative plaster cornices. They descended the wide, creaking front staircase, peeped into the drawing room then walked through the dining room back to the sitting-room.

The house was a time warp, original fireplaces, wood panelling and Georgian cupboards and alcoves. Much of it must have been closed up for years; the faded and peeling wallpaper was from the thirties or forties. Eddie pulled away a couple of layers to expose Victorian paper, early Victorian, his knowledge or all things old was encyclopaedic. Janice was choked, with work the house would be absolutely beautiful, and it was a blank canvas, no memories, no ghosts, but for who?

Janice had spent last night worrying about Brooklyn, the girl in America. Eddie had talked about Chin and Ellen, and Lamarr and Maybelle Potts, but said very little about Brooklyn. Janice looked at Eddie in despair, he had no idea of fashion and even less of colour, there was no way he'd chosen the clothes he was wearing. The realisation was crushing: today he was going to be kind and let her down gently.

They had lunch on the patio, a weed-filled area of cracked concrete and uneven paving slabs outside the kitchen door. Eddie had placed a Georgian mahogany tilt top table and two Regency dining chairs in the centre and set it with good china. The sandwiches were Frankies' best, and he made Earl Grey tea in a china teapot. Janice was confused, why was he making such an effort, and why did he keep looking at her? She was close to tears, and would have to leave for her interview soon.

"Why all this!" Janice knew she'd snapped at him, but it was either that or burst into tears. "Who's it all for?"

The unreadable face that Janice was so used to seeing disappeared, Eddie was hurt and it showed. Then he opened his eyes wide and smiled sadly at her, just like he'd done in the horrible little room in Gladstone Street.

"I always was a fool." Eddie shrugged. "I assumed you liked Jane Austen, Georgian houses and Georgian furniture because you were Lizzie Bennet come to life." He paused. "And I hoped you might like me..." His voice tailed away.

"I do, but..." Hope replaced despair in an instant and Janice blurted out the question uppermost in her mind. "Who bought you those clothes?"

Puzzlement replaced the hurt on Eddie's face. "Roxy said I looked like a bag of washing, she sent me out with Gary..." He stopped as Janice began to cry.

"You have no idea of clothes and no colour sense, I thought you had another woman." She gulped out the words between sobs.

Eddie grabbed her hand. "Another woman!" The shock in his voice was obvious. "You thought I had another woman?"

He released her hand and hurried to something hidden in the long grass. A moment later he was standing in front of her almost stupefied with embarrassment.

"I had it made ..."

The grey slate house sign had 'Pemberley' engraved on it.

Eddie held it out to her. "Turn it over, there's engraving on the back too, I know I have no right to ask but..."

Janice turned the sign over and read the engraving with disbelief. "You don't mean ...?"

Eddie tried to smile. "I meant it when I gave you your locket and I mean it now." He paused, the smile gone.

But his eyes were still open, beautiful kind eyes that melted her inside just like they did all those years ago. Then Eddie was staring at his watch, the one she'd given him for his twenty-first birthday, the one with the engraving on the back that she'd meant too.

"Your interview, you've got to go for your interview. Promise me you'll come back as soon as it's over. Please!"

It was beyond belief, Eddie was pleading with her, she should be pleading with him, but she had to go, they'd worked hard together for thirteen years for this opportunity. And there was something else she had to do, something she should have done ages ago.

CHAPTER 17

Hard times again

THE ACCIDENT

It was always the same, if you'd had a really bad day at work and were desperate to get home the road would be blocked by a breakdown or accident. Dave glanced at his watch, six o'clock, he'd been crawling along the Canley bypass for over an hour. He could see blue lights flashing in the distance and an articulated lorry slewed across the road. Drivers were staring, twisting and lifting themselves in their seats to get a better view. Dave hated rubber-neckers at accident scenes, he would look straight ahead.

His bad day had started early, it was Sharon's birthday and he'd called in on his way to work as he'd made the effort to buy a present rather than post a cheque. He needn't have bothered, Sharon wasn't interested in his present, she was furious with him for finishing with Sue. On reflection, the two were very much alike and had become firm friends.

"What possessed you to choose that collection of weirdoes over Sue?" Sharon had prodded him despite knowing he hated being prodded. "She took the trouble to introduce you to some proper musicians, but you didn't want to know, did you?"

No, Dave didn't, he'd tried to be enthusiastic but playing cabaret music at cabaret volume to self-important worthies who were more interested in talking to each other than listening wasn't his thing. Dave didn't argue, it was her birthday, he'd bitten his tongue and gone to work.

Work started badly too, Vinnie Proctor was in prison, Chief Superintendent John Powers was under investigation for possible corruption, and Jerome Proctor, Bendigo Windsor and their friends were flexing their economic muscles against anyone who dare suggest they were fraudsters. That clearly included Dave, he'd lost two service contracts from companies owned by Proctor and Windsor.

The final straw came at lunchtime – Dave had gone home to collect some papers and found out why Sue hadn't returned his key, she'd spent the morning collecting her possessions and trashing his. An emergency locksmith had fitted new locks, but Dave was desperate to get home to assess the full extent of the damage.

Dave saw two ambulances race away from the scene and the traffic started to move. His resentment at the delay disappeared when he saw the state of the car embedded in the side of the lorry – the firemen had cut off the roof to free the occupants. Then he was angry with himself, his intention was to look straight ahead, but couldn't drag his eyes from the macabre scene. A further indication of how serious the accident was that an inspector was supervising the scene not a sergeant.

As he gained a clear view of the wreckage Dave's heart came into his mouth: he recognised the car as Janice's blue hatchback! He swung wide and pulled through the bollards, scattering several before squealing to a halt beside a police car standing with its doors open and lights flashing.

Inspector Grant Pithers stepped briskly over to him. "Sorry, Dave, I know you're a mate, but you can't stop here."

"The car, the blue hatchback, it belongs to a fried, a really good friend…"

Dave knew he was shaking, he felt sick and Grant's serious expression didn't help. "I'm sorry, Dave, he didn't make it, the impact was massive."

Grant had said 'He' not 'Her', Dave felt momentary relief and gulped hard before asking.

"Was there a passenger…"

Inspector Pithers beckoned to a sergeant clutching a clipboard and muttered to him. The sergeant glanced at the clipboard then at Dave.

"The driver Andrew Fox was certified dead at the scene." He paused before continuing. "His passenger Janice Fox is alive but badly hurt, she had to be cut out." The sergeant grimaced at his inspector. "Those idiot firemen didn't help, the bastards love blood and guts, they were joking about finding a severed foot on the floor."

A & E

Canley General Hospital's Accident and Emergency Unit had two rooms for relatives at opposite ends of the department. Dave was sitting in the blue room musing on whether this was coincidental or planned, whether there were occasions when relatives needed to be kept apart. He couldn't think of one, but then he couldn't think of anything much at the moment; the doctors trying to stabilise Janice had sent him away.

He wasn't feeling good about himself. As he'd rushed to his car, eager to escape the accident scene, a woman police constable had shouted to him.

"Mr King, wait a minute!" Dave had swung round, angry at being delayed. "Grant says you're a friend of Mrs Fox?" The WPC was clutching something heavy wrapped in a cloth. "Would you take this to her, she was asking for it, and do you know someone called Eddie?"

WPC Edison had comforted Janice at the scene whilst the paramedics were working on Andy. "She was confused and kept drifting in and out of consciousness, but she kept asking for Eddie and for her sign. She passed out before I could get his phone number, but I found this in the car."

She unwrapped a grey slate sign with 'Pemberley' engraved on it. She turned it over, read the words engraved on the back 'To Lizzie with love Fitzwilliam' and smiled ruefully.

"Her Eddie is obviously a romantic."

Dave had been puzzled. "Romantic…?"

WPC Edison had given him a pitying look. "Jane Austen's book 'Pride and Prejudice'? The hero and heroine are Fitzwilliam Darcy and Lizzie Bennet, and his estate is called Pemberley."

Dave should have known that Janice would want Eddie, he'd put the sign in his car and reached for his mobile telephone.

Dr Amelia Stone was good at her job and thrived on the adrenaline rush of A & E work. Unfortunately, her private life didn't have the same excitement, plain nurses in heavy shoes attracted more attention from the male doctors than her. Perhaps they couldn't stand the competition, envied her ability.

Her latest patient was stretching her ability, the injuries to her legs were very severe, particularly the right leg, and she'd lost a great deal of blood. To make it worse she was panicking, her pulse was racing and she was hyperventilating, making it difficult to stabilise her. She needed someone to calm her down whilst they were waiting for Mr Large, the consultant orthopaedic surgeon, to arrive.

She turned to a nurse. "Fetch Mr Film Star from the relative's room and get him to hold her hand or something, and someone will have to tell her that her husband's dead, we can't avoid it for ever, she keeps asking for him."

Dave's heart sank as he listened to Dr Stone, Janice needed an immediate operation but the surgeon had been delayed, his job was to keep her calm until Mr Large arrived.

Dr Stone consulted a file. "I assume Eddie is the husband, Andrew Edward Fox?"

"No." Dave shook his head. "He's Andy. Sorry, he was Andy. Oh shit! Anyway, Eddie's someone else, I phoned him and he's on his way."

Time for Dr Stone to shake her head, the girl was nothing special, although to be fair it was hard to look special strapped in a spinal board and neck brace, but she had a husband, Mr Film Star and a boyfriend.

Dave had made matters worse – one glance at Janice's legs and he'd turned away, sick to his stomach with shock. He made the feeble excuse that he had to ring Eddie again and walked away. He hadn't actually spoken to Eddie the first time, Ellie had answered the telephone, made sense of his gibberish and told him she would organise everything. What was there to organise? Her calm voice had told him.

"You're not talking to Eddie in that state, you'll frighten him to death. Bob will tell him what he needs to know and drive him to the hospital. I'll organise telling Mike and Roxy, her mother and sisters and anyone else who needs telling. I'll tell Sophie myself, she will be upset." She'd paused. "I assume you haven't contacted anyone yet?"

No, he hadn't, the only thing on his mind was getting Eddie there to take over the responsibility.

Janice knew she was panicking, everyone kept telling her to calm down, but why should she? In two hours she'd gone from having everything she'd ever dreamed of to nothing. When Eddie gave her the sign he was shaking, unable to say more than a few jumbled words. What she'd interpreted as stupefied embarrassment was nothing of the sort, it was fear. The unbelievable truth was that a man who would walk forward and fight armed maniacs without a backward glance was frightened she would hurt him!

She'd put the sign in her car and rushed off to her interview expecting a gruelling interrogation, the final hurdle after thirteen years of evening classes, examinations and grudging promotions. It wasn't, the partners were more interested in how well she knew Charlie than her ability to do the job. After ten minutes they'd handed her an offer letter with the sole proviso that she pass her final examinations.

Janice had signed the offer letter, handed it back and asked for the remainder of the afternoon off. She then telephoned Andy and told him he could have all the collateral in their house and all the contents if he went with her to a solicitors that afternoon to formalise their separation and start divorce proceedings. He agreed, but insisted on driving them there in her car. Once on the bypass he'd demanded the car as part of the deal; his had failed the MoT. She'd refused, it was the car Eddie had spent a pile of money on. Andy had been drinking, she could smell it in on his breath, and he was driving very fast trying to frighten her, then the lorry was in front of them.

At the last minute Andy swerved so that her side of the car would take the main impact. His attempt failed, a tyre burst with a loud bang and dragged the car round so that his side hit the lorry. What did it matter now, the hospital staff could be as reassuring as they liked, but she'd heard the fireman joke about the severed foot in the car. Dave had looked away white faced and shaking after a brief glance at the remains of her legs. She wanted him to come back so she could get him to stop Eddie coming, she didn't want him turning away like Dave had done.

Dr Stone was frustrated, the neck and spine X-rays for Mrs Fox had gone astray. If she could release her from the spinal board and neck brace and let her see for herself she still had two feet, she might calm down. Mr Film Star had been worse than useless, totally unable to hide his shock at the state of the girl's legs, hopefully the boyfriend would do better. At that moment the door flew open and an unimpressive figure in tee shirt and jeans appeared.

Janice heard Eddie's heels clicking on the tiled floor, he would look at her legs and be desperate to go like Dave. And she would let him go, it would be for the best, she would be no use to him as a cripple.

She heard a nurse whispering something and Eddie's controlled tones in reply but couldn't make out what they were saying. Why wouldn't they remove the neck brace, she wanted to see the damage for herself.

This couldn't be right, Eddie looked carefully at her legs with no sign of shock before ignoring the blood all over her face, leaning over and kissing her gently. Now he was holding her hand and smiling, looking rakish with smudges of blood on his cheek.

"I've lost a foot, I heard the firemen…"

Janice closed her eyes not wanting to see his expression change.

"Janice! Sweetheart! Open your eyes and look at me." Eddie's voice was soothing. "I have to admit your legs are a bit knocked about, but you definitely have two legs and two feet."

Janice opened her eyes slowly, the smile had faded a little, but still no shock or revulsion.

"Would I lie to you?"

"You would to protect me."

"Surely you can feel them, they must hurt like hell?"

The nurses had said that, but Janice had heard about people experiencing pain in amputated limbs. She heard Eddie talking quietly to a nurse; he'd hardly moved, he was still holding her hand, but she couldn't see his face.

His face was back, directly above hers and smiling. There was a glint in his eye, he seemed almost amused and was flexing the fingers on his right hand.

"Now, can you feel that?"

He was tickling her left knee, it wasn't a stab of pain or a nerve twitching, it was rhythmic tickling. As soon as she said yes, he was tickling her right knee. Then he was gently wiggling the toes on her left foot.

"Can you feel that?"

"Yes." Janice could hear the relief in her own voice as he moved to wiggle the toes on her right foot. It didn't matter that the pain was excruciating, she had two legs and two feet.

Eddie was looking at her again, the glint still in his eye. "Wiggling your toes would have been enough but I thought I'd have a feel of your knees while I had the chance."

"Eddie! Will you behave."

Eddie had never said anything even slightly risqué to her in all the years she'd known him, and he'd called her sweetheart! Janice heard herself laughing, overwhelmed by a mixture of relief and amazement. Eddie was laughing too, and the nurses were looking at the monitors with relief.

A LAST GOODBYE

Bob appeared a few minutes after Eddie, delayed by parking the car. Dave could have done with some company, but Bob had gone outside to answer his mobile telephone and hadn't reappeared. Janice had gone through to the operating theatre and Eddie was in the gents washing blood splashes off his jeans and tee shirt. Dave paced up and down the corridor outside the blue relatives' room, trying to pull himself together.

"Where's Eddie?"

Bob was back, closely followed by Deborah. His tone was sharp, surprised to see Dave by himself.

"He's in the gents washing off some blood splashes. Janice is in theatre, she's going to be OK. They were smiling and laughing..." Dave shook his head.

It was Deborah's turn to speak sharply. "Is Eddie OK?"

Dave looked surprised. "Of course he is, he's used to blood and guts, isn't he?"

Now what? Why were Bob and Deborah eying him with contempt.

Bob had gone to the gents to check on Eddie, and Dave was in the blue relatives' room feeling inadequate. Bob, Ellie and Deborah had found out where all relevant people were and appointed appropriate messengers to tell them the news. Mike was on a train to a taxation course in Edinburgh, Gary would get him to come back and meet him at the station. Roxy and Jim were on holiday, they would wait. Ellie was on her way to tell Sophie, and Hilda Lomax was babysitting so Jimmy could tell Barbie and Janice's sisters and bring them to the hospital if they wanted to come. Ellie would get Sophie to telephone Charlie, it would make her feel useful and mature.

"Now, your job!" Deborah was talking slowly and firmly. "Andy's mother is in the green relatives' room. Go and tell her what a great guy Andy was, how he was your best mate and can you do anything to help. Be convincing and make sure she stays in the green room well away from Eddie. Bob will keep a look out for Andy's brothers."

Deborah stared at Dave. "Which bay was Janice in?"

"The one on the left."

A grimace from Deborah. "Was she on one of those yellow spinal boards?"

Dave nodded. "Yes, with a neck brace and pads on either side of her head."

"Did she have blood in her hair and on her face?"

Dave wondered where this was going. "Yes, Eddie asked that. Why?"

"Jilly was in the same room on one of those boards with blood on her face and in her hair."

Bob returned looking worried, Deborah ushered Dave out of the door to find Mrs Fox then turned to him.

"How is he?"

"In control, as always…"

"And!" Silence from Bob. "Bob! Loyalty's all very well, but I can't help if I don't know."

"He's like he is after his nightmares, he's talking normally but it's like he's not there. If you didn't know you'd think he didn't care."

Deborah hung her head, Eddie had been like that when she, Jimmy and Stan Orton were screaming at him after Jilly had been killed. Then she thought he didn't care, now she knew he was hurting so bad he'd switched off. Eddie appearing in the doorway interrupted her thoughts, he looked normal, he sounded normal, completely in control.

"Has Andy's mother arrived?"

Deborah nodded slowly. "Yes, Dave's gone to…"

Eddie interrupted. "I'd better put in an appearance."

Bob was quicker than Deborah, grabbing Eddie's arm to stop him. "No! For Christ's sake she's just lost her son."

Eddie eyed him sadly. "I know, Bob, so she'll need someone to blame, someone to hate, it will make it easier for her."

Now Deborah was angry, particularly so because she knew Eddie was right. Blaming him, hating him had helped her get over Jilly's death. She pushed him fiercely towards a chair, then pushed him again, looking to Bob for support.

"Not this time." She shook her head. "You're not taking the blame this time, we won't let you."

Eddie refused to leave the hospital, even though he knew Janice would be in theatre for hours, so Bob had gone to fetch him a change of clothes. Before leaving he scoured the hospital vending machines and produced an Eccles cake and a cup of tea. Deborah watched Eddie eat and drink mechanically wondering what to do next. Suddenly he looked up and smiled, but he was looking through her as if she didn't exist.

Deborah knew she wasn't sensitive, her strength was practicality and realism, but everyone had their moments and this was hers.

"It was the same room, wasn't it? The one Jilly was in."

Eddie's eyes moved slowly back to her. "Yes."

"Could you sense she was there?"

A long, long pause before a single word. "Yes."

"Is she here now?"

Deborah didn't need an answer, Eddie was looking through her again. She couldn't feel anything, but then she hadn't been traumatised time and time again until she couldn't distinguish between hallucination from reality. She pretended to see, tried to put right the wrongs of five years ago.

"I think she wants to say goodbye…"

Mike arrived shortly before midnight and with Gary. By early morning it was clear that Janice was out of danger, although rambling and incoherent from the effects of the anaesthetic and morphine, and the nurse in charge insisted they go home to rest. For Eddie that meant the farmhouse – before leaving for her interview Janice had plucked some wildflowers from the garden and put them in a glass in the kitchen. Her simple gesture made the farmhouse their home and Eddie wanted to be there.

In any case he couldn't stay with Mike, he knew what would happen after a major shock. He was right, the terrors started almost as soon as his head hit the pillow, Jilly on a yellow spinal board crying out to him. He ran down dark corridors into bright lights time and again, with Jilly's cries becoming ever more desperate. Suddenly a change, Janice on the spinal board calling out to him and more dark corridors, more bright lights and he was running so fast he couldn't catch his breath. Now Janice's face was decaying like Jilly's did and he could hear screaming. The screaming was getting louder and louder, and there was a bright light in his face. He was awake, it was him screaming and the bright light was the bare light bulb hanging from the ceiling. Eddie closed his eyes, opened them again and stared at the glowing bulb. The images began to fade, but that couldn't be right – they should take ages to fade! Eddie looked round, the images were definitely fading, he could see Desmond eyeing him quizzically from his position curled up on a chair in the corner. Had he made his peace, had the terrors become simple nightmares? Eddie hoped so, nightmares were OK, even normal people had nightmares.

BETTY

Betty couldn't understand people who drifted aimlessly from job to job; she'd enrolled as a student nurse forty-five years ago and still loved nursing. A few months ago, she turned sixty and could have retired but chose not to, husband Norman had two years to retirement and there would be no pleasure being at home without him. Was she just lucky, choosing the right career and the right man? Probably, but she'd never been attracted to feckless charmers with Brylcreemed hair and false smiles. Betty smiled to herself, few people under forty would know what Brylcreem was; today that sort of man used hair gel. Her smile faded, both her sons-in-law used hair gel.

Working beyond sixty had its benefits, managers were keen to retain an experienced nurse and allowed her discretion with her work and shift patterns. Betty preferred long term nursing, it could be depressing with demanding, ungrateful patients feeling sorry for themselves, but mostly it was rewarding to work with appreciative patients struggling to recover from major trauma or illness.

Betty had gained her latest patient by default; other nurses had avoided her. Not that there was a problem with the girl, she fell firmly into the appreciative category, the problem was her boyfriend.

"Don't you know who he is?"

Yes, Betty did know who he was, she'd lived in Canley all her life and read the newspapers. She also knew who Neville Webster was and it didn't seem fifteen years since Yvonne Webster came screaming to her door after finding him hanging in the garage. Betty had run back with her but was too late. Normally she wouldn't have been, Betty had seen many potential suicides and knew the difference between a cry for help and a genuine attempt. Neville's was a cry for help, and he'd simply been unlucky, he was a heavy boy who'd used a strong rope that didn't stretch, placed the noose at the side of his neck and allowed too much slack. As a result, he broke his neck rather than slowly choking. Neville hadn't left a suicide note because he hadn't intended to kill himself, he knew what time his mother came home and had left the garage doors open to ensure she found him quickly.

The Websters were a timid, unworldly couple. They suspected that Neville was being bullied and had complained to his form master. He assured them that Broad Street didn't have a bullying problem and suggested that Neville make a greater effort with his fellow pupils. Neville's death shocked them into action, they questioned his friends, saw through their denials and determined to do something about it. They wrote an open letter to the Canley Herald, accusing the headmaster, his staff and the governors of gross negligence and named the ringleaders of the bullies. They didn't know Jerome Proctor owned the Canley Herald and his friend Bendigo Windsor owned the company John Webster worked for. A writ for libel was followed closely by a redundancy notice and the Websters were a broken couple. Betty was Yvonne Webster's confidante at this dreadful time and tried to persuade her to fight for justice, but the Websters had two other children to support and no fight left. Proctor offered a deal, a job many miles from Canley and withdrawal of the writ if they signed a retraction, and they took it.

A year later Doreen Morris came screaming to her door, two suicides in one street and one nurse to call on for help before an ambulance arrived. Betty read Juliet's letters and saw they contained the same facts the Websters had been compelled to retract. Juliet also named Eddie Stagg as a hero, the only person who'd tried to help. Betty never read the Canley Herald again, preferring the dispassionate voice of the Advertiser.

Betty didn't know Stephen Napier, but she would have recognised his hanging himself as a cry for help not a serious attempt to kill himself. Unlike Neville Webster, Stephen used a rope that stretched, placed the noose at behind his head and only fell a short distance. His father found him before he choked to death and his only lasting physical injury was a scar around his neck. Like his father, Stephen was short and round but without his father's charisma. Sir Charles thought that an expensive boarding school would be the making of his son, but instead, merciless bullying drove him to attempt suicide. It was a rude awakening for Charlie, not just the shocking realisation that he did not understand his son, but the realisation that his influence was as nothing when the culprits were the sons of an Earl, an impossibly rich merchant banker and an MP. When he met Eddie in HM Prison Padmoor, he was looking for a cause where his influence would count, and found it.

Following problems with staff performance some years ago, Betty was co-opted onto a review panel charged with examining in depth recent appointments of auxiliary nursing and cleaning staff. She found several instances of fake qualifications and fictional glowing references. Dismissing the worst offenders didn't cause her any heart searching as they were both unreliable and incompetent. However, she also found two girls with references and job histories that appeared genuine but were unusually alike. Betty went back through previous years and found two more girls with similar references and job histories. Unlike the fakers who had been dismissed, all four girls were reliable, hard working and eager to please, so Betty kept her suspicions to herself and talked to the girls informally. Eventually they told her about the man who'd rescued them from an appalling life, found them a place to live, provided plausible references and job histories and never asked for anything in return.

NOT MY BOYFRIEND

Saturday afternoon, not everyone's choice of shift, but as Norman had gone to the football, Betty had volunteered. It was a busy shift, Canley General's visiting hours were 2pm to 4pm and 6pm to 8pm, and at weekends visitors came in droves. Thankfully Betty's ward was relatively quiet, long-term patients had fewer visitors. Her first call would be on her new patient, a girl who'd hesitantly asked Betty to change the name on her notes from Mrs Fox to Miss Newton and kept a house sign in her bedside cabinet. Unfortunately, Janice was in tears, a total change from yesterday, but mood swings were common with patients on high doses of morphine.

"Isn't your lovely boyfriend here yet?" Betty tried to sound cheerful.

"Do you mean Eddie?"

Betty smiled. "Well, how many lovely boyfriends do you have?"

"Eddie's not my boyfriend, he's my best friend, but not my boyfriend."

It had been different for Janice in A & E, her decision to tell Eddie to go away had evaporated when he smiled and held her hand. Since then, she'd had time to think – Eddie deserved better than a tall, thin girl with a big nose and shattered legs. When he visited yesterday, she'd told him to go away and make a life for himself.

"You've not had an argument, have you?" The concern in Betty's voice was touching and Janice was in tears again.

"I'm going to be a cripple, Betty, I told him to go away."

"Well, you're a silly girl, but I don't think he'll take any notice."

"It's five past two and he's not here…"

Betty looked round; someone was running along the corridor. Running was not allowed in Canley General corridors and Betty drew herself up to issue a reprimand. Moments later, Eddie skidded to a halt outside the door, clutching a box of chocolates.

Betty sniffed. "You may be late but I'll have no running in my corridors." She smiled at Janice, then looked sternly at Eddie. "We're a bit upset today."

Mr Large had inserted metal plates in Janice's legs and they were both raised in splints until the wounds healed, giving severely restricted movement. Eddie would hate it, he hated being restricted and hated having his head below the level of his legs even more. Janice needed her backrest raising; he would ask Betty.

"You'll have to lift Janice first." As Eddie stared at her, Betty gazed skywards in the universal gesture of despair. "Lean forward, get Janice to put her arms round your neck then lift gently. Support her with your right arm round her back and move the backrest with your left."

Betty paused in the doorway, the lifting process had come to a halt, they were staring at each other and holding their breath.

"Eddie! Janice! You've got to breathe."

No response. Betty sighed and left; love was a powerful emotion, but it rarely led to asphyxia.

Early visiting was over and Betty found Eddie waiting for her at the nurse's station. "I wanted to thank you for being so nice to Janice, but it would be best if you stopped being nice to me because…"

Betty interrupted. "Because you're Canley's very own violent maniac Eddie Stagg?" Betty smiled and continued. "But if I stopped being nice to you, your girls would never talk to me again!" Her smile went. "I know who you are, I helped cut Neville Webster down when he hanged himself. I comforted Doreen Morris when she found Juliet, and I read her letters." She paused. "There are at least four of your girls working here, I persuaded them to trust me, and they told me all about you."

Late visiting was over and Betty was looking forward to going home to a good home cooked meal. Like many men of a certain age, Norman had taken to fancy cooking, all very well, but it took him forever to prepare a meal, which meant Betty had time to look in on Janice before going home. She knew Janice and Eddie hadn't died of asphyxiation – the last time Betty looked in, they were talking and Janice had put on some lipstick.

The corridors were quiet with the visitors gone, so Betty would spend a few minutes with Janice rather than disturb Norman in the throes of a cooking marathon; instead, she would arrive as he was about to dish up.

"How are we now then?"

The dazzling smile came as a bit of a shock, dazzling smiles were rare from those incapacitated after major surgery.

"I'm very well, thank you, Betty."

"And how's your lovely boyfriend?"

"Do you mean Eddie?"

Betty smiled, this was going to be a running joke. "Well, how many lovely boyfriends do you have?"

"Eddie's not my boyfriend, he's my fiancé."

CHAPTER 18

A second chance

THE LOCKET

"I love you, Eddie."

Apparently the most popular time to die of natural causes is between three and four in the morning. Perhaps popular wasn't the right word – death and popularity were not obvious bedfellows – but Eddie knew what he meant, it was the time when the human body reached its lowest ebb. Eddie had done much of his thinking between three and four in the morning, woken by nightmares, too tired to start work but too frightened to go back to sleep. Brooklyn said he shouldn't make important decisions when he was tired, frightened and alone, and she was probably right. However, one decision he'd made in the middle of the night a few weeks ago was right: he must tell Janice he was half mad, a monster and a killer, before declaring his love for her.

However, the four words he thought he'd heard Janice say took away the little sense he had. He was holding her, trying to rearrange her pillows and lift her backrest at the same time, and she just said it. He remembered staring at her like an idiot for a few seconds before telling her he loved her too and always had.

Eddie couldn't dissuade her, she dismissed his years of fighting, battering and maiming with a shrug. He took a deep breath and went for the big one, describing the fight in the grubby hotel room, the fat man dead on the floor and how he would have killed Weasel if Brooklyn hadn't screamed. Her response was incredible, she was more concerned about his relationship with Brooklyn than the fact he was a killer.

"I don't care if you've laid waste to half of America so long as you love me."

Then he remembered her tears at the farmhouse when she thought he had another woman. He didn't, he wouldn't, he couldn't!

Then euphoria took over, he was on his knees looking for a lipstick she'd dropped, he looked up at her, took her hand and proposed. She was speechless but nodded her head and they just stared at each other. Within minutes guilt and depression almost overwhelmed them both, bleak memories of wasted years and the prospect of universal condemnation. Andy wasn't even in his grave and the vile, baseless rumours that he'd been disloyal to Jilly would all resurface.

As a responsible manager, Deborah didn't abuse Canley City Council's flexitime scheme. To the contrary, she did more than her fair share of early mornings, late afternoons and delayed lunch breaks, but today she'd finished early, she wanted to visit Janice before Eddie arrived. On the surface, Eddie was as controlled, emotionless and unreadable as ever, but her new insight made her think he was worried and confused. In contrast, Mike was trying to be controlled and unreadable, but couldn't hide the fact he was pleased about something. Deborah guessed what had happened but needed to know for certain, and repentance was good for the soul.

"When you were in the operating theatre I spoke to Eddie." Deborah paused; this was difficult. "At first he was rambling and hallucinating, seeing things I couldn't see, but afterwards he talked to me." She stared at the floor. "Jilly always said he was a kind boy who would do anything, take terrible risks to protect his girls. I didn't believe her, I was convinced he was a monster, I could always feel an undercurrent of repressed violence in him." She raised her head. "That night Eddie was frightened, not for himself but for you, it wasn't that obvious but I'm getting better at reading people since I learned about body language. Anyway, the awful thing is that it was the same undercurrent I've always felt; it's not repressed violence, it's fear, Eddie's frightened all the time and deliberately messes up his body language to hide it." She gave an embarrassed laugh. "The man I've hated and feared for years is just a frightened boy. I told Roxy and she laughed, she's always known. I'm ashamed of myself, Janice, please tell me you're together so I can be happy for you."

Janice didn't reply, instead she reached into her bedside locker and took out her locket. "Do you recognise this?"

"Yes, it's your Nan's pendant, it's beautiful."

Deborah had never seen Janice without it, but it must have been damaged in the accident, the top loop was bent and the large central blue stone was twisted in its mount.

Janice shook her head. "It wasn't my Nan's and it isn't a pendant; it's a locket, Eddie gave it to me for my twenty-first birthday." She smiled sadly. "He loved me then, but I didn't know; I loved him but pretended I didn't because I wanted him to find someone special. When I met Andy and let him take my place in the band, it hurt Eddie so much he fell out of love with me. It was before he met Jilly, he was never disloyal to either of us."

Deborah gripped her hand. "Does he love you now?"

"Yes."

"Do you love him?"

"I've loved him since I was seventeen, I told him two days ago and he couldn't believe it. I persuaded him it was true, and he proposed. Now he's full of guilt, he thinks that everyone will hate us."

Deborah shook her head. "Not those that matter."

Delancy's the Jewellers kept late hours. Young Mr Delancy, a man of around fifty, showed little surprise when Deborah produced Janice's locket and asked to speak to Mr Delancy Snr. Janice didn't want Eddie to know the locket had been damaged and Deborah had offered to take it to be repaired. Apparently, Mr Delancy Snr had made a point of serving Janice personally on the few occasions she'd visited the shop and suggested Deborah ask for him.

Mr Delancy Snr appeared quickly and asked sharply.

"Could you tell us who you are and where you got this jewel?"

Deborah was startled by his intensity but replied, "I'm Deborah Orton, my friend Janice asked me to bring it in, she's been in an accident."

"Ah!" Mr Delancy gave a sigh of relief. "I do apologise for my tone. I believe Miss Newton is recovering well from her injuries?"

Odd, how did Mr Delancy know Janice wanted to be known as Miss Newton, not Mrs Fox? He continued quickly with a statement that was almost a challenge.

"But then Eddie is caring for her and he is a very caring young man, despite his reputation." As Deborah nodded her agreement, he smiled. "I repaired and engraved this jewel for Eddie many years ago, I will repair it myself and reset all the stones, not just the sapphire." He peered myopically at her. "Good quality stones deserve good, firm mounts."

"I thought the stones were paste."

Mr Delancy seemed quite shocked. "Goodness me, no! Eddie would have no truck with paste for Miss Newton, the diamonds are unexceptional, but the sapphire is a particularly fine Ceylonese example."

Young Mr Delancy left, flicking down the closed sign and locking the door behind him. Mr Delancy Snr prised open the locket and carefully placed the two photographs inside it in an envelope which he sealed and handed to Deborah.

"I think Miss Newton would like to have these with her." He smiled ruefully. "Alice told me about the accident, but we hope some good will come of it."

"Alice?"

"I beg your pardon, I assumed you knew that Alice Popplewell is my sister. She's mentioned your name, I believe you are doing voluntary work in West Town with Miss Bailey." Mr Delancy paused and took a deep breath. "I was not surprised when she told me that Eddie had saved the West Town Walk-in Centre from closure." His tone took on a bitter edge. "Not that he will ever get any credit for it, or for any of his other projects in West Town, he would be an extremely wealthy young man if he didn't give most of his money away."

He explained: "Eighteen months ago, Canley City Council's Environmental Health Department inspected the kitchens and day rooms at the Walk-in Centre and served an Improvement Notice on the leaseholder, the St Nicholas Church Ladies Charity. It was a scam, some corrupt council members wanted to force the closure of the Centre so their paymasters Proctor and Windsor could buy the lease at bargain price, demolish the building, build a block of flats and make a fortune. Their plan was thwarted at the last minute when someone outbid them, completely renovated the property and leased it back to Alice and her ladies with no increase in the rent. Philanthropists are very rare in West Town, so Alice asked our nephew who is a solicitor to try and identify the buyer. A long and convoluted search eventually led to Agamemnon Properties, a division of SIKO (Canley) Ltd, which is Eddie."

A VISITOR FROM AMERICA

Mr Large authorised the removal of the splints from Janice's legs and the indignities of immobility were over. Afterwards he told her as sympathetically as he could that, despite his best efforts, she was likely to be around an inch shorter than before the accident. He had no idea that throughout her teenage years she'd gone to bed each night hoping that something, anything might happen to make her a little less tall. The downside was that her right leg was now shorter than her left, a permanent limp was inevitable.

Tomorrow she would start physical rehabilitation, basically learning to walk again. Mental rehabilitation had already started, Canley General had a trauma counselling unit for patients and close relatives. Janice had been offered counselling after seeing Eddie's fight with Vinnie and the others thirteen years ago, but she wasn't particularly traumatised then or now. Conversely, Eddie was traumatised then and now, but boyfriends, particularly those condemned as brutal streetfighters, didn't qualify.

Afternoon visitors had become fewer as the days passed but it didn't matter, Eddie came every evening, always staying until the last minute.

"You've got a visitor." Betty put her head round the door. "Not someone I've seen before, a nice young lady called Brooklyn?"

Betty disappeared before Janice could question her. Panic set in, everything had been going so well that Janice had almost forgotten about Brooklyn. Why had she come, had she already seen Eddie? No more the meek and frightened Janice, Eddie was hers and she would fight for him, there was no way she would greet this girl lying on a bed. Janice struggled to the edge of the bed and tried to stand up, clinging to the bed rail for support. The effort was too much, darkness started to close in, she saw movement then everything was black.

The girl was strong, she caught Janice, picked her up bodily and placed her gently on the bed. Everything beyond the girl's concerned smile was a blur, and why was she calling her 'Janith'? Janice tried to sit up and the girl moved forward to help. She wasn't small and pretty as Janice had imagined, she was tall, heavily built and, even without the lisp, reminded her of Juliet.

"You look as though you've seen a ghost?"

Janice had seen a ghost, and laid another. Brooklyn spoke slowly, her voice a curiously soothing mixture of Essex English, American drawl, speech training and a struggle with her speech impediment.

"Eddie's not here, he..."

Brooklyn interrupted. "Good, I came to see you, not Eddie."

Brooklyn was in England with Lawrence laying her own ghosts, visiting her mother's grave and attempting a reconciliation with her family. She'd been partially successful – her father and brother were cold and dismissive, but her sister was desperate to regain contact. Whilst in England she'd decided to seek out Janice for a specific purpose, she was considering a permanent career change back to trauma counselling and wanted to meet the girl who would know if her counselling had helped Eddie.

"I haven't got long, Lawrence is waiting outside in the car, I told him I'm visiting an old friend."

"How did you know where to find me?"

"Carole, your PA." Brooklyn smiled broadly. "She must be a very good friend as well as a colleague, I had to jump through every hoop in the world before she would tell me anything."

Janice was still puzzled. "But how..."

"E-mail, your home computer is set up so all unanswered mail is forwarded to your office."

"Those weeks with Eddie were a nightmare for both of us." Brooklyn shivered. "I tried to put his head back together, but I could only scratch the surface."

"You did something, the Eddie that came back was different, less haunted..." Janice gave a bleak smile. "I think you've found your niche."

Brooklyn looked guilty. "Did he tell you about the fight?"

Janice whispered backm "He told me he killed one of them, he said he had no choice."

"He didn't, they had knives, they would have killed us both." She shook her head with disbelief. "It was all over in seconds, I got the impression that the only difference between that fight and all the others was that someone died." She looked away and missed the shock on Janice's face.

THE SILVER HATCHBACK

The red estate car had let Eddie down again, another obscure electrical fault draining the battery overnight. Perhaps it was a hint to change the car – the red estate would always be associated with Jilly, it wasn't fair on Janice to keep it.

Others were clearly having similar thoughts, Dave's telephone call sounded rehearsed.

"I'm not touting for business but I know you're busy and probably don't have time to look round ..."

Dave was a good guy but not particularly sensitive, someone must have primed him, probably Mike. It didn't matter, whoever it was had got it right and Dave was being generous, Eddie could have any car he had in stock at trade price, and he would take the red estate in part exchange.

"Thanks, Dave, but I don't want the red estate to stay in the area..."

"Yes, I can understand that." Dave sounded genuinely concerned, perhaps he was more sensitive than Eddie gave him credit for. "We go to an auction in Doncaster regularly, I'll make sure it's sold there, not locally."

Air-conditioning, electric windows and a CD player, cars had changed a great deal since Eddie had bought the red estate. Janice suggested he buy a hatchback, SIKO now had two vans and another strong young man to help Bob in the workshop so could transport anything bulky for Eddie. SIKO was expanding rapidly, the purchase of the Methodist Chapel was complete, and Eddie was delegating more and more to the reliable and indefatigable Bob and Ellie.

A crisp October evening, Eddie had left Janice talking to Betty and was driving home along the Eltham Road. The transition from the Lower Eltham Road to the Upper Eltham Road was marked, the untidiness and neglect that characterised the fringes of West Town giving way to open countryside dotted with substantial dwellings. The farmhouse was definitely a substantial dwelling. Eddie tried to be dispassionate but had to admit he got a buzz parking in the drive, knowing it was his.

Chuck Berry was singing 'Johnny B Goode' on the CD player as Eddie rounded the bend that revealed the farmhouse. One look and knew something really bad was about to happen. Why did bad things so often follow good things and really horrible things follow really good things? Life was really good so something really horrible was probably imminent.

There were two cars parked immediately outside the farmhouse. The first was obviously a police car with chequered paintwork, headlights blazing and blue lights flashing. The second was unmarked apart from a single blue light flashing on the roof. Eddie tried to be calm, he drew up slowly, pulled into the drive and was surrounded by three uniformed officers as soon as he opened the car door. All three were wearing high visibility jackets and stab vests, two were gripping large batons with side handles, the other pointing a Taser at him. Two others in plain clothes stood behind them, the shorter of the two wearing a very expensive looking camel overcoat.

Camel overcoat man wasn't local, his accent was South of England with a serious public school affectation.

"I am Detective Chief Inspector Marcham." He flashed a warrant card at Eddie. "Are you Edward George Alonzo Stagg?" Eddie nodded. "Then I am arresting you on suspicion of complicity in the murder of Duane Edward Altman. You're not obliged to say anything unless you wish to do so, but it may harm your defence if you do not mention when questioned something which you later rely on in court. Do you understand the caution?"

For a moment Eddie had hope, he'd never heard of Duane Edward Altman and said so. The second plain clothes officer, a tall friendly looking man, spoke out of turn.

"Better known as Big Eddie…"

Inspector Marcham silenced his sergeant him with a fierce look and Eddie was expressionless.

CHAPTER 19

Back from the brink

REVENGE OF THE RED ESTATE

Dave met the pizza delivery man at the showroom entrance. It was hard to determine who was the most surprised, Dave or the pizza man on his moped as Dave didn't like pizza that much and the delivery man was clearly uneasy about delivering to a closed car showroom. Work was no substitute for pleasure, but home and the Golf and Squash Clubs had lost their attraction. His splendid new house at Eltham was precisely that, a house not a home, and Dave was unhappy with the attitude of most fellow Club members. So what if John Powers diverted resources from scumbags in West Town to protect decent people! So what if Vincent Proctor had slapped a couple of tarts about and snorted a bit of coke! So what if Jerome Proctor had greased a few palms to get contracts and there had been a few dubious insurance claims! From the few brief conversations he'd had with Eddie, Dave knew it was much more than that, it was widespread major corruption, but he and Sir Charles Napier were being obstructed at every turn.

Now his office smelled of pizza, and spreadsheets showing a successful business had lost their attraction. Dave climbed wearily into his car, he wouldn't visit Sharon tonight, he would cut straight through to the Upper Eltham Road and home. If the lights were on in Eddie's farmhouse he might stop briefly and ask about Janice.

The Canley Central Police Station cell was depressingly familiar, but this time Eddie couldn't complain about his treatment, DCI Marcham had done everything by the book. He and his big Sergeant made an interesting team, fast track career professional supported by down to earth human being. The Custody Sergeant was busy, so a young constable had relieved Eddie of his belt and shoelaces and locked him in a cell. Apparently, DCI Marcham had enquiries to complete before interviewing him.

Eddie thought hard, Marcham's words were 'suspicion of complicity in the murder of Duane Edward Altman', and his sergeant had said 'better known as Big Eddie'. A flood of relief washed over Eddie as he realised this was nothing to do with the fight in the New York hotel room. He wasn't complicit in that murder, he'd bashed the fat man's head in with a chair, and he was Fat Eddie not Big Eddie. Eddie felt himself grinning like an idiot; that had to stop, he was still in some sort of trouble.

Thirty minutes later the young constable brought Eddie a mug of tea, eying him warily as he handed it over.

He paused in the doorway. "I expected you to be bigger." He paused. "You look sort of ordinary, are you really him?"

Eddie replied with a question. "What's Marcham like?"

The constable hesitated and looked round before replying. "Detective Chief Inspector Marcham and Sergeant Price are from Headquarters, Marcham's one of the graduate fast track lot." He hesitated. "But he's straight enough not like some…"

He stopped abruptly as he heard footsteps in the corridor. Moments later Sergeant Price's big frame filled the doorway, Marcham was ready to interview him.

Eddie was familiar with the routine, two sealed tapes unwrapped and placed in the Neal tape recorder. Switch on, wait seven seconds for the warning siren to finish, all persons present to identify themselves and a repeat of the caution. Did he want a solicitor, a Duty Solicitor could be provided free of charge? No, he wanted to know what he was supposed to have done. Eddie felt curiously relaxed, this time he hadn't done it, whatever it was.

Marcham's interview technique was straightforward, no good cop bad cop silliness or attempts to lure Eddie into making false statements.

"Yesterday evening at around 9pm two men were talking in North Street, Stanford when a red estate car mounted the pavement and ran both men down. One man, Duane Edward Altman, died of his injuries at the scene. The second, Raymond Powers, was seriously injured and is presently in hospital under police guard."

Eddie struggled to assimilate the facts. He didn't know Altman but, of course, he knew Ray Powers.

Marcham continued his unemotional explanation. "Raymond Powers identified the car as being identical to one owned by you and that the hooded man at the wheel was your size and build. An eyewitness stated that Altman had his back to the approaching car and Powers was facing it. As Powers tried to run, his legs collapsed under him, otherwise he may well have avoided the car." Eddie nodded, that was doubtless the leg he'd injured during the fight outside The Heron.

"Our enquiries show that you left Canley General Hospital shortly after 7.30pm?" Eddie nodded again. "For the purposes of the tape, Mr Stagg nodded in agreement. Which would give you ample time to drive to Stanford and mount this attack."

"I sold the red estate a week ago."

Disbelief from Marcham. "Who to?"

"Kings of Canley, I dealt with the owner Dave King…"

Marcham interrupted, clearly annoyed. "Would that be the Dave King who's been banging on our front desk and making phone calls for the past half hour?"

He paused as the interview room door opened and he was handed a message. Marcham read it quickly and grimaced before continuing.

"Where were you at 9pm yesterday evening?"

"At Robert Stephenson Comprehensive School."

Eddie had left Janice early, picked up Sophie and a load of band equipment in a SIKO van and driven to the school. He'd hired the school hall for the first rehearsal of 'The Retro 5'; Sophie, Mark and three friends had formed a band. His alibi was cast iron, but innocent people shouldn't have to provide alibis.

A knock on the door heralded another message. Marcham scrutinised it carefully before looking up.

"Your solicitor, Stephen Napier, has arrived and insists on seeing you immediately." He scanned the earlier message again. "And Sir Charles Napier QC left an earlier message stating that he would personally review all paperwork to ensure total compliance with the provisions of PACE."

Stephen's brusque assertiveness startled Eddie as much as Marcham, there wasn't a shred of hard evidence to connect Eddie with the hit and run incident other than the well documented animosity between him and Powers. If Marcham attempted to hold or question Eddie further, he would risk action for false arrest. Within minutes Stephen and Dave were leaving, and Eddie was waiting for his belt and shoelaces. Marcham told them that a police car would take Eddie home.

"This is off the record." Eddie, Marcham and the big Sergeant were alone in the Custody Suite. "Are you happy with that?" Eddie nodded, still surprised by Marcham's open hostility. "Myself, Sergeant Price and my team have gone through your vile past. Whilst you may not have personally run down Altman and Powers, I do not accept you had nothing to do with it. When I arrested you, I said 'complicity in the death of Altman'…"

Eddie interrupted. "Off the record or on the record, I had nothing to do with it."

Sudden anger from Marcham. "Just as you didn't attack Powers and Windsor outside the Heron Public House four years ago?"

Eddie's reply was slow and controlled. "Twelve good men and true decided that they attacked me."

A sneer and a change of subject. "You're a familiar face in West Town, aren't you? In fact, so familiar that some say you run West Town!"

"I don't." Eddie couldn't see where this line of questioning was going.

"You batter and maim anyone who gets in your way!" Marcham thrust his head forward. "You're a violent gangster, or at best a vigilante and I don't like vigilantes, I didn't like Charles Bronson in Death Wish, and I don't like you."

The atmosphere was icy, Eddie wasn't interested in Marcham's opinion of him, but Sergeant Price was different. He turned to him with a benign smile.

"You're a family man, aren't you, Sergeant?" Price gave a puzzled nod as Eddie inspected a suspicious patch on the front of his jacket. "My eyes aren't great, but my nose is pretty good, a child's been sick on you. A child, not a baby, babies put it on your shoulder or down your back; boy or girl?"

Sergeant Price beamed. "Girl."

Eddie's tone changed, instantly hard and uncompromising. "What would you do if some pimp plied your daughter with alcohol and drugs then sold her over and over again to any pervert who would pay? Form an action committee, write to your MP, tell the local police when you know for a fact they will do nothing about it if you came from West Town? Or would you batter the bastard senseless to make sure he and others like him never showed their face in West Town again?"

He stopped abruptly, the smell of the patch on Sergeant Price's jacket reminded him that only a year ago a startled Dave watched as Sophie clung to him in floods of tears then vomited down the front of his shirt. In a few months she would be fourteen, the age Roxy was when she ran away from her children's home and fell into Jed's clutches. Eddie had no conscience about what he'd done to Jed and men like him, Roxy and many of the other girls were children and those men had shown them no mercy.

Marcham construed Eddie's silence as weakness and snapped. "Don't insult me with trite justification, I've read the local intelligence reports, you've left carnage everywhere you've been." He shook his head. "God knows how you've got away with it, but this time you won't…"

He took a pace forward, jabbing his finger, spluttering with rage. Eddie's response was as fluid as ever, he turned side on, weight moving onto his toes, hands moving up to his chest. Price and Marcham went into slow motion, it seemed ages before Price lurched forward to protect Marcham, his face a mask of concern. In contrast ,Marcham moved backwards, fear on his face as he reached for the panic button. Eddie was ahead of them, Sergeant Price saw his second movement and dragged his Inspector's hand away.

"For Christ sake, sir, he's put his hands in his pockets."

Eddie sneered. "I wasn't going to hit you, I just wanted to see what would happen if I threatened to." He pointed contemptuously at Marcham. "You with all your mouth went backwards and your sergeant moved forward to protect you."

Marcham stuttered as he spoke. "If I'd pressed that button this room would have been full of officers in thirty seconds."

"In thirty seconds I could put both of you down and hurt you so badly you wouldn't get up again." Eddie stared at Marcham. "But I don't hurt fools..." He turned to Price. "... and I certainly don't hurt honest family men." He shrugged. "Yes, I've hurt perverts, pimps, drug pushers and their minders, but if your lot had been there to protect the girls I wouldn't have had to." He pointed at Marcham but spoke to Price. "He cannot grasp the fact that records and reports are only as good as the people who write them. If they are written by bent coppers or weak ones looking the other way to safeguard their pensions, they can be rubbish. I bet neither of you has set foot outside this station apart from going to arrest me. I suggest you take a walk round West Town, see for yourself there are no CCTV cameras and no police patrols. Talk to the locals, to Alice Popplewell who runs a charity at the Walk-in Centre, to Jim Lutkin who runs a boxing charity trying to stop youngsters fighting on the streets, to Roxanne Bailey the Coordinator for the Canley Confederation of Children's Charities and her boss Gerry Burchnall OBE. Then try to explain how Powers, Proctor and Windsor have got away with fraud and corruption for years without collusion from police bosses, council bosses and God knows who else. You need to do more than read falsified paperwork if you want the truth." He paused then added. "And despite supposed supervision by external officers, how did the DVDs seized during the raid on Vincent Proctor's home end up being inadmissible because of damaged seals? And why was the VHS video tape found at the scene never examined? And why are the Proctor and Windsor families so desperate to have them all returned, what secrets are they hiding?"

HOME TRUTHS

For Sharon, life didn't begin at forty, it was the beginning of the end. She'd been dwelling unhappily on her forthcoming birthday and yesterday's staff appraisal had brought matters to a head. Her new boss was thirty-two, female and had written 'Sharon is a competent worker with years of good service ahead of her' at the foot of the appraisal form. Damned by faint praise indeed, where had the glowing words of years ago gone 'young, thrusting, dynamic?'. Or was Sharon deluding herself, she hadn't even got an interview for the post of Coordinator to the CCCC.

"They gave the job to that tart Roxy. I complained, I couldn't believe she'd fulfilled the essential criteria on the Person Specification. They told me the selection process was scrutinised by the City Council and pulled my application to pieces, they made me look stupid."

This was a Sharon Dave hadn't seen before, the confidence that bordered on arrogance had gone. He had no idea she'd applied for the Coordinator's job and could feel the double blow to her confidence, being refused an interview then finding Roxy had been appointed. Dave had been on a high, proud of his part in securing Eddie's release from custody. He wanted to tell someone, Sharon was convenient and he hadn't noticed her depression.

For the first time in years, they were talking instead of arguing and the biggest shock was that she still loved Kenny, Sophie's father.

"I always thought he'd come back, and if Sophie was beautiful and talented he'd stay."

A new perspective on Sharon was opening, insecurity fuelling a desperate need to be popular and successful, and a growing fear she was neither.

"I hate that man." She spat the words out. "He's battered and horribly injured people since he was at school, anyone else would be in prison but not him! He's got everything, money, influence, powerful friends and my daughter. Then you come here and boast about helping the psychopathic bastard."

There was more than a grain of truth in what Sharon was saying. For the past year Dave had tried hard to like Eddie, see the good in him, but couldn't. It wasn't about jealousy, the fact that Jilly and Janice loved him, or his amazing commercial success, he simply didn't like the man. Others might be able to look at him and not see someone capable of appalling violence, but Dave couldn't.

Sharon moved on, talking about the injustice of giving a man like Eddie a brain. "I know he's clever, too bloody clever, unnaturally clever. And he's a good teacher too, I've seen him with Sophie and Janice, doing their coursework for them." She shrugged. "I know you think I'm hard on Sophie, but she's not clever, above average perhaps, but definitely not clever." Sudden anger. "He tells her she's beautiful and clever. But she's not, she's plain and ordinary, that fool has given her unreal expectations and one day she'll realise what she really is, fall flat on her face and be miserable."

Dave protested. "But the Hay commendation certificate…"

"That was him, for Christ sake, Professor Hay recognised Eddie's style, he wanted to find the mad genius…"

The problem with false allegations was that, on occasion, it could be difficult or impossible to prove they were not true. Eddie was in no way complicit in the attack on Altman and Powers, but his reputation and his known hatred of Powers had damned him, he was guilty until proven innocent. Challenging the allegations could be counter-productive, the resultant publicity could cement the allegations in people's minds. For the time being, and perhaps forever, he had killed and got away with it.

The telephone intruded into Eddie's thoughts. He looked at his watch, Janice's watch, it was too early for the telephone to bring good news. Thankfully he was wrong; the warm New York drawl instantly cheered him.

"Hey Eddie, what time is it over there?" Chin was excited, he had good news, but it was a reminder of a bad experience. "The police have found Weasel in a dumpster…"

To be precise they'd found parts of Weasel in a dumpster, but enough to make a positive identification, Eddie was off the hook.

Unlike New York, murders were rare in Canley, news of Eddie's arrest quickly made the newspapers and his release on bail excited disbelief, rumour and speculation. The truth was that Ray Powers had developed a drug habit and was massively in debt to his supplier Altman. Seeing Eddie's red estate in Dave King's compound sparked a plot in his mind to kill Altman and have Eddie blamed for it. Ray should have escaped unharmed, the hooded driver was instructed to give him time to run, but his damaged knee let him down. He persisted with his allegation that Eddie was the hooded driver who tried to kill him, that Altman was an unintended victim and Eddie had got away with murder. To be fair, Eddie had got away with murder, but not that one.

MRS MORRIS

Canley High Street had gone continental with pavement cafés open in summer and on bright winter days. Eddie was standing by a shiny aluminium table staring down the High Street to catch a last glimpse of Janice and Sophie. They were being secretive, and Eddie suspected that their shopping trip was to buy his Christmas present. Janice could walk short distances on crutches now, but a shopping trip necessitated a wheelchair with Sophie as propellant.

Eddie knew he was smiling, he had good reason to, and a nearby voice startled him. "Does that smile mean I'm forgiven?"

The last time he'd spoken to the middle-aged lady addressing him was thirteen years ago in the converted loft above the garage in Gladstone Street. He'd seen her many times since, but she'd always hurried by, head down.

"Forgiven for what?" Eddie was genuinely at a loss – Mrs Morris didn't need his forgiveness, he needed hers.

More wasted years, two people assuming guilt and both wrong. Eddie and Mrs Morris sat outside in the weak sunshine sipping coffee, sheltered from the elements by etched Perspex screens.

"Juliet didn't think you'd abandoned her, she knew your mother had died." Mrs Morris was choosing her words carefully. "I knew your mother slightly, we had some mutual friends."

Eddie wasn't concerned whether Mrs Morris knew his mother or not. "But you ran from my room in tears, you couldn't bear to look at me?"

"Oh Eddie!" Mrs Morris was almost in tears. "I was crying for you! Everything you'd done for Juliet and all those others, and you were in that horrible little room by yourself." She hung her head. "I felt so guilty, I assumed that Juliet told you in her letter that we were so obsessed with our new grandson we ignored her. We knew she was unhappy, but we did nothing, it was our fault she died."

Eddie shook his head slowly. "There was nothing in Juliet's letter about a nephew, and no criticism of you." He paused. "And no-one, and I mean no-one, should ever cry for the likes of me, I'm a monster and not worth crying for, never have been never will be…"

Mrs Morris interrupted angrily. "Don't say such a thing, over the years I've cried for you more times than you can imagine."

A second coffee and Mrs Morris was being positive. Eddie should call her Doreen and she wanted to tell him about her grandson, Juliet's nephew. "I've been such a silly woman, I went back to work full time after Juliet died and hardly saw him." She was close to tears again. "Part of me blamed him for Juliet's death and I avoided him. Thankfully his other Gran had more sense, they're very close." She stared at her coffee cup. "A few months ago she had a real go at me, called me a wicked woman ignoring him for so many years, and she was right. I'm getting to know him now and he's a really lovely boy." A sad smile appeared. "Things have changed since my day, his best friend's a girl." She grabbed Eddie's arm with sudden enthusiasm. "Would you believe it, they've got together with some friends and started a band."

Eddie stared at Mrs Morris lost for words, why hadn't he seen the obvious? He didn't have a lisp, his head wasn't too small for his large frame, but he had that same glow inside that Juliet had.

"Eddie! Are you OK?" Doreen was worried, Eddie had been staring blankly at her for ages.

"Yes, I'm more than OK." Eddie gave a confused smile before continuing. "Your grandson's called Mark, isn't he, and his best friend is called Sophie."

It was Mrs Morris's turn to stare blankly.

Eddie struggled to come to terms with the fact he'd known Juliet's nephew for years and not recognised him. He heard Mrs Morris give a disdainful sniff as two middle-aged ladies stared disapprovingly at them sitting together and hurried past.

"That's your reputation in tatters." Eddie forced himself back into the present, away from the awful picture of Juliet in her best blue dress on a plastic sheet.

"They can bugger off!"

Her vehemence made Eddie smile, a genuine smile this time. The response was a confused look from Mrs Morris. There had been a few such looks, particularly when he'd stared blankly at her on discovering Mark's identity.

"Eddie, you know I said your mother and me had a mutual friend…?"

If you like your countryside flat and featureless, then the Fens were the place to be. Eddie didn't, but nonetheless was heading deep into the Fens. Civilisation as he knew it had ended a few miles east of Peterborough at Kings Delph railway crossing. Next was Whittlesey, a dismal place with the appearance of normality, but a town whose sole claim to fame was an annual Straw Bear Festival had to be suspect. Further east place names echoed a bucolic idiom: Burnt Fen, Turves and Rings End. Eddie turned off the main road onto a side road with black land crisscrossed with drainage ditches and pumping stations on either side heading for Chatteris.

The approach to Chatteris was depressing, long rows of drab council houses, with many front gardens littered with caravans and rotting sofas. Eddie followed faded signs to the town centre to be depressed again. For all the world, Chatteris had prepared itself for a Royal visit or something similar forty years ago, only to have the visit cancelled. In their disappointment the residents must have lost heart and neither improved nor decorated the place since.

Unexpected modernity, red traffic lights, Eddie braked gently to a halt to allow a particularly repellent example of local manhood to cross the road. He'd clearly been shopping, but long arms and a pronounced forward stoop caused him to drag his bags along the pavement and onto the crossing.

Eddie gulped as the man turned and leered at Janice in the seat beside him, thick matted eyebrows met his hairline without any noticeable break for a forehead. The apparition made Eddie think that the lurid stories of inbreeding, incest and animal molestation in Fen towns could be true.

"Eddie! The lights are green."

Janice seemed entirely unmoved by the Fen Tiger; was it just him, his mind playing tricks?

Juliet never asked Eddie why he sat in a bus shelter on Mayors Road rather than go home. She didn't need to, she guessed that boys who dressed in charity shop clothes were unlikely to have a caring home to go to. Doreen Morris confirmed her suspicions when she told her daughter not to mix with Eddie, a boy with a bad reputation and an alcoholic mother. Eddie and Doreen would never rid themselves of guilt about Juliet's death. Being caught shoplifting was the final straw that led a desperately unhappy girl to sacrifice her life, hoping to put right the wrongs in her world, but both could and should have done more to help her.

A few days after their meeting in Canley High Street, Eddie met Mrs Morris again to hear about the mutual friend she'd spoken about. The obvious was only obvious when you knew the truth. In the same way Eddie hadn't recognised Mark as Juliet's nephew, he hadn't considered the fact that his mother, father and Charles were all fairly short and heavily built. Eddie was neither, he was a similar build to John Renton-Thorpe and had the same startling blue eyes. Mrs Morris had worked with John, seen him with Eddie's mother and suspected they were having an affair.

Finding Mrs Renton-Thorpe wasn't difficult, it was hardly a common name. Eddie trawled through the internet moving gradually away from Canley and the first Renton-Thorpe he found was John's widow, now living in Chatteris. She wasn't particularly surprised by his telephone call, uneasy and suspicious but prepared to speak to him. John had died five years ago, she knew about his affair with Margaret Stagg and her claim that she was pregnant with his child. He thought it was a crude attempt to ensnare him and left the area.

"Outfield Road!" Janice spotted a street sign by a post box. "She said turn left by the post box."

Their visit was brief, Mrs Renton-Thorpe met them at the door, invited them in, looked Eddie up and down then snapped.

"Look at me, and don't squint your eyes up!"

She turned away after a few seconds. "John wasn't an obviously attractive man, it was the eyes that did it…" She stared at Janice. "You know what I mean, you're a very attractive girl, you wouldn't normally be with an ordinary boy like him. And don't bristle at me, young lady, I bet you didn't consider him until one day he looked at you all big blue eyes you could drown in."

Mrs Renton-Thorpe made it clear that she wanted no further contact from Eddie for the sake of her children. "John was a good man who made a mistake, we all loved him dearly and I don't want anything to change that.'

His mistake had huge repercussions for Eddie with his mother seeing John every time Eddie opened his eyes. She clearly blamed Eddie for John ending their affair and moving away. At the door, Mrs Renton-Thorpe answered one last question, John's full name was 'John Meridew Alonzo Renton-Thorpe'. Was it unrequited love or did Margaret want her husband to find out and hate Eddie as much as she did?

MORE NEWS AND NORFOLK

A New Year and the newspaper readers of Canley wanted something new, not the endless good guy, bad guy bickering between the Herald and the Advertiser. Anyway, corruption wasn't that interesting, particularly to those who had benefited from it directly or indirectly. For them corruption had happened since the dawn of time, and they didn't care about the human dross in West Town or insurance companies' profits.

Ray Powers was in a bad way, the impact of the red estate had thrown him against a wall with tremendous force, breaking his back and paralysing him from the waist down. John Powers asked for and was granted early retirement, ostensibly to allow him to care for his disabled son, in fact it was to get his pension before an enquiry took it away.

Vincent Proctor was released from prison on licence after four months, but such was the public's disinterest in him that even the Herald relegated the story to page six. Within days he was back in Canley society and actively pursuing the case to have the DVDs and the VHS video seized by the police returned to him.

The letter did not come as a complete surprise, Charlie had told Eddie that DCI Marcham had spoken to him at length and Roxy had spent a whole day showing Sergeant Price around West Town. However, the fact it was hand delivered by a courier on the eve of Eddie's next meeting with Charles and Stephen Napier and Doug Bracken was a surprise. Charlie said there had been a major breakthrough and would reveal all at the meeting. Eddie tore open the envelope to find two close typed pages signed by DCI Marcham.

Dear Mr Stagg,

Everyone I have met over the last few weeks, from Sir Charles Napier to Octogenarians at the Walk-in Centre, have called you Eddie, not a single person has called you Mr Stagg. Despite this, and the outstanding charity work you have done in the area, I cannot bring myself to do so. Whatever the provocation I cannot and do not approve of vigilantes and you are an extremely violent vigilante.

You and West Town owe a huge debt to Bob Price, a man who instinctively knows more about people and policing than I will ever do. He persuaded me to talk to Sir Charles and allow him to spend time in West Town to see if your allegations were true. To my amazement, Sir Charles has nothing but praise for you and everything you said about West Town is true. There are no CCTV cameras, if residents or shopkeepers install their own that in any way cover the streets they are mysteriously torn down. Sgt Price saw no police patrols, but when I covertly inspected records afterwards they showed regular patrols.

Sir Charles said that you were convinced that blackmail was at the heart of the power held by Powers, Proctor and Windsor and that it dated back years. He also identified the extreme lengths the Proctors were going to in trying to recover DVDs and a VHS video tape which was held in the secure store in the Canley Central Police Station. More suspiciously, the family had taken out an injunction to prevent them being viewed once they were ruled inadmissible at Vincent Proctor's trial. Even Sir Charles' influence could not get this injunction removed and their return to the family was imminent.

My personal life has been one of privilege, and to mitigate my conscience I joined the police force to hopefully give something back. On the death of my father last year I became an Earl and my close relatives include very prominent politicians and members of the judiciary. I used every scrap of this influence to gain access to the DVDs and VHS tape and made many enemies in the process.

The venue for your meeting tomorrow has been changed, it will now be at Scotland Yard with very senior independent police officers present along with technical experts. The VHS tape has been deliberately damaged and one DVD appears to be encrypted but the technical experts are confident that all the material on them can now be viewed.

Apparently, Sir Charles will collect you and his son early tomorrow morning and I and the indefatigable Bob Price will meet you there.

Yours sincerely

Peregrine Marcham

When Eddie had first set foot in Cromwell Road and Gladstone Street the area was awash with street prostitutes and brothels. Jerome Proctor was not a pimp but knew someone who was and the value of blackmail. He hid secret cameras in an exclusive and discreet brothel that could also procure young girls, anyone caught on his cameras would be doubly damned, not only consorting with prostitutes but under age ones. That someone was John Powers, then an Inspector, and one of their first victims was his boss, later to become Chief Constable. Proctor was no fool and in a well-organized sting tricked and filmed Powers to make himself all powerful.

The final part of his plan was to keep areas of Canley and Stanford free of CCTV cameras and police patrols to allow unobserved dumping and recovery of goods stolen to order. He wanted pimps and drug pushers to move in, thinking anyone investigating corruption in the area would assume the origin was sex and drugs and he had no involvement in either.

The video was a grainy copy, the faces were much younger but still recognisable, senior police officers, local and national politicians and wealthy businessmen. The encrypted DVD eventually gave up its secrets, more of the same, just more recent. The other DVDs were Vincent Proctor recording his abuse of young girls, some consensual but mostly not. As the VHS video was a copy then the encrypted DVD was probably a copy as well. A search of Jerome Proctor's home discovered a hidden safe; he refused to give the combination so it was cut open to reveal the original VHS video and the original encrypted DVD. The roundup of blackmailers and the blackmailed began in earnest.

CHAPTER 20

Norfolk and the Blonde

NORFOLK

O nce Janice could walk without crutches, she and Eddie decided to take a short break and looked for somewhere reasonably close without memories, good or bad. An evening with tourist guides found Cromer, the Jewel of the Norfolk Coast with faded Victorian splendour, a pier with a lifeboat station, a legendary lifeboat coxswain in Henry Blogg, and the Hotel de Paris.

As Victorian opulence metamorphosed into Edwardian elegance, steamboats moored up alongside the pier bringing wealthy holidaymakers to Cromer's smart hotels. The smartest of them all was the Hotel de Paris, an imposing red brick Victorian Gothic building perched on the cliff above the pier. In Edwardian times a succession of horse drawn chaises brought the holidaymakers from the pier to the hotel. Eddie and Janice arrived on a fine Saturday morning in the silver hatchback.

Oddly, for a man born so far inland Eddie loved the sea, the look of it, the sound of it, even the smell of it. Perhaps it was because his first sight of the sea had been on his first holiday, a day at the coast with Jilly. There had been no holidays for the young Eddie, his parents continued their drunken debauches in Spain, leaving Eddie with the cheapest childminder money could buy. After his father's death, Margaret holidayed with Charles, leaving Eddie alone in the house; Charles didn't take her out of love, she was simply a cheap babysitter for Charlotte and Phillip.

Eddie's later trips to the coast were as a proper little family, he and Jilly taking Sophie with them to play on the beach and splash in the sea. Eddie understood the unhappiness of an unwanted child, rejected by her mother for being insecure and sickly. What he would never understand was how amazing girls like Jilly and Janice could be happy with him.

Janice pondered as she watched Eddie staring at the sea from the bay window of their room. Lots of girls had successful second marriages contending with jealous ex-husbands, vindictive ex-wives and troublesome weekend children. She had no such problem, no ex-spouses, and the weekend child was Sophie, with the possible exception of her friend Mark the most thoughtful teenager ever. And there was no jealousy there either, Sophie wasn't Eddie's child.

Even if Janice didn't love Eddie as much as she did, living with him was easy, apart for two things. At home he was kind, caring and thoughtful, just as she'd expected. And he had no bad habits, he was tidy, never left dirty clothes lying about, put the lib back on the toothpaste, didn't leave the toilet seat up, didn't channel hop with the TV remote control, and insisted on doing his share of the household tasks. A welcome surprise was that he was sentimental and romantic, but a major surprise was that Eddie was funny, a strange offbeat sense of humour, but never dark and definitely never cruel.

Away from home, Eddie was how he'd always been: edgy, eyes everywhere, reacting to noises, sudden movements, even flashes of light. The streetfighter always anticipating trouble, a constant reminder of the two things Janice found difficult, his nightmares and his trollops. The nightmares were relentless and mostly about violence and Juliet and Jilly's death. She had no issue with those about Jilly or Juliet, but had serious issues with those about violence as they were caused by the traumas suffered fighting knife wielding maniacs to protect prostitutes. Janice didn't mean Roxy, she was different, she meant the trollops who were doubtless the architects of their own misfortune. Why did he risk his life to protect them, and why did he insist they were innocent victims and his friends?

One day she would talk to Roxy about it, but in the meantime she had a problem coming to terms with her guilt. Janice had been a selfish lover, when she'd cried herself to sleep night after night thinking about Eddie, she was crying for herself, wanting him come and wipe away her tears. She wasn't crying for him, alone, unhappy and frightened. Eddie was the perfect dream, the kind boy with beautiful eyes in that horrible room in Gladstone Street. Without the nightmares and the trollops, the reality would be as wonderful as the dream.

The hotel food was ordinary, and it was full of pensioners – a coach party had arrived in the afternoon. As much as Eddie empathised with old ladies, they decided to venture out; they'd seen a pub, the Kings Head, not far from the hotel's rear entrance.

They were in luck, the pub had live music, a local band 'Adam's Experience' mixing Sixties covers with Eighties hard rock, and they were good. It was strange being thirty and possibly the oldest customer in the pub, but the youngsters were remarkably polite, squeezing along the benches at the side of the room to give Janice a place to sit. Two songs 'Some might say' by Oasis and 'Down, Down' by Status Quo showed the band's versatility but exposed their musical differences. The guitar player liked the overdriven sounds and complex chord structures of Oasis, the bass player preferred the three chords, head down and go for it style of Status Quo.

At the end of the first set the two warring musicians adjourned to the car park to discuss their musical differences. Two passing police officers took exception to the robust nature of their robust discussion and Adam's Experience became a duo; a drummer and a singer. After a hurried consultation with the landlord the singer nervously approached the microphone.

"Is there a guitar player in the house?"

Sunday morning, Sharon was at work trying to impress her new boss and Dave was keeping Sophie company. He'd been reflecting on his long heart to heart with Sharon, particularly her conviction that Eddie was giving Sophie false hope. Decision made, he would talk to Sophie himself, he was more sensitive than Sharon so would be able to let her down gently, not hurt her feelings.

Ten minutes later Dave realised he'd made one of the biggest mistakes of his life. Supposed maturity and years of people watching had taught him nothing; he was a hopeless idiot.

"You've been talking to Mum, haven't you?" Sophie wasn't in tears; Dave had hurt her so badly she was beyond tears. "She's been telling me the same thing for ever. I'm not stupid, Uncle Dave, I've got a mirror, I can see I'm plain. And if I was really clever like Eddie and Roxy, I'd be top of the class in everything, but I'm not. I am top of the class in English, even Professor Hay says I'm good and he wouldn't lie to me." She stared at him, eyes wide open. "Eddie thinks I'm beautiful and clever because he loves me. I know it's not true but it doesn't matter ..." She gave a loud sniff, tears were imminent. "... Eddie would still love me if I was really ugly and really stupid."

Dave tried damage limitation. "But your Mum loves you and I..." He got no further.

"Mum was going to give me away to Eddie and Jilly. When Jilly died Mum wasn't sad, she was angry because she had to keep me." Sophie paused to blow her nose. "She's nicer to me now Professor Hay gives me free lessons and she found out that Charlie was a Sir. She was horrible to him when she thought he was a gardener."

Her tears finally came. "Apart from Eddie, Roxy's my most favourite person in the world and Mum says she's a tart and I mustn't see her again."

So there it was, Sharon was taking her anger and disappointment out on Sophie and Roxy? But a question.

"I thought you liked Janice?"

Sophie was indignant. "Of course I like Janice, she's really, really nice and she makes Eddie happy, but that doesn't mean I can't like Roxy a little bit better."

No, of course it didn't, silly Uncle Dave. Then he was saved by the bell, his mobile phone was ringing, the call display said Eddie.

"Yes, of course, love to. Can you speak to Sophie, she's a bit upset."

Eddie was staring at the sea again and Janice was examining herself in the unforgiving light of the bathroom mirror. She wasn't entirely dissatisfied, her confidence had been boosted by Eddie's obvious happiness and constant compliments, but her grey hairs were becoming tiresome. It was the Newton Grey – her father went completely grey in his twenties and had coloured his hair all his life. She'd had a few grey hairs for several years but the accident had made them proliferate. Janice smiled to herself remembering Roxy's words 'Eddie goes for tall, skinny blondes, so two out of three's not bad'. Perhaps it was time for three out of three.

Last night there had been a guitar player in the house – Janice persuaded Eddie to play. The drummer wasn't Mike, the singer wasn't Dave, and it wasn't the wall of sound she was used to hearing from Eddie's big Marshall and his home-made compressor, but he was happy. Towards the end of the first number the drummer gave up the unequal struggle of trying to lead and followed Eddie's crashing chords just as Mike had done for so many years. After a few songs Janice attracted Eddie's attention and volunteered to play bass for a couple of numbers. Eddie was thrilled, he knew she couldn't stand for any length of time so helped her onto a high stool and handed her a bass. When he'd finished staring at the sea she would suggest he rang Mike, Dave and Jimmy.

THE BLONDE

Saturday evening and The Roadrunners had a gig playing at a sixties dance in Broad Street School Hall. Ostensibly it was a good gig, the hall was freshly decorated, had a raised stage with professional lighting. Eddie's memories of Broad Street School as it was years ago would never leave him, but if Janice and Mike could live with the memories then so must he. The first set was going well, a full dance floor and a buzz of excitement. The combination of good music, Roxy's flair and Deborah's attention to detail had made The Roadrunners charity gigs for CCCC an instant success.

Emily was standing in the bar feeling conspicuous, let down and angry. It was the story of her life, always the bridesmaid never the bride, always the one left holding the dirty end of the stick. After eight wasted years trying to make her relationship with Colin work, a new job in a new area offered a chance to start again. It wasn't working, she didn't like Canley that much, and her new colleagues had just let her down badly.

Winning the raffle prize, eight tickets and a reserved table at the dance seemed like a great opportunity to get to know them. She decided to use the prize to take the three members of her team and their partners to the dance. There had been some whispering and Emily suspected she was being set up with a blind date using the eighth ticket. She wasn't, and if she hadn't held on to the tickets her promised lift would not have arrived either. Her colleagues had bought a ninth ticket, she was playing gooseberry with four couples. The colleague sent to fetch her when they arrived at the dance without tickets left her in the bar, saying she was going to find the others before buying a round of drinks. That was twenty minutes ago, Emily decided to buy her own drink and find their reserved table.

At least the band sounded good, her colleagues had enthused about them, apparently the singer was tall, dark and handsome and they had a girl bass player. Emily smiled sardonically, she probably had close cropped hair, tattoos and muscles like the village blacksmith. Childish perhaps, but Emily had always been sensitive about being tall and well built. Tall girls weren't perceived as feminine, they didn't have doors opened for them or coffee fetched for them from the machine. Not quite true, stick thin supermodels were perceived as feminine, it seemed that their skeletal frames conveyed fragility and restored femininity.

Emily had always been intimidated by clever, attractive and talented girls. One out of three was fine, two out of three was just about OK, but three out of three was intimidating! Emily bought her drink and lost most of it as she was jostled at the bar. The man offered no apology so she walked wearily towards the front of the hall to find their table before she was jostled again. Now her miserable evening was complete, their reserved table was empty and the bass player wasn't a muscle bound Amazon, more like a blonde supermodel sitting on a tall stool playing a bright red bass. Her friends were right about the singer; Mr Tall, dark and handsome and the blonde were probably an item.

At the end of the band's first set Emily returned to the bar to find her colleagues already there drinking and talking amongst themselves, they'd walked past her on the other side of the hall. Enough was enough, she wouldn't buy another drink, she would phone for a taxi and go home. The bar was packed with people pushing and shoving, trying not to spill drinks held at shoulder level. Emily stepped back to avoid a man clutching three pint glasses.

"Shit!"

Emily felt a flood of cold liquid wash over her head and shoulders, she'd stepped back into another beer carrier. It was her fault, it was always her fault, she would apologise and walk away. She turned to see Mr Tall, dark and handsome staring at her. Odd, very few men looked at her twice, most didn't even look once, so why was he staring? Odder still, he was apologising, refusing to accept it was her fault. Emily argued, insisting she'd stepped back into him, but he would have none of it, making eye contact all the time. Tonight, she was wearing her glasses, the ones with lenses as thick as the bottom of a bottle, she didn't wear contact lenses any more as they made her eyes sore. One of the few good things about moving to Canley was losing her nickname, she'd been 'Specky Spencer' all her life and hated it.

The singer was called Dave and was being charming and concerned. Emily sniffed, that would stop when his guilt faded.

"Your top's soaked, I'll get one of the girls to loan you a cardigan."

He was insistent, leading her towards the front of the hall. This was silly, the blonde wouldn't appreciate him turning up with a girl covered in beer.

Now he'd stopped to talk to a small man who Emily recognised as the band's drummer. He smiled and shook his head.

"No, Deborah's not there, just Eddie and Janice..."

Emily saw an odd look on the singer's face but felt relieved, blonde supermodels might be called Deborah or Debbie or Debs, but not Janice.

Wrong! As they walked towards a table on the edge of the dance floor Emily saw a flash of blonde hair. A few more steps and there she was, but she was holding hands with the guitar player, the one who played standing in the shadows at the back of the stage.

Dave stopped abruptly and called out. "Eddie, it's Dave."

The guitar player was already on the move, dropping the blonde's hand and whirling round to face them. The movement stopped as quickly as it started and he stepped back to help the blonde to her feet. Close to she was very attractive but not stunning, and she looked approachable. A pity, Emily wanted to dislike her.

"Dave! What have you done?"

Emily warmed to the blonde, she'd assumed Dave was in the wrong.

"I spilled my beer…"

The blonde turned and smiled sweetly at the guitar player. "Eddie, would you fetch the towel from your gig bag, and my red jacket?" Dave got a scowl. "We're going to the ladies to wash away your beer. You'll have to start without me, Eddie will play bass so you and Jimmy will have to cover the guitar playing between you."

Emily's dislike of the blonde had been rekindled, she was far too striking in her sleeveless white trouser suit and her walk was affected, she wiggled when she moved her right leg. If her intention was to look sexy it was working, men could hardly tear their eyes away. Minutes later her dislike evaporated again, Janice was being extraordinarily kind, washing away Dave's beer and drying her hair with the guitar player's towel.

She held out her red jacket. "I have to buy big sizes because I have wide shoulders." She stood back and smiled. "It's pretty obvious Dave likes you, I know he's a clumsy oaf but give him a chance."

What a stupid comment, her give him a chance, tomorrow he wouldn't even look at her. Emily was annoyed, the blonde ought to get real.

"It's easy for you to say that, I mean look at you, you've even got a sexy walk."

Emily could see she'd touched a nerve, but Janice was sad not angry. "It's a limp, Emily."

"Sorry?"

"The walk, it's a limp. I was in a bad car accident a year ago, I learned to walk again but I can't get rid of the limp." Janice spoke with a sudden intensity. "It's all a front, Eddie keeps telling me I'm terribly attractive, so I dress up and pretend and everyone seems to believe it. Look behind the hair and the nice clothes and you'll see a tall, thin girl with a big nose and a limp."

The music started, the rumble of the bass penetrating to where they were standing. Janice stood back and swallowed, she was close to tears.

"That's Eddie, he's such a good bass player."

Emily had been a bit dreamy about Colin for the first week or two, but it didn't last - Janice and the guitar player must have just got together.

Emily was feeling conspicuous again, but for a different reason this time. Janice may have wide shoulders but her jacket was a trifle snug – without a top under it Emily was showing rather more boob than she was used to. She was getting glances of her own now, including one man leering openly down her cleavage.

The band were coming to the end of a number, Dave had seen them and was waving and singing at the same time. Now he was speaking into the microphone, saying something about our ladies being back, ladies not lady.

Janice squeezed her hand. "Now, watch what a tall, thin girl with a big nose and a limp can do when someone believes in her."

She walked towards the steps in the centre of the stage apparently brimming with confidence. A moment later there was a boom as Eddie thumped the red bass down onto its stand before leaping off the stage to help Janice up the steps. It looked theatrical but Emily now knew that steps without a handrail were a major challenge to Janice. Standing for long periods was impossible; playing bass sitting on a stool wasn't an affectation, it was a necessity. The crowd loved it, applauding as Janice climbed the steps on Eddie's arm, and cheering when she kissed him before he retreated into the shadows.

Janice left Emily with Deborah who was married to Jimmy, the guitar player with the boy next door good looks standing to Dave's right. She introduced Emily to Gary, very smart, absolutely charming, clearly gay and quite open about being with Mike the tiny drummer. They were treating her like an old friend, better in fact as Emily didn't have any old friends.

Gary loved dancing and soon had Emily on the dance floor. After two dances he led her back to the table full of apologies because she didn't have a drink and was instantly gone to the bar. Deborah confided that she neither danced nor liked music that much, unusual for the manager of a rock band. Time was speeding by, the band were about to play their last number. A colleague approached, stared at the red jacket and asked if she wanted a lift home. It was the first time any of her group had spoken to her all evening and it gave Emily some satisfaction to politely decline. As she went to sit down, she heard Dave's amplified voice.

"Emily, wait!" She swung round to see Dave whisper something to Jimmy before returning to the microphone. "Our last number is Eric Clapton's 'Wonderful Tonight'. Jimmy's going to sing for us and I hope Emily will make my tonight wonderful by dancing with me."

Emily gazed round, expecting to see some other Emily standing behind her. Scenes froze in her mind; dancers parting as Dave walked towards her, open mouthed astonishment on the faces of her colleague and Deborah glowing with pride as Jimmy started to sing.

TAKE A NICE GIRL HOME

Reliable staff didn't like the boss turning up unexpectedly, Dave didn't usually work on Sunday mornings so if he went into work the sales staff would think something was wrong. Instead, he rattled around his big new house in Eltham trying to think of something to do. He hated DIY and was useless at it, he liked gardening even less which left …another cup of coffee.

Ten years ago, Dave had watched Jilly walk out of Broad Street School hall hand in hand with Eddie and hoped that one day he would take a nice girl home full of hope for the future. Ten years of bimbos, trollops and Sue, and it had finally happened, Jilly was an impossible dream but Emily was real.

Last night he'd walked her to her front door and behaved like a gentleman. That was a first, and it made him think about how he'd condemned Sharon as easy for having fewer sexual partners than him. Chauvinistic bigotry wasn't dead, it was alive and well and called Dave King. Emily hadn't asked him in for coffee and he hadn't wanted her to, nice girls didn't do that on a first date. He'd arranged to see her on Tuesday, a long time to wait.

Weekdays weren't a problem, after a hard day's work and cooking tea, Emily was happy to curl up in front of the television. Saturdays weren't a problem either, the hustle and bustle of household tasks and food shopping. Sundays were different, everything stopped, Sundays were for families. She had an open invitation to Sunday lunch with her parents but only went every three weeks or so, she didn't want them to think she hadn't made a life for herself in Canley. Today's Sunday lunch would be a microwave meal for one.

Last night had been an education – her colleagues were not her friends, in fact they weren't even good colleagues. On the other hand, she'd met Janice, and Emily was sure they would become friends, they were meeting for lunch on Wednesday. Dave wouldn't last, when he recovered from his guilt he would phone and cancel their date on Tuesday. Men like him wanted trophy girlfriends who didn't argue, an ordinary girl with a mind of her own was not for him.

Apparently, Janice and Eddie had been together since her accident a year ago, they must have the real thing, they were still besotted with each other. Emily couldn't quite understand why a really attractive girl like Janice was with a nice but ordinary boy like Eddie. The thought started Emily wondering why Deborah had said she shouldn't be frightened of Eddie and why Dave had stopped and called out before approaching him?

The telephone disturbed her train of thought, Emily recognised the voice, it was the call she'd been expecting, just a day early.

"Emily, it's Dave. You know we agreed to…"

She interrupted. "It's OK, Dave, I understand."

"Understand what?" Dave sounded puzzled.

"You want to cancel?"

"I don't want to cancel, I was hoping we could go somewhere today, a pizza or something." He laughed. "Can we change that, I'm not that fond of pizza."

Two weeks and Colin was a distant memory, her colleagues treated her with new respect and Dave wasn't a male chauvinist pig. He hadn't tried to impress, he'd listened, asked about her and gone to Sunday lunch at her parents. No coercion, she said she was going and he'd offered to take her. This afternoon he was returning the compliment, they were visiting his only relatives in Canley, his sister and niece. Afterwards they were having dinner with Janice and Eddie.

Emily was learning about the good and bad areas of Canley. Sharon lived on the Lower Eltham Road close to West Town, a poor area and not a place to walk after dark. However, the road seemed quiet, the houses well maintained, and Dave was very casual about leaving his car on the road outside. The interior of the house reminded Emily of the one she'd shared with Colin, not in layout but in the conflict between tidy and untidy occupants.

Sharon had the King good looks but not Dave's personality, she typified the girls who used to intimidate Emily, those with two or more of the clever, attractive or talented trio. Perhaps Emily was changing or perhaps Sharon only had one of the three; despite her confidence, Emily wasn't intimidated.

Sophie had just returned from a creative writing course, her suitcase forgotten on the floor while Sharon interrogated her about it. The King good looks had skipped a generation, Sophie was tall, nicely dressed but rather plain. Dave's attempts to interrupt the interrogation eventually met with success, but Sharon's only other subject was herself and Sophie seemed preoccupied.

"How about some tea?" Dave sounded strained.

No reaction from Sharon; instead, Sophie jumped to her feet and moved towards the kitchen, followed by Dave. Emily needed the loo, if only to escape Sharon.

"The cloakroom toilet's broken, you'll have to use the bathroom." Sharon pointed vaguely upstairs. "Second door on the left, past Sophie's bedroom."

Upstairs was no tidier than down with a pile of dirty washing by the bathroom door and a coat and scarf draped over the banister rail. Emily peeped into Sophie's bedroom out of curiosity and answered a question – she was the tidy one, it was immaculate. A bright red bass similar to Janice's was on a stand in the corner and Emily stepped forward to look at it. A picture on a chest of drawers caught her eye and she smiled, Sophie must have kept a memento from her childhood, a fairytale princess cut from a storybook. A pace forward brought a shock, the fairytale princess was real, a photograph on a bedside table showed her holding hands with Sophie and Eddie. A second photograph was no surprise, Sophie with Dave, Sharon and what must be her grandparents. A third brought another shock, a group picture with a beaming Sophie surrounded by the impossible pretty girl, Eddie, Mike the tiny drummer and Roxanne Bailey, the rather scary Coordinator from the CCCC who'd presented Emily with her raffle prize.

Emily heard a door bang and someone talking excitedly on the telephone in the hallway. She hurried from the room and walked slowly down the stairs to be greeted by Sophie. She was a different girl, waving the telephone excitedly, her face alight with pleasure

"Eddie says you're having dinner with him and Janice tonight, he says you're really nice?"

An enjoyable evening had been marred by Dave changing the subject every time the conversation strayed onto anything to do with the past. Janice had become subdued, her happy chatter of the early evening slowly evaporating. Eddie's offbeat humour had disappeared too, he'd become edgy and protective. Emily started to worry; despite their obvious devotion there was a definite sadness about Janice and Eddie. Something was wrong, Dave knew and wasn't telling her.

"What about that cat then?"

Part way through the evening the door had opened silently and the biggest cat Emily had ever seen in her life stalked into the room. He'd glared balefully at her, arched his back and spat at Dave, then leapt onto the settee, walked across Janice and flopped down on Eddie's knee.

"Dave!" It was her assertive tone. "Stop prattling on about the bloody cat and tell me what's going on."

The car swerved slightly as Dave took his eyes off the road. Emily sighed, she'd done it again, men didn't like assertive women, Colin hated her being assertive.

She softened her voice. "It's something from the past, isn't it? And why has Sophie got a picture of Eddie with an impossibly pretty girl on her bedside table?" Now she was assertive again. "If you don't trust me then we're going nowhere, and don't tell me you don't know because you do!"

They were approaching a roundabout, Dave drove slowly all the way round and set off back towards Eltham.

"Haven't your colleagues said anything?" He grunted. "I bet they're being really respectful!"

"I thought that was because I was with you?"

Dave gave a grim laugh. "I'm flattered but no, after the dance you were chatting to Eddie like he was an old friend…"

Emily interrupted, another character trait Colin hated. "Well he's s a nice boy and easy to talk to so long as you're not taken in by his silly laconic, tough guy act."

Dave laughed openly. "That's no act, people who mess with Eddie's friends tend to wake up face down in an alley with their legs broken."

Emily squeaked. "You mean that nice boy's violent."

More laughter from Dave. "You really don't know, do you, and why do you keep calling him a nice boy?"

Dave's house was like a show home, eye-catching but characterless and cold. Emily shivered with nerves not cold, Dave was clearly upset.

"They're in here somewhere."

He was scrabbling about in a cupboard, fumbling and cursing under his breath. Eventually he emerged clutching a bundle of newspapers

"I've put them in some sort of order, try to reserve judgement until you've read them all and I've explained."

The stories were horrifying and conflicting, sensational accusations in the Canley Herald and cautious support in the Advertiser. A brief report in a national newspaper sided with the Advertiser and carried a statement from a Sir Charles Napier QC recording his unequivocal support for Mr Stagg and praise for his charity work in Canley's West Town. Emily went back and forth trying to make sense of it all and realised she knew the girl pictured in an edition of the Canley Herald described as a 'Red Haired Tart' and accused of being Stagg's partner in crime.

"That's Roxanne Bailey, she presented me with my raffle prize and Sophie has a picture of her with Eddie and Mike and that girl." Emily threw the papers down. "I don't want to read any more, just tell me."

Dave shrugged and quietly recounted an appalling story of rejection, bullying, violence, guilt, betrayal, brutal revenge and an accusation of murder. Then hope, a heartening story of friendship, loyalty and love. Two friends who found to their complete surprise that they loved each other and always had, now mourning their lost years and the deaths it had taken to bring them together.

"I don't like him, Emily, I never have, all that icy control and repressed violence..." Dave paused. "Eddie, Mike and Janice were at school together, they're inseparable..." He paused again. "My previous girlfriend said they were like a freak show 'a psychopath, a gay midget and a stick insect'. She made me choose, them or her."

"And you chose them."

Dave nodded. "Yes, it's not just Mike and Janice, it's Sophie; Eddie is her most favourite person in the whole world." He shrugged. "And apart from Eddie, Roxy is her most favourite person in the whole world."

Emily spoke softly. "You thought I might ask you to choose?" She paused as Dave nodded. "Well, I won't, and I can only imagine what it took to make a nice boy like Eddie do such things..."

Dave interrupted, shaking his head in puzzled amazement. "Why do you keep calling him a nice boy?"

"Would that pretty girl, or Janice, or Sophie or Mike or all those other girls love him if he was a monster, can't you see he just pretends..."

Dave interrupted again. "Eddie's a big silly who pretends a lot…"

It was Emily's turn to be puzzled. "Sorry?"

"Sophie was four when she said that…"

CHAPTER 21

A Final Dream

WORRIES

All her dreams had come true, well all but one, and that would come true in a few weeks' time. Janice had a beautiful home, a job she enjoyed, a smart car, fashionable clothes, a close female friend and, most importantly, Eddie. Was she happy? Of course she was happy, she was happier than she could ever have believed possible, but that didn't stop her worrying.

At seventeen she'd fallen in love with Eddie in the horrible converted loft over a garage in Gladstone Street. She'd cried herself to sleep for years pining for him and worrying about the awful girls he mixed with. Equally, she'd worried about the stories of men being found in alleys with terrible injuries and that Eddie was responsible. The Broad Street School enquiry report stated that Eddie's violence was 'An extreme response to an extreme problem'. The pimps, drug pushers and perverts in West Town that Proctor, Powers and company allowed to flourish were an extreme problem and Janice had come to terms with Eddie's extreme response to them. She'd also come to terms with his killing Fat Eddie in the hotel room in New York – it was him or them.

Most of Canley believed that Eddie was responsible for Duane Altman's death, that he'd been caught up in Eddie's attack on Ray Powers. They believed that having got away maiming Ray in the fight outside The Heron, he'd decided to finish the job. Janice didn't believe a word of it, Eddie was not capable of premeditated murder, and was distraught that Jilly's car had been used as a weapon.

That left the worry that never went away, his girls. One day she would have a heart to heart with Roxy, even meet some of the girls, speak to them face to face. Janice had spoken to some of them on the telephone – Eddie wasn't secretive with his mobile phone, often leaving it lying around, and was happy for her to answer it if he was in the garden or the shower. All the girls spoke slowly and clearly, gave their name, apologised for troubling her and asked if they could speak to Eddie please. When he called back he didn't leave the room and spoke to them without the slightest embarrassment. It should have made the worry go away, but it didn't.

They used a landline to make and receive international calls. Janice regularly answered these calls and often spent as much time with the callers as Eddie. Mostly it was Chin or Ellen, but sometimes it was Maybelle Potts. Janice would always remember the first time she answered a call from her, the long pause before the hesitant enquiry 'are you my boy's Lizzie'.

CHARLOTTE AND HILDA

Local government wasn't where Charlotte expected to begin her career, but Canley City Council under the dynamic leadership of new Chief Executive Steve Carter wasn't the Canley City Council of old. Their graduate entry scheme didn't guarantee fast track promotion, but it offered an opportunity for rapid progress to those with ability and the desire to work hard.

Steve Carter believed in mentoring, shadowing experienced managers and getting your hands dirty. He also believed that potential high flyers could learn a great deal from able junior and middle managers. However, Charlotte still felt a little aggrieved that she would be shadowing a junior manager, Deborah Aston. She wondered why Deborah was occasionally co-opted onto the department management team above more senior managers. Steve Carter must value her down to earth approach, so Charlotte decided to be positive and accept that Deborah had something valuable to give. Her first task was shadowing her at a management team meeting, but the rest of the week would be spent with Deborah's small team located in the Town Hall basement.

The room was depressing, a storage area converted into office space by fitting a false ceiling, strip lights and a few studwork partitions. Three side walls were windowless and the few windows on the fourth side looked out onto a row of recycling bins pushed up against a high brick wall. The meagre light that crept through the windows had to be permanently augmented by the strip lighting, a recipe for depression. Surprisingly, a brief inspection suggested a happy office, the room abounded with well-kept pot plants, bright posters and personal knick-knacks.

"You must be Charlotte, we're here to show you around."

It was one-thirty, Charlotte expected everyone to be at lunch but Deborah was ahead of her, she'd telephoned Angie and Sue and asked them to wait. This could be interesting – when the boss was away their staff tended to tell tales about them. Angie and Sue did tell tales, but they were positive ones, they liked Deborah.

"I know she seems really steady and sensible, but she manages a Rock band!" Angie looked from side to side like a conspirator. "Come on, I'll show you."

Angie led Charlotte into a small office constructed from half glazed partitions in the corner of the room and pointed to a pin board covered with photographs. At the bottom was a publicity photograph for a band with Deborah standing proudly among the musicians. A face jumped out at Charlotte, and she quickly scanned the other pictures on the board. The face appeared several times; Deborah must know, there was no way she couldn't know.

Charlotte declined an offer to join Angie and Sue for a late lunch and waited until she heard Deborah's heavy footsteps in the corridor.

Deborah saw Charlotte's face. "Is there something wrong?"

Charlotte nodded. "Angie and Sue showed me your photographs and…?"

"You saw the pictures of your uncle?"

Charlotte had recovered from her surprise, an afternoon filing, tidying the stock room and shredding documents gave her time to think. She'd recognised other faces in the photographs, including the pretty girl who'd come to their house many years ago. Charlotte remembered coming home from school to find her talking to her mother, shortly afterwards her father came home, shouted and raved like he always did, and she never saw the girl again.

Her father was mercenary, selfish and egotistical. Their names reflected his egotism, he was Charles Philip Stagg, she was Charlotte Philippa Stagg and her brother Philip Charles Stagg. Like so many long suffering women her mother had stayed with him for the sake of the children. When they finally split up three years ago her father had been a pig about the divorce, hiding money in offshore bank accounts and telling lies about his income, pension fund and investments.

Eighteen months ago, a Mr Chilvers came to see them. He was very polite, saying that he'd been instructed by her uncle to recover money from her father, but had been told not to do so if it would prejudice their education or wellbeing. It wouldn't, the divorce settlement was a one-off payment, their mother knew better than to trust their father to pay maintenance. The visit made Charlotte think about her uncle, showing concern for relations he hardly knew was not the stuff of psychopaths.

"What's he like?"

Charlotte was studying the picture Deborah was most proud of, the publicity photograph for The Roadrunners charity dances, with her identified as manager.

Deborah moved alongside her. "Different, and impossible to get to know if you have preconceptions, it took me ten years."

"Dad said he was a violent maniac, a dangerous psychopath. He made us read those terrible stories in the Herald."

Deborah sniffed. "I wouldn't believe everything you read in the Herald." She sniffed again. "Yes, he is very dangerous and very violent if you're a pimp or a drug pusher, or if you hurt one of his girls, but apart from that…" Deborah shrugged and pointed to Janice in the publicity photograph. "You really need to talk to Janice, his fianceé." She moved to an old picture. "That's her a few years ago."

Charlotte peered at the pictures. "That's never the same girl!"

"I can assure you it is." Deborah laughed. "See what living with a violent maniac has done to her!"

Hilda Lomax was at Frankies Two, sitting outside at the table furthest from the shop. It was in partial shade, but from there she could see the top of Eddie's workshop peeping above the trolley racks in the supermarket car park. Hilda was nervous, not about having tea and cakes in the middle of the afternoon, but because she was waiting for an admirer.

She jumped when she heard footsteps and looked round; it wasn't Bill, he would be on time, not early or late, but precisely on time.

Hilda peered at Eddie's workshop again and smiled, her Bob was now a company director, Eddie had promoted him again. SIKO and its many offshoots were still growing, and she'd met Bill as a result. Eddie had bought a derelict cinema on the edge of West Town and converted it into an auction house. Bill had retired early from the Civil Service and taken a part-time job with Eddie as an auction porter/handyman. On his free days Bill ran SIKO subsidised tea dances in the converted cinema, Bob persuaded her to help, she'd met widower Bill and they were now walking out together.

Bob told her that the SIKO group of businesses were like a family, giving priority employment to Eddie's girls, Jim's boys and vulnerable youngsters recommended by Roxy. SIKO also supported a string of West Town charities and subsidised regular events for West Town residents. Their charismatic auctioneer and Bingo caller was very much part of the family – the retired Sir Charles Napier QC was as fond of Eddie as all the others. Hilda liked Sir Charles and his son Stephen very much, she loved Mr Chilvers and Gary and would never understand why they liked Eddie. Hilda didn't, she was as frightened of him as she would be of any other dangerous violent man with a permanent undercurrent of brooding menace.

EDDIE'S GIRLS

A daydream became an impossible dream for Janice when Eddie met Jilly. It reappeared four years later when Jilly was killed, tainted with guilt but still wonderful. The dream was always the same, Janice would arrive at a church in a beautiful white dress and see Eddie waiting for her with Mike at his side. The music would start and Eddie would turn and look at her with love and kindness in his eyes.

The eyes should have told her straight away, even part-time monsters would not have kind eyes. It took Jilly a few minutes in a fire exit corridor at Broad Street School to find the real Eddie. It took Juliet an hour in a bus shelter on Mayors Road to find him. Roxy needed a few hours to be certain after he beat Jed and Errol to a pulp in the grubby yard in Gladstone Street. Four-year-old Sophie took about fifteen seconds. Janice, stupid and disbelieving to the bitter end, took fifteen years.

In the end, Roxy found the real Eddie for her and finally ended her worries. Janice had been thinking about Roxy, reflecting on how difficult it was to picture someone so clever, articulate and in control as a victim. Eventually she plucked up the courage to tell her so and, surprisingly, Roxy wasn't angry. Instead, she said Janice should go with Eddie and meet the girls, the ones she'd repeatedly condemned as trollops and architects of their own misfortune.

With Canley Police and City Council purged of corrupt officials, West Town was being transformed with CCTV cameras, new developments and visible police foot patrols. It remained a poor area but in every other respect it seemed normal, safe, unexceptional. They went to the walk-in centre to meet Alice and her volunteers, then to the West Town café next to the supermarket. The girls that dropped their bags of shopping to run and throw their arms around Eddie weren't clever, articulate and in control like Roxy, just ordinary, artless girls with big smiles and trusting faces. Their stories began differently but ended much the same, trusting men who said they loved them before being betrayed, their confidence destroyed, abused then put on the street. Later they trusted Eddie who protected them, housed them, found them jobs and never asked for anything in return. All had seen him batter pimps, their minders, drug pushers and perverts to a pulp, but none were frightened of him. They drank tea, ate bacon sandwiches, talked excitedly about their jobs and showed him pictures of their children; Eddie was their hero.

She met Nadine and Krystal who ran the West Town café. Agamemnon Properties, one of Eddie's companies, owned and maintained the building and leased it to the girls at a hopelessly uneconomic rent. In return, they provided good food at affordable prices and secure employment for the more vulnerable of Eddie's girls and Jim's boys. Nadine was a bit like Roxy, clever, articulate and seemingly in control; Krystal was younger, eager to please and clearly vulnerable. In reality, neither Roxy nor Nadine were in control, they were simply copying their hero, pretending to be in control. One thing that had never crossed Janice's mind was the possibility that Eddie might be a victim. Could a hero, iceman, fearless streetfighter and unsmiling man with a bad reputation be a victim?

Ask the child routinely beaten and locked in a windowless boxroom for having nightmares, not crying out because he knew it would bring another beating. Ask the boy sitting in a bus shelter watching others go home to loving families, constantly told he deserved beatings because he was bad. Ask the teenager watching his world spiral into a nightmare of violence because he couldn't bear the thought of anyone being as lonely and frightened as him. Ask the young man fighting psychopaths with knives and iron bars in back alleys knowing that every bloodstained contest would stay in his mind and haunt him for ever.

Professor Hay said Eddie's essay 'The role of emotional repression in the novels of Jane Austen' was a work of genius. His pleasure at finding Eddie after a twelve-year search was enhanced when Eddie told him he'd written many more essays. Many were written in the dark hours before dawn, Eddie woken by nightmares and concentrating hard to erase images of Juliet waiting patiently to die on her plastic sheet, or of girls tortured and abused by pimps and perverts, or Jilly dying in agony in a bus shelter. Professor Hay read them all and was astonished at their sensitivity, insight and developing maturity. Eddie offered him a deal, the copyright and publishing rights if he would speak at next year's Tacoma Flat's literary festival and find a publisher for Roxy's book 'Diary of a Prostitute'.

Charlie, another man with a brilliant mind, was equally in awe of Eddie's multi-faceted ability but more amazed that he had managed to remain sane. The both agreed that individuals with such brilliant, sensitive and easily damaged minds should never be exposed to the harsh realities of the real world, they should be closeted in academia, protected and revered.

Finding that Eddie's girls were not trollops did little to ease Janice's worries, it simply rekindled the dark thoughts that had always been there. A few days later she went back to see his girls by herself, to drink tea and ask the questions she could not ask with Eddie there. It started well, they asked if he ate proper meals now and had stopped working so hard. Then a whispered question raised the demon that had haunted Janice since she was seventeen 'Were his nightmares any better?'. How did they know about Eddie's nightmares, he had them at night, in bed! Lewd tales about Eddie and his tarts had always abounded, Andy loved repeating them. Janice had tried not to listen but …!

The café was empty, the lunchtime rush was over and the teatime rush was yet to start. Nadine had been bustling about clearing up, now she was standing over Janice looking menacing.

"Roxy said you'd be back, and she said I should knock some sense into you." She saw the expression on Janice's face and snorted. "I don't mean literally, for Christ's sake." She sat down opposite Janice and leaned back. "You're still not totally sure about him, are you? You think he's two people, nice when he's with you, then goes off and maims a few pimps and shags a few tarts!"

Janice didn't think it, she feared it.

Nadine spoke slowly and precisely. "Eddie only hurts people when he genuinely believes it's the only way to stop them hurting his girls. I'm not saying he always gets it right, he's not likely to, he's been off his head most of his life." Her voice took on an edge. "How about a story? A fifteen-year-old girl is being sold to the highest bidder. Her pimp is giving her a beating for refusing to go with some fat old pervert when there's a knock on the door. Her pimp opens the door and she sees a young man standing there. She's relieved, he looks nice, ordinary, so at least he won't hurt her. The pimp says 'You a punter?' and the man replies 'No I am your nemesis'. The girl didn't know what nemesis meant but the next thing she knew her pimp was on the floor and the man was kicking the shit out of him.

"The man calms her down, tells her to pack her things and takes her to a big old house that looks like a building site. He's really kind, feeds her then shows her to the only decent room in the house and says there's a bolt on the door if she wants to lock herself in. The girl can't believe it, he should be shagging her and telling her he's in charge now. She can't sleep so creeps downstairs and sees the man asleep in an armchair and watches him. After a while he wakes up screaming with a nightmare, so she runs back to her room. In the morning the man makes her breakfast, goes on his computer and sorts out a Benefit claim online giving his address. He says she can stay with him until he finds her a place of her own and will find her a job, a proper one, no sex work.

"Later then her world falls apart, the man says he wants her to meet a friend. She's been there before, her first step to prostitution was doing a favour for a friend." Nadine laughed out loud. "The friend was Mike, and the girl with nothing and no one suddenly had two of the nicest men in the world looking after her, and neither wanting anything in return." Nadine paused. "I forgot something, the day after the man took the girl home she gets a visit from a hard-faced tart. The tart tells her that if she ever did anything to hurt the man, she would tear her fucking head off!"

Janice stared at her. "Roxy! And the girl was you?"

"No, it was Krystal, and lots of others. I was much earlier, the first one after Roxy." Nadine looked away. "One day, only a few years ago, I looked at Eddie and Roxy properly and didn't stop crying for a week. He's just a nice boy so frightened of anything and everything that he ends up frightened of nothing and she's crying inside all the time." She gripped Janice's shoulders. "Go home and look at him, forget everything you think or suspect or fear, just look and all you'll see is a nice boy!"

THE FINAL DREAM

This time the dream began differently. The beautiful white dress was the same, but she was inside a car, not outside a church. The opulent leather upholstery and burr walnut trim of the car seemed familiar, and so did the driver in his immaculate chauffeur's uniform.

Janice lurched forward as the driver of the dark blue Bentley braked sharply to avoid a youngster wobbling out of a side turning on a small motorcycle.

She felt a reassuring hand on her arm. "You OK, Janice love?"

Janice recognised the voice and the face, but what was Jim doing in her dream? She peered round and shook her head, the car was familiar because it was Charlie's car and it was Charlie in the chauffeur's uniform.

Jim squeezed her arm gently and smiled. "You've been miles away for the last few minutes, were you daydreaming?"

Their interview with the earnest young vicar at St Nicholas Church hadn't been the trial they expected. He confirmed there was no theological barrier to his marrying a widow and a widower and, following Alice Popplewell's glowing recommendation, had dispensed the usual lecture on regular church attendance and repenting past sins.

Janice had Eddie, a beautiful white dress on order and a church, so the rest didn't matter. She envied girls with close families who rallied round icing cakes, making bridesmaids dresses and relatives happy to travel to the wedding from faraway places. Envy was pointless, her mother and sisters claimed a prior engagement before she told them the date, and her father and Nan...

But family did not have to be blood relations, suddenly she was surrounded by lovely people wanting to make her day special. People did travel from faraway places, Chin and Ellen from New York, and Lamarr and Maybelle Potts insisted on making the long journey from America's mid-west.

Reality was better than the dream, Jim led her into the church and she could see Eddie waiting for her with Mike at his side. The music started, Eddie looked round and the love in his eyes took her breath away.

"Do you, Edward George Alonzo Stagg...?

Janice didn't remember any more until the vicar smiled and pronounced them man and wife. Then they were walking past a sea of smiling faces, so many people genuinely happy for them. Jimmy hanging on to Deborah and looking strained, but Janice loved him for coming and trying to smile. Gary beaming with Charlotte on one arm and Carole on the other. Betty and Alice smiling under big hats, Roxy and Sophie clinging to Mark with tears in their eyes. Bob and Ellie looking wistfully at each other – it was about time Bob made an honest woman of her. Dave and Emily all loved up, they would be next. A group of Eddie's girls dressed in their best clothes, dabbing their eyes and throwing confetti.

Outside pairs of Jim's boys, most wearing a suit for the first time in their lives, patrolled each approach to the church. Immediately outside the church the most able of Jim's boys guarded each entrance. Inside the church, security had been supervised by the professionals, Chin, Jim and Billy Wells. Purging Canley of corruption had made Eddie many enemies, nothing would be permitted to spoil her day.

Janice knew she was crying but it didn't matter, she'd spent half a lifetime thinking this would never happen, but it had.

LUXOR

The battered Peugeot taxi dropped them outside their hotel, the driver nodding to the armed guard at the gate before driving away. Their tour guide had stressed the need to travel by taxi and keep to public areas. Eddie wanted to visit the market again, the guided tour had been all too brief, so they'd returned by taxi to smell the spices, feel the rolls of silk and marvel at the variety of goods for sale.

In the cool of the early morning, they'd crossed the Nile to visit the Valley of the Kings, returning to the hotel before noon to rest. Even now, in the late afternoon, it was hot and Janice was looking forward to the air conditioned cool of the Luxor Sheraton. As they walked across the courtyard, four musicians sitting by the door began to play. Two beat drums with curious hook-shaped sticks, a third blew a bulbous, bell ended pipe, and the fourth played what looked like a single string violin.

The musicians sat outside the hotel twelve hours a day, seven days a week, playing to welcome guests as they approached the main doors. They considered themselves fortunate, the streets of Luxor were unforgiving and poor, the money they earned kept them and their families in relative comfort. All played with extra enthusiasm for the tall blonde English girl – not to encourage her to give them a few coins, she would do that anyway, but hoping she would smile for them.

All avoided eye contact with the Englishman, the troubles had brought men like him to Luxor, dangerous men who saw everything and revealed nothing.

Christmas many years ago had brought a present from her father that Janice had always treasured. 'The Wonders of Egypt' had maps and line drawings but no pictures, so her sisters didn't consider it interesting enough to steal or destroy, leaving Janice to read it in peace. Egypt was a place of wonder, a honeymoon touring Egypt was her final dream.

Tomorrow they were flying to Aswan, spending two nights at The Old Cataract Hotel where Agatha Christie wrote 'Murder on the Nile' before cruising back to Luxor. Tonight, they would eat in the hotel, it was too dangerous to stray outside at night, but who would want to, the Sheraton had a veranda overlooking the Nile serving freshly barbecued food.

The hotel was quiet, the troubles had driven many tourists away, but the management intended to entertain the guests they had; a keyboard player and a guitarist had set up on the patio beneath the veranda. They sat and listened and talked and planned, they had fifteen years to catch up on, then the guitarist announced 'Wonderful Tonight'.

Eddie wasn't a dancer, most musicians weren't, and Janice had never had the chance, boys didn't ask tall girls to dance. Now she couldn't, her damaged legs weren't up to serious activity, Eddie had carried her through much of the Valley of the Kings, and she'd resigned herself to never dancing. Eddie must have read her thoughts, he helped her down the steps to the patio and they stood on the dance floor with two other couples. They clung to each other and shuffled about in time to the music, it was magical and Janice wanted to cry again.

They were staying in a bungalow a short walk from the hotel's main building. After the dance Janice was very tired and her legs hurt, so they walked slowly to their room past a pond packed with golden carp and covered with white water lilies. A few surprised-looking pink flamingos stood in a corner of the pond, their eyes appearing to follow them as they ducked under a palm tree onto the path to their bungalow.

A slowly rotating brass fan in the white painted dome above the main room kept them cool. A small lizard, a gecko, clung upside down halfway up the dome, and the hotel staff had turned down their sheets and left chocolates on their pillows. Janice wasn't self-conscious with Eddie any more, he didn't see a tall, thin girl with a big nose and badly injured legs, he only saw the girl he loved.

That was a gift from Juliet – Janice had accidentally found her letter whilst looking for an envelope. It was as beautiful as a suicide note could be, Juliet loved the Eddie who never saw a big, unattractive and ungainly girl, he only saw his friend. Juliet had gone to her death happy, convinced that her gesture would vilify the bullies and make Eddie a hero. As she lay on her plastic sheet waiting patiently to die, Juliet was thinking of her unsmiling man with a bad reputation, clutching Al Stewart's Bed-Sitter Images album he'd given her. Janice recognised the source of the last line of the letter 'When you're alone just think of me once in a while', it paraphrased the last line of Swiss Cottage Manoeuvres. Janice would not be jealous if Eddie thought of Juliet once in a while.

Janice felt Eddie stir in his sleep and looked at him, fearing it was the start of a nightmare. It wasn't, he settled, and she closed her eyes. Most people looked relaxed and childlike in sleep, but Eddie didn't; he looked strained and troubled. Sleep was a battleground where he fought his greatest enemy, his own mind. The nightmares were easing, last month Eddie had broken a record and gone three consecutive nights without them. Thankfully, the old man still came for his shoes. Thankfully because even Eddie's guilt-seeking mind couldn't think of anything he'd done to provoke that one. Janice felt Eddie stir again, selfishly she wanted him to wake, she wanted to tell him how happy she was.

It was a nightmare, but Eddie had woken before the images had taken hold. Now he was awake watching Janice relaxed and childlike in sleep, blonde hair spread on the pillow. Suddenly she woke, gave a dazzling smile and asked him a question.

"Oh Eddie, is it possible to be happier that this?"

He answered and, seconds later, she was asleep again. Eddie was pleased, if she saw his tears she would ask why and he didn't want to tell her.

It only seemed like yesterday that the prettiest girl in the world woke in the night in a hotel room in Lido di Jesolo and asked him the same question. His answer then was the same and as true as it was now.

"I don't think so, sweetheart, I really don't think so."

Eddie felt the tears warm on his face, it was good he could cry now but the tears would never wash away his guilt. How could he be with someone as wonderful as Janice and think of another woman, even Jilly. But how could anyone have wanted another woman, even Janice, after being with someone as wonderful as Jilly?

A tear dripped off his face onto the pillow. He was crying for Janice, the girl he'd loved since he was fifteen, for her years of unhappiness and her worries about the restraints her damaged legs imposed on her. He was crying for Jilly too, his fairytale princess, a beautiful life cruelly cut short. And for Juliet, a lovely girl who had thrown away her life in a hopeless gesture. And for Roxy and his girls, their childhoods stolen by perverts. It was good he could cry for them, but he must never cry for himself, he wasn't worth crying for, never had been, never would be.